taking ronnie to the pictures

taking ronnie to the pictures

gary ley

seren

seren is the book imprint of
Poetry Wales Press Ltd
Wyndham Street, Bridgend, CF31 1EF, Wales

© Gary Ley, 1998
The moral right of Gary Ley to be identified
as the author of this work has been asserted.

ISBN 1-85411-193-0

A Cataloguing in Publication record for this title
is available from the British Library

*The publisher works with the financial support of the
Arts Council of Wales*

Printed in Plantin by
The Cromwell Press, Trowbridge

San Antonio, Texas

He first noticed the smell of smoke when he was telling Ronnie about his goats. She was eight and liked animals. She sat on the sofa with her feet stretched out onto the chair by his desk. He smiled and told her how tall the goats were, how he picked them because they were father and daughter and how the largest goat had seemed to smile at him when he first glanced its way.

'What are their names?' she asked. She liked asking questions about names. At her age they were important in any characterisation. They somehow went with laughter and sadness and dictated the need for sympathy or hatred. To her, Mavis was cool, Jenny was Ok, Trevor was peachy, Michael was boring. There was no clear logic for that. It was something to do with sound. 'Let me guess!' she said. 'Let me guess!'

He sat back. He let her guess. While he waited, he thought how he liked it when she got excited. Somehow her whole body wriggled with anticipation and she always pulled herself into a different position. He watched her move her legs and sit up. 'Matilda!' she shouted.

'Who's that? The father?'

'No, silly. The daughter.' She laughed. A soft laugh. It took its time coming and going. 'The big goat could be called Francis,' she added.

'My name,' he said, clarifying the child's response. 'What about Ronnie? That would be a good name.'

'No,' she said adamantly.

'Ronnie in my country would probably be a man.'

'Yeh, men can be called Ronnie. But Ronnie's no name for a goat.'

He went to the desk and grabbed what, to Ronnie, looked like a large book. 'Here,' he said, offering it to her. It was a photo album. He smiled as she stopped at a photograph of the smaller goat jumping over a fence, then at one of the larger goat grazing down on its front knees and finally at one of the large goat sitting in a kennel-like box lazing away an afternoon. She laughed as her eyes followed the goat's neck. It was placed against the side of the box. It stretched upwards allowing the goat to stare into the roof of the box. She tried to imitate the pose.

'That's clever,' he said, sniffing the smoke again. He thought nothing of it. He knew that Brad, Ronnie's father, had probably cut away the growth from the path to the main road and had left it to burn. His head shook at that. He thought how he had told Brad of the dangers of the dryness of the summer vegetation. But Brad never listened. He

5

always smiled and said 'Good idea. Hey boy, that's right.' Then two weeks later he'd cut the grass again and pile it up and leave it to burn away as he mended the truck or put away the chickens.

'Do they fight?' Ronnie asked, making faces at the large goat.

'Of course.'

'Why? We don't fight.'

'We're not goats.'

Momentarily she looked confused, allowing the point to make its way through her mind.

'Look at the photo two pages on,' said Francis, breaking up her thoughts.

'They fighting there? Why do they fight?' she asked, hurriedly turning the pages.

Again Francis told her to have a look. He sniffed hard and looked up towards the tarpaulin that made up the tower's roof. There was something acrid about the smell now, something more pungent than anything the burning of a piece of wood or a bundle of grass could produce.

'Tell me about them!' pleaded Ronnie. 'Please!'

He told her about the way, when he had bought the goats, he and his friend Owain had found it difficult loading them into a van, how they had gone for a cup of tea and returned to find the goats sitting in the back of the van waiting for them. 'Smiling,' he said, describing the look on the goats' faces. He told her how the small female goat had taken to travel and had sat patiently enjoying the rhythm of the van's movement and how the large male had refused to relax and had stood up all the way, brushing into the female on every corner, disturbing her to the point that they would confront each other and bow their bodies into a head butt. Then he stopped. He sniffed hard again. 'I want to look outside a minute,' he said. 'You look at the photos two pages on. You'll see my van there.'

In the seconds that it took him to climb up to the roof, a sense of panic arrived. He scrambled up the ladder, missing steps, shouting 'Shit!', forgetting the presence of Ronnie. His limbs began to tremble as his brain told his legs to move more quickly, to make the ground to the top of the ladder in a split second not half a minute. When he reached the top, he peered over the rim of concrete. Plumes of smoke were rising to his left. They were beginning to reach his level and block his view. 'Christ,' he mumbled as the need to act hit him. 'Come on,' he said, sliding down the ladder. 'You've got to come.'

'Why?' asked Ronnie.

'Just come.'

The sudden change in his movements scared Ronnie more than any depth of smell that was creeping into the room. Even the sight of the smoke failed to move her. She thinks it's fog, thought Francis, remembering how last January she had been in the tower when he had left the tarpaulin off and fog had swirled in. He remembered her laughing as she climbed down the outside ladder not being able to see anything.

'Where's your jumper?'

She pointed.

'Come on,' he said, drawing it over her head.

'Why? I'm enjoying this.'

'Ronnie!' He didn't want to frighten the girl so he smiled and knelt down beside her. 'You bring that,' he said calmly.

'The photo?''

'Yeh. Look I'll carry it.' Francis took the photo album and held it in one hand. With his other hand he drew her to the inside ladder. 'Now you try to climb the steps more quickly than you've ever done before.'

'Quicker than last time?' she said.

'Yeh'

'What's in it?'

'A buck'

'Five bucks. I'll do it for five bucks.'

He watched her try to scramble up the steps, then told her to take her time. Her right foot missed a step. Then her left slipped off a rung. He thought she would cry, but there was too much profit to be made for tears. 'And down the side,' he said, when she reached the rim of the tower. As she climbed down, he surveyed the smoke. They were on the south side of the tower now, but the smoke was creeping around it like a pair of hands. He imagined it squeezing the tower. It was then that Ronnie cried.

'Put a hand over your mouth,' said Francis, 'but keep going. You're doing fine.'

She coughed.

'Over your mouth,' urged Francis. 'And keep going. Come on. You can do it. Hey I'll buy you a goat. Your own goat. Yeh, the male. Like the one I had. Now keep going. That's it. Good. Good. Just ten steps to go. Ten steps that's all.' As he spoke he thought how the outside ladder had been built for an eight year old, how the steps were tightly together, how Ronnie's feet slipped into place while his toes stubbed against metal. 'Good, good,' he kept saying. 'You're nearly there. That's it. You're down.' He saw her feet touch the ground. He moved more quickly to be alongside her and held her hand.

'Keep your mouth covered,' he said insistently. Momentarily he stood still. He wondered what to do, whether to leave her and investigate or to take her with him. He couldn't leave her. 'No,' he heard her say. He was almost dragging her now. He moved to his left towards the wood.

He had moved five paces when he saw it. The breeze had moved up the path that was a clearing in the wood and gestured the smoke away. Suddenly it moved quickly and dived up and over the flames that had created it. There was something lovely about the movement. It was like a veil in the wind. He watched it settle and rise up again. The flames followed it. They smacked into the roof of the house. Black smoke rose off the roof.

'Shit!' he said. 'Who's home? Ronnie, who's home?'

She coughed as her father's car exploded.

*

Francis was in the valley below Brynlas, the family farm in Wales. He was watching a stream. He was learning how the water, rushing around edges, created lips and lines, like eels moving. In pools he had seen leaves and reflections. Then his father called. He rushed back to the farmyard. His father was watching the animals and talking. 'After the rain they lay eggs see.'

'Who do?' asked Francis.

'The flies,' said his father. 'Remember? I told you last week. Said I'd show you so you'll know what to look for. Now come here. Watch carefully. And don't bloody fidget.' His attention turned back towards the sheep. He let his head turn his body as his eyes inspected a lamb. 'That one, see?'

Francis laughed. From his height he couldn't separate the lambs. They were a mass of bodies crushed together with heads popping up staring out over each other's backs.

'Why do they lay eggs?' asked Francis.

'The rain,' said his father, looking around again having lost the suspect.

'The rain?' echoed Francis. The answer didn't satisfy him.

'See that's the sort of thing you don't need to know. What you need to know is what to bloody look for. Rawness, that's what you need to know.'

'Rawness?'

'Yes. Look. I'll show you what bloody rawness is.' With the words his father swooped. 'Got you,' he said, catching hold of a lamb and dragging it over to Francis. Francis watched his father drop onto one

8

knee. He held the animal with its back clutched to his chest. The lamb was up on its hind legs. His father let its head dip away to the right. It looked towards the other lambs. 'Come round here son. See?' In one hand his father held a hand shears. Francis watched as the two blades clipped wool away. There was blood on the fleece. His father was getting to the cause of the redness. 'There it bloody is. That's rawness.'

Francis learnt that in days maggots could eat a sheep.

'Where the hell are they?' his father was saying. 'Oh look at this. Buggers. They've gone a hell of a way down. Look. See? Now that's what bloody rawness is.'

Francis was looking away.

'Oh Christ. Pass me that son. Francis! Hey, come on, pass me that will you? Bloody hell, what you doing now? You listening? Fluff your bloody feathers son.' His father had stopped and was pointing beyond Francis in the direction of the sheep dog that was sitting prick-eared, watching and wondering, down on its haunches, ready to launch itself if needed.

'The dog?' said Francis innocently.

'What do you bloody mean the dog? Will you bloody wake up? The bottle, the bloody bottle. There! Behind you!' Francis picked up the bottle of dettol. He watched the liquid being dabbed onto the lamb's skin and listened to his father's coaxings. 'You buggers.... This will sort you out... There you are.... Serves you right.... There you are.... Serves you bloody right....'

The same day he went with his father to a hillside. A neighbour had called to say they had seen a sheep struggling.

'What are we looking for?' asked Francis.

'What do you mean what are we looking for? The sheep that's what we're bloody looking for. And if we can't find the sheep we may find the dog –'

'Dog?'

'It's a dog that's hurt the sheep.' His father was carrying a gun over his arm. He was dressed in the same pork pie hat and checked shirt and brown trousers that he had worn earlier in the farmyard, but he had added a plain waistcoat and green wellington boots. From a distance he looked a gentleman. Francis remembered thinking that. He stayed in the tractor and watched him. 'Should have brought the horses,' mumbled his father, returning to the tractor. 'I want to go up there.'

'Can I come?' asked Francis. His father seemed a little shaken by the response. It was as though it was rare. It was certainly unexpected.

'Up there? No you bloody can't.' His father placed the shot-gun behind the driver's seat. He ignored the look of disappointment on Francis' face. 'I've told you about up there. It's dangerous. Do you ever bloody listen? Eh? Haven't I bloody told you? Course I bloody have.'

Francis looked out from the tractor at the adjacent wood that ran up the opposite side of the valley. He let his gaze drift up to their farmhouse, Brynlas. Then he dropped his eyes and focused on an old cart left at the base of the valley. One broken plank had been turned up like a snub nose. At the same time he saw his own nose reflecting in the side window of the tractor. He saw his father looking straight ahead.

'Go up there?' his father was saying. 'I've told you that side of the valley is full of bloody mine shafts. You know what shafts are? They're bloody holes. Holes in the ground. Holes big enough for little bloody boys to fall into.'

'Perhaps the dog will,' suggested Francis, trying to be helpful. His father wasn't listening.

'Bloody things. Adits are alright see. They're like caves. I've showed you one of those. Remember? There's one just above that bit of woodland.' Francis' father nodded in the direction of the wood. 'They're alright. You can walk into those. But shafts. Well it's the little ones see, the ones a bit of bloody soil and grass has covered up. They're the buggers. The sheep run along them and the soil gives way. Right through they go. Find one or two a year up there. Trapped.'

'Dead?' asked Francis.

'Oh aye. They can't bloody get out, can they? Not once they're in. How the hell are they supposed to get out?'

Francis listened and looked at his father once. The roughness of the tractor on the path made his father's head bob awkwardly as he spoke. It reminded Francis of the jerky movements of puppets he had seen on television. He briefly turned his father into one of them and laughed.

'Bloody funny, is it?' snarled his father without looking Francis' way. It stopped the laughter immediately. 'And you want to go up there,' he added more to himself than Francis.

'You could take me,' suggested Francis, his enthusiasm overcoming the need for quietness. 'You've taken me before.'

'Not chasing dogs I haven't. And not up top, up to the bloody shafts. And I'm not bloody starting now. You hear me? It's bloody dangerous.' Francis' father moved his head, again glancing up the hill. 'Go up there,' he muttered, before shouting, 'What the hell! What's he doing here?' The exclamations were directed at a black collie that ran across the front of the tractor. They returned a smile to Francis's face. He knew his father had never gained any sort of proficiency at directing the sheep dogs. 'Ivor!' his father was screaming, shouting out the dog's name. 'Get back 'ere. Ivor!'

The next day there was a phone call. His father was out and his mother who took the call seemed shaken. There was a lot of 'Ahs' and 'Ohs' in the phone conversation. When she put the phone down she stopped for a second and looked blankly at Francis. He knew it was a sign that she was making a decision. He watched her sit down again. She sat in the kitchen chair. It was the chair Francis liked. It was round topped and the wood was patterned with leaves like a garland. The arms of the chair were loose. They were breaking away. Francis had thought it was as though they were expanding with her as she moved towards middle age.

'Francis, you seen Geth? Is he about?'

Francis remembered telling her that Gethin was in the shearing shed, sweeping it out, getting it ready for the shearers' visit the following month.

'Now Francis,' said his mother, returning with Gethin. 'You go with Geth. Mrs. Thomas just phoned. She's found the sheep. It's dead. Probably just as well. Now your father's out looking for the dog and I've got to go into the village. It's Thursday see.' Francis nodded. He knew that Thursdays meant a gathering of women and chatter and cakes and activities. His mother had taken him when he was younger. He had enjoyed the fuss and the cakes. 'Can't get your father, so Geth will have to go over to the Thomases and you'll have to go with him. There Geth,' she said, passing him the car keys. 'You'll need to take the small trailer and you'll have to drop me in the village first.'

Gethin, Francis' cousin, was even quieter than Francis. He was a big lump of a man. Twenty two and fair, but overweight and willing to work all hours for Francis' father whenever he could. Francis thought his father used him. He had witnessed his mother asking his father whether Gethin enjoyed the work. He remembered his father's words: 'Gethin? Geth? Geth like the work? Course he bloody likes the work. Wouldn't miss it for the world Geth. Bloody loves it.'

As they travelled in the car, Francis remembered thinking how it seemed odd he could recall his father's words so precisely. Anything associated with his mother's thoughts and ideas were much more imprecise. It was as if he didn't listen to her, as if she was less important. He thought that she seemed like him, insignificant, dwarfed by his father. He studied her agitation while they travelled in the car – she

11

cursed Gethin's driving once and shouted at Francis for chewing the neck of his tee shirt. 'More revs,' she kept saying, trying to speed up the journey. 'Now you know what to do?' she asked twice, showing her concern that in Francis' father's absence she was doing the right thing. At the Thomas' the sheep was on its left side, lying in an out-building. 'They've put it here for us to pick up,' said Gethin, who liked stating the obvious. He undid the back of the trailer, released the hinges and dropped down the end. Francis walked over to the sheep. One leg had completely disappeared. Its head was intact, its eyes staring out. Francis imagined it was looking at the two holes the dog had gouged out.

'Insides have gone,' said Gethin, looking into one of the holes. He shook his head.

'So what do we do?'

'We put it in the cart. We drag it back. I'll bury it,' said Gethin slowly.

'No you bloody won't.' The voice behind Gethin's was Francis' father's. 'What you bloody doing over here in the car?' Gethin didn't answer. Francis recognised the silence and the tone of the words. 'She should have waited. She should have bloody waited. She knew I'd be home in an hour. Bloody woman.' Francis' father stared at the sheep for the first time. He put his left hand on the sheep's remaining front leg and left his right arm dangling, balancing his movements. He dragged the sheep passed the car and around a corner to the tractor. 'You come here. Round this side,' he said to Gethin. Francis' father put the sheep down and switched his grip to the back leg. 'Grab that,' he said, directing Gethin to the other back leg. 'Now.' The word sig-nalled the synchronisation of an activity that involved picking up the sheep. They swung it together. One swing gathered momentum. The second allowed them to throw it onto the back of the cart the tractor was dragging. While he watched, Francis thought how his father would munch his mouth when angry, pouting almost. It could go away like a gesture. He knew it could also quickly return to reinforce a point. 'Bloody dogs. They don't know when to stop. That's their bloody trouble.'

'I'll come and help you bury it –'

'Bury it!' Francis' father scorned at Gethin's words. 'Leave it with me. That's why I was angry with Mairwen. I knew you'd do some-thing bloody daft like bury it. Especially with him in tow.' The him was Francis. It made him want to hide away. 'What the hell's he doing here anyway? He's too bloody young and too bloody daft to be deal-ing with dead animals.'

'So where you going?' asked Gethin.

'I'll drop it down by the old cart. Somewhere clear.' His father bolted up the trailer and looked at the sheep again. 'At least there's a bit left. Might draw the dog back. If the bloody buzzards give him half a chance.'

It was lunchtime the next day when Francis' father saw a dog in the farmyard. It was over by the duck pen, head down, sniffing. It pounced, scattering the ducks who quacked noisily. 'You bugger!' Francis' father shouted, running into the yard. 'You bloody bugger!' His cry drew Francis out of the farmhouse. 'He'll be going home.' Francis' father seemed quite definite. His words drew a look from Francis as he watched his father move towards a drake that was washing itself. His father threw his hands out over the top and in front of the drake. It froze. He grabbed it. 'Shut up,' he said as the drake hissed. It looked alert now, the fine feathers on its head raised. It kicked and struggled in Francis' father's hands. 'Bloody bird. Keep still will you? Still! There.' He placed it in the pen. He began to round up the others. 'Follow the dog,' he shouted to Francis.

Climbing the hill, Francis thought of the dog. It was his friend Owain's, the son of the farmer who worked the land adjacent to Brynlas. Owain had kept the dog from a puppy, helping train it to work on the land. Owain didn't always like the dog. It had made a habit of periodically falling out of favour: once by biting the head off Owain's favourite toy; another time by being sick on the floor of Owain's bedroom. But he knew Owain loved the dog. That showed. He groomed it to the point that its sheep dog status was almost disguised. Francis laughed at that. He pictured the dog as he walked up the hill. All black. Well nearly all black. Some white splashed on its ears and muzzle. Actually quite a lot of white. Its shiny coat brushed and brushed. Silky. It was a good natured dog, playful to the extent that Dilwyn, Owain's father, said it hadn't grown up.

He was linking what he knew of the dog with its appearance when it came into view again. It was sniffing a line of ducks. Francis thought how it was another game. A snarl confirmed that. The misplaced aggression did nothing to change the soft look of the hazel eyes. He watched the dog move away, come back and then walk towards him. The sight of his father coming up the lane disturbed the dog. It lost a little of its playfulness as it contoured the hill, disappearing near some gorse bushes.

'Don't you move,' Francis' father issued the words between breaths. 'Good,' he said, settling beside Francis in the hedge.

'There's four ducks.'

'The bugger's collecting them. Right.' The sharp words indicated the dog had returned. It was back by the ducks, sniffing and pulling at them, correcting the line as though they were hunting trophies on a wall. It was touching the last in the line when Francis' father took aim and shot.

Francis watched his father put the dog into a bin bag and leave it on the ground. His father made no attempt to stop and consider what was going on. He moved with a sense of service and precision. It was like watching a butler cleaning shoes.

'These are alive!' shouted Francis, seeing three of the ducks had their eyes open. He held them up one by one, their heads slumping as he lifted them. He recognised their heavy breathing and shaking. It was the sort of movement they made after accidents: twice tractors had run over ducks in the lane: the survivors had acted in such a way. His father said they were in shock. 'Panic attacks,' he said. The fourth duck was dead. The dog had bitten into it too deeply. The white feathers near its tail were red with blood. 'Must have thought they were sheep,' remarked Francis' father seeing the location of the bites. 'Nipping their legs. Stupid bloody dog.' He shook his head. 'Put it in with the dog,' he ordered. He was still dispassionate, working out what was necessary. 'We'll need boxes,' he concluded. 'Will you get them?'

Francis was surprised by the question. He was normally told what to do and how to do it. He shook himself. 'Ok,' he said slowly.

'Oh hell. Not now.' Francis' father's words greeted the sight of Dilwyn, Owain's father, coming across the field towards them.

'Seen a dog?' he asked when he was ten yards away.

'Your bloody dog? Aye. It's here. Dead.'

'Dead?'

'Aye. It was collecting ducks. Probably killed the sheep too.'

'Probably!' stormed Dilwyn.

'Aye.' Francis' father's tone was adamant. 'I saw it bothering them earlier. Didn't twig it was yours.'

'Never done anything like that before.'

'What you bloody saying? Eh? Look it was on my land, killing my ducks.'

'I'm saying you should have let me deal with it. God I was only over there. You must have seen my tractor.'

'Aye.'

'So?'

'What do you mean so?'

'I'm saying you should have let me deal with it.'

'And what would you have done?' Francis' father had a glint in his eyes now. He was enjoying this. He liked debate. He liked battle. The land gave him the right here. He felt on top, confident of his position and the justice of his actions. My land. My ducks. His dog. His dog killing my ducks on my land. The logic couldn't be questioned. It couldn't be denied.

'I'd have tied it up.'

'Tied it up!' scoffed Francis' father. 'You bloody would have, wouldn't you?'

Dilwyn shook his head. 'You should have told me,' he said insistently.

'This is my land. I look after it.' There was a touch of exasperation about Francis' father's tone. The ground had been gone over. He knew that, but there was something that he needed to add. 'It's always been like that. Remember your father? When he caught me nicking apples.'

'That was forty bloody years ago.'

'He gave me a good hiding.'

'You deserved it.'

'Aye,' agreed Francis' father contemplatively. 'Exactly. He could have taken me home, couldn't he? Eh? My father could have sent me to bed.' A shake of his head was used for effect. 'See? Nothing's changed. That's what I'm saying. Nothing's bloody changed.'

★

Francis spent some time in hospital having his lungs cleaned out. It had seemed a good place to be. He spent most of the time lying out flat with his eyes closed, thinking. Memory had taken over. It seemed like a heavy attachment to his mind, holding him down, changing his sense of things. It seemed to reorder the experience, to change it into something positive that steadied him and allowed him to reappraise not only the fire and the deaths, but the whole span of life that had brought him from Brynlas to Texas.

'Time to eat.... Francis.... Frankie. Hey Frankie....' The nurses had taken to calling him Frankie. It was unprompted and he disliked it, but he didn't object. He just smiled. Out of weakness, he thought, coming round at mealtimes. Soup, soup and soup. It was all he managed. Not that they minded. They just smiled. In a knowing way. In a way that said, 'Ok. You just do your best.' It was a reassuring smile. It demanded a response. So Francis smiled back. As best he could. He forced his cheekbones to move. He slid them up. The pressure folded his face.

'You Ok? No pain?'

He shook his head. There had never been pain. He just seemed helpless. Baby like, he thought, lying there, the nurse washing him, grooming him, feeding him. All he did was push up his cheekbones and nod or shake his head.

'Let's get you up. You ready? Ok. Let's go.' He was heaved up onto one of the pillows that was turned to accommodate his back. His head slumped momentarily until he realised the need for control.

'Your favourite today.'

'Mushroom?'

'Yeh. Mighty good one too. Had some myself. Here we go then. Open wide.' The spoon was lifted and pushed towards his lips. He took in the liquid, gulping in his throat to pull it down. He felt it trickle, the taste staying in his mouth, his tongue spreading it around.

*

It was at night the arguments were at their worst. They woke Francis up. Sometimes he moved to the landing outside his father's room. He could hear more clearly there. The whispers, the sighs, the shouts. He wondered why he listened. He knew he shouldn't be listening, that the words weren't for his ears, but he liked picturing his parents, hanging looks of malice and tenderness onto expressions.

'You did what? Oh God...' He knew his mother's exasperation well. Sometimes it was reserved for him, normally when he emerged untidy or returned from school dirty. She'll kill me, he would think, but it was never half as bad as he anticipated and quickly his mother's softer side would dominate. 'That's Owain's dog. What will I say?'

'Say I shot it. I mean I bloody did, didn't I? It was eating our ducks. Killing our sheep.'

'You sure? Another sheep went tonight.'

'Another dog.'

'Another dog.' His mother tutted. Francis imagined her looking away, her eyes becoming cold, steely, filling with disgust. 'That dog was harmless.'

'Harmless! It killed a duck.'

'It was young. It was playing. That was an accident. Christ it didn't know any different.'

'Look. This is my land. That dog was on my land. It was killing my ducks.'

'Our ducks. Our land,' whispered his mother, correcting his father.

'What?'

'Nothing.'

Francis pictured the head shaking, the mute loyalty, the resignation. He put expressions on the imagined faces. He predicted the conversation, the way it could twist and turn, where there would be a pause or sighs of disbelief . She'll be on about the village next, he thought, working his way into his mother's mind. Closing his eyes he crossed his fingers. Somehow it was important that he should be right.

His mother's tone rose. 'I'll go round and see Mary and Owain.'

'Why?'

'To apologise. To say how sorry we are.'

There was a shuffle in the bed now. His father, thought Francis. His father pulling himself together, gathering his wits. 'We're not bloody sorry. There's nothing to apologise for. It's sorted. I've seen Dilwyn. The cows are back in the field.'

Francis smiled. The cows are back in the field, he thought. He liked that. He had expected some such saying to creep in. His father used sayings like alliteration. They softened sounds, broke up the hard economical way he spoke.

'Bloody hell you know what he wanted? He wanted to tie the dog up. Bloody nonsense,' his father scoffed. 'Never done it before, he said.'

'And it won't do it again now, will it?'

'Bloody armhole,' mused his father. Armhole was one of his derogatory terms. Francis smiled at the expression. He knew it meant someone who was useless or awkward. 'Look it would have taken all the bloody ducks.You know that. And what would it have got next, eh? I mean a taste of blood. A dog's never the same after a taste of blood. You know that. Dilwyn knows it too. I had to bloody kill it.'

'Which you well and truly bloody did.'

A silence followed. That was usual. Francis began to think of it as a ritual. The roles clear, animal like. He would wait for a minute, checking it wasn't just a pause and then crawl back to bed. Sometimes the words would re-emerge, changing topics perhaps or qualifying something. If they did they were more vitriolic, sometimes ending peculiarly in sounds Francis couldn't comprehend. Such sounds would draw him back. He would try to look through the keyhole. A key normally blocked the way. Once the door was ajar. It gave him the chance to peer in. He didn't understand what he saw. His father was on top of his mother breathing heavily, making noises in his throat. His mother was quiet. Francis was more interested in his father's back. He had never seen his father with his shirt off. Even in summer he kept his shirt on. Francis could see why now. What a covering of hair he had. It was like a fur, thick and full, darkening his back below his shoulders. It was wet with effort. Francis saw the perspiration dripping down his back. The rhythm reminded him of a fairground ride, only this was more vigorous. It ended with a groan; his father seemed to collapse.

'You always do that,' his mother said quietly.

'You enjoy it.'

'Oh yes.'

'You do. You bloody do.'

'And you use it. We argue, then this.'

'I like arguing,' laughed his father.

'You plan it, don't you?'

His father's laugh became stronger.

'You bloody plan it.' His mother was hitting his father's body now. Francis could see her fist coming down on his chest. It made his father laugh even more loudly. 'You just don't care, do you? I've always got to sort it out. Always me. I do this, I do that.'

'You bloody enjoy it.'

'Oh yes. I enjoy it.'

'Forget it mun. Owain'll be alright.'

'See. That's what gets me. I mean how do you know? How do you make that out?'

'He's a farmer's boy.'

'Not everyone's like you.'

'And what does that mean?'

'It means some people care.'

'Oh I care,' objected Francis' father.

'Oh yes, you care. You bloody care.'

'I do.'

'Yes you do. You care about the sheep. You care about the land. You care about this building. You care about the past.'

'Yes.'

'What do you mean yes?'

'I mean yes, you're right. I care about the past.'

The arguments became worse. Any humour disappeared. His mother sounded more angry. Bitter almost, thought Francis. It aged her. It gave her a sorry expression that seemed frail and delicate.

He still heard them at night. It was the same old lines, though they were somehow abbreviated. 'I want to stay, I want to go' became 'I'm staying, I'm going'. There was a degree of bluff and brinkmanship now, a dangerous game that traded insults. 'Primitive,' his mother called his father. 'See sense,' she'd say. That was an expression she

18

had transferred from Francis to his father. 'See sense. We can't stay forever. God we're middle aged now. You thought about old age? You thought about being up here without heat. We should move down. There's a lovely spot down by the road. I pictured our house there the other day. It's just big enough for a house.'

'What do you mean without heat. We've got bloody heat.'

'You can't cut wood forever. It's hard. You puff and blow now. We should have oil. I've told you that, but you want to keep it as it was.'

'I've told you oil's bloody noisy.'

'Noisy?'

'Oil is.'

There was a pause. Francis imagined his mother biting her lip, thinking that it was all down to Francis' father wanting to keep the place as it had always been. Like when his father and grandfather were here. Bloody mad he is, she must have been thinking, bloody mad. 'Well I'm going one day,' she whispered.

'What?' There was a moan and the sound of turning over in bed. A yawn followed.

'I said I'm going. When Francis goes.'

'Really,' said his father in a lazy, drawling way. He sounded half asleep.

'I am.'

Some sense of seriousness seemed to tug at his father. Francis heard more movement in the bed. It was his father sitting up. 'So you're going when Francis goes.'

'Yes.'

'Well you'll have to wait a long bloody time then.'

'How do you make that out?'

'Because Francis isn't going anywhere,' said his father quite adamantly. 'He knows when he's well off. He knows this is his.'

The response was laughter.

'What's so bloody funny?'

'This. Him wanting this.'

'And what's wrong with this?'

His mother didn't respond. She knew what she wanted to say, but thought better of it. When she could, she avoided provocation. That was policy. That was politic.

'Come on,' his father was saying. 'What the bloody hell's wrong with this, eh?' After the words there was a vague noise, a stirring in the throat, a pent up, angry sort of noise. His father called it indignation. He didn't like the word anger. He said it was too strong a word for what was normally just mild annoyance. Francis waited for the

19

expletive that was like a clearing cough. But it never came. Instead the vague sound continued like an uninterrupted murmur. It played behind another push from his mother.

'We could have had central heating,' she said.

'Of course we could have had bloody central heating.'

'We could have had a shower. A new kitchen, I suggested that last year.' The pause came with a moment of reflection. Francis sensed she was checking facts, asserting control over issues. She seemed to be ordering them too, establishing what she had suggested and then underplaying the excuses or the silences he had issued. 'I asked for a cooker. Remember? That was July 4th. Ena phoned. You said you liked the calor cooker. You said you like the way the heat varies, the way cakes are never the same. Very inventive you are when it comes to excuses. Very inventive.'

'Nothing wrong with that,' mumbled his father. The pitch told his mother she was winning. It made Francis picture the superior look on her face. He knew it well. The look that came with instruction or correction. Her nose dominant, her eyes half closed as though they were hiding. 'Well?' she said.

There was no reply.

'Well?'

Francis listened hard. He expected to hear a regularity of breathing that signalled his father had fallen conveniently asleep.

★

Francis heard voices. A doctor. A nurse too. The doctor was reading his chart out loud. 'Blood pressure's low.'

'It's been low all the time.'

'That normal? We checked out his doctor? Got his notes?'

'He's English.'

'Oh hell he's the guy. Jesus.'

'The water tower.' The nurse was nodding when Francis opened his eyes.

'You're kidding. How'd he get here? I mean what's he doin' in Texas? Shit I mean in a water tower. What the hell's he doin' in a water tower in Texas? I mean this guy's from England for chrissakes. Gee.'

Francis couldn't move his head to see the other side of the bed. His concentration stayed with the nurse. She was shrugging now.

'Vacation, I guess.'

'Hell of a vacation,' the doctor said, laughing a little as he put the notes back at the end of the bed.

★

Francis heard of America before England. His mother showed him photographs of her sister Ena. Ena was ten years older than Francis' mother, but they were very close and wrote to each other once a fortnight. Ena had met a Canadian soldier in the war. She had moved to Swansea and was in the RAF, doing service with the air defence systems guarding the town's docks. A Canadian based at the local airport saw her in a shop, so the story went, and forced information out of a mutual friend. Where she lived. Who she was. Who she liked. Eventually the Canadian invited Ena, through the friend, to his twenty first birthday party. They were married within a year. Francis' mother went to Swansea to be a bridesmaid. She showed Francis the wedding photographs. The men looked like gangsters in a Hollywood film, all pin stripes and wide lapels. His Aunty Ena looked like his mother and, in the photo, Francis' mother looked like Francis. She always joked about that.

'See where you get your good looks from?' she would say, laughing.

Francis would blush, knowing he shared his mother's sharp bone structure and gaunt look. He preferred it to his father's round, squat features, but it was all too angular to approach ever being called handsome. It was distinguished though. Characterful one could say. Francis frequently did, defending himself. He thought it seemed a positive outlook. Realistic, he thought whenever he reconsidered the view.

The old photograph always brought such a reappraisal. New photographs of Ena did too. As did photographs of Nina, Francis' cousin who was about his age. 'Two years older,' Francis would say, objecting when his mother loosely tied them. Two years seemed a significant difference in Francis' early years. Yet he liked Nina. He admired her, relishing her American experience with its freedom and expectations. It seemed so open-ended compared with Brynlas which seemed to lay Francis' life out before him. The hills, the buildings, the sheep. When he surveyed it, he sometimes shook his head. It wasn't always attractive.

He remembered feeling that when he was quite young. Eight perhaps. Maybe younger. His father, who had called him into the kitchen, was standing by the table. Like a headmaster, thought Francis as he sat down. His father pointed to a photo album on the table. 'This is yours,' he said. 'I've labelled the photos. There's names on the back. Dates too.'

There was something very serious about the occasion, something almost sombre. Francis stared at the album. He turned the pages.

Brynlas. Brynlas. Brynlas. The house recurred. Sometimes it framed people. Sometimes it was left by itself showing off a window or a coat of paint or a new outbuilding. 'Me. My father. His father,' said Francis's father, identifying the people in the photographs. The house was behind them all. It was like a gene being passed on. It brought with it a sense of fate. It was the first time Francis had been aware of that. He smiled at his father, expecting more. But nothing was offered. A half smile came and went as though it was sanctioning a pact, confirming an agreement.

After that America provided relief. It came in through the letterbox. Ena would write to Francis' mother and Nina would write to Francis. Francis enjoyed her letters. He would look at Pittsburgh, PA, on the map and trace the route over the Atlantic. To him it was all about geography. The open space of America. The industry. The wealth. The differences. They were what attracted him. The trust. The freedom. He sensed they were qualities he had wanted. Perhaps they wove a magic when he was younger, perhaps they provided a picture of what could be obtained. Perhaps it was just the magic of the words being written in America. In America! Imagine that, he would think when he was in Brynlas. It was difficult to imagine. All those miles. All those days of travel.

'Post,' his mother would say on the days when the mail brought him a letter.

'For me?'

'From America.'

'Nina?'

'You like her letters.'

So much did he like them that he would hide them away quickly, leaving his mother to curse his bad manners. Sometimes she would call him back down. 'Francis! Back here. Now. You hear? This minute. You answer me in future. You hear?'

His mother bought an atlas of the United States. She got it out when Ena wrote. It placed events, set holidays.

'Their next door neighbours have gone to live with their son in Richmond. Now where's that?' The atlas would be used then. The reference at the back would find a map.

'Virginia. Now that was capital of the South.'

'The South?' asked Francis.

'The South. In the Civil War.' Her explanation was beyond Francis. His eyes were pulled together, screwed up. They showed his bewilderment.

'The North fought the South. Union and Confederates.'

'Why'd they fight?'

Such questions always highlighted the limits of her knowledge. They always caused her to bite her lip and look down. A flurry of activity said 'I don't know' as she turned pages and read words.

In time his mother's knowledge of the States grew. Its geography settled in her mind. Where the individual states were, where it was cold, where most people lived, where there was coal and oil. Everything was placed in relation to Scranton, PA. California was too distant. New York close. Washington accessible. It was as though she was centring herself, making Scranton, PA, a second home.

Francis liked all that. He enjoyed her knowledge. He learnt too. They played games with each other. State capitals, for example.

'Colorado?' asked his mother.

'Denver.'

'Yes. California?'

'San Francisco.'

'No.'

'L.A.'

'No. Sacramento.'

'Sacramento,' he scowled, never understanding the logic of state capital designation, why the largest city was frequently overlooked. It made him move on, turning the page and dwelling on something trivial. Dates of joining the union, population density, crop production. Most maps were considered. None of them bored his mother. That always surprised him. She was always tolerant when it came to the States. At least she was tolerant until Francis considered the technical side of map-making. She always forgot his interest in maps. It always emerged to surprise her.

'Look at that!' he'd gasp, turning the atlas to face her. Pie charts, dot maps, bar graphs, flow line maps were all marvelled at. He would work through the ideas then. 'Can I go?' he'd ask, moving up to his room to play with pen and paper and perfect a skill. 'Look! Look!' he'd shout, moving back to his mother. She would still be there, taking in the shapes and patterns and reading the accompanying notes. 'Lovely,' she'd say.

'What you reading mam?'

'America remains a dynamic country where there are fewer inhibitions to expansion and enterprise than in Europe,' she said, smiling at Francis. 'It means it's exciting,' she added, explaining. 'Different to Brynlas.'

★

'More tests?' Francis could speak now. He could put together words, managing an economy similar to his father's. He was surprised by the fluency of the conversation, the way leaving out the trimmings didn't affect relationships. No weather. No talk of television or pets or favourite food. No sport. No music. Attachments came from manner, from smiles and movements and intimacies that related thoughtfulness.

'Just checking you now. I'll sit you in the chair, yeh? Until they're ready. Won't be long. There.' The nurse held him as he moved across from the bed.

'Ah.'

'You like that?'

Francis nodded. 'Makes a change.' He watched the nurse make the bed.

'Hey you seem better. That's good. You'll be out soon. The doctor's concerned about one or two little things. But we've had details from England.'

'Details?'

'Your notes.' The nurse looked up and smiled. 'You've low blood pressure, you know that? Bet you do. You'll never die of a heart attack.'

'Lucky old me.'

The nurse laughed. It was a stuttering laugh, coming and going between glances sent Francis' way to check there was a touch of humour supporting his words. The slight smile he let loose gained confidence. 'I reckon a day or two. That's all they'll need. You've been lucky.'

'So everyone says.'

'No permanent damage. That's good, yeh?'

'Very good.' Francis smiled again. It was a fuller smile now. Something more than cheekbones. There was a warmth about it. A glow in the eyes. A glimpse of teeth, perhaps. There was a weakness though. A weakness that welcomed sleep.

★

'I've been thinking about the future.' Francis' words were delivered slowly. They had to be said. Francis knew that, but he had been putting off the moment. He wondered why. The words were quite easy to say. It was the reaction that worried him. His father would make it clear there was nothing to think about, that all he had to do was carry on. That's what his father was doing. Carrying on. It was like a religion, somehow gratifying, satisfying, consoling. Francis felt

24

none of that. It left him cold. All he could think was the world was large, much larger than the cycle that had captured him. He wanted to step out of it. He wanted to break away.

'What's that?' His mother had been eating toast, reading the cross-word clues.

'The future.'

She laughed.

'What's funny?'

'The future.' She looked up, over her reading glasses. Their presence gave her an even greater sense of seriousness. 'So what are you saying?'

'Well,' pondered Francis.

'You've been thinking. I can tell.'

'How?'

'I know you. You've come to some sort of decision.'

'I have? I mean I have.' Francis tried to sound more definite. His mother's intuition had thrown him. Momentarily he had lost control. He felt a need to regain it.

His mother looked serious. 'It's because you've left school. End of a chapter, I suppose.'

Francis nodded. A silence closed in. It seemed like a natural break, but there was unfinished business, there were things to say. They made Francis fidget. He thought of what his mother said, how he had stayed on to do A levels and failed geology and just passed geography. All because of maps, he thought. Staying on. He shook his head. At least it had kept him out of his father's way. He worked the weekends. His father was somehow less evident then. There were distractions at weekends. 'Well what I've been thinking, I mean what I've thought...' He spooned marmalade out of a jar and spread it on his toast.

'Yes?' prompted his mother. 'You want to try something else, yes?'

'How'd you know that? I mean, yes. Yes I do.' Francis looked a little shaken. He had rehearsed what to say, but all the talk about not being sure of farming seemed redundant now. He smiled. He laughed nervously.

'So you want to go....' She gave him a long, hard look. Aggressive, thought Francis, recognising it. He wondered whether it came from dejection, from disappointment.

'Well...' He didn't know what to say or how to pitch his words. The silence let a gloomy air permeate. It set faces. Long looks, thought Francis, sharing his mother's oppression. He shared her submissive responses too. He waited for her.

'I don't blame you. I wish I could have tried something else. That's why I act. That's why I do the crosswords.'

'Crosswords?' mumbled Francis, struggling to follow his mother's flow.

'Clues,' said his mother slowly. 'They take your mind away. Beats sheep. Beats lamb prices. Beats your father.' She laughed loudly. It was rare to hear her respond so freely. 'So where will you go?'

'The States.'

'Oh to Ena and Nina. That will be wonderful. They'll love that. Stay with them. Try to find work. Ena always says the farms there are short of hands in the summer. You'll get work easy.'

Telling his father was much more difficult. He had considered asking his mother to tell him. She would do it. He knew that. She would do it well too, picking the right moment, the moment when his father was tired or drunk or obsessed with some ongoing concern like killing the dog or an infection amongst the sheep. There was usually something convenient that could be used. A distraction or a mood, thought Francis. His father was full of moods, but Francis couldn't read them. His mother could. To him, for some reason, there was no telling, beyond a glum look, what a bad day would do to his father. Sometimes he shouted and thumped the table, emphasising what was wrong and what should have happened; other times he just fell silent, listening to the radio. He would even try to smile then. That confused Francis. What is concealed? What is explored? he would ask himself.

He first tried to tell his father on the way to market. They were in the lorry that came for the sheep, talking weather and prices. His father seemed subdued, reflective almost. It made Francis fear nostalgia, the call back to how it was and had been. Francis disliked all that. He thought it selfish of his father. He thought that he should have realised neither Francis nor the driver, a quiet man called Peter, could relate to the long tales and the cry that it had always been better.

'Aunty Ena wrote the other day,' said Francis, trying to change the subject.

'Ena?' Francis' father sounded surprised. He looked perturbed. His eyelids arched, his eyes opened. Francis imagined his thoughts. Why Ena? What's she got to do with sheep? He would recognise the contrivance. It made Francis move quickly.

'She wants to come over again.'

'God.'

'What do you mean God?' asked Francis, tracking the evolution of a distraught look on his father's face. It was probably riding over thoughts of previous visits, of lost time and wasted days.

'God. That's what it means. What do you think it bloody means?' He looked Francis' way and met a shrug that said no idea. 'It means everything comes to a bloody halt. That's what it bloody means.'

'Bloody women,' said the driver feeling a little left out.

'Aye vaccinated with a gramophone needle that Ena,' said Francis' father confirming the driver's opinion.

They all laughed, though Francis feared it may cause the conversation to peter out. He tried another slant. 'Said she'd bring Nina again.'

'Oh that's it. I see. I bloody see.' Francis' father's face lit up. 'You like her, don't you? You've got your bloody eye on her.'

Francis smiled. He wanted to point out what a disaster the last visit had been, how he had built Nina up into an icon, an imagined being who had fed his sexuality and then collapsed his confidence in it. None of that was Nina's fault. He knew that. He also knew he would always be uneasy with her, that her role in his adolescence was inestimable and could easily have been more profound. His lack of maturity killed that.

'She's a nice girl. Cousin though. You remember that. Inbreeding cross continents is still bloody inbreeding. Isn't that right?' he asked the driver.

'Wouldn't mind seeing her again,' remarked Francis. 'She said she'd show me round. The States I mean. Pennsylvania.' Francis stopped. He could see his father wasn't listening, that he had broken off to await a response from the driver. Nothing came.

Francis told his mother of his attempt to tell his father. The drive to mart preceded other attempts. One by one he listed how he had been hi-jacked, losing control. His mother laughed. To her it was familiar and predictable. Manipulation she called it. But it wasn't that. It was more instinctive, less calculated. Something rather simple, perhaps just a manner of speaking.

'He talks over me,' moaned Francis, sitting at the kitchen table. 'I mean I wanted to ease him in.'

'Gently?' His mother was filling the kettle with water.

'Yes.'

'You can't do that. He doesn't respond to that.' His mother paused to think of the uncorrupted quality that maintained plain talk and straightness. 'He'll just take over,' she said. 'He sets the agenda. He runs the ship. You must have noticed that. The way he sort of sets you back down in reality. He's good at that.'

'So how do I tell him?'

'You mean how do you break it to him?'

27

'I suppose.' Francis thought how such news needed to be couched in softness, something to land in, something to take away the awkwardness. 'You know he doesn't like Ena?'

'He's never said.'

'You can tell by his tone.'

'But he's said he likes her.' Francis recalled occasions, conversations.

'Oh yes. He says that, but I can tell. He doesn't like the interference. She wants to do things he doesn't want to do. Walk, talk. That's what she'd want to do.' His mother laughed, acknowledging the problem, understanding the turning back, the walking away. 'Still that's his problem. He could have been like Ena. He's missed out. You have to try something. That's life. He's jealous of that.'

Francis looked doubtful. It wasn't that he disagreed with his mother's words. He agreed fully with what she had said. It was just that he couldn't fit his father in the frame of what she was advocating.

'He has the valley mam. He has Brynlas,' he said coming to his father's defence.

'I'm not so sure of that,' said his mother quickly. 'I think this place has him.' Again she laughed. It was as though she was thinking of the image, the place gobbling him up. It seemed to stay with her as she poured boiling water into the teapot. She left the tea to stand, moving to a chair, sitting down, staring briefly at the crossword clue that was facing her. 'Invisible idiot,' she said. 'Three, Two, Four, Three, Two, Four.' She looked back Francis' way. 'Doesn't it tell you something?'

'What?'

'All the talk of place.' She laughed. 'Place. His loyalty to it.'

Francis pulled a face. He was bemused now. The conversation about Ena still hadn't detached itself. It left him a step behind, refocusing, fumbling with thoughts, turning them over, testing their significance. A raised eyebrow invited his mother to move on.

'Just tell him,' she said finally. 'You can't cushion anything. Just tell him. See what he says. He's full of surprises your father.'

'He'll understand?'

'Oh now that I don't know. Just tell him,' she said again. 'I did that when I was pregnant with you. And that time when I crashed the car.' She shook her head. 'Just tell him. Chances are he'll just say yes. He doesn't really know how to react.'

'Why?' asked Francis, intrigued now.

'Because nothing of any importance ever happens to him.' She sighed. It gave her time to reconsider the way he was and had always been. 'Oh a lamb dies, a tractor goes wrong, a horse goes lame. Those are the crises. He understands those. You going to America. Nina coming here. It doesn't mean a thing to him. Not a thing. How could it?'

So Francis told him. He told him when his father was cutting wood, when he had taken off the bright blue ear muffs that he wore for chain sawing and had picked up the axe, when he was grunting with effort and breathing deeply.

'You want a go?' His father looked up, smiling. He had sensed Francis' presence. The hovering irritated him. 'Hear my bloody chest? I should be fitter. It's at my age you bloody need to be fit. Go on you have a go.' He spoke as though he was assuming Francis' eyes were on the bright orange chainsaw and its rounded edges. It was on the floor next to him on a piece of paper that soaked up particles of oil. 'It's easy to use,' he said, hoisting the axe again. Francis watched it reach the position where its head was at a right angle to his father's back. From there it was thrust forward. 'My father wouldn't let me use this til I was your bloody age. Said it was dangerous. That's bloody dangerous now.' He pointed at the chainsaw. 'Funny how things change. Still,' he said, raising the axe again.

'I've not come for that.'

'Oh it's all bloody formal is it?' He brought the axe down. It held in the wood. 'Bloody wood.' He puffed as he lifted up the wood and hit it against the ground. The wood splintered, freeing the axe. 'So what you want then?'

'I'm going to the States. Mum said I should tell you.'

'Did she now?' His father brought the axe up again and puffed heavily.

'I'm going for a month or two. May stay longer if I can get work.' Francis paused for a second. He was surprised at the time his father was giving him. 'Nina says it's easy to get work. She says there's all sorts of work. Of course I'll try to get farm work.'

'Of course,' laughed his father as he brought the axe head down. There seemed to be more venom in the blow. It cut straight through the wood.

'I'll be alright. I'll stay with Ena. I'll enjoy seeing Nina. I'll find it interesting...' It seemed like one of the longest phases of talk Francis had ever engaged in with his father. Few interruptions occurred. His father had continued to wield the axe, grunting and groaning as he raised it up and let it fall. Perhaps his mother was right. Perhaps his father would say little. Perhaps he would just accept it. Francis thought of a number of possibilities as his father lowered the axe and dropped it on the ground. He walked away quickly. Francis followed.

'It will do me good. I'm sure it will.'

'Give you chance to find yourself,' said his father.

'Yes.'

'Give you chance to think.'

'Yes.'

'Make you realise what a bloody paradise this is.' His father laughed to himself. 'I'm going for the tractor. You get me some fencing out of the barn? There's a bloody hole down by the road. Want to move the sheep down there tomorrow.'

Francis watched his father move away. He thought of what his mother had said. She was right, he thought. She was bloody right. He clenched his fists, wanting to scream with delight. 'Yes, yes, yes, yes,' he said to himself, astonished now at his father's calmness. He just smiled, he thought. No anger, no vitriol. He just walked away. He thought how his father's body language said little more than there's work to be done. He looked purposeful. Nothing more. And Francis looked dazzled, shaken by the ease of it all. All that energy, he thought, all those restless nights. His mother had been right. Thank God.

After telling them, Francis led them both along. His father told him of his plans, how he was going to involve Francis more and more, giving him specific responsibilities. His mother told him how she had written to Ena, to tell her he would be coming over and what he planned to do. 'Look out for work for him,' she had written, suggesting he would stay for a month or two.

Francis smiled at them both. He was smiling all the time now, enjoying the way he had been elevated, how he had suddenly seemed more precious. His parents overdid it. They made him feel like a baby, not quite in his mother's arms or helpless on the floor, but certainly a toddler being penned in. 'I want to go,' he kept saying under his breath. They never understood the accompanying looks. They were meant for them but they were too busy organising, making plans, enjoying expectations. Francis didn't want such intrusions, not in this. This was his. He kept telling himself that. This was his. It wasn't something that could be shared or offered. It couldn't tolerate regulation. 'Why don't they see that?' he kept saying to himself. It's easy. But they didn't see it. They just wittered on. And he made plans for travel. He set the ground rules. One: no visiting. Two: no being met at the airport. Three: no staying in Scranton, PA.. Four: Scranton would be avoided and used in emergency only and even then only as a last resort.

He smiled at the rules. He knew his mother particularly would abhor them, so he kept quiet about them, always going along with what was said. That was the easy way. He even added a PS to a letter his mother had written to Ena, saying, 'See you soon,' even though he knew full well he would pass through Scranton or even avoid it completely. 'Pass through,' his mind said, its association compelling him to look at it, to see whether its Americanness was as pronounced as the images Nina had conjured. It was a fiction he now believed in. It was what he expected America to be.

'They'll come to the airport. They'll want to meet you,' said his mother one day, breaking up his thoughts.

'To New York? There's no need for that,' Francis said abruptly.

'Oh they'll want to. I'm sure they will.' His mother seemed insistent.

'But it's a long way mam. This is America we're talking about remember. Big distances.'

'Scranton to New York? No.'

Francis quickly thought of ways around that. He wanted to arrive and settle and write an apology, making up a story about some man or woman offering him work in Lubbock, Texas or Sacramento, California. Work in one of the place names he liked. Louisville, Kentucky was another. Durango, Colorado. Reno, Nevada. He made a list of them. Any of them would do. He would be happy there, given work and a room. He would promise to call in to Scranton on the way home via JFK New York. 'Thought I'd see New York,' he added, explaining his sharpness. His mother's stern look turned into a smile.

'Yes. Of course,' she said. 'All that way and not seeing New York. The Big Apple. Oh yes, it makes sense.'

'I think so,' agreed Francis. They were back on common ground again. It made everything seem smoother. 'Three days in New York and then onto Scranton. I'll need flexibility for that. So tell them I'll just turn up. I'll get a bus. There'll be several a day from New York.'

'You know?'

'Oh yes. I've got the timetables upstairs. They sent them to me.'

'You've planned it well,' said his mother in a complimentary way. It made him smile. How right you are, he thought, beaming a smile that gave little away.

★

A telephone interfered with his thoughts. It rang and rang. He was aware of it, but it seemed peripheral, nothing to do with telling his mother or father of his trip to the States. They were separate. He couldn't move from where he was, with them, in his mind. So he stayed and somehow he got used to the tone.

It went then. Someone answered it. Someone stopped it. That allowed him to return fully to the hills. He could hear a voice calling like his mother used to when it was time to come in and he would shout, 'Five minutes'. And she'd agree and come out again in ten minutes when he would have to apologise and go in.

'Francis! Francis!' The voice's rhythm was set by a hand that was rocking his shoulder. It was pulling him back into the world of the telephone and bed and window and white walls. He opened his eyes.

'Hey you with me? Frankie!' A smiling face greeted his return. He saw the prominent cheekbones first, then the sockets of the eyes, blue eyes, young eyes, like pools somehow rippling as he transferred worlds. He saw himself in the eyes. 'Phone. International call. From your home, I guess. Little old Wales.' The phone was pushed towards him. He shuffled up on the bed, coughing to clear his voice. He gestured to the nurse to puff up the pillows and prop him up.

'Hello?' His voice was croaky. It was curious. It seemed strange, even to him, but there was a confusion of location settling over him. It bothered him. He shook his head.

'Francis?'

'Mam?'

'How are you? It's lovely to hear you. Your father's here. And Gethin. And Uncle Gwyn. How are you?'

'I'm fine.'

'We thought we'd try and get you. We've been phoning, talking to the hospital. You're very lucky.'

'Yes.'

'Listen. I'll get in touch with Ena. See if she can get to see you?'

'No mam. No, there's no need.' The mention of Ena seemed to pull Francis round. He was suddenly thinking quickly. 'I'll be out soon. I'm Ok, really. They've just cleaned out my lungs a little. Smoke. I expect they've told you that.'

'But Ena'd like to be there. I know she would.'

Francis laughed. His mother's geography was Welsh in scale, compact and manageable. Long distances were in tens of miles in her world. Francis realised that. It stopped his laughter.

'I'll get her to phone.'

Francis sighed. 'There's no need. I'm fine.'

'You sure?'

'Yes. Really.'

'Now you're not just saying that?'

32

'No. I mean yes. No, no. No I mean no. I'm fine,' he snapped, cursing himself as he realised how anxious his mother was. All that way and this happens, he thought, assessing how she would view it. 'Look mam, there's nothing to worry about. My lungs were affected, but they're fine now. I just breathed in some smoke.'

'Yes, they said that. They told us it could have been worse.'

'It could have been much worse,' said Francis, thinking of the fire and the deaths.

'But as long as you're Ok.'

'Listen, I wish you could see me then you'd know I'm fine. I'm having the best of attention. I'm being well looked after. You couldn't do better.'

'Can't believe that.' The comment seemed to shake his mother. It seemed too normal – her looking after him. It conjured breakfast time meetings and summer picnics in the fields. The distance between them suddenly shrank. It made her voice become edgy. 'Your father's here.'

'How is he?'

'He's fine.'

'Put him on.'

'He's out in the kitchen at the moment, making a coffee. He's shouting. Hear him? Says he sends his best.' She laughed at the growl that accompanied her words.

'Says serves him right, I bet.'

'No. Course he doesn't. He's very concerned. Wants you home.'

Francis didn't hear her comments. He stared forward, loosening his grip on the phone, thinking how he would have liked his father to have been in the fields. He would have been listening. Now it would be difficult for his mother. Why didn't she lie? he thought, why didn't she say he was out? Not in the kitchen, thought Francis, not so near. Not near enough to come to the phone, a voice in his mind was saying. Why didn't he come to the phone?

★

Moving from the periphery to the centre was a shock for Francis. He had never expected it. He never thought the respect he gave others would be reciprocated, that he would be treated like a hero. 'You really going?' was the question they asked. 'Yes,' he'd say, feeling there was no way back, that he was committed to moving on. Still he enjoyed that. He liked answering the questions 'Why?' and 'When? and 'Where?' And he felt big when someone said, 'I could never do that.'

His mother derived benefit too. She felt proud. She smiled at friends knowing they were talking about Francis' trip. She reminded them of Ena and Nina and how well they were doing. She said it was in the blood. There was a warmth in that, a satisfaction. Like sitting in front of a fire you have built and started. It made her glow. It fuelled questions too. It made her want to glean information that could be used. 'Three days in New York' was a good prompt. It made her friends coo. And that nourished her. It made her search for more.

'You know when you return?' she said to Francis one day at the kitchen table.

'Yes,' said Francis, knowing by the tone that something was about to be asked. Some information or favour, he thought.

'Well when you return I was wondering... well could you... I mean you don't have to if you don't want to, but it would be nice...'

Francis laughed. He was unable to contain his surprise at the way he had unsettled his mother. She suddenly seemed almost in awe of him. He wondered why.

'Could you give a talk?'

'Me!' Again he laughed.

'A sort of review of your journey. It wouldn't take long and you'll be taking your camera, so there'll be lots of photos. It's easy to talk around those. I mean they work like a script. You know. And this is. .. Ah and it was by here that....' His mother illustrated the technique perfectly. The fact she believed he could carry it off intrigued him. She had never shown such confidence in him before. It made detachment seem rather virtuous. Yet, at the same time, he believed, for all the attractions of his new life, there was bound to be a reaction. It couldn't just be allowed. Nothing worked that way. Even Francis, with his limited experience, knew that. So where was the interference? He expected it to come from his father, but there was nothing but smiles from him. Short, sweet smiles, smiles from the mouth. They seemed more manufactured than eye-based smiles. He could almost sense the effort going into them. He could almost hear the voice in his father's mind saying, 'Smile.' At the same time they indicated some sort of misplaced satisfaction. This was the boy making his mark. His father admired that. Manly. That would play on his mind, particularly as he was going around blaming himself, saying he should have given Francis more scope. That made Francis' plans seem almost traditional rather than avant garde. It made it seem as though the hills had wrong-footed him. I'll get you, it made Francis think when he saw the smile come and go. You wait, he'd think, considering the first phone call or letter home from New York. Frequently he considered that first letter home, what it should say, how he should say it. Lie to tell the truth, he thought, deciding he would have to come up with something that would make it clear that he would be staying longer. An invitation, perhaps. An offer of a job. A job for a few months. Maybe a year. A full year, he thought.

★

It was on his eighth day in hospital that Francis heard he could return to the tower. Maybeth, the nurse he liked best, told him after breakfast. 'The doctor says Ok, you can go,' she said. Her words left his mind flinging up birds and bulging clouds, providing him with the sort of scenes that he would lie in bed and watch from the tower. He thought how he could do that, how he could roll back the tarpaulin that made up the roof of the tower and see the clouds scud by. Sometimes birds would sit on the concrete rim of the tower and stare in.

Maybeth brought him his clothes. He dressed slowly. He kept thinking of the tower. He compared it with Brynlas. His role in its creation killed the contest. He thought how everything in Wales had been inherited and how he would fail to change the inheritance. Then he thought of the way he had warmed the inside of the tower and given it his smell, the way he had made the inside ladder, the way he had found the furniture and cabled in electricity. Each of those thoughts moved slowly. They penetrated. They led him on. He dwelt on things occasionally. He spent a long time thinking where he found the wood for the ladder, how Brad had smuggled home two strips of wood that were painted red and had what looked like Russian markings. He remembered shaving off the signs and building on the rungs, painting them white. Then he remembered the furniture, how it needed to be small enough to carry up the ladder, how he had found chairs and bought a bean bag and Brad had found a mattress. He remembered too the desk he had constructed inside the tower, the desk where Ronnie would sit. She would visit most evenings. It was his pictures she liked most, his pictures of elephants, leopards, lions and giraffes. She particularly liked the giraffes. Francis would use double pages and extend the neck of the giraffe he was drawing onto the second page and have them wearing silly hats or saying silly things. He thought how he would use such drawings as warm ups, how they would precede his efforts to draw cartoons. Fred cartoons were his favourite. Brad had bought him an album of Fred cartoons at Christmas. That had surprised Francis. He had only been in the tower three months and hadn't expected a present. The gift was wonderful. He laughed

35

through Christmas and then started making up his own Fred cartoons. Ronnie would come to see them.

She had been visiting when the fire broke out. In hospital he had been trying to appreciate what Ronnie made of the fire, whether she had realised what was happening and how she would react to the realisation. The memories helped. They helped him recall what it was like being Ronnie's age. He had been eight when the dog had been killing sheep, when he had been to Thomas' farm to pick up the carcass. Such memories brought him closer to Ronnie. He punctuated the memories with thoughts of the day of the fire. He kept retracing the way Ronnie had fidgeted and coughed and the way danger had suddenly numbed her. He thought of his encouragement and sensed he had probably done all he could to move her on. It was that thought that made him smile. It was like an unrelenting focus. 'Ten steps to go,' his mind kept saying, 'ten steps to go.' He wondered how he had managed to let the encouragement rise above the confusion of perceptions that had been hitting him – the smoke, the warmth, the sizzle of fire. They were like punches. Feelings followed, but somehow he had managed to urge Ronnie on. And she had kept going.

The tower smelt of smoke. He sprayed it and bought pot-pourri and placed it in little dishes that were like offerings to gods. It was the smell on his books that annoyed him. He had only three books. He had bought them for his father and had been meaning to send them home. They were books on cowboys and indians and the Wild West. Eventually he took an aerosol and sprayed the covers and then flicked through the pages allowing the aerosol to send in flowers of the forest. After that he sprayed his clothes. From his clothes he went to the map on the wall by his mattress. It was a 1:25,000 map of Brynlas and the surrounding hills. The map took him back. He translated its lines and symbols into streams and trees. He knew each of the trees. But it wasn't that that made the map special. It was special because it had come with him. It was the only thing from home apart from a portrait of his father that his mother had sent him for Christmas, a ceramic pig he had had since he was five and the album of photos that he had shown to Ronnie.

The portrait of his father also smelt. He sprayed it and smiled. It seemed an odd reaction. Looking at it made him wonder why his father had stayed at Brynlas, why he hadn't left. Others, much less articulate or intelligent, had moved to the city and developed new skills. His father could have done that. A little nurturing would have fashioned new thoughts and created a new man. Instead he had come back to his family after the war and, as his father had said, looked into the eyes of the land. He remembered his father telling him how it had been, how he had doubted he would recognise it or it would recognise him. But they were like old friends saying hello spontaneously and shaking hands. He settled then; he marked out his territory and stayed.

Fifty years on, his father was still in awe of the land. He said it made him vulnerable and self conscious, that it took away ambition, that all it left were the needs of security and survival. He would say that unpretentiously, yet he knew his experience was to be Francis', that the line of history went on and on. His father saw it all as pure, as uncorrupting, as allowing access to myths and references. Francis thought how in certain fields his father would say, 'Your great-grand-father liked it here.' Francis often wondered how his father knew that, then, accepting it, he thought how it was like saying nothing had changed.

The photograph always brought all of that back. It reminded Francis of the look that would accompany his father's words. It was always the same. It was drained. It was raw. There was no conceit. It was like looking at a bare field.

Apart from the smell there was surprisingly little damage to the tower. The wind had fanned the flames north and the tower being forty or so metres south of the house had escaped damage. Francis spent the first two days after his return to the tower thinking of such things. His only visitor was Davison, the ranch owner. He had called to see Francis on the morning of the second day and had quite a shock when he saw where Francis lived. He said he had never quite figured out what Brad had meant when he had told him that Francis was living in the tower. He thought it was some quaint, old English expression for home. He laughed when he told Francis that, but he should have known better: Brad and his wife had three children and two bedrooms: he should have appreciated the squeeze and worked out the implica-tions. If he had, he told Francis he would have offered him something better. In fact that was why he had called. Before Francis could say anything Davison was offering him a cabin down by the water hole over the other side of the ranch. He said it hadn't been lived in for some time, but that he had sent a man over and the man had said that no-one had been in sleeping rough or drinking. Francis said he had a home and smiled.

It was when Francis was on his way back from saying goodbye to Davison that he stopped and stared for the first time after the fire at the cottage. There was little left now – a charred frame with fallen timbers creating barriers and little pieces of debris that were shrivelled pieces of Brad and Pam's life. He tried to interpret shapes, to fill them up, to give them a full, lean, useful look. It was when he saw a toy that could have been the boys' or a piece of furniture that Brad had been doing up in his shed that Francis felt the need to wonder about the people. He wondered what they were doing when they smelt the smoke or saw the flames. Then he thought it was obscene to put the people he knew into that situation, that the people he knew were more at home on the balcony on a summer's night. That is how he decided to remember them. It took their suffering away from him. And he was thankful for that. All the same, he began to flail for connections between the ash that lay outside and the flames that greeted him when he and Ronnie stood by the edge of the wood. He remembered the penetration of the streak of yellow and the way it touched the roof and provided a commentary on the main action that was going on inside. No chance, it said. It was speaking to Francis, telling him to pull Ronnie away, to leave the scene and settle for what he had. Yet, instead, he had dragged her towards the fire. He remembered his feet burning through his shoes, the heat charring his trousers. He remembered the scream from Ronnie that pulled him back. That was enough to stop him for a second before he retreated. In that second he thought he saw Brad, but, before he could call out, the core of the shape turned yellow.

When he returned to the tower, he sat back and drank milk and thought over Davison's offer. It was that first sense of detachment that allowed him to sit at the desk and tidy the papers on it. It was the first time he had approached it since the fire. Even finding a photo of the goats lying on its surface, upside down, did not deter him. He moved it to one side and took out his sketch book and looked at the image of Fred that two weeks ago had been emerging. It was October. Fred was walking out on to the bough of a tree to reach branches and collect leaves. Below the tree Fred's neighbours were all out sweeping up leaves. Francis' caption read: 'Fred decided to make a pre-emptive strike'. Francis laughed at that. He did a double take, rereading each word. Did I write that? he thought, shaking his head.

The confrontation was necessary, essential in fact. He had found something that was linked with the fire. He needed now to recall the detail that had sat him at the desk and had let him draw Fred tiptoeing on a branch. He struggled, but, as he knew it would help him recall the fire, he tried hard. Eventually he had to apply logic. He thought of Saturdays, of their pattern, how on some Saturdays he went to town and returned mid afternoon. Then he remembered helping Brad on the morning of the day of the fire. He remembered Pam asking them to clear some bushes that had covered a back window. He tried to recall the time they had finished and whether he had gone straight back to his desk and the cartoon.

He looked at the drawing again. It seemed finished. He checked the date in the bottom left hand corner. Saturday May 20th. The day of the fire. The date made him wonder how much of the day was missing. For some reason it was important now that he knew it all, that he learned from the experience. He believed it was the distance of such experience from the predictability of Wales that made it seek attention. He believed that somewhere within it were clues that could provide an explanation.

It was when he was shaking his head, showing a little disgust and tension that he saw the bag that Davison had left. He thought how Davison had brought it in and put it down and had gone without mentioning it. Francis was sure it was for him. He had expected it to be full of fruit or the sort of things a sick visitor would bring. He was surprised when he found a series of local papers. They were bundled together by a piece of string. Francis reached for the penknife at the side of the bed and cut the string that rolled the paper up like a carpet. He took his hands away and watched the papers spring open. He pulled the first paper out and stared at a story about storms and then at one of a killing outside the governor's palace in San Antonio, then at plans for road developments and stories of rain and subsidence and of a protest by the Hispanics that had ended in violence. It was the next page that uncovered the mystery. 'Blazing Inferno' was the headline. 'Four die engulfed by flames.' According to the paper an explosion was heard, followed by leaping flames that burnt the fringing trees. Details followed about Brad Stubbs, his wife, Pam, and their two boys, Denny and Paul, aged ten and six. It was the next line that shocked him. It mentioned Ronnie, aged eight, who had survived. It said she had been with a family friend, a foreign national who lived nearby. 'Nearby?' Francis said, thinking of the vagueness of the term.

The following day's edition had a fuller account and photographs of the burnt out shell of the cottage. The water tower was in the background. Francis was shocked at the amount of debris that was in the photograph. It was much more than he had seen when he had returned from hospital. He stared at the guttering he and Brad had taken down, at the series of cans Brad used as water butts, at the stray odds and ends that the fire had gutted and left like bones. The paper said the fire chief was making a full investigation and that the police were treating the incident as suspicious.

It was the word 'suspicious' that shocked Francis. It made him think of the visit he had had in hospital from the police. He tried to work out the slant that the policeman who saw him had taken. It had seemed routine. All those questions about time and place and what he was doing and why. At the time he had answered naturally. After all there had been nothing to alarm him. The questions were straightforward and the policeman's manner was light, though direct. Everything Francis had said had been accepted and the policeman never returned.

Francis wondered why. Why hadn't he returned? He had deserved another visit. He remembered how, when the policeman had gone, he realised he had forgotten to tell him how, once outside, after a failure to reach the cottage, he had taken Ronnie back into the wood and tied her to a tree. He also forgot to tell him how he had then returned and had got much nearer, how the heat had burnt his feet and the smoke had covered his breath. It was the smoke that had driven him back. He remembered how it had fanned behind him, how there was nothing but black and the sound of his coughing. He had run back to Ronnie. He wasn't ashamed of that. It was all he could do. Besides, if the wind had shifted around, the smoke would soon have reached Ronnie.

Much more had come back to him. The stimulus had worked in that respect, though in other ways, as he reread the story, some of the words worried him. He saw now the police were suspicious, not just tidying things up in the routine sort of way that involved report writing and statement taking. That realisation made him restless. He had to call on a voice in his mind that kept saying they hadn't returned, that all must have been well, as well as it could have been given the fire and the deaths.

He thought too of his position. He was working illegally. He thought how he had schemed with Brad and Pam to overcome any inquiries from the authorities, how he was to become a cousin of Pam's if anyone inquired. That should have worked well because Pam's mother was an orphan who had only the one child. She was fifty when she died and was from Fort Worth. That much was true. Pam built on it and decided that she was third generation Welsh, that she had traced her family back. It was then she had discovered Brynlas and made contact. Francis' visit had followed that initiative.

He smiled at that. He thought the story feasible. It made him think of Pam and Brad as he would remember them. He thought of a normal Sunday in the cottage. Brad watching a video of some football game. The Broncos probably. Denny on the computer, saving the world and screeching and being shouted down by Brad. And Paul, the

40

serious boy and scholar who had already taken a keen interest in Abraham Lincoln and Napoleon Bonaparte and who had already lost Brad who tried incessantly to get him to hold a bat or pitch a baseball for his father to hit into the wood. Pam would be cooking or washing or making up lists. Pam lived on lists. Every day was detailed and structured. There was a Saturday list and a Sunday list. Every day had a list.

Francis found it difficult to launch that normality into the chaos of flames. He tried. He had the children scattering to exits, screaming and crying. Pam sat frigid, disbelieving. Brad became violent, squabbling for position, trying his best to remember the geography of the room. Then Francis learnt that there wouldn't have been time for any of that. He learnt there was an explosion. He wondered why neither he nor Ronnie had heard it, why the smoke had arrived without a sound. But the newspaper was adamant. It blamed the fire on a faulty gas cooker. He read it was the third fatal gas stove fire in the state in the last twelve months. Warnings followed from the fire chief about buying second hand stoves. Francis reread the sentences. A fire inspector had discovered a fault and was preparing a full report. After that, the story deteriorated into small human accounts of friendships with Brad. 'A careful man who loved his family dearly' was Davison's description. Francis flinched at that. He wondered about the word careful. To him it seemed a strange choice of word, but then he thought how all small town America may have merited the adjective. He was shaking his head at that as his eyes read on. 'What!' he exclaimed, 'Fritz!'. The paper told him that Brad's friend Fritz who had been on his way to see Brad had been two hundred yards away when he saw smoke rise above the trees. The paper said Fritz had been lucky, that every Saturday he brought his video over to Brad's to watch some tapes of football games, how twice a year Brad and Fritz went to Denver to see the Broncos. It also told him that it was Fritz who found Ronnie and an unconscious foreign national, a friend of the family, who had tried to get into the cottage.

Francis should have sat back and thought of the implications of Fritz finding him. Instead he found himself recalling his first meeting with Brad. It had been in San Antonio. Francis was between buses. Brad had been on an errand for Davison. Brad had sat by Francis on a bench. He was waiting for Pam. They had decided to make a day of it, to nose around town and walk by the river. He was looking up and down the sidewalk trying to catch a glimpse of Pam who had drifted away to make a phone call. Once his eyes caught the gaze of Francis.

'Nice day,' said Brad, finding it necessary to say something.

'Yes.'

'Hey where you from boy?' Brad quickly seized on the soft sounds of Francis.

'Wales.'

'Wales? Shit, where the hell's Wales?'

Francis laughed. He liked the directness of Americans, the way they cut across formality.

'Oh I know. Wales, Alaska,' suggested Brad.

'No —'

'But they have whales in Alaska boy. Big whales. Saw it on the nature programme. Big fat whales. An' they can move them whales. They had guys on asking them why they killed them. Why they killed them! That's like asking me why I work on a ranch—'

'England,' said Francis. He was laughing, thinking how American narrowness worried him and how for the first few inquiries he had stayed firm and never mentioned England, then he had drawn maps and put arrows pointing to Wales. Now he had given in. For the sake of his patience he was willing to give himself to England.

'Ah Wales England,' said Brad with a surprising degree of misplaced certainty. 'Gee that's a long way boy. How'd you get here? Train?' Brad laughed at his own words. He chortled, then laughed more fully. 'Get it? Train.' The explanation was unnecessary, but it allowed Francis an opportunity to join in.

When the laughter died down, they started a conversation about people and places. The idea of rural came up and why Francis had left Wales. It made Brad sit up. The argument Francis was forming seemed to advocate change and insecurity and the constant maelstrom that developed could be viewed as exciting or disturbing. 'Hated the structure' he was saying, 'the routine.'

'There's routine here boy,' countered Brad. 'Hell there's routine everywhere. You ask the guy who sold you those cookies —'

'You want one?' Francis felt obliged to make the offer now that Brad had mentioned the cookies that were on Francis' lap. Brad declined with a wave of his hand.

'He's up at six,' continued Brad, 'warming his baking tray. Now where's the maelstrom in that?'

'Ok, Ok, but —'

'But what?'

'Look I've just met you —'

'Yeh. So?'

Francis' turn of words were clever. They were using the geography of the street, pointing out the uncertainty. He stressed the point again, allowing Brad to realise the unpredictability.

'See it's all about not being sure who you are going to meet. Like the cookie man meeting me –'

'And what's so great about meeting you?'

Francis laughed. He shook his head. 'That's not the point.'

'Oh. And me meeting you. And you meeting me.' Brad nodded, realising what Francis was trying to say.

'And you never know the consequences...'

The consequence was moving into the water tower. Realising that, Francis put away the papers. He sat back, put his feet up on the chair and stared at the wall. He recalled Brad showing it to him. He thought how Brad giggled his way through his promise to straighten it out, to clean it up and make it liveable in. At that point he should have realised what was coming. Instead he and Brad had sat on chairs and talked farming. Brad gave Francis a history of subsidy and post-World War Two support and Francis matched his knowledge with words about the Hill Livestock Compensatory Allowance. It was then that Brad suddenly stood up and said, 'So how about staying?'

'What here?' Francis replied in such a derogatory way that Brad had moved to the ladder and had started to climb. Francis called him back and apologised, saying that he hadn't expected the offer. 'I'd like to stay,' he said.

Francis tried to think what it was that made him say that. He thought of Brad, tall all American Brad. His most noticeable feature was his wide smile. It filled his face. It was a face for pleasure Francis thought, yet Brad controlled it. Beyond that, Francis tried to find something in the relaxed chat of their first meeting. He was trying to find something that he liked or some promise of what life would be like. But he found little there. Very quickly he turned to the tower. Now, looking around it, Francis thought that the only thing that was Brad's, apart from one or two chairs, was the graffiti on one section of the tower's round wall. He remembered Brad telling him how he had laid out the decoration of the room around the words, how he had placed the mattress and the cushions to lie under them, how his desk faced the mattress to allow him to stare at the words.

Whenever Francis looked at the words he recalled Brad, standing by the ladder, saying, 'You like my decoration boy?' He remembered his explanation too. 'All that white. Thought it would brainwash me. I mean you hear of things like that. So that's there as a distraction.'

Francis read the graffiti out loud. 'Think of it young man. You who are rubbing along from year to year with no great hope of the future...'.

'Think of what?' Francis had asked.

'Now that's the question boy,' Brad had replied laughing. 'It can be whatever you want it to be. It's just the idea of keeping space in your mind free, of making room for dreams. Jefferson said it.'

Francis thought how it said a lot about the tower, but he realised that it was the two maps draped either side of the graffiti that had first attracted him. They had gone now. Brad had taken them. At the time he had sensed Francis' interest.

'Like them?' he had said.

'Oh yes,' Francis replied enthusiastically. 'I love maps. I love their colours. I love their language.'

'Their language?' laughed Brad. 'War's the language of these maps.'

'War?' shrugged Francis, beginning to look more closely. He tried to take the detail in quickly. He saw blocked lines on topography, blue and red, the shape of gold bars, straight and long, bars facing each other. That told Francis. 'Battles' he said.

'Yeh,' laughed Brad. 'The Civil War boy. Richmond,' he said, pointing to the map closest to him. 'That's Vicksberg over there. That's how they were on those days.'

Francis saw that in the top left hand corner of the map there was a date. 'Is that significant?' he asked.

'Oh yeh. Things change in war.'

'And the names?' asked Francis, moving closer to the maps.

'Generals. That's Jackson,' said Brad interpreting the direction of Francis' attention. 'Stonewall Jackson. You heard of him boy?'

Francis nodded.

'He used to suck lemons and keep one hand in the air to keep balance.' Brad sniggered. He enjoyed the line. It was well practised. 'Gee they were real characters. I mean Clinton, Gore. What they got? I tell you what they got. They got nothing. They wouldn't have made it through that war. God no. Ol' Clinton in 1863 wouldn't have been able to hide away. I mean the Union was going down then. You know what Lincoln said −'

'In 1863?'

'Yeh'

Francis shook his head.

'He said if there's a worse place than hell I'm in it.' Again Brad laughed to himself. It wasn't an attractive laugh. A little man's laugh, thought Francis, listening to the air that blew out through Brad's nostrils. The noise increased as Brad turned round. He looked at the map of Vicksberg. Alongside him Francis studied an intensity that should have been reserved for combat. It was as if Brad was there, he thought.

'Clinton would have been a confederate, wouldn't he?' remarked Francis, thinking over the conjecture.

'What?' said Brad, moving out of thought.

★

Francis had always liked maps. It was something he had come to understand at an early age when his primary school teacher, Mrs. Jones-Ellis, had made Francis and his classmates draw their journeys from their home to school. She had liked Francis' map. She had said it was advanced. It was the first time she had used such a word for Francis. She said she liked it because it was the only map to see the land like a bird. Francis had imagined looking down on the land, drawing Brynlas as a square, the outbuildings as smaller rectangles, the track as two lines, the road as two lines with the road markings down the middle.

The evening his mother told him what advanced meant, he decided he liked maps. They became the first things he drew. Quickly he went on to make up landscapes and buildings and roads. He created a town. Then one day his mother came home with a book and gave it to him over tea.

'I've a present for you,' she said, smiling his way. 'Don't tell your father. He'll think it's your birthday.'

'And is it?' asked Francis excitedly.

'No. of course it's not.' His mother was laughing. She felt down on to her lap where she was hiding the present. 'See no ribbons and no pretty paper,' she said, holding up a book.

'What is it?' shouted Francis excitedly. He tried to reach across the table and touch the book.

'Ssh! Quiet. Your father'll come back in.'

'He won't mind.'

'Oh he will. Here.' Francis' mother handed him the book. Francis gazed at the cover. A map of the world. It made him smile. He liked the world. He particularly liked South America. It reminded him of an ice cream cornet. He began to read the words on the cover. 'My... first... What does it say? Mam, what does it say? Oh come on mam.'

'You try,' she said.

'Aa.'

'Good.'

'Ta...la..Aatala.'

'Atlas,' said his mother. 'Atlas. A book of maps.'

'A book of maps. A book of maps! Wow!' shrieked Francis excitedly.

Maps came to fill Francis' room. He liked their colour most. He saw them as a form of decoration and, without understanding their intricacies, came to possess a geology map, a land use map and Ordnance Survey maps at a variety of scales. He hung them haphazardly around his room, so he could lie on his bed and look east and west and north and see different features of the same place. That was an essential feature. All the maps had Brynlas on them. Some named it. Some had the outbuildings.

One map in particular became his favourite. The geology map. It seemed a fine map, more of a work of art than the others with a delicacy of lines and angles and special symbols. One day, coming home from school, he found his father in his room looking at it.

'Nice, isn't it? Colours and things,' said his father slowly. 'I can see why you like it.'

Francis stayed by the door staring in. He wondered why his father was in his room. His father never came to his room.

'So what does it bloody mean?' His father waved a finger over the map as he spoke.

'The colours are different rocks.'

'Ah.' His father nodded. 'I see.'

Francis thought how there was much more to tell, but his eyebrows were flickering. He knew what that meant and thought how sometimes it was his breathing that was affected and how sometimes the palms of his hands began to perspire. He thought of the ways his father troubled him, how he made him feel uneasy. Why is he here?, he thought, why is he in my room? He watched him move to the next map.

'Land use,' said Francis.

'It's wrong –'

'What?'

'It's out of date. That's not fallow.' His father pointed at a spot on the map. 'What's the bloody point of that?'

Francis didn't answer. He watched his father move on to the 1:25,000 map. Again there was a shake of the head. 'Can't make head or bloody tail of this,' he said. 'Oh I see. There we are. Well, well...'.

Francis stood still, observing. He wanted to chime in and talk about detail and perspective, but somehow he told himself it was best to stay silent. He watched his father turn and face him.

'Your uncle's coming.'

'To stay?'

'Yes. He's not well. You mustn't bother him. He's not that strong.'

Francis nodded. He knew his Uncle Gwyn quite well. He liked him. He could talk to him.

'Your mother wants you to tidy the room up. You'll have to sleep downstairs. Or on the landing. On the landing, I expect. The maps will have to go. I'll want to paint the walls.'

Francis made no objection. He had learnt there was no point. He allowed a flicker of anger to strain his face. His father saw it, but was unmoved.

'Your uncle has photographs and things. He'll want to put those up. Ok?' The question was posed to impose the words on Francis. It made him see the necessity to comply. 'You can keep that,' his father added, as though he were playing a game. He smiled, acknowledging the good behaviour of his son. 'I mean that one can stay on the wall.' He was referring to a map of medieval Wales that was framed and under glass. 'You can keep them all, but not on the wall. Not for now. Alright?'

Francis kept the maps folded up in his briefcase. At night he would take them out and unfold them. No-one understood the importance of the maps. They grew with Francis. He came to understand their language. He would rush home and check features, correlating geology with landscape and land use with soil. In his mind a web of relationships grew.

Discovery of such secrets gave Francis delight. He would tell his friend Owain of the maps, of the way he had tapped into their code. In time Owain became less interested. His own talk of youth clubs and football and girls in turn was unappreciated by Francis. Owain told Francis to come along. 'Try it out,' he would say. And Francis, out of loyalty, would try it out. He had gone to the youth club and the football training, but with others he had little to say. All he would do was sit or stand in a corner and join in when he was told to. He showed no enthusiasm. Then one day at the youth club Owain realised Francis was missing. He found him in the car park.

'Francis!' he shouted.

Francis ran. He felt threatened and self conscious. It was a piece of behaviour he couldn't explain. As he ran, he thought of his predicament: a teenager without words and just when he needed them. He thought how everything was becoming complicated and how he wanted to stop the music and the dancing and turn on the lights and examine it, how he wanted to describe and explain. Yet language had deserted him. He blamed the threats, the taunts, the innuendoes, the oppression. It had all created turmoil; only the maps provided a calmness. He thought how he would look at them, how he would lay them out on his bed, how he could now visualise landscape, how he could discern progress in his study of them.

★

Francis had been back in the water tower four days when Fritz called. He was sitting at his desk, drawing, composing a Fred cartoon. Fred was in a garden. There was sunshine. It was June. Fred was getting ready for his holidays, toning up his tan. As the ideas came, Francis' pencil shaded in detail. Fred was lying on a lounger, sun-glasses on and sun cream in hand, but the moon was out and the stars were shining. The caption read: 'Fred decided to put some extra hours in on his tan.'

Francis was putting a twinkle on a star when he heard a voice crying out.

'Hey! You there! Anyone at home.' The cry almost became musical. 'Francis! Fran-cis!' A face peered over the top of the tower's rim. 'Hey treehugger. Where the fuck are you? You avoiding me? You little foreign shit.'

Francis smiled. He had a soft spot for Fritz. He found him amusing. 'Avoiding you? How could anyone avoid you?'

'Yeh that's right. How could anyone avoid me? Can I come in or what?'

'Yeh, come on in. You seen this place?'

'Nah. He never let me in here.' Fritz let loose a long smile. He looked around. The smile was still on his face when he reached the bottom of the ladder. 'What was the fuss about? His secret place I suppose. Somewhere where he could drink his beer and pick his nose. Know what I mean? Ok?' Fritz had seen Francis' disapproving look. He looked around again.

Francis looked at the blond haired man's cool blue eyes. He wondered how Fritz, racist and fascist, could be so likeable.

'Had to come and see you,' said Fritz. 'Do you mind?'

'Why should I mind?'

'Oh I don't know. All that's happened. It sort of turns the mind. Makes you want to forget.' Again he looked around the room. 'Tried to see you yesterday,' he said continuing, 'couldn't get an answer.'

'At the shops,' said Francis, gesturing to Fritz to sit down.

'Thanks.' Fritz's small fat frame eased its way into a chair. The chair creaked and shook. Fritz continued to talk. 'What you doin' at the shops? I can buy you what you want. I'm in town every day. You

48

just tell me. Hey what you reading?' he asked, seeing Francis turn the pages of the paper.

'I'm reading about you.'

'Me? Oh the man who raised the alarm. Yeh, yeh, yeh. What do they fuckin' know?' Fritz laughed. He parodied what he told the reporter. 'The man who ran. My heart nearly fuckin' popped. You know how far it is back to my van?'

Francis listened and again built up an image of the events. 'So you heard the bang?'

'Saw it. There wasn't much of a bang. I guess there was more to see than hear. I mean everything fuckin' came out. You get me? The house sort of jumped up and then sat back down again. These going?' Fritz was referring to a packet of nuts.

'Beer?' asked Francis, sensing a need for hospitality.

'Yeh. My throat's like Arizona. Brad had his beers in the water channels cooling when it was like this. He had all sorts of fucking bright ideas.' Francis placed a can in front of Fritz. The small, round perspiring man nodded and smiled. He pulled hurriedly on the ring and smelled the beer. 'Good. Hey man you're looking after me. I'll come again. You know anything about football? I need a Saturday friend now. Fucking Brad.' Fritz shook his head and drained the last drops of beer from the can. 'Why'd they do that to him?'

'They?'

'Yeh. All those fucking gods and fairy godmothers. All those shits who look after us. Why they do that? He was alright. He was a good guy.'

'So did you try to go in?' Francis redirected the conversation.

'What? To the cottage? It was a fucking fireball. Did I try to go in? Hey who do you think I am?'

'So what was it like?'

'I told you. The flames shot through it. There was a bit of a wait. A second or two. Then it just went up. Didn't even hear screams. The explosion must have knocked them out. Pam must have been blown to bits. I mean she was always cooking.'

The image had no effect on Francis. He was comparing notes, surprising himself with the realisation that he and Ronnie must have been there at the same time as Fritz, though they had missed the explosion that Fritz had described and he couldn't recall the ferocity that Fritz's words conjured. For Francis there had been a seepage of smoke, nothing more. Just a gentle realisation and then an alarming piece of logic that this was different, more pungent and more tickling in the nose than any summer garden fire could generate.

'Funny enough I was thinking of Brad just before you called.'

'I'm always thinking of him,' remarked Fritz. 'And Pam. And the kids. You seen Ronnie?'

'No.'

'Neither have I. We should see her. Make the effort. We owe it to her.'

Francis agreed. 'We'll see her,' he said more positively. 'Did they have anyone? Family I mean. Anyone local?' As he spoke Francis thought how he knew Pam's mother was an orphan. He knew little about Brad's background.

'There's a brother in Mobile and a sister down the road.'

'Where Ronnie is?'

'That's the one. She never spoke to Brad. Thought he was a shit because he voted Republican and hated niggers. She'd hate me,' joked Fritz. 'I'd hate her too. She's a do-gooder. Married a South African. See what I mean? At least she divorced him.' He laughed again. This time Francis joined in. It reminded Fritz of his presence. 'So how'd you meet him?'

'Brad?'

'Yeh. You never told me. Not properly.'

Francis told Fritz the story of his first meeting with Brad. As he spoke, he thought of his first meeting with Fritz. He recalled the way Brad kept a log of times when people passed on the main road. He used them like a bus service. He'd scamper down through the woods and wave them down when they were passing. Francis remembered Fritz in his van coming towards them, beeping them.

'You're gonna get run down one day,' Fritz said, greeting them.

'What do you mean?' laughed Brad.

'One day I'm gonna have my fuckin' ulcer and you're gonna flag down Duane or Ricky –'

'Who the hell are they?' Brad found it difficult to contain his laughter. Having sat in the front alongside Fritz, he turned around and pushed his hand into Francis' ribs. It made Francis nod knowingly.

'They're the other fuckin' drivers and man they don't stop. They don't stop for nobody. You'd be a piece of shit in the road man.' Fritz smiled. He looked into the mirror. 'Who's the pretty boy then? Is he a wet back? You been swimming across the Rio Grande boy?' Fritz looked in the mirror to see Francis' smile. 'He joined you? You fuckin' treehuggers.'

'He's a nice Englishman. Aren't you boy?' replied Brad in a knowing way. Something about the delivery told Francis that the English had been discussed on some previous journey between Brad's and town. A laugh from Brad confirmed Francis' suspicions. It sniggered coldly.

'Well he better be nice,' joked Fritz. 'I got all the equipment for dealing with guys who ain't nice and you English got a lot to make up for. Look what you done to us. Giving us all those niggers an' things.' He shook his head, applied more pressure to the accelerator and left Francis sniffing at the gas-like smell and looking over his shoulder at the equipment in the back of the van. Fritz was a ratcatcher or, as he called it, a vermin control officer. 'Goin' from bad to worse America,' said Fritz. 'It's so fucking violent. Even the language is violent. You fuckin' noticed?'

'Yes,' said Francis, issuing his first word.

'You English don't say much –'

'Reserved,' laughed Brad, cutting into Fritz's words.

'Heinous crimes all over the fuckin' place and all they do is give me fuckin' parking tickets. If I stopped here, they'd give me shit. And you English fuckin' started it.'

Now it was Francis' turn to laugh. It was the first sign of strength he had shown and Fritz warmed to it.

'Hey, he's alright. No wonder those English always win fuckin' wars. They've a way with words –'

'But he ain't said nothin',' laughed Brad.

'Exactly. But he knew when to come in. When to say, hey what's all this shit. You don't do that.'

'I do,' objected Brad.

'No you fuckin' don't. You listen to all the crap God gives you. And all you do is say yeh and laugh. And that's why I like you. It's good for a man to find a fuckin' gook who'll laugh at his jokes. Hey man you laughed when I said I got an album full of parking tickets.' Fritz paused as Brad laughed again. 'See. You're laughing now. You'd laugh if your granny's butt was on fire –'

'I wouldn't.'

'You fuckin' would. He wouldn't,' Fritz scoffed, looking in the mirror at Francis. 'So Mr. Englishman, what's your name?' he asked.

'Francis,' answered Brad.

'Hey you're alright Francis. Do they call you that? Not Frankie?'

'No,' said Francis, shaking his head. 'Francis.'

'Ok. Francis. Yeh I like that. Francis,' repeated Fritz practising the name. 'Hey Francis you're Ok.' Fritz thrust his hand back Francis' way and shook hands.

'You don't mean that,' sighed Brad, putting one foot up on the dashboard of the van. He leant forward to play with the radio.

'I do. And you can fuckin' stop that. You know I never have it on. Not while I'm driving. If I'm parked up, Ok. Play the fuckin' radio. Sing along. Pretend you're the boss. But when you're driving, eyes on the road,' remarked Fritz, staring directly at Brad. 'Where've you come from Francis?' he asked.

'St. Louis,' said Francis.

'St. Louis. Hey that's my fuckin' home town. East St. Louis I'm from. You go there? Hey, what am I saying? Did you go there? Course you fuckin' didn't. No-one ever goes there.' Francis saw the slightest movement of Fritz's face. It suggested he was trying to turn towards him. 'Hot there?' he asked.

'Eighty five degrees.'

'Yeh, that's St. Louis. Fry fuckin' eggs on your car in summer. Lovely city, what d'you think?'

Francis nodded and said, 'Yes, it's nice. Very friendly.'

'See. He fuckin' tells the truth. Not like you.'

'I tell the truth,' said Brad, sounding a little aggrieved.

'Like hell you do. You've got the truth hidden away. And don't you fuckin' know it.'

It was the last few sentences that stuck in Francis' mind. At the time he had let it pass, thinking it was Fritz's way of sounding smart. Brad and he had enjoyed the banter and had learned how to build it up so it became ridiculous, but somehow believable.

'That was good. What beer was it?' Fritz belched and answered himself by picking up the can. He sat back in his chair and relaxed. 'It's nice here,' he said, looking around again. His face softened to a degree Francis had never before witnessed. 'He must have liked you,' he added.

'Brad? Why?'

'Because this was his place. Fuckin' treehugger. He spent a lot of time up here. Mostly doin' nothin'.' Fritz laughed. 'This was the only thing he had plans for. Last I heard he wanted to turn it into an observatory. A fuckin' observatory. Now is that a plan or what? He had big ideas Brad. Fuckin' big ideas. Did he talk to you about it?'

Francis shook his head and went to the fridge for another beer.

'Yeh,' said Fritz accepting the offer. 'He wanted to put a fuckin' telescope in here. He said it was the tower that made him realise about stars and life and he fuckin' believed what he told himself.' Fritz laughed loudly and spluttered beer out on to his lap and the floor.

'Hey I'm fuckin' sorry,' he said, bending down and pulling out his handkerchief. He started dabbing at the floor. 'I'm so fuckin' clumsy. Betty says I'm not house trained –'

'What was so funny?' asked Francis.

'Oh just that he said that when he died he wanted to be shot into space. You know like them human cannon-balls at the circus, only on a fuckin' bigger scale. Bang and out he'd fuckin' shoot. All over the fuckin' universe. Hey they'll be landing on Mars in a hundred years time and what will they find? They'll find fuckin' Brad.'

Francis shook his head. He liked Fritz's openness. He liked his way of smiling, the way the side of his face would open up and his chin would shake with the small sound that followed. He thought what a delight it was to find such new friends and considered how in Wales it was difficult, how friends were there like the stream and the fields. He thought too how in Wales the process of getting to know each other was less intimate because there were always others to intervene and families to approve or disapprove.

'Hey, I'll have to go'. While Francis thought, Fritz had caught the time on his watch as he cleaned up the floor. 'Christ I nearly forgot why I came over,' he said, standing up. 'I wanted to know if you wanted to go to the funeral. The arrangements were in the paper.'

Francis looked a little concerned. He hadn't thought of the funeral. It made him think how he would feel outside of it all, how funerals were such a distinctive part of culture, of the way people interrelated.

'What's the matter?' asked Fritz, sensing Francis' concern. 'Not guilt is it?'

'Could be,' said Francis thoughtfully.

'Look you're alive. Forget it. The funeral will help.'

Francis doubted that. He wanted to say so, but he knew how Fritz would react. He sensed there would be little sympathy.

'I'll pick you up at ten,' said Fritz, making the decision for him. 'Tell your boss. He'll want to go. I expect he knows about it. He'll know how important it was to Brad. God and country and all that shit. Christ.' Fritz wittered on. He realised Francis wasn't listening and checked his words. 'So I'll pick you up yeh?'

Francis smiled. 'When?'

'Wednesday. Are you listening to me?'

'What time?'

'Didn't I say? Ten, I'll pick you up at ten. I'll call here, Ok?'

'Fine,' said Francis, thinking it was best to agree and let the idea fix in his mind. He could always find an excuse later.

Francis went outside and waved goodbye to Fritz. When the squat figure disappeared behind a tree, he stayed and listened to the wind moving through the bushes. Such movement was rare here. It was mostly still. When it was windy he thought of Brynlas. For a moment he remembered the rain drumming, drops catching on the tips of leaves, white spots marking the black bark, running away like blood. At another scale, there was the spray of trees around Brynlas. The debris after the storm of 1987. The trees felled by the wind lying against each other like wounded soldiers. He remembered the way the realignment changed the pattern of light that reached the house. The way the old boughs developed a fur. The way the bark broke up and flaked into an orange rot. He remembered the leaves always agitated, like a bad nerve twitching against the light.

Somehow, out of that, something told him he should go to the funeral. It wasn't the past, it was the present that pressed him. He felt a need to see Ronnie and say hello and check she was well and coping. Brad's sister would grant him that. He was sure. He also decided it was an opportunity to suggest that he should see Ronnie, perhaps take her for a burger or to the zoo. He thought how he could show her goats and giraffes, all the things he drew. He began to make plans, to make lists of all the things they could see and do. As he stood there at no time did he think that Ronnie or Brad's sister may opt to forget the past and leave the farmhouse and the water tower behind. He was too positive for that, though he did allow other thoughts to come and go. For a time Fritz's words about Brad stayed with him. He wondered when it would be appropriate to mention that to Fritz. He thought how Fritz was so transparent that it would only take a sentence to sense whether it was a throwaway remark or something more substantial. It also made Francis realise that that was why he felt so at ease with Fritz. He liked the straightness.

Standing in the wood also made Francis aware of Brad's influence on place. The niches and pathways around him all related back to Brad. He had created them. But it was more than that. Francis associated them with conversations and walks they had had. Conversations, particularly from the days just after he arrived, seemed to linger in the shade. They never failed to come to him. Now, standing south of the cottage, where Brad had made Denny and Paul a tree house, he remembered how Brad had sat in a chair. 'Good place to come and think this,' he had said. Francis remembered that, as he spoke the words, Brad had sat up and looked around. He had seemed to be taking note of the paths that led off into the wood. 'This is the centre of it all,' he had added.

'The centre?' Francis said.

'All the paths meet here boy. Don't ask me why. I mean you'd expect them to meet at the house. Must be important to me, I guess. Yeh, that's it. This place is like the tower. It's where I think.'

'So you need to get to it.'

'Yeh,' Brad said, smiling. The realisation seemed to relax him. He laughed a little and fell back into the carved out tree trunk that had fallen across the path. He corrected his position to show the trunk's versatility. 'Hey I'm not laughing at you. Just some thoughts. You know. About thinking, about being private.' Francis watched him and imagined the view when Brad's back was flat against the bark and his eyes were following the birds that were jumping from tree to tree. 'Good place to come and think I guess. I think of Pam, the boys, Ronnie. All the important things boy. I think of God too. You religious boy?' Francis didn't reply. He didn't need to. Brad moved on. He shut his eyes. 'You know I remember a t.v. show on the other week. The Texan Weave it was called. You know I'm not sure what it was about. Gee what am I saying boy. Makes me sound daft. Don't know what it was about.' He laughed again. 'Still one week some guy came on – a baseball player, I think – and I said yeh man that's right, that's what I think. Not that I knew it before. I mean I knew it, but I sort of couldn't think it. Get my drift?'

Francis nodded and smiled reassuringly. Brad smiled back. 'What did he say?' Francis asked.

'All sorts of things boy. I remember sitting there thinking this man knows. But there was one bit, one little bit that made sense.'

'Just one bit?'

'Well, you know, one bit's enough. It's all you need.'

'And what was it?'

'He said he believed in the random nature of life.'

'The random nature of life.' Francis took his time repeating the words. He was thinking that it expressed nothing more than modernity.

'Yeh. That's my theory. I'm one of those guys who starts on the bottom rung of the ladder and it breaks. That's me boy.'

'And me,' Francis added.

'Not that I mind. Cause I got God.'

'And this man was at the top?'

'Oh yeh, the guy was the best. I remember thinking at the time, Jees I'm in good company. Then I looked at my pay. One hundred and seventy eight dollars. There's the proof I thought. A random life.'

'So you come here and think about it.'

'No I come here and don't think about it. I'd shoot myself if I thought about it. Jesus! Think about it!' Brad laughed at that. He sat back on the trunk again and giggled. 'Worst thing is,' he said, continuing, 'I can never find any talent. It's there see, it must be. That what makes it random boy. The difficult bit is finding it.'

The memory of the wood and the conversation was still with Francis on the day of the funeral. He even extended the recall to include their walk around the wood's perimeter and their invention of all sorts of possible talent that Brad could possess. By the time they had returned to the water tower Francis had bought Brad a piano and sent him to the moon. 'Prefer to stay as I am,' Brad had said, walking away. 'A simple man.'

Fritz turned up late and was hurrying when Francis was imagining Brad walking away. 'You ready?' Fritz asked. 'I should have told you to wait by the fuckin' road.'

'Your idea,' replied Francis.

'Yeh, yeh, yeh. And it was my idea to marry Betty and to get a diploma in poisons and to vote for Kennedy in 1960. Life's full of shitty ideas.'

Francis laughed. As he hurried about the tower, putting on a tie, he took a long look at the respectable looking Fritz.

'What's so fuckin' funny? I bought this for my cousin's wedding.'

'And when was that? Nineteen forty five?' said Francis with difficulty through his laughter.

'Hey man what is this? What have I done to you? Fuckin' treehugger.'

Francis pointed at Fritz's tie.

'Ok, Ok, look it's a nice tie –'

'It is,' said Francis nodding.

'Gee thanks,' said Fritz knowing there was much to pick up on. 'Come on then. We going?'

'Think Ronnie'll be there?' Francis asked, as they climbed down the ladder from the tower.

'Don't know,' said Fritz in front of him. 'I've been thinking about that. Would you have gone if you were eight? You don't know do you? So what's your next stupid fuckin' question? Make it snappy. We'll be fuckin' late the rate we're going. And I can't speed in the van.'

'Van? You got the van?' Francis' tone displayed the fact he couldn't believe what he was hearing. He had expected Fritz to have sufficient sensitivity to bring the car.

'Yeh. What's wrong with that? I had no choice. Betty needed the car. Taking the kids to have their teeth cleaned. Now what's the fuckin' problem?'

'You don't see it, do you?'

'See what?' said Fritz reaching the bottom of the ladder and striding towards the road. 'Ok don't tell me, let me work it out for my fuckin' self. I mean am I dumb or something? What is the fuckin' joke?'

'Come on.'

'Yeh.'

'The van.'

'Yeh.'

'You've got the van?'

'Yeh.'

'But it's called Hired to Kill. It's got that on its side. It's your firm's name.'

'Sure. Got a good ring to it, don't you think?'

'Fritz this is a funeral we're going to.' Francis laughed loudly, freely.

'Hey you should laugh more often. You've a good laugh. I like it. Yeh. That's good. Just as well I've got the car,' he added, smiling wickedly Francis' way.

Fritz was unusually silent driving to the funeral. Francis kept glancing his way, waiting for a word. When he realised nothing would be forthcoming he settled back Brad style, putting a foot up on the dashboard. He looked out of the window. He thought of funerals he had been to, of funerals he had seen. He recalled the sight of upturned earth, the sound of the slop of water as the coffin was lowered in. He could see the minister, Thomas Jones, waiting by the grey wall, looking gaunt, his mouth set back, his chin long and pointed, his grey hair like a rising wave, two furrows on his forehead like plough marks. Francis thought how he always seemed to be looking beyond the mourners, waiting for something more important, more permanent. Whenever Francis approached him he expected to see moss furring over his dog collar. The land seemed so much part of him.

'Be there soon. Hey did I tell you my boss has been to England? Said when you're driving you've got to use your directionals all the time. All those fuckin', err, what do you call them? Those round things. You know.' Fritz looked at Francis. There was no recognition on his face. 'You know,' he insisted. 'Those roads that go round.' He drew a circle in the air.

'Oh roundabouts.'

'Yeh roundabouts.'

Fritz's words speeded up Francis' thoughts of Wales. They moved Francis inside Bethesda, the chapel, where the congregation spoke to God in Welsh. Francis wondered about that, whether it made any sense to Him, whether He wondered about the sound that was muffled by the stones and the rain, whether He was more impressed by the humanity of tears and the warmth that came from turning out, from standing in groups and saying nice things. Something about that made Francis laugh.

'You English,' cursed Fritz. 'Funerals funny eh? We laugh at Steve Martin and the Marx Brothers. Hey you had that comedy *Four weddings and a Funeral.* Gee that was good. That bit when...'

But Francis wasn't listening. He was thinking how in Wales it was only on days of weddings and funerals that people spread out over the scene like sheep, how everything then seemed occupied, lived in.

The Texan funeral was different. The people were dressed for the land. It proved Francis' belief in some sort of environmental determinism. He confirmed that by sweeping his eyes around the crowd's white shirts. His eyes stopped drifting when they settled on the vicar. Again a contrast. This man looked open, less abstracted and more part of the day. He sang the hymn, his voice weak and lost in the straining notes.

Francis didn't sing. His eyes continued their tour of the chapel. There was no sign of Ronnie. That surprised him. For all of Fritz's logic, there was something about Ronnie's spirit that was so indefatigable that he expected her at any moment to walk in. No fuss, he thought, just an appearance and a quiet look at who had come and what was going on.

Without Ronnie, it was Francis who adopted the quiet look. After the vicar, he tried to look for the round face and wide eyed, prominent, statuesque look that had been Brad's. He found appropriate stature, but side on or from the back, couldn't match the geometry of the face. He was just settling on a tall man in the second row for Brad's brother when his peripheral vision found Davison. Francis immediately connected him with Brad. He thought of their relationship, the deference Brad had shown, the loyalty Davison had shown in trying to help his employee. He remembered the way Brad had told him he had gone to Davison for help at Christmas and the way Davison had given him a bonus. Brad had labelled him a good employer. Perhaps such praise would be extended now he was here and had taken Francis on, giving him a job on a weekly basis and, although Francis was turned away some weeks, most weeks he had worked. All this interfered with the thrust of Francis' thoughts. He wanted to apply Brad's ideas on the randomness of life. Here was a man on top, a man who had found his talents. But Francis wondered what talents. It wasn't like a footballer or a writer, the skills were less obvious. Perhaps luck had just picked him out. To Francis that seemed the ultimate in randomness. It put Davison on the top of the tree. And it made Francis reserve judgement and listen to the words of the priest.

He enjoyed what he heard. The eulogy was predictable, picking on the things that were clear, missing the things that happened out of sight. It made Francis see it was the solid that was held and valued. So Brad was a family man, a good father, a carer of community, the man who organised the building of the extra schoolroom, the man who drove the Sunday school children for their summer treat. He thought how the words could have been given perspective by reference to the way Brad would fight his corner and how the characterisation that was being conjured could have been lightened by reference to his practical jokes.

Such thoughts made Francis think what he would have said. He would have made it lighter. More anecdotal. He thought of suitable stories. Some made him smile. They said much more about the nature of Brad. It made him seem real. In particular he thought of his first drink with Brad. They had gone to the small bar in town. He couldn't remember its name. Oscar's rang a bell, but other names came to him too. He realised it didn't matter. It was what went on inside that was important. Fritz had taken them. They had drunk some beers. It was then the fight happened. Francis had never before been in a fight where windows were broken and chairs were thrown, but something between Brad and a tall, grey haired man named Jim had simmered to the point that Brad had told the man to 'cut the tongue'.

'Tongue,' Jim had said, standing up. 'You can't hide from truth. I seen ya. It's the truth. As I stand here, so help me God, it's the truth. You been playing around. You been seen. Now I know. And you know. The only person who don't know is Davison. If he knew you'd be gone.'

Francis had continued to drink. He had treated it like a movie scene. He had expected someone to come between the squaring-up men and shout 'Cut!' and applaud the delivery of the accent or the nervous movements that had accompanied the words. Instead there was Jim and Brad edging towards each other, looking angry.

When Brad hit Jim, Francis realised that the fury of Errol Flynn and the movie tradition had been concocted to create suspense. There was little suspense about the crack on the chin that Brad dealt Jim and the way Jim had collapsed on the table. Francis had expected the table to give way and all the others in the bar to join in. Instead the instant silence soon filled up with talk. Only a barman moved. He rushed across to revive Jim. 'Hey man, you crazy or something. There was no need for that, no need. You better drink up and go. Yeh? Get what I'm saying?'

'He was foul mouthing me, lying,' shouted Brad. 'No-one does that. I got a wife and kids. I got pride man. No-one foul mouths me, Ok?'

'Ok man, Ok.' The bar man pushed Jim back in the chair. He watched Brad make for the door. Francis had smiled and said nothing. He finished his drink and followed Brad and Fritz.

What surprised Francis was the way Brad had recovered. When Francis had caught up with him, Brad was marching down main street, moving more quickly than normal and looking more serious, but Francis somehow sensed that Brad had already recovered. It was a sign that he had done it before. At the time Francis thought that it was also a sign that Brad was in the right.

'Shit,' said Brad, walking quickly.

'Hey I'm staying. You guys want a lift back. I said I'd meet Betty here at ten outside Morris.' Fritz's words were met by a wave that intimated Brad was walking home.

Francis looked up and saw the shop sign 'Morris the Realm.'

'Morris the Realm,' Brad was saying when Francis caught up with him. 'Makes me laugh. You know Ronnie can't say it. Can't say the realm. So what she says is Morris eleven. Morris eleven,' he laughed.

Brad took Francis on what he had called the shortest route. It crossed fields and followed tracks. While they walked there was no mention of Jim. The talk was of parents, of childhood, of work. Francis remembered talking until Brad had looked at a field. He said it was Davison's land, the start of the ranch, that from here he knew all the short cuts.

'Follow me boy,' he said. 'This little ditch here kind of cuts off the long corner.' Almost immediately they were confronted by what looked like an ordinary fence. 'Shit!' Brad looked distraught. He stopped for a second and thought.

'What's wrong?' Francis asked.

'Electric boy.'

'Electric?'

'The fence. Strong current too. It's the perimeter. There's normally cattle here.' Brad stayed thoughtful throughout the delivery of all his words. 'Still,' he finally said, coming out of thought.

'You sure it's electric?'

'Yeh boy. It's electric. I put it up.' Brad sniggered.

'Better go back to the road then.' Francis turned and began to walk away.

'No, you stay here. There's no need for that.'

'You sure?' Francis said, turning round.

'Look I know a way. You push your bag down on it.' Brad paused to point to a spot on the wire. 'I'll scamper over.'

'And that will work will it?' Francis' face had continued to show concern.'

'Yeh. No problem. I'll go first.'

'Ok.'

Francis placed the carrier bag containing his jumper, diary and money on the wire. He watched Brad slowly and carefully move his left leg over the fence. His right leg followed. 'Ok, your turn boy.'

'Right,' Francis said anxiously. 'You hold it then.' He looked at Brad's gentle smile that was now on the opposite side of the fence.

'Sure boy,' came the reply.

Francis watched him settle the bag on the wire. He saw Brad exert downward pressure. 'Come on boy,' Brad urged. Smiling, Francis threw one leg over the wire and was about to move his right leg when he heard the beginnings of a worried whisper. 'Oh!' Brad exclaimed, watching the wire slip and jump up between Francis' legs.

'Ow! Bloody! Bloody! Bloody!' Francis jumped and screamed and vaulted forwards. He felt a pulse, a shock, but it was all imagined, all conjured out of the circumstances and the trickle of concern that had touched Brad's face. The concern had gone now. A snigger replaced it. 'You thought... Didn't you?.. You sort of imagined.... I know.... I know...' The words were interspersed with sneers and the sniggering laugh Francis now considered unattractive.

'You bugger,' he said, standing up and collecting himself. 'You bloody bugger.' A laugh followed the curse. 'I'll get you,' he said, chasing after Brad who ran ahead of him, still laughing, still enjoying himself.

The last hymn was unknown to Francis. The tune seemed flat. The words were about place and change and tradition and what should be valued. They made Francis think of the conversation with his father when he was waiting for the taxi to take him to Brecon for the bus to London and Heathrow. What his father had said had shocked him. Certainly it made him see the distance between them, how he hardly knew his father's thoughts and beliefs.

He remembered they had been talking about the countryside, about the future of the farm. His father couldn't understand what Francis disliked. Francis said compactness. His father said 'What?' Francis said 'Not the farm.' His father said 'What then?' Francis said 'Society.' It was then he spoke of wanting to take the mask off, to reveal the true face and he commented how everyone in the country was like a police force making sure the mask stayed on. He remembered the pause at that point, how he had closed his eyes expecting his father to walk away. Instead his father was nodding, agreeing. His father then spoke of his only holiday abroad. A trip to Paris. He spoke of the quays and the wharves, the kiosks and the arcades, the squares and the traffic. He spoke of the parks and the buildings. Francis knew what he was saying. And Francis agreed. He shook with excitement. He smiled and smiled, and laughed, and said 'yes.'

In the car park Fritz had waited for Francis. People were milling around, talking. Nobody showed any inclination for driving away.

'What did you think of it?' asked Francis.

'Ok. But they made him sound like a fuckin' saint. They hid his skeleton away –'

'He's got skeletons then?'

'We've all got fuckin' skeletons.' Fritz didn't expand. Francis had noticed the way Fritz quickly controlled his words about Brad's weaknesses. He wondered how he could draw them out.

'Didn't mention Jim McDonald,' laughed Francis.

'God no.' Fritz laughed too. 'Jim McDonald. There's a hundred Jim McDonalds they could have mentioned. This is cowboy country. What you expect? Kissing and cuddling. A lot of people would have liked to have laid out Jim McDonald. Why do you think the bar was so silent? They were fuckin' amazed. Jim McDonald had beaten the shit out of half of them there. If I could have reached his chin, I'd have laid one on Jim McDonald.'

'And a lot of people would have liked to have landed one on Brad I guess.'

Fritz smiled at Francis. 'Hey that's not a bad assessment. You're learning.' As he spoke he opened the car door.

'But why?' asked Francis.

'You getting in?' said Fritz, ignoring him.

Fritz drove to the outskirts of San Antonio. Large houses were set back off the road, shaded by trees, secluded and private. They made Francis think how Brad had struggled in a rented home, a bedroom short, and how every little repair job had to be squeezed out of Davison, how the people here wouldn't miss the dollars for a tile or gate. Eventually they stopped by a drive that already had a trail of cars.

'Here we are,' said Fritz, slowing down the car and stopping it. 'Better go in and say hello. It's etiquette.'

'You know this sister?' inquired Francis.

'As well as you –'

'Meaning?'

'Meaning I just fuckin' met her. You saw me outside the Church. I said I'm Fritz Semmler, how are you? She said ah Fritz, a friend of Brad's. I said no, a friend of the family. Sorry, she said. I said, look I'm really sorry. I said Brad was a good guy, a rough diamond, but, at heart, a good guy and I said Pam was a fine girl, a real nice lady, then she said –'

'Ok –'

'Get it?'

Francis nodded a reply.

'Now let's get in and get it over with.' Fritz began to head off towards the house. After five yards he stopped and turned to Francis, who was following him, saying, 'Now no fuckin' seducing the sister. You hear me? I've got to get home and play with the kids. Otherwise Betty'll kill me.'

Francis didn't reply. He looked away, across the open garden, passed the well planned borders and the shrubs and dwarf trees that looked over each other's shoulders and were trained to sweep across the grass. The house behind was a long bungalow. Francis thought that like the garden and the neighbourhood it was individual, sweeping in a curve and disappearing around a bend rather than a corner. He could hear voices around the back.

'They're in the garden,' whispered Fritz. He drew Francis along the path that followed the shape of the house, stopping occasionally to stare in. 'Look at that!' he gasped. Francis' attention was drawn to a window that framed a sculpture of a man by a staircase. It was upside down, falling with the most magnificent hands catching hold of the earth. 'Some place, eh?' said Fritz, moving on.

'Hello.' The tall blonde haired woman Francis had seen Fritz conversing with in the churchyard met them at a corner. She forced a smile. 'Oh God, did I make you jump? I'm so sorry. Look, you just grab what you want. There's food over there. And drink there.' She paused between the sentences to indicate precisely where she meant. Fritz nodded a recognition of the locations. 'You'll know some of the friends and some of the family. Any introductions give me a call. Yeh?'

Again Fritz smiled. He watched the blonde haired woman move away. 'Drink or food? And where do we fuckin' sit?' Fritz whispered, smiling at a man who had waved his way.

'You know him?' asked Francis.

'Na. Never seen him before. He smiled at me –'

'And you smiled back –'

'Hey what am I supposed to do? This is America remember. Come on let's get some food.'

They sat in a niche, eating and talking to two of Brad's workgang, saying hello to people who wandered across from time to time. They talked about the old days and Davison and his plans and about the ranch's cottages, about whether Brad's cottage would be rebuilt.

It was a little later when they were talking about football and the coming season that Francis saw his chance to have a word with Brad's sister. She was standing at the bar, ordering a drink. Francis excused himself and stood behind her. He admired the elegance of her shoulders and her straight back that was draped by her thick blonde hair. He looked around her at the counter and the pink shade and the ice boxes and bottles that were spread out beside the barman.

'Sir,' said the barman when the woman moved away.

'No, no, I'm fine,' said Francis. He curled up his mouth as if to say sorry and moved after the woman. 'Hello,' he said, moving alongside her. 'I'm Francis. Francis Williams –'

'You're the man from England,' she said. 'We owe you a thank you Mr. Williams.'

'What for?'

'For saving my cute niece. For at least leaving us one part of the family.'

'How is she?'

Francis' question stopped the woman. She sipped her drink then held the glass at her side. She smiled at him. It was a wispy, insignificant smile. Francis thought it had no depth, but he felt obliged to smile back.

'Oh come on you probably know her better than I do, Mr.

Williams.' She stopped and took another sip. 'You see we didn't get on.'

'People are different,' said Francis.

'Oh it's not what you think.' The woman laughed at his words. 'We didn't grow apart because of this. This didn't bother him.'

'What was it then?'

She laughed. 'This is his funeral Mr. Williams.' She waited for some sign of recalcitrance on Francis' face before continuing. 'But not to put to fine a point on it, he was no good Mr. Williams. Heavensakes you know how it is. You like some people and you don't like some people. Brad I didn't take to.' She stopped to take in the look on Francis' face. 'I'm not kidding. I mean I know he's my brother. I tried to like him. Gee I'd like to be able to say he's a swell guy. But I can't. That's the way it is.' She shrugged. 'Was,' she corrected herself quickly. 'God.'

Francis bit his tongue. He knew his perspective was tainted by the way Brad had taken him in and got him a job. Francis thought quickly through the points he could have made. 'He helped me,' he said responding. He wanted to continue. He remembered the humour of their initial exchanges, though he recognised as quickly that, as time went on, Brad became more morose. His obsessions seemed to take over.

'He helped himself too.' The woman's smile infuriated Francis. It was arrogant, concealing, almost patronising. She started walking again. 'Let's agree to disagree' she said.

Francis didn't argue. He thought it wasn't the occasion to delve. He thought of Ronnie. 'How's Ronnie?' he asked.

'She's delightful. And she's fine.'

'So what happens to her?'

'We're keeping her here. We love her Mr. Williams.'

Francis nodded his head. He knew it was what Ronnie deserved. He knew that she was the ideal child, the sort of child that made people want children of their own.

'She'll like it here.'

'You think? You like it?'

'The garden's lovely.' Francis swept his eyes over it to find a feature to praise. 'The path round there. I mean the shrubs.'

'No you mean the path,' said the woman somehow knowing what he meant.

'Yes the path.' Francis looked at the tall, tapering evergreens that flanked the wide path.

'See the gravel. The gravel that cuts into the path. It's the shadow of the plants. Different times for each side. At three mid summer the gravel is the shadow for that side.' The woman pointed to the furthest row of shrubs. 'Oh I forget for the other side. It's gotten a symmetry all of its own. Cute, yeh?'

Francis smiled and agreed with a nod, though he didn't really understand the concept she was trying to explain.

'You seen *Last Year in Marienbad*?'

Francis thought quickly. Seen, seen, seen, he thought. Film. Last year in... Where? It rang no bells.

'It's European. French, I think. Have to check when I go in. Sort of looks French. You know what I mean? It's gotten that look.' She smiled, nodding as though she were refocusing her mind, her eyes staring at the Christmas tree hedges that bordered the path around the side of the house. 'Wanted to paint it. Wanted to put down boards and paint in the shadows. That's what they did in the film. You should see it some time.' She smiled fully. 'Nice talking to you.' Again the woman began to walk away. Ronnie, thought Francis, Ronnie.

'Is she here?' Francis called after the woman.

'Ronnie?'

'Yes.'

'Yeh she's here.'

'Can I see her?'

'Well that's kind of difficult,' said the woman, turning. 'I mean she's here but she's not here, if you see what I mean. She's out. At a friend's. She's got a cute friend called Rhoda. They sing together. In the choir I mean. Rhoda keeps tortoises. Ronnie loves them. I thought it was better to let her stay away. She's very emotional and not very mature. I thought it was the only way. She wouldn't have coped. But if you call me, we'll fix something up.'

'I'd like that. Perhaps I could take her to the zoo? I could show her the goats. She loved mine.'

The woman smiled. The coldness seemed to move away. There was something genuine about the smile. It was as if Francis had said something that had quantified just how close he was to Ronnie. 'So they're your goats are they? Those goats.' The woman laughed.

'What's so funny?'

'Mr. Williams she loves those goats. They're all over the wall of the bedroom I've put her in. They've made it her room. All she's been asking me is what's their names.'

'Didn't I tell her?' said Francis.

'I think you had other things to think of.' Again the woman smiled. By now her features had warmed. Francis thought how the gaunt look had been put away like a hat or a pair of shoes, that she now looked relaxed, as if, for the first time, she was coping with the day.

'Toggie and Zoon,' said Francis revealing the names.

'Toggie and what?'

'Zoon. Nice Welsh name,' joked Francis.

The woman laughed. It was a shrill, no nonsense sort of laugh that came and went. It didn't linger. 'I'll tell her,' she said. 'Toggie and Zoon.'

'The big one's Toggie –'

'Right,' she said, turning away. She checked herself and stopped to look into the small hand bag she was carrying. She picked something out of its middle section. Francis watched her snap the small black bag shut. 'Hey here's my card. Give me a call at the end of the week, I'll see what I can do.'

Francis accepted the card and returned the smile. He looked at the name. Zelda Stubbs. Horton Publishing, he read. He at least got that right. Publishing or marketing was what he would have predicted. He thought, too, how appearances were deceptive, how all he had thought at the chapel and in the garden about snobbery and importance had been replaced by something softer and more worthy.

Francis began to look forward to seeing Ronnie. That night he began to plan how he should act and what he should say. He thought of presents and dismissed them. He thought of visits. The zoo was a possibility. But the cinema seemed better. He remembered how Ronnie had told him she liked the Disney characters she had seen in books, how she fell in love with Bambi when she was six and how she had always wanted to see it on the big screen, how it would have made her feel the characters were there with her.

She had mentioned that on her first visit to the tower. It occurred about three to four months after Francis had moved in. Up until then, he saw her only when he called at the cottage for milk. On such visits, 'Hi' was about all she managed to say. That's why her appearance in the tower had shocked him. He had been sitting at his desk, drawing. Fred had put on his best suit and was looking to fall in love. It was spring. March. Daffodils were in bloom. Toggie and Zoon were dancing. The sap was up. He had just finished drawing Fred staring at himself in a mirror and was writing the caption, 'Fred fell in love with the best looking person he could see', when she came down the steps. Francis had jumped. He hadn't realised that, prior to his occupation, Ronnie made visits to the tower, that she had got into the habit of visiting her father there, that she knew how to climb up the ladder and enter the tower.

Ronnie laughed. 'I surprised you,' she said, climbing down the inside ladder. 'You didn't hear me –'

'I did –'

'No you didn't. My daddy says I walk like a lamb. Do you know what that means?'

Francis shook his head. Ronnie did an impression of a gambol. It was sufficiently loose and uncoordinated to be impressive. 'Very good,' laughed Francis.

She smiled and looked at the drawing on the desk. 'Who's that?' she asked. 'It's not you.'

'How do you know?'

Again there was nervous laughter and a shake of her body. 'It doesn't look like you –'

'Oh I don't know.'

'No it doesn't. He's got no hair. He's tried to drag it forward.'

'Has he?'

'Yes. Look.' Ronnie took a longer look and absorbed the detail. She tried to make sense of it. 'Is that funny?' she asked.

Momentarily Francis wondered what to say. 'It's meant to be,' he eventually answered. 'But that doesn't mean it is.'

'What do you mean?' asked Ronnie.

'Well what I find funny, you may not.'

'I see,' said Ronnie, after a pause for thought.

Francis remembered how at that point he had felt the need to change the subject. His mind worked hard thinking and rejecting topics. As it was, Ronnie did it for him.

'You've changed it,' she said, referring to the layout of the tower. 'It's like a house now.'

'Lived in?'

'Yes.' The expression on her face showed her excitement. There was a ferment of ideas there, the world of the dolls house was being transferred to Francis' space. It left Francis bewildered rather than enlightened. In the silence he assumed she was planning some sort of scheme, devoting areas to uses and thinking of functions.

'So you've been here before,' said Francis moving to the fridge. He offered her a can of orange.

'Gee thanks. Dad never had drinks. But he never lived here. He used to come here to think.' She laughed at that. The laughter stopped and started again when she took another look at the drawing of Fred. 'You're good,' she said. 'When I grow up I'd like to be an artist.'

'You could be a designer.'

'What's that?'

'A designer? It's someone who plans how to use something. Like you planning where to put the mattress and the fridge in here.'

As Francis spoke, Ronnie's eyes moved from the objects he mentioned and tried to take in what he was saying. Francis thought of her visits to her father. Why Brad encouraged her to climb the tube ladder and why he wanted her to set foot in his space was beyond Francis. But then perhaps it was a case of her wanting rather than him, perhaps he would spin yarns and tell her that Pam was waiting. Francis thought how there was little she could have done in the space, how the tower without windows and toys would have seemed like a giant can, a five minute exploration. He looked at her again. The smile she gave him made him think that perhaps her interest lay in her father, perhaps she just wondered what he was up to.

'Can I draw?' she asked, taking a pencil.

'What here?' said Francis, wondering what she meant. He thought of correcting her English, but overlooked it and passed her a clipboard. 'Go ahead,' he said.

'Would you draw me?' she said, accepting the clipboard and starting to line in a shape.

'I don't think I could –'

'Why not?'

'You're pretty. I wouldn't do you justice.' His words had the desired effect. They made her retreat. They made her seem reluctant to go on with her sketch.

'Ok,' she said accepting his words. 'Can you draw a giraffe then?'

'I'll try,' said Francis more enthusiastically.

'I like giraffes.'

'Ones like this?'

'Yes,' squealed Ronnie as the sketch took shape. She watched a long neck emerge on the sheet. 'Yes!' she squealed again as Francis perfected the exaggeration of an eyelash and developed the full prettiness of the eyes.

'They have lovely faces, giraffes,' said Francis.

'Do you know one?'

'I've seen one.'

'At your home?'

Francis laughed. The idea of a giraffe making itself at home in Brynlas amused him. For a moment he considered his father's reactions – what it was worth, how much it weighed, how much grass it ate. The practical considerations.

'What was it called?' asked Ronnie quickly.

Francis let the first name that came to mind suit the animal. He went for a little alliteration. 'Giovanni,' he said.

'Giovanni the giraffe,' said Ronnie. 'Yes,' she squealed again.

Francis had a lie in the morning after the funeral. The light through the tarpaulin told him it was a fine day. It reminded him of the day he left Wales. Again he thought of his last conversation, how his father had shocked him. The interior of the tower gave the thoughts geometry. He set them in Brynlas' kitchen. He imagined his mother's wooden chair, the checked table cloth, the spread-open paper, the pen on the crossword. He thought of his mother doing the crossword. 'Half man stuck on desert island,' she'd say, appealing to his father for help. 'Ten letters begins with d.' His father would never answer. He would sit by the half finished loaf that was left by the butter. He would shake his head to the sound of a knife cutting through bread. Francis remembered the sound. He sucked and blew imitating it. Then he remembered the stove, modern and out of place, and the round mirror by the phone, his mother watching herself through conversations. Above her there were shelves. They were untidy but clean with jam jars and basins.

At breakfast in Brynlas the conversation always centred on time. There was never the scope for the sort of words his father had used when they were waiting for the taxi that was to take Francis on the first stage of his journey to America. Rather, the day would be outlined, working out what Gethin would do, whether Gwyn would help, arriving at contingencies if Francis' mother needed the car or if Francis needed to be picked up from school. Only when that was sorted out would they reminisce. Then they would talk about the great events that would make his father grasp his cup and say, 'Yes, yes...', like the arrival of electricity at Brynlas in 1960. 'Candles before that see. Used to bang three nails in the wall and slot a candle in. Bloody messy. Wax everywhere see. Wax bloody everywhere.'

For each event or piece of recall, Francis was able to place his father's words. Always his father's, he thought. Always those eyes remonstrating. He saw them when he looked in the mirror. He didn't look like his father, but, somehow, his expressions and reactions were similar. In particular any resemblance emanated from the way he smiled. He used his eyes. His father used his eyes. They somehow opened and warmed. They showed delight and surprise. And like his father they pulled at his features, making them lighter. They set up looks too. Looks that were linked with events. Francis laughed, remembering the morning that he announced that, like his friend Owain, he wanted to keep ducks.

'Dad let him have them,' his mother had pleaded. 'You've been on about him having responsibilities, about him having things to do.'

'Aye useful bloody things,' his father had said. Francis remembered the look that accompanied the words. The way his short nose stayed still between his eyes and the way his small mouth, close to his nose, seemed tied to a finger that wagged its way through conversations.

'But I've said you could pick up some ducklings next week. And you could pick up some Bibby from the farm supplies when you're over there. They'll need a new box too. The one from the last lot's had it.'

'Bring me a bucket of sand and I could sing him the desert song,' muttered Francis' father, looking more and more disconsolate. 'How old is this bloody boy?'

'Oh go on. He needs a challenge' His mother at least tried, but she was never very persuasive; she certainly was never persistent.

'There's no bloody go on about it. Where you going to put them? You thought about that? Which field? They'll have to be close to the bloody house. You moaned when we had those bloody muscovies in the front yard. Shit everywhere, you said, shit everywhere. So where we gonna put them? Can't have bloody ducks over the other side of the farm, can you? And they'll have to have a field of their own.'

'Why?'

'You know why.'

'Why you smiling?' Francis' mother was almost laughing.

'Teeth girl, teeth. You know you can't keep sheep and horses.'

'But he wants to keep ducks.'

'Oh Christ!' his father erupted. 'Look. Bloody look.' He smiled and pointed to his mouth. 'A horse has got a full set. You know that. One nearly bit you on your birthday once...' A pause allowed Francis' mother to smile. Francis recollected her telling him of an incident near the postbox at the main gate to the farm. She had offered a horse a piece of her sandwich over a fence and it had bitten through the bread to her fingers. 'Uppers and lowers see,' continued Francis' father. 'Means they're more efficient. They can get it lower down.'

'So?'

'So there's nothing bloody left. And ducks graze it lower still. So no. No bloody ducks. You hear?'

71

It was a two mile walk to the nearest telephone, a walk through the woods and then along the main highway to a secluded rest area where there were parking spaces and a phone booth. It was a walk Francis had undertaken wholly or partly several times with Brad. Thoughts of those walks now couldn't penetrate the lists Francis was compiling in his head. Lists. Lists of things he had to do. Pam made lists. But he didn't think of her. It was his mother he thought of. She made lists too. Realising that made him consider how rarely he now thought of Wales. Occasional fleeting comparisons didn't really count. They were nothing more than an outer skin, the inner feelings that had affected Francis were much more closeted. Ronnie had provided the break. She was a meaningful focus. Her softness seemed colourful compared to Wales' greyness, her vulnerability was more seductive than the clear-cut answers provided by Wales. It was all he didn't know that now dominated. More than anything the intimacy Ronnie had shown during her first visit to the tower came to intrigue him, the way she had known where to step and turn and be so precise in her normally loose movements, the way she had appreciated all the changes in decor and fittings, the way she was so well versed in what her father did in the tower. It made her or the tower seem full of trickery. They or her or it concealed meanings and mixed up truths.

Francis didn't dwell on the implications of that. Rather, he focused on the father-daughter relationship. Brad and Ronnie. There was nothing strange there, yet somehow putting it in the context of the tower shook the basis of the relationship. Why the tower? Why meet there? And why did Brad allow Ronnie to climb up to the tower? Perhaps Brad had no choice. Perhaps it was something that Ronnie liked doing. But Brad seemed too forceful to allow his daughter to face such danger. He remembered occasions of sharp words like when Denny had soaked Ronnie in spring when she had her best clothes on and when he found Ronnie had been taking chunks of fresh bread to feed a bird that had taken to skipping across the balcony. Brad hadn't held back then so why should he allow Ronnie to climb up the tower and why should he allow his peace to be disturbed?

'Tell her about the giraffes,' Francis said over such thoughts. 'Tell her about the new pictures. About the cartoons.' Another list took over then. A verbal list. 'The drawings,' he said as he dialled Zelda's number. When Zelda said hello he pictured her face and tried to place her sitting down by the phone on the patio near the spot where he had tried to ask her about Ronnie.

'You said the end of the week,' said Francis quickly.

'I'm glad you phoned –'

'You are?'

'I forgot the goat's name.'

'Toggie?'

'No, the other one.'

'The female? Zoon. It's Greek for animal. Or is it Roman?' Francis asked himself.

'Of course.' Zelda sounded relieved. 'Zoon,' she repeated. Francis pictured her writing down the name. 'That's cute. Ronnie says you draw cartoons.'

'Does she? She remembers me then?'

'Remembers you! As I said at the funeral, her bedroom's like a shrine to you. Goats everywhere. Is that healthy for an eight year old?' Zelda was laughing now. That had encouraged Francis. He thought how at the funeral she had taken so long to warm to him. It seemed now that she had settled, that she was comfortable with him. He asked if she was alright. She said yes, admitting she was glad it was over and that the funeral had provided a sense of relief, that it ended an immersion in feeling. She said she had come out of it numb, that the sadness and loss had released a feeling of great terror, but that now she was noticing the most subtle things about death, the things that the shock that draws you to the point of total breakdown covers up and hides.

Francis listened to her points, saying 'I see' periodically. He thought how he needed to show her he was still there. When he started saying 'mm', he sensed she thought his contemplation was a show, that he really wasn't that interested. 'Listen to me,' she said, finding an excuse to change the subject. 'And all you want to know is whether you can see Ronnie. God I go on –'

'Can I?' said Francis hurriedly.

'Hey you're cute. So polite you English.'

'I'd like to see her.'

'Yeh, yeh. Whenever you like.'

'I'm not often passing,' said Francis.

'I hadn't thought of that. You haven't got a car, have you?'

'No.'

'So how will you get here?'

Francis admitted he hadn't thought of that. It led to a series of pauses before Zelda suggested she could bring Ronnie to him or take him to her.

Francis interrupted that trail of thought. He asked how Ronnie was, how she had coped, whether she had realised what had happened.

'I don't really know,' said Zelda answering the last question. 'I mean at eight. It's not really fair is it. Gee I mean it's everything to an eight year old. But there, I'm speculating. To be truthful I haven't asked her. I don't know what to say. I mean I have said things, but whether I've said the right things. I guess that's another question. Still she's a cute kid.'

'So what have you said?'

'I told her the truth. At least I did in so far as I said they're dead. But whether she understood that. I'm not sure. Gee I'm not sure I understand it myself. I still expect to see them. And that's daft because as you know I hardly ever saw them.'

As Zelda spoke, Francis thought of the difficulties, of how easy it was to paint something other than reality, of escaping it to the extent that you are left free of it and find it indistinguishable from what is not real. Something less than the truth, however brutal, may let all sorts of demons wriggle free in the future. That worried him. 'You've done everything you could,' he said suddenly, cutting into her words.

'Oh I'm not so sure.' Zelda sounded less than convinced. 'I've felt a little helpless. I guess I've needed advice. Still the priest was kind –'

'The priest?'

'Yeh. He came and spoke to Ronnie.'

'Why?'

'Oh the funeral.' Zelda's excited, hurried words stopped suddenly. Francis wondered what the priest had said, what he had told the impressionable child. 'I guess he wanted to reassure her. Tell her what had happened and what would happen –'

'Going to heaven.' Francis thought how, for all the spirituality that was supposed to be part of Wales, he was a rationalist. He would have preferred the priest to have stayed away and kept all the secrets he may have revealed with him. 'I expect he told her what he had said,' remarked Francis more reasonably.

'What he said at the funeral?' Zelda surmised. 'Heavensakes,' she said laughing. 'I didn't recognise Brad. I guess Ronnie will. She loves him.'

'I suppose it's good that she'll remember the good in him.' Francis spoke slowly as he recalled the sermon. Its focus was a wall Brad had built for the local school. The priest had compared it with the way he had built his life: the way he was an organiser, a carer, the way he did things by himself for the sake of others, his selflessness, his self effacing manner. The priest had said too much. For Francis it all seemed appropriate and balanced. For Zelda it was misplaced.

'The bricks were his arms,' she laughed, somehow knowing Francis would also be replaying the words. 'Independent, determined–'

'Campaigning,' added Francis.

'No harm to others...no thought for himself –'

'Perhaps it's for the best,' said Francis, mulling over the likely effect on Ronnie. 'She needs to remember the best in him.'

'And as it's come from a priest, well. She probably thinks he's some sort of Jesus Christ. God knows that priest turned Brad's wall into a miracle.'

'Why not,' said Francis. He thought how the priest was providing a poem Ronnie would grow old with, how it was a myth, how it was his words rather than anything real that she would call up when she wanted to cherish her father.

On Saturday Francis felt restless. He decided that it was the potential of meeting Ronnie that excited him. It was the same sort of feeling he had encountered before travelling to the States and before making the decision to travel. It was the potential for change that excited him, somehow it seemed to almost crackle through him. It certainly made him sit up and sense a mix of excitement and danger. There was a degree of enchantment in that. It made him feel captivated, almost converted to the uncertainty his new life offered him.

When he finally settled, he sat in the chair by the desk. Ronnie's chair, he called it. It was where she would sit when she called. It seemed appropriate he should sit in it and make lists of questions he would ask her, of places he would take her. Everything he planned demanded a degree of control that was beyond him. It was Ronnie who would be in control. She would set him free or anchor him, allowing him access to her thoughts or depriving him of all he felt he needed to know. It was that that made him deride his lists. He pushed them to one side and turned to face the table and the ceramic pig.

'Hi!' A call from Fritz broke up the thoughts. It made Francis put down the pig like a guilty boy. He composed himself and called back, inviting Fritz into the tower.

'Just passing,' shouted Fritz unnecessarily as he climbed the ladder. Francis hurriedly looked about the tower. He threw a newspaper from the table to the bed and covered over his workpad on the desk.

'Hi,' said Fritz again. He was manoeuvring round to let his legs find the rungs of the inside ladder. 'Great day out there. The sun's streaming through the trees. Good protection you get here. Nice 'n cool.' He talked his way down to the floor.

'Beer?' asked Francis. A smile came to his face as he left his chair and moved to the fridge. Fritz took his place on the chair. He puffed a little. Flickers of warmth spread into a full smile as he accepted the beer. 'Fucking hot,' he remarked, swilling it down.

'I thought you were away this weekend.' Francis had remembered a remark Fritz had made casually at the funeral about a visit to a sister-in-law.

Fritz was caught mid swig. A kind of serious playfulness came over his expression as he implored Francis to wait. He belched. 'Sorry. That's good.'

'So what about your visit?'

'Put off. Or rather put back. Sally's dog has run away.' His words disappointed Francis. They pre-empted the chance of his running through a multiplicity of possibilities. 'Fuckin' animal should have been put down years ago. It's all fleas and whimpers. Run away. Hey that's funny.' Fritz was laughing wildly. 'It couldn't fuckin' stand up the last time I saw it. It sort of rode around on its butt. She used to polish the floor to help it move. Now it's run away. Those fuckin' pills she was giving it must have worked a treat.'

Francis smiled. He liked their intimacy now. It had nothing of the awkwardness it once had.

'So I thought I'd come over and see how you are. Whether you're ready –'

'For what?'

'Work.'

'Work?' Francis made it obvious he didn't catch the drift of Fritz's words. He screwed up his eyebrows and tried his best to look puzzled.

'Davison's manager flanked me down yesterday. I thought I was fuckin' speeding. This guy shot up behind me and waved me over. I saw it wasn't the cops and then I recognised him. Said he tried to see you but you weren't in. I said, what's new. He said Davison wanted you to work next week –'

'I'll go over there.'

'Yeh, I should. Keep on the good side of him. He can be a fuckin' pain. Brad learnt that.'

'How?' asked Francis, half expecting Fritz to remember the discretion he normally applied when speaking of Brad. It was no surprise when he bit his lip. He realised he had already said too much. The regret was in his eyes. Francis saw that. A look of disaffection came and went. It was a wry look giving away a thought that seemed to make Francis think he should take the explanation that was about to be offered at face value. There was some restraint when he started talking again. Francis noted it and thought how for Fritz speed was essential in conversation; the coupling of ideas, the disconnections were paramount.

'He got too bossy. Started telling people what to do. Turned himself into a foreman,' said Fritz, shaking his head in a knowing way. 'Overruled orders. Did jobs in the wrong sequence.'

'Doesn't seem very much.'

'It wasn't. Said he worked by the weather. He probably did. But Davison wanted some painting done down on the perimeter fence by the road. To impress some friends that were coming. The sun shone and Brad messed around with the fuckin' animals, dipping or clipping or something –'

'And the friends came –'

'Yeh. Davison went wild. Threatened to get rid of him. Brad smiled. He was always fuckin' smug. That's what I thought when I first met him. I met him here. Hey did you know that? On this road. For some reason he waved to me. Must have seen me go by day after day and I must have been smiling. I do that when I'm driving along. I'm thinking of something that's gone on. I saw him in a bar then. Oscar's. He bought me a drink. I wouldn't have fuckin' known him. In fact I said so. I said who the hell are you. He said I'm the man you pass every day. Then I knew. I never passed him again. I couldn't after that. We got on straight away.'

Francis smiled. 'No ups and downs?'

'No. Why should there be? You get on or you don't get on. That's how it is with me. You different?'

Francis shook his head, though the truth was he was more doubtful. He believed in evolution and change. He had to. And such principles applied to relationships. He believed in mysteries and uncertainties and that fragments of values and outlooks would be put together or taken apart, moving the ground of relationships.

'You see he knew his faults,' Fritz continued. 'He knew his weaknesses. He tried to correct them. That's why I liked him. Fuckin' treehugger.' Fritz fiddled nervously with the sketchpad in front of him. He turned it over. The cartoon of Fred staring into the mirror confronted him. 'Hey I like that –'

'Thank you,' said Francis warmly.

'Hey, it's good.'

'There are better ones,' added Francis unnecessarily. There was no reason for defence.

'It's fuckin' funny. You're clever.' Fritz laughed again. A grin stayed on his face. 'This your character? He needs more hair. People like people with hair. You know they like more slender figures too. But he's cute. What d'ya call him?'

'Fred.'

'Too fuckin' old. Get with it. Call him something schmaltzy. Duane or Brad or something. Hey how about Matt? Matt's cool....' Fritz paused to run over the joke again. 'So he stares at himself and says...' Francis sat back staring, letting Fritz enjoy the moment.

'Hey you got too much talent for sitting up here and working for Davison.' Again he looked at the sketchpad and fell silent. Francis offered him a second beer. While Fritz pulled on the ring he wondered whether it was time to press Fritz to reveal Brad's indiscretions, to tell him why his sister disliked him, why people acknowledged some problem that created a basis for bias. Francis heard Fritz say 'Ah' as he enjoyed the beer. He was stalking like a predator now, trying to find the words that would vibrate with each other and spark a response that was anything but a dismissal.

'Hey, how d'ya get on with Zelda?' The question had broken through Francis' thoughts. It had moved the conversation away. Francis felt stranded, anxious to draw Fritz back and question him. 'You seeing her?' asked Fritz. Francis realised the moment had passed, that it would have to be reserved for another time and beer. Instead he answered Fritz. He told him about his phone conversation with Zelda and, in turn, Fritz told Francis again about Davison's desire to get him back to work. Then Fritz almost shouted: 'Hey look at that!' referring to the time. 'Listen, I'll have to go. Kids! Do this, do that. Take them, pick them up. You know what fatherhood is? A fuckin' taxi service. Still. See you soon, yeh?'

Francis nodded. He watched Fritz go, thinking how he was someone who could set agendas and control situations. When he was with Fritz, Francis felt like a disciple, but somehow that wasn't right. He knew he was much more than that. He had chosen Fritz. He had left Wales. He had confronted fear. He had broken conventions. That made him different. It set him apart from the people he had known in Wales. At that point he pictured them. In chapel. In pews. It was as though they were in a pen, like lambs waiting to have their ears clipped. They seemed controlled, conditioned. And they were an irritation now. They were like a fly on the face. He felt them there, but wanted them to move away and, although he did little to move them on, somehow, after some time they were relegated, placed behind other ideas and schemes. On this occasion, as he stood staring after Fritz, Brad replaced them. He wondered how someone so active and friendly as Brad had instilled such disrespect in people. He thought over all he had heard, the references made by Zelda and Fritz, the way people dismissed Brad with a fleeting word or a condemning look. But no-one lingered, no-one explained, everyone disengaged. It made Francis believe that, whatever the problems Brad had with people, they must have been recent. Certainly there was no sign of time healing, there was no-one willing to balance something in the past with what had gone on since. It made Francis think that whatever Brad had done, it had overwhelmed, it had eclipsed.

'You know I've been meaning to ask you about the sculpture –'

'Everyone does.' Zelda laughed. She and Francis were sitting in the room into which Francis had stared on the day of the funeral. He could see it now. The upside down man with the enormous hands. 'I like it,' he said.

'You do? No-one else does.'

'Really,' said Francis, giving himself the time to take a long look. 'Why?'

'Because it's about perspective, about getting a view of things, of people I guess.' Zelda turned around to take another look at the sculpture. It was behind her. She let her gaze slide across the coffee table to the French windows and the sculpture on its left side. The exaggeration of her scrutiny of the room suggested she was considering how bare it was, how there was almost a complete lack of ornamentation – no mementoes, no gifts, just the sculpture. That added to its impact. She stared at the shape: the out-of-control, flailing legs; the bent torso that seemed to be straining; the sucker like hands glued to the earth. She laughed.

'What's so funny?' asked Francis.

'That you like it.'

'Don't you?'

'Yes, yes I do. Very much.'

'Well why can't I?'

'No reason.' She looked back his way. She seemed a little uneasy as though she didn't want him to continue. She searched for a way of changing the subject, but Francis moved on too quickly.

'I like it because it reminds me of home. Or rather it reminds me of what people thought of me when I was home.'

'You walked around like that,' laughed Zelda.

'I walked away like that,' smiled Francis. 'I'll tell you about it one day. Who made it?'

Zelda seemed to want to avoid that question. She fidgeted and cleared her throat as though she was debating whether or not to tell

Francis the truth. 'Nick Chatwin,' she said. 'A friend. Well actually a lover, an old lover. And a husband. An ex-husband. A South African. And a shit –'

'Oh I'm sorry.' Francis sounded defensive as though he hadn't wished to pry.

'There's no need to be. Truth is truth.' She broke away to sip the coffee. 'Do you like this?' she asked. 'Indonesian. Javan, I think. Can't make up my mind.'

Francis offered no opinion. He drank the coffee and smiled. It seemed to be an affirmative response. It let him look at the khaki, cotton-dressed woman who sat demurely in front of him. Her slender frame impressed him. Her calmness intrigued him.

'Yeh, you're right. It's fine.' She sipped the coffee again.

'He's talented,' Francis spluttered, returning his attention to the sculpture.

'Oh yeh. Don't I know it! It's awesome. Kind of frightens me. I guess I knew it would come between us. I mean I'm too straight, too narrow to ever match him and his talent.'

'It troubled you?'

'Yeh. Talent breeds ego. At least it did with Nick. His ego was so developed. I sometimes wonder whether in his case ego bred talent.' Zelda's voice was stronger now. Francis sensed the memory was livid, as though it was with her, like a taste, strong and clear. She was savouring it, sitting expressionless opposite him. 'Gee that sculpture. He used to say it said it all. That there was nothing left to say. Meant nothing to me.' She looked at the sculpture again, turning her head to appreciate the stylised features and the line of the man's fall. 'He kept seeing things differently,' she said. 'That was his talent. Not this.' She dismissed the sculpture. 'It was the way he was capable of saying something different. God knows how he did it. ' She turned away again and stared back at Francis. She laughed. 'There. God, am I going on?' She held her hands up. They framed her face. 'And all you want to know about is Ronnie –'

'You're not going on,' Francis insisted.

'Are you going to stay at the tower?' The way she changed the subject surprised Francis.

'Haven't thought about it,' he said.

'You like it there, don't you?'

'Yes,' admitted Francis.

'Why?' she asked.

It was Francis' turn to feel uncomfortable. He thought about mentioning how he had felt the need to break away, how he hated moulds and models and preferred flexibility. Then he stopped himself. He knew it was too early for her to understand. He grinned. 'It's home,' he said softly.

'Guess it is,' she said.

Such sensitivity surprised him. He had expected her to laugh at the squalor. 'How did you know about it?' he asked quickly.

'The fire. Ronnie,' she said, explaining.

Francis told her how he had met Brad and how he had explained to Brad about his search for the unknown and the unpredictable, how Brad had suggested Francis should take the risk of stopping off at the tower.

'That was Brad. Unknown and unpredictable,' said Zelda. 'And you were taken in.' She shook her head in an almost disparaging way.

'It was what I wanted,' said Francis. 'It was all I couldn't find in Wales. No one ever came along there and asked you to stay. No stranger anyway.'

'And you stayed?'

'Nearly nine months.' It was Francis' turn to sound affected. He thought how quickly the time had passed.

'Bastard,' said Zelda caustically. Again she showed no sympathy for Brad. Francis watched her shake her head. He let her mind justify the assessment; and he saw his chance. In his mind he double checked whether an inquiry now would seem spontaneous. He thought it would.

'Why'd you say that?' he asked.

'He was,' emphasised Zelda. 'As simple as that. He was.' A silence followed. Again something had put up a barrier. 'Hey I haven't mentioned Ronnie. You come all this way on spec and you haven't asked.'

'Didn't like to,' said Francis.

'You won't believe this.'

'She's not here.'

'At a friend's,' explained Zelda. 'Won't be back till tomorrow.'

Francis stayed silent. His disappointment was obvious.

'Shouldn't worry.' Zelda smiled reassuringly. 'She wants to see you. All last night she spoke about Toggie and Zoon and your drawings. God have you got some giraffes to show her? If you haven't you need to get working.'

'I will,' said Francis, standing up. He pulled at his shirt, straightening it.

'You're not going?'

'I should get back.'

'Things to do?'

'Sort of.' He watched Zelda get up. She walked out into the hall and returned with a coat.

'You off too?' he asked.

'Yeh. Got to get milk and cookies. Brad's place is on the way. Say, why don't I give you a lift home?'

At the edge of the woods, where Fritz had stopped regularly to pick up Brad on his way into town, Zelda pulled into the side of the road.

'Nice car,' Francis said, reaching for the door handle. Zelda leant across to stop him opening the door.

'Hey you got a minute? I mean there's something I'd like to say.' She grabbed his hand and pulled it away from the handle.

Francis looked bewildered. A touch of worry crept in as he considered possibilities. 'About Ronnie?' he said, sensing she was about to talk about what had happened and how Ronnie had reacted.

Zelda laughed. It eased the tension she felt. She slid back in her seat, sighed and looked out into the road. 'No Ronnie's fine. About Brad.'

'Brad?' pondered Francis. He couldn't work it out. He waited for clarification. Then he thought of the evasion. Fritz, Zelda. They all knew something. It made him feel it was time now to push for a revelation. 'Yes, you're right,' he said, coming out of thought.

'Right? What d'ya mean right?' Again she laughed. She shook her head and looked directly at Francis. She waited for a response. She seemed to sense his anger and knew that he suspected something, that he sensed people were hiding the truth.

'You all know something,' exclaimed Francis. 'Something that's bad. You, Davison, Fritz. You all know.'

'Oh come on –'

'No. You do.'

'So?'

'So why not tell me? What's the problem? Is it that bad? I mean Ok, he always wanted to be top dog. Number one.'

'Yeh a real goody goody, Brad.'

Francis shook his head. He thought over all she had said, all the names she had called him, all the anger and frustration the mere mention of his name seemed to impose. 'But you know that's not so. Ok he took me in at first. But I saw him fight. Ok he was a rough diamond, but he tried.'

'You don't know.' There was something emphatic in Zelda's voice now. It sounded out-of-place, too serious. Francis found it rather disturbing, that whatever Brad had done could censure the attractive lightness of her conversation.

'Ok then.'

'What do you mean?'

'I'm waiting.'

Zelda fidgeted a little, wondering what to say, how to tell on her brother and reveal the way he had been. 'He beat Pam,' she finally said.

'Beat Pam?' Francis took in the words. Beat Pam. It wasn't what he was expecting. Somehow Pam had never entered the rush of thoughts that were still seething in his mind. Now she did. He replayed the arguments, the difficult moments he had witnessed. 'What do you mean? You saying that he hit her?'

'Yeh he hit her. Quite badly.'

Francis stayed quiet for a second. He remembered the fight at Oscar's, the way the silence had fallen with the punch, the way Brad had recovered. He couldn't transfer such drama to the cottage. He wondered what could have precipitated it, how gentle Pam could have riled Brad. It seemed unbelievable.

'He beat her several times,' said Zelda, continuing. 'Heavensakes she was hospitalised once. The police nearly got called in. Pam wouldn't have it. I told her too. Fritz did too –'

'He knows?'

'Fritz? Oh yeh. He was a pal of Pam's. You ask him.' She paused and looked away. Francis sensed a little fidget of uncertainty. It was moved away with a smile. 'He must know. I mean I don't know for certain because I've only just met him, but Pam liked him. She told me. She thought he was cute. And Pam talked to her friends. Talked and talked,' Zelda emphasised. She made it sound as though she didn't approve. 'She'd have told him,' she said.

Francis nodded. He decided to think of Fritz later, to concentrate on the characters he knew and try to see how their characteristics could stretch to such behaviour.

'It was awful. I told her to have him put away. But she thought it was something to do with her. It screwed her up. She couldn't work it out. But it happened again and again and again. Sometimes he'd stop for months. They were great then. Happy, smiling. Then he'd flip. And she'd think the same thing. Some sort of inadequacy on her part. Women have some wild ideas.' Zelda stopped. She took in the blankness of Francis' face. He stared straight out. Occasionally he shook his head as some thought came and went.

'We talked to him. All of us. We tried to get him to see someone, to get some therapy, to work it out –'

'Why?'

'We thought it best.'

'No, why'd he do it?'

'Hey, how do I know? I guess something just snapped. Boy did he lose control.' Zelda knew she was failing to find the words. She waited, hoping Francis would find some direction.

'How often did he do it?' he asked.

'Six, seven times. From what we know. Nothing recently. It was when the kids were young. Denny was a baby. I think he felt he couldn't provide for them. Not properly. I mean they were a bedroom short. Two Christmases he went berserk.'

'You help?'

'Of course. Until Pam told me to keep away –'

'Why'd she do that?'

'Who knows. She never explained. Pride, perhaps. I gave them money now and then. Well I could afford it. I was doing well. Still am.'

Francis smiled and nodded. He urged Zelda on. He wanted to know as much as possible.

'Once Denny came to see me. He was my favourite. So cute.' She smiled at the memory. 'He said he wanted this software. It wasn't much. A little more than I'd have normally given him, but I got carried away. I went into this shop to get what he wanted and I bought this and that. Little extras, nothing more. They bought him the computer on credit. I mean I should have known better –'

'But what's wrong with that?'

Zelda shrugged. She was glad Francis had seen it her way. From the look on his face she could tell he too would have managed such a gift. She sensed he liked generosity. He shook his head. 'I mean I don't see it. I can understand pride. Yes, I can. But you're family. Surely he could take things from you. He could see how difficult it was –'

'He went wild. Hit Pam. Said she was begging. Said she had come round to me. Poor old Pam. He hit her black and blue. All over. She blamed me.'

'Pam did?'

'Yeh. She was so loyal. She loved him.'

Francis sat back and let his head fall onto the head-rest. His eyes looked up into the roof of the car. He thought how little he had known, how the people he had called friends were suddenly transformed.

Zelda watched him and became nervous. She moved her legs, sat up and fidgeted. 'You alright?' she eventually asked.

'Yes.' Francis let his head drop. He smiled at her.

'What's that for?' she asked, sounding more cheerful.

'For telling me.'

'You're shocked?'

'A little.'

'You weren't the only one,' said Zelda. 'After that, I didn't speak to them.' She decided to go on and relate the full story. 'Denny came around. They didn't know. He'd come round when Paul bored him. Too bright Paul. Denny'd come and swim in the pool and have tea and tell me what was going on.'

'So you didn't know Ronnie?'

'Not really. Saw her at the family reunions. Hey she's lovely. Like Denny. Ever so like him. Sweet. Sincere. You alright?' Zelda sensed Francis' sudden movement. He had rubbed his chin, shaken his head and tugged on the handle of the car door. The erratic movements seemed to worry Zelda.

'I'll call you,' he said. It had been too much to take in. Francis gave Zelda a reassuring smile. It was forced but somehow it calmed her and made her sense he would be alright. 'Can I phone you Thursday?' he said, turning around as he was walking away. 'I'll be in town. Shopping day,' he explained.

Zelda smiled.

He called in the following night. He couldn't keep away. The revelation had kept him up all night and his subsequent tiredness made him phone through his apologies to Davison. Davison's secretary said it was alright to leave starting work until tomorrow. 'Still a bit shaky,' explained Francis. 'Some sort of delayed shock, I guess,' said the secretary.

After that he spent all day thinking of Ronnie, thinking of the environment that had nurtured her, of the difficulties she must have faced before the fire and the deaths. Hope she's there, he thought on the way to Zelda's. Hope she's back.

She wasn't. 'Stayed over,' said Zelda. 'They've been so good. She needs the company. I'll get you a drink. Beer?'

'Coffee,' said Francis. 'I need a clear head. Back in work tomorrow,' he explained.

'Lucky you,' laughed Zelda, moving towards the door.

Her absence gave Francis the opportunity to take a good look around the room. Immaculate, he thought, apart from the piles of videos in the corner. One pile had fallen over. Colours peeped from their sleeves. A mass of orange. One was pink and blue. One was a series of red waves. Francis imagined titles. He thought how the line of colour was like a freeway into a city. Each one vied with the next, trying to outdo it, trying to draw the eye to sample. The mish-mash appealed. It did its job, moving him off his seat. A shuffle in the corridor sat him back down.

'Can't see them,' Zelda mumbled, re-entering the room. 'Must have put them down. You seen them?' she asked, noticing Francis was out of his chair. 'My new shades. You seen them?'

'We're indoors,' laughed Francis.

'So?'

'Well...'

'They tone things down. You look real sort of Latin through them. You know that? De Niro like. You do.'

Francis laughed. He thought how the shades told him there were no boundaries to her purchasing. Somehow he found that unsettling. It wasn't that structures were threatened, which they were, rather it was the unpredictability of what would be threatened next. He wondered what it would be, whether there would be an order.

'You look worried,' Zelda remarked, noting the serious expression on his face. She moved alongside him with his coffee. She too stared at the videos. 'Don't you like De Niro? You push your hair back. Come on let's have a go.' She reached towards him. 'There. That's it.' She held back Francis' fringe. Now that's real De Niro like, yeh. That's a cute look. Cool. Now if I had my shades on you could be him. You like De Niro?'

Francis nodded.

'He's the man. That smile. Gee that smile. God!' She was opening her mouth now, giving a look of amazement. 'Can you do it?

'What?'

'His smile.'

Francis laughed nervously. 'No. No I can't.'

'Go on.'

'No. No I can't. Really.' Francis laughed at the disbelief that confronted him. 'Something to do with being Welsh.'

'Hang ups?'

'No. Nothing like that. It's just that we're not good mimics. We're... well we're sort of quiet.'

'Really?' Zelda's eyes left Francis. She looked around the room. 'Where the hell did I put them then? The bedroom. When I changed. Yeh, yeh.'

She wandered away. Francis felt a little relieved. He sipped his coffee and looked around the room again, passing the videos and the sculpture. He put his cup down on the coffee table. He looked at its top. Tidy papers. Some untouched looking magazines. Only a copy of Halliwell's Film Guide looked used. It was face down, open at a page. Francis moved over and picked it up. Thumb prints, he thought, coffee stains marking pages. It was open on the B's. Francis' eyes peered down the list. He couldn't resist a game. Which one had she been looking up? *Blackmail?* Too old thought Francis. *Blackjack Ketchum, Desperado.* Too wild thought Francis, laughing.

'Hey what's so funny?' asked Zelda re-entering the room. 'Not these I hope. Hey what do you think?' She was wearing her shades now. They made her move confidently as though they were grooming her or making her walk at ease. Her shoulders bobbed. She strutted. Francis admired the exaggeration.

'You are what you wear,' she said, taking them off flamboyantly, then replacing them. 'So what you looking at? Oh Halliwells.'

'I was guessing which film you were looking up.'

'Remind me,' said Zelda, sitting down.

'Begins with B.'

'Here.' She held out an arm to accept the book. A laugh greeted the recognition. 'Can't you guess?'

'I was trying to.'

'*Blade Runner*,' she said with a smile. It was a knowing look. It seemed to demand or expect a response. A smile too, thought Francis, taking it in. 'You seen it?'

Francis shook his head.

'Oh you should. Come over one night. God you haven't seen it. Where the hell have you been? You been to LA?' She waited for a nod before continuing. 'Then you'll love it. I mean gee you'll really appreciate it. It's set in LA in 2049 or 2059 or something. You know thinking about it it's not much different to LA now.' She laughed at that. 'God there's one scene where this replicant –'

'What?'

'Replicant. A sort of robot, I guess. Anyway this replicant called Thora or Dora, something like that, is dressed up as a sort of model, you know those things they have in shops –'

'Mannequins?'

'Yeh, yeh. That's it. Well she's one of those and she dies smashing through windows in a shopping arcade. What an image, eh?'

Francis found his first day back in work difficult. He kept thinking of Zelda. Zelda, the modern woman. In publishing. Thirtysomething. Single. Attractive. A way with words. An ability to find one comment that could create a crisis. He wondered why she hadn't followed him from the car the night before last after she had told him about Brad, why she hadn't realised the effect her news may have on him. It wasn't as though she didn't know him. Ronnie had taught her a lot. The closeness. The tension. The goat and giraffe drawings. She knew so much, down to details of conversations and Fred cartoons. That should have conveyed sensitivity. So why tell him? Or rather, why tell him in that way?

Francis couldn't work it out. He tracked back conversations, stopped words, interrogated meanings, but there was always too little to go on. The only thing he and Zelda had spoken about was Ronnie and the sculpture in the lounge and farming. He remembered the way she had announced she was an ecofeminist. That had silenced Francis. He thought it trendy, something that brought with it a welter of opinion that would be forced on him. He was right. Zelda had spent a good five minutes talking about the connection between the domination and oppression of women and the domination and oppression of the environment. Francis had tried to stay with the conversation, but when she called for anti hierarchical systems, he was lost. 'That's what I'm doing,' she kept saying, switching her ideas to the publishing company she was directing. It was then he fully realised how important image was to her and how the American sense of image was stronger than anything Brynlas had offered. He compared it momentarily to respectability. That was the all important role of image in Brynlas. Convention. But that was something very different. It kept you in the crowd without separating you out. Zelda had to stay in, but stand out. That was tricky.

Francis was conceding that at the end of the day when he was walking home. He was pleased when he heard Fritz's van drawing up alongside him. 'What you doing here?' he asked.

'Passing.'

'Out this way?'

'Yeh. Hey what's with the questions. I thought I'd see how you are, that's all. That's Ok, isn't it? You getting in?'

Francis smiled. He was grateful. A day digging ditches had been a shock to his body. He felt its stiffness as he bent down to get into the car. He sighed as he felt the seat's comfort.

'You alright?' Fritz asked.

'Tired.'

'So what you gonna do? Sleep?'

Francis laughed. He liked the way Fritz made things clear. He began to believe it was American. Fritz telling him what he wanted, namely a conversation, a conversation about Zelda and Ronnie and what Zelda had said, about how he had learnt that Brad wasn't quite the generous buddy Francis had imagined. Thoughts of the brutality returned. He began to wonder what Fritz knew. He wondered when he should ask.

'I've been thinking,' Fritz was saying. He took in Francis' laugh. 'Oh I know it's a fuckin' miracle and that you're surprised and that you're going to say something clever like what's that –'

'I'm not.'

'Aren't you? Well I don't fuckin' believe you.'

'You think you know me.'

'I do.'

'Oh yeh.' Francis was still laughing.

'Right.' Fritz was riled now. Francis knew a tirade of abuse could follow. Certainly Fritz would try to be clever. He would change direction or say something that would shock Francis. For once Fritz took his time. It surprised Francis.

'You've forgotten what you were going to say.'

'No I fuckin' haven't.'

'You have,' asserted Francis.

'Hey, how can I fuckin' forget what I'm going to say when I never know what I'm going to say? That's why I talk all this fuckin' garbage.'

Again Francis laughed. He found the cosy conversation reassuring. It was like a root, bedding him down. He knew he should wait for Fritz to move the conversation on.

'Listen, what I wanted to say was have the car. I mean have it when you take Ronnie out. When you take her to the movies.'

'Fritz I could kiss you.' Francis leant across in a moment of fun. He put his hand on Fritz's knee.

'Hey! Hey!' screamed Fritz. 'What you doing?'

It was when Fritz pulled over at the spot where Zelda had made her confessions forty eight hours earlier that Francis felt he should ask.

'Zelda told me something,' he said confidently.

'You saw her?'

Francis told Fritz of their meetings, of how Ronnie was away and how Zelda had run him home the first time they had met.

'She dropped you here?' said Fritz, checking what Francis was telling him. Francis suddenly seemed nervous, as though he didn't have a total belief in Zelda's words. He knew Fritz's reaction to what he was about to say would tell him much.

'Zelda said Brad beat Pam.' He looked directly at Fritz. There was no noticeable reaction. 'Several times,' said Francis. Again no reaction.

'Once she was hospitalised. Almost got the police involved.' Yet again no reaction. Fritz was still, staring forward. Francis sensed a mix of loyalties was restraining him or pulling him a number of ways. 'Zelda only saw him at family reunions after Pam told her.'

'I know.' Fritz suddenly spoke. His seriousness struck Francis. It was something he had never seen in Fritz before. All the lightness had gone. It was as if there was nothing else to say.

No elaboration followed. Fritz told Francis to arrange to see Ronnie next Wednesday. It was the day he went with Betty, his wife, and another couple to dancing lessons. Normally Francis would have laughed at the normality of that. It seemed un-Fritz-like, but the circumstances kept him quiet. He told Fritz he would check with Zelda and let him know. Then he left the car.

He had walked only about thirty yards when Fritz called him back. 'Ok, Ok. Yeh I'll have a drink. That Ok?'

In the water tower they drank beer and talked about Zelda. Fritz made Francis tell him exactly what Zelda had said. The repetition gave him time to consider what he should say. He began to listen again when Francis was summing up.

'I thought she'd follow me,' Francis was saying. 'I don't know why. I mean I don't know her. But I know she's sensitive. I mean she seems sensitive. So I guessed she'd have worked out what it would do to me. I mean you don't live with a family for nine months without getting to know them.'

'I think she just felt she had to tell you,' Fritz said slowly. He paused. 'I guess she thought about you and Ronnie, about you seeing her again.' He paused again. Francis took in his words. He nodded, noting the worry or concern in Fritz's voice. He wondered what it meant.

'I guess it was time to tell,' continued Fritz. He took a swig of beer and allowed more thoughts to direct his words. 'She wouldn't have expected you just to go. She got that wrong. She probably wanted you to stay, to talk it over. It's important now. It affects Ronnie. The way she behaves. The way you should see her.'

'You sound as if you know her –'

'Ronnie?' said Fritz a little confused.

'No, Zelda.' Francis was surprised by the ease with which Fritz was interpreting Zelda's behaviour.

'In a way I do –'

'From one meeting?'

'From what you've said.'

'From what I've said!' laughed Francis.

'Well...' Fritz stalled. It made Francis sense Fritz was holding back, keeping something from him. That made him angry. More secrets, he thought. Somehow Zelda didn't matter now. The scale of importance had changed. This was a friend. Someone he knew he trusted.

'You know something,' he finally said. He set his eyes on Fritz. 'I don't believe it. Zelda. Now you. You knew about Brad, didn't you?'

'Yeh.'

'So?'

'So it didn't seem important –'

'Didn't seem important!'

'Relevant. I meant relevant,' protested Fritz. 'He'd changed.'

Francis considered the relevance of that. He realised that a year ago the family would have been different, more cohesive, more responsive. He wondered whether then they would have allowed him in, whether he would ever have lived in the water tower.

'He'd improved,' said Fritz.

'How'd you know?' asked Francis suddenly concerned about the beatings.

'I saw it. The marks on Pam. Her hospitalisation. He had to tell me. I guess he knew I knew. It was better to be open.'

'He told you? How could he tell you? What did you say?'

'I called him shit brain. Then I walked out. But the kids looked scared. Nobody told them.' Fritz paused again. He let his put-upon expression meet Francis' gaze. It held a touch of shame. 'All that priest said,' Fritz started to laugh. 'All that good. Brad the wall builder. For most of the time he was banging his head against a fuckin' wall. Jees he was knocking it down, brick by brick. But he changed.'

'By the time he met me?' surmised Francis.

'Oh yeh. But by then it wasn't the same. How could it be? Pam hated him. She wouldn't show it, but all her respect...well it had fuckin' gone –'

'Did you talk to her?'

'Yeh. I got to know her. I called when he was out. During the week. Some Sundays too, when he'd go to Church with the boys and Ronnie. Pam worshipped Sundays. Time to herself, she'd say. It was a Sunday when she told me about Zelda. About what Zelda said. I agreed. She should have left him. He could have killed her the mood he was in.'

'But she stayed.'

'Yeh. Because of the kids. He was alright to them. I mean she actually said he was a good father. Lousy husband, good father –'

'And was he?'

91

'Oh come on. You saw him. He was amazing. Got a bit anxious over Denny, but for all the right reasons. Yeh, he loved them. But he knew he'd fucked up. And he knew she could never love him again. Not after what he'd done. Sometimes I think his conscience got to him. I mean he couldn't get round Pam by then, so it told him to be good with the kids. And he was.'

Francis nodded. He exhaled, then breathed in heavily. He let Fritz's words settle. He stored them away and considered them. He began to make judgements. About Zelda. About Fritz. But mostly about Brad and Pam.

'She didn't believe it,' he said quietly.

'I know,' said Fritz, his voice almost breaking.

'Hey what's wrong?' Francis sensed Fritz's vulnerability. He watched the warmth almost form a tear. It was shaken away with a smile.

'Sorry,' said Fritz.

'Why?'

'Oh I don't know. Being silly.'

Francis laughed. He thought how Fritz's hard talk and hard eyed view of the world was such a cover, how he had made such a good friend.

Francis drew that night. It somehow developed from writing on a calendar. June 22nd. Taking Ronnie to the pictures, he wrote in red, underlining it. He took two paces back. 'Taking Ronnie to the pictures,' he said, reading the red words.

In the morning he ate breakfast and looked at a cartoon he had drawn. It was summer. Fred was buying a pair of second hand cricket pads. The caption read: 'Fred had decided to open the batting for England'. Between mouthfuls of toast, he turned back to it and laughed. He liked it. He shook his head, picking up his jacket and heading for the ladder.

'Brad,' he said, taking the first step up. He had made an agreement with himself. Consider Brad in the morning and Pam in the afternoon. Use the time. Use the journey to work. So all the way to work he thought not only of the fights and the aggression Brad had shown, but also of the way he called Pam 'love'. She was his cowgirl. His Marilyn. In a strange sort of way it impressed Francis. Even through the arguments he had witnessed, he had never suspected a split, never imagined such a rift in the family had occurred. Arguments were normal.

Arguments were Brynlas. His father and mother. That was his model. It had been easy convincing himself Brad and Pam were like them : a unit, integral to each other and their identity. It had been inconceivable to split them. And that was down to Brad and the job he had done, the way he had sold an image. Even in their first meeting in San Antonio everything Brad said suggested a togetherness with Pam. He had referred to 'us', said she was with him and mentioned little things in speech patterns like 'As I was saying to Pam'. The reality was a distance. Something difficult, something cold.

Francis thought of that. He considered incidents close to the cottage, the domestic scale. Again there was no indication. He thought how rarely he had seen them in the same room, how rarely he had witnessed a word between them. But there was nothing there to worry him. He had assumed an intimacy. It came out of Brad saying 'love' or 'dear' or even 'Pam'. He said it with warmth, with respect, sometimes with a longing.

Passing the tree house and the chair helped Francis refocus. He thought of Denny and Paul collecting wood with Brad directing them. 'From over there,' Brad was saying. 'Hey you guys, what did I say?' He shouted after them. 'That's it.'

Francis had laughed at the way the boys' energy and excitement overcame their comprehension.

'They're wild,' said Brad, turning back to Francis. 'I mean what are they gonna be like when they're twenty?' He shook his head. 'You like kids boy?'

Francis found the question difficult to answer. He smiled and shrugged, trying to make it seem he hadn't heard. The reality was he was scouting about inside for opinions. For some reason he found the topic daunting. Threatening too. It somehow emphasised Wales and loneliness. The only child in the hills.

'I love them. God's gift boy. Like women. Like food.' Brad looked back after Denny and Paul. 'Turn left!' he shouted, directing them to the store of wood. 'Left,' he laughed, watching Denny turn the wrong way. Brad sniggered. 'Don't know left from right. Guess he's no genius. Unlike his brother. Now he's bright. Real bright.' He laughed again to himself as other thoughts confirmed his opinion. 'Left, left. That's it,' he called after the boy, still struggling, enjoying the confusion of movements, the stops and starts and the inquiring looks that were relayed back as the boy searched for confirmation. 'Do it to annoy him I guess,' said Brad. Francis nodded. He knew the way Brad employed ruses. 'Still couldn't do without them. Pam realises that –'

'What do you mean?' Francis had missed the point.

'I wanted them. I had to convince Pam. For a while, I thought she wasn't going to oblige.'

'Female independence –'

'Oh yeh. You can say that again boy. Particularly with Denny. I think she wouldn't have minded another girl, but she convinced herself it would be a boy.' Brad broke off to pass Francis another piece of wood. He watched him measure it and mark it with a pencil. 'And she was right,' he said slowly.

'She's good with them,' remarked Francis before putting the pencil back in his mouth.

'Yeh. Very good. She's a natural, boy. A natural. I guess she thought two's enough. A lot of women do. My sister backed her up. Now she's a feminist. Can't stand feminists. I mean God made us like we are. You can't undo His work boy.' Brad decided to sit down. He leant against a tree. 'It nearly split us up –'

'You?' Francis took another measurement. 'You seem so happy.'

'Oh come on. You've seen our rows boy.' But nothing more was said. The boys returned clutching wood and to keep their enthusiasm Brad decided to race them back to the wood store. Francis watched them speed away. He tried to recall Brad and Pam's arguments, but they seemed no different to what he had witnessed from the landing at Brynlas. Normal, he thought, absolutely normal. Jokes and jibes, nothing too serious, nothing threatening, nothing that could split people up. He imagined them kissing, making up.

'Hey Father Christmas is here. Hey! Hello. Anyone at home?'

Francis was inside the tower having lunch on Saturday when he heard the words. He knew it was Fritz, but he wondered what the announcement meant. He left the ham and tinned potatoes and climbed to the top of the ladder. He peered over the tower's rim. 'You're mad,' he said, laughing and looking down.

'Well I got to have someone to watch the football with. So here I am. –'

'How are you going to get that up here?' asked Francis. He laughed again and shook his head at the sight of Fritz puffing and panting as he placed the television he was carrying on the ground. 'And what's in the bag?' In one of his hands Fritz had held a plastic bag.

'Everything you need,' said Fritz. His hand delved into the bag. 'Voila,' he said, pulling out a small aerial that he placed on top of the television. 'And this,' he added, producing an extension lead.

'Ah I see –'

'Yeh. Easy eh? I throw this up to you and you plug in and we sit out here –'

'In the rain,' said Francis, thinking of the forecast he had heard for the weekend.

'Maybe.' Fritz started to unwind the lead that had curled its way around the aerial. 'You'll enjoy it,' he said. 'Big game today. You coming down?'

'You come up. Have a beer. I'm having my dinner –'

'Dinner?' said Fritz, as though he recalled the way Francis had his dinner at lunch time.

'There. Have a beer,' said Francis when Fritz appeared.

'That television going to be alright?' asked Fritz. He looked concerned.

'Have an onion.' Francis accelerated his eating and broke off only to point Fritz to what was available. He thought how eating with someone was the ultimate in acceptance and socialisation.

'Spoken to Zelda?' asked Fritz, slicing himself some bread.

Francis shook his head. Fritz leant across to reach the butter. 'She was nicer than I thought she'd be. I mean I had her marked down as a trendy young thing. Pam told me she was –'

'An ecofeminist,' remarked Francis, remembering the most embarrassing moment of his time with Zelda.

'Yeh. That's how she painted her –'

'Pam?'

'Yeh'

'Pam was nice,' said Francis, contemplatively. 'I liked her. Respected her.' Francis listened to the sigh from Fritz and thought how he knew Fritz liked her too.

'I was thinking of Brad and the boys yesterday, of building the tree house. I remembered him telling me Pam wasn't too keen on having Ronnie.'

'She wanted some time of her own. She used to act,' said Fritz.

'Did she?'

'Yeh. That's why she always kind of wanted Ronnie to perform. All that singing. Sweet voice Ronnie.'

'So where did Pam perform?'

'Locally. She was good. I saw her once. I had to go. She made me. Brad fucked up and went berserk. He wouldn't fuckin' go. Couldn't be bothered. Said she had two sons, a daughter and responsibilities. But Pam was independent. She wasn't having any of that. Course Brad made it worse, telling her what to do.' Fritz scoffed and shook his head. 'He enjoyed that. He liked to be in control, telling Pam to do this and do that. He even tried that with me.' Fritz paused, then forked a potato and started again. 'And the men in his gang. And you, though in a different way –'

'How?'

'Coming here. That was enough.'

Francis pushed his plate away and moved his chair back. He brushed his hand over his mouth, moving on a piece of potato. He thought how Fritz had got it wrong, how he couldn't understand the philosophy that had pushed men out of Wales. He smiled, thinking it wasn't worth pursuing such thoughts. He tried to think of a way of changing the subject. 'So did he know?' he asked. 'I mean did Brad know that you went to see Pam.'

'Yeh I told him.' Fritz looked up. He wondered what Francis meant. He doubted his intentions. 'Pam asked me. I told him. Of course he fuckin' knew. He asked me ten times a day. You going tomorrow?, he'd say. You going? Why you going? You think she's good up there on the stage? He was awful. He couldn't fuckin' bear it.'

'I bet she looked good. I mean up on stage. She was a good look-ing woman.' Francis wondered what he was saying. The remark had somehow just emerged. It caught Fritz off balance. He gave a strange look, another piercing look. His bewilderment was obvious. Francis sensed he was wondering what was being hinted at. It made him fork another potato and jab it into his mouth, then he narrowed his eyes and gave Francis another long look. He couldn't catch Francis' eye. That seemed to frustrate him. He sighed and chewed harder on the potato.

'What are you trying to say?' he eventually asked.

'What do you mean?' Francis was shocked by the menace in Fritz's tone. He was almost snarling.

'I mean what are you trying to say. You understand?'

'I'm not trying to say anything,' insisted Francis.

'You sure?'

Francis nodded. He had never seen Fritz so agitated. He wondered what it meant as he watched Fritz shake his head and stare at the plate. His fork chased a small potato around the plate. Then he stopped sud-denly and put the fork down. Francis watched him put his elbows on the table and clasp his hands together as though he were going to pray.

'Look are we gonna be honest with each other? I mean it doesn't matter now. They're fuckin' dead. So we may's well say what we mean.' Fritz looked up. His look of amazement had somehow trans-ferred itself to Francis' face. 'What I mean is let's lay all our cards on the table. Let's not play any games.'

'No games,' agreed Francis, still shocked by the way Fritz had reacted.

'No fuckin' games,' repeated Fritz thinking over what he had precipitated.

Francis nodded at Fritz's strong words. Somehow, for once, he had become the provoker. That made him smile. He decided he liked it. It made him feel more in control, though he wondered for a moment exactly what he had provoked.

'Ok then. You fancied her.' Fritz sounded as though he was summing up rather than asking a question.

'In a way.'

Fritz laughed at Francis' response. He shook his head and flung it back, looking up at the tarpaulin. 'No games remember? You fancied her. Yeh?'

'Yeh. Ok. Nothing wrong with that is there?'

'No. Nothing at all –'

'And you did,' suggested Francis, sensing the source of Fritz's edginess. 'You really liked her, didn't you? That's what all this is about.' Francis waited for Fritz to respond, to bite back, but nothing was forthcoming. He wondered what thoughts were turning over in Fritz's mind. Again he saw emotion in Fritz's eye. For the second time it surprised him. 'You had an affair with her, didn't you?

'I said no fuckin' secrets didn't I? I'm a sucker, eh? Ok. We made love. Just the once. It brought us close. It had to happen. I felt so sorry for her. She needed someone. Brad was wild.' He waited for a response, staying still in his chair. Francis smiled. 'I began to hate him. No, not hate. Despise perhaps. He had so much. Lovely wife, kids. Everything. Yet he was so wild. Then one day she just turned up. Said she couldn't stand him. That he'd shouted at her over food. She was spending too much, making nice things. He said he'd buy the food. Then he hit her. She needed me. She was like a little child. Just standing there, crying.'

'You're a nice man –'

'Oh yeh, so's Bill Clinton,' laughed Fritz making little of Francis' praise. He pushed the plate away and laughed to himself. He thought how it all seemed such a long time ago, how the recent events had changed his perspective of time. 'So now you know,' he said, standing up. 'Now no telling anyone. And no more secrets. Everything open, Ok?'

'Ok.'

But there was a secret. A big secret. And Francis had to keep it. That night he thought of the time he had drifted down to the house to borrow some sellotape and a scissors. He was packing a parcel to send home. A present for his father. A book on black cowboys. Cowboys were his father's only interest in the States. He remembered him watching *High Noon* and *Shane* and shouting on the heroes and shooting at the bad guys. It all made Francis believe that the reason he wasn't allowed onto the northern hills of the farm had little to do with lead mines and subsidence and more to do with the way out on the hills with Bess and the sheep his father became a sort of Gary Cooper or Alan Ladd. He came to believe in that. He really believed that his father's sobriety was acted, a deferment of pleasure until he felt the sweep of the west wind up valley and he could kick into horse-flesh and gallop away.

'You sending that home?' asked Pam when she was looking for the sellotape.

'Black cowboys,' explained Francis.

'No such thing,' said Pam.

'Oh there are. It's all in here. Lots of them.' Francis waved the book and displayed the face on the front cover. 'It's for my father,' he explained.

'You said you didn't like him,' remarked Pam, bending over a cabinet, peering into the contents of an open drawer. 'You said he frightened you. You said he sort of stood over you. That's what you said. So don't you like him? I mean he's your father. Doesn't that mean anything?'

Francis thought of ways of modifying her misinterpretation. She hadn't quite grasped what he had previously said. 'Don't understand him,' he said. 'I like him. Yes, I think I like him. At least I hope I like him. I like to think I like him –'

'What?' Pam couldn't keep up with the wittering.

'I just can't talk to him.'

'You tried? I mean have you made the effort? That's important you know. You haven't given up have you? You shouldn't give up. Never.' He sat down. He watched Pam close the drawer and heard her mutter something to herself about Brad's workshop and a store of sellotape. She left him for a minute. The interrogation transferred. He asked questions of himself, thinking how it seemed like the long nights he had spent at Brynlas, how he would practise approaches and think of interests and try to find what his mother would have called the right wavelength.

Out of the thoughts came the memory of following his father out to the storeroom where he kept the mix for the horse and the goats. He remembered standing by the door, watching the stocky frame of his father transfer bags of mix into bins. He could still sense the richness of the smell. Molasses dominated. It was an oily, clear, strong smell. His father was talking, muttering. It was animal talk, ridiculous talk, meant for Toggie and Zoon and Bess. He couldn't make out the words, but that didn't matter. It was the intimacy that affected him. The softness. It was something that outside in the open air his father somehow lost. He told Pam about it when she returned. He said that it made him seem more hopeful, that it gave him a target, something to gain.

'Parents,' she said, sitting down at the kitchen table opposite Francis. 'I guess there's always clashes –'

'You think?'

'Oh yeh. Different generations, different lives.' She became thoughtful for a second, but soon burst into a smile. 'Your tape.' She pushed the sellotape across the table to Francis. 'I'm in town tomorrow if you want me to post it.'

'Oh...thanks,' said Francis.

'It's no trouble. I've got some mail to pick up. Do you want to pack it here?'

'No,' Francis answered quickly. 'The paper's in the tower.'

'Bring it over later. Whenever you've finished.'

'You sure?'

'Yeh,' said Pam smiling broadly.

Back in the water tower, Francis considered Pam's brief comment. It made the hostility he felt for his father seem inevitable. He wondered about that. He knew it controlled the way he approached his mother, the way she was manipulated by his father, the way one word from him would mould her response. Because of that he had always known that his father was crucial to their harmony.

The thoughts upset Francis. They interfered with the writing of the birthday card. 'To dad' he had started. Then the thoughts took over. They made him think of the overly possessive disciplinarian that his father had turned into. He imagined him sitting at home, opening the card and dismissing it. He anticipated the response. His mother saying, 'It's from the boy.' His father nodding, nothing more. The lack of commitment hurt Francis. It made him curse the hills and religion and tradition that always had him returning to the image of his father baling mix into bins and talking almost baby like to the animals.

Sometimes it made him want to be one of the animals, to be much more part of his father's life.

'With love, Francis' he finally wrote, failing again.

When he returned with the package, Brad let him in. The children had gone to bed. Brad was watching a film. 'Outside,' he said, waving Francis through. 'Good film. You seen it boy?' Francis shook his head. 'Go through,' said Brad. Francis watched Brad and the screen long enough to witness an old man being beaten up. The screen was full of laughing faces. Brad was sipping a beer. 'Through there boy,' Brad said again, sensing Francis was taking his time. 'She's baking.'

Pam was drinking. She sat by the kitchen table. A smell of bread filled the room. 'Hi,' she said, looking up. The word was accompanied by a smile. Francis took it in. He thought how welcoming it was. Like a mother's smile. He smiled back.

'I've got it.'

'Yeh.' She put out a hand and waited for Francis to pass her the package. He did it slowly wondering for a second what she would do with it. She sat staring at the address. 'Drink?' she asked, still staring at the words and thinking of a far away place. Francis wondered how she saw it. 'Looks cold,' she said, answering his thoughts.

'What does?'

'This place. Brynlas.' She stopped to listen to Francis laughing at her pronunciation. 'Sounds cold. Hey what's so funny? Brynlas, I've heard you say it. Brynlas.' She ran her finger underneath the word as she said, 'Sounds like ice. A big bucket of ice.'

'That's the drink,' said Francis, sitting down.

'Ah yeh, you haven't answered me though,' she said in a mocking way. 'What d'ya want? You can have scotch, beer, juice. Try the juice. Mango. You like juice?'

'Beer,' said Francis, spying a row of cans on top of the fridge. He thought it was a sign there were several cans chilling in the freezer.

Pam laughed. She looked around the room, staring at the door, passed the food cupboards and then to her right passed the sink and the window. She turned. Behind her she saw the washing machine and the tumble drier and more surfaces and cupboards. 'Where the hell's?'

'The fridge,' said Francis.

'Oh yeh,' laughed Pam. She put her right hand in front of her face and waved a finger. It was meant to say no.

'No beer,' interpreted Francis.

'Brad's. You mustn't touch Brad's. Nothing of his. His beer. His food. His car. His body.' She laughed loudly at that. 'Particularly his body.'

'Perhaps I'd better –'

'Go? No, I need company.' She stood up and went to a cupboard and found a tumbler. 'Here.' She placed it in front of Francis. 'Scotch. You're a scotch man. It's your drink. From your country.' She poured a generous portion. 'Go on. Be social,' she urged.

Francis took a sip. He smiled. He felt more uncomfortable than at any time since he moved into the water tower. The feeling made him realise how little he had seen of Pam, how their meetings had been so polite, so ordinary.

'Ssh. You hear that?' she asked.

'What?'

'Listen.' Pam pointed upwards. 'Flies,' she said. 'You noticed how big they are this year. Those cans of spray aren't big enough to knock them out. They're huge this year....' She lowered her arm and looked at Francis. 'Hey you like that?' She watched Francis take a second swig. 'Yeh. You can tell me about your country. Or your family. Hey what about your father? You didn't get on with him, did you? Did he hit you?'

'Hit me?' Francis was defensive now. A hard look said 'no'.

'Did you ever think he would hit you?'

'No.'

'Hey you're good. You'd be a good witness. If I ever need a witness, I'll call you. Yeh.' She raised her fist and smiled. Francis smiled back. He thought how there was something wild about her grin. It was wicked. And it came and went. It told him a quick mind was working behind the tired features. She shook her hair as he watched. It fell out of a ribbon. She pushed it back onto her shoulders. 'Shit,' she said. 'I must look a mess. I mean I never look good. Not real good. My hair sort of falls everywhere. You noticed? You must have.'

'No.'

'Oh you have. You're just saying that.' She raised her hands to try to tie back her hair, smelling her elbows and the back of her wrists as her hands began to work. 'God, I smell of dough.'

'It's a nice smell. Reminds me of home –'

'Brynlas,' laughed Pam, her features changed as she remembered what Francis had said. It brought a serious look to her face. 'But why? I mean you keep saying how you wanted to leave.'

'Oh come on, some bits of it are nice –'

'Home?' said Pam doubtfully. She accompanied the word with a half shake of her head. It was as though half way through the motion

101

some thought had changed her mind. It made her take another swig of the whisky. 'You ever think how dangerous home is? All those emotions. All those things contained, sort of held in.' She tossed back her head and shook her hair. It was that movement that made Francis realise how it was wild and loose and long and much curlier than he had imagined. He realised then that it was always tied up, frequently hidden underneath a hat.

'And you never thought, God he's going to hit me? You never considered violence?'

'No.' Francis managed to sound surprisingly categorical.

'You should have,' said Pam.

'Why? Your father hit you?' Francis' response was suddenly less easy. He was trying to understand the direction the conversation was taking.

'My father!' Pam laughed again, louder and wilder than ever before. Francis was trying to understand what he had said, how it had unsettled Pam. He was about to ask her about it when Brad came into the room.

'Hey I'm listening to a film in here. Can you keep the noise down? Your laughter's so loud.'

'My laughter, see –'

'I don't care whose laughter. Hey come on the boys are in bed.' The fact there was a salvo of machine gun fire as he said his words only moved Brad to say, 'An' I'm missing the film.'

'Yes sir,' said Pam, trying her best to look downtrodden and used. Brad took one look at her and raised his eyes at Francis. He began to back away.

'I'd better go,' said Francis feeling suddenly even more uncomfortable. He sensed there was little else he could do and that it was his presence that had disturbed the evening.

Pam waited a second expecting Brad to respond. When nothing was offered, she said: 'No, there's no need. Don't listen to him. I don't. Hear that?' She raised her voice so that the sound would follow Brad through the door. She watched him move away.

'I think it's time –'

'Oh go on then.' Pam seemed disappointed. She seemed at a loss, contemplating how she should react. 'I'll post it, don't worry –'

'You'll want some money.' Francis began to fumble in his pocket.

Pam waved a hand in the air. 'Forget it,' she said.

'You sure?'

Again she waved her hand. Francis said thank you and walked away.

He felt a little difficult with her after that. A formality resumed. It was as though they had revealed too much and one or the other or both had felt a need to take a step back. Occasionally, if he wasn't working or was late or delayed, he would see her taking the children to the school bus. They met it on the road. She would walk down talking children's talk and then walk back more slowly. It was then she would stop, sensing how the light crept into the woodland, changing textures and tones. Once she called out, 'Hi. Great day.'

Francis had been mending the canvas top to the tower. He was shaking the water out, draping it so it would dry. 'Yes, warm.'

'I guess for April. I'll have to open the windows in the garage. Get all those old insects out. You noticed them? They're just waiting there. Ready to go. You seen them?'

Francis shook his head. He wondered what she meant. He rarely visited the garage. It never crossed his mind that she was speaking generally.

'Must be waking up time I guess. That's kind of nice don't you think?'

Francis turned and faced her. He was smiling now. He wondered what to say.

'Sometimes I feel like sleeping through. In the fall. The first cold. Oh.' She shook, imitating a shiver.

'Must be hard waking up again,' remarked Francis.

'Oh I don't know. Couldn't manage it at this time. Too cold.'

'Too early,' suggested Francis.

'Yeh. Now if I could wait until lunch time and the sun was shining. Yeh I'd be keen. Guess I'd like to be one of those flowers that only opens its petals when the sun shines. I'd like to keep myself to myself the rest of the time.'

'Just as well you live here then.'

'Why?'

Francis regretted the words. He had forgotten Pam's lack of experience of anything but San Antonio and its suburbs and the wood. It was pointless drawing in anything else, particularly Wales. Anything else was alien, exotic perhaps, but Francis doubted that. He might just as well have been considering the moon. It made him wonder how she formulated perspective.

'Oh I think I get what you mean. The wood. Hiding away. Yeh. It's easy here.' She smiled and walked on by.

Another time the morning was greyer, less welcoming. She moved more quickly. She couldn't avoid Francis. He was climbing down the ladder, moving as quickly as he could.

'Hey you're late,' she remarked.

'Working on the field by the wood today.' Francis threw out an arm indicating a direction. 'Taking a tree down. The foreman's bringing the chain saw over. Said I'd see him at nine.'

'See,' she said with a little laugh.

'Yeh, but I'm not late.'

'But I am. Thank God the bus was late. Thought I'd have to take the car. No room for a cup in that. You noticed?'

Francis smiled. He wondered what she meant. His smile conveyed that, but Pam was preoccupied. She shook her head. She blinked some thoughts away. 'God that car. Brad wanted a new one, a real fancy one. With a catalytic converter. You heard of those things? I read about them. Gee they're dangerous. Go in a corn field and you won't come out with one of them. They'd set fire to it. They get so hot.' She emphasised the 'hot', pursing her lips and blowing. 'Can I walk with you? Would you mind?'

Francis smiled. He was taken by surprise. They had mostly avoided each other. Occasional nods of acknowledgement were necessary when they noticed each other. Words were only spoken at distances less than thirty metres and then they normally were limited to 'Hi'. Sometimes 'How you doing?' was offered, but very little else.

'You have letters?' she asked, turning to move his way. 'I mean from home. You must have. You get many?'

'From Wales?'

'Yeh. What's it like?'

'Wales?'

'Like here?'

'Here? Oh no, nothing like here.'

'Hey you're very definite."

Francis laughed nervously. He thought quickly, trying to find a way of explaining his words away. 'Well it is different. Very different. Every country's different. Different place, different values, you know.'

It was Pam's turn to nod. She smiled too. She was thinking how already Francis' words had afforded a comparison that closed down differences. Place, she thought. 'Is that significant?' she asked. 'Place. I mean does it mean much to you? I guess in LA or New York or even San Antonio place is no great shakes. It's a country person's thing. Don't you think? You a country person? You are, aren't you? I can tell,' she said before he had chance to speak. Francis wondered how she knew. 'Country people value place,' she said, continuing quickly.

'See we've something in common. All this travelling's changed you. That's your problem. Staying here will sort you out. You miss anything? You must do. I'd miss things. But that must kind of tell you something. So come on tell me what you miss.'

Francis thought how he needed to respond, how it was difficult, how miss could be categorised in different ways. Positive and negative, he thought. Then he began to break the barrier down and just drew up a list. Family came first. Its security. Its outlet. It was still near. The Stubbs. They were a family, but they had more stresses and cracks in their relationship. Things could be exploited and opened out, he thought.

'Come on, you guys that come over here must miss something.'

'Family,' said Francis.

'Family! No kidding? Jees they're not so great. I never ever,' she emphasised, 'see my family. I used to. But not any more. Brad does. He sees his sister and brother once a year. Once a year.' She shook her head. 'Used to go into San Antonio at Thanksgiving for a get-together. God there'd be twenty or thirty of us there. Distant cousins and things. The same on July 4. Fireworks and family. Turkey and pumpkin pie at Thanksgiving. And I don't miss it. Ain't that an awful thing to say? I don't miss it at all.'

It was a week after he had taken over the parcel when Francis next saw Pam. It was a fine evening and she was on the veranda knitting. Francis walked across and stood on the steps leading up to the veranda. Pam greeted him with a smile.

'Lovely evening,' he said.

'Sure is. Makes you feel good. Keeps you sober,' she laughed, trying to make a reference to their last meeting. It worked, dismissing the embarrassment. That pleased her. It was part of her plan, to try to project herself differently to Francis.

'You're always knitting.'

'Kids,' she said. 'Fighting, playing. They're always breaking things. You must remember?'

Francis nodded. He remembered his mother in her favourite kitchen chair, drinking tea and knitting, looking up over the top of her glasses. He found a surprising amount of pleasure in the image.

'An' I just kind of like it. Out here on the deck. Me and the stars. You ever look at the stars? Aren't they fine? Real pretty Southern skies are best. Should take a trip, I guess. Hey you're smiling,' she observed.

Francis thought how Pam was always wordy. Normally she struggled to contain herself. That frustrated Francis. So many questions, he thought. He was sure she was bright. He had always felt that. Occasional observations confirmed it. 'I am,' he said, remembering the need to respond. 'You know I never think of my mother, I never see her. It's always my father –'

'Same with me,' she drawled, sounding much more gentle. 'Pig that he was.' She shook her head at some thought. 'You going out?'

'No. I'm drawing.'

'You draw?'

Francis laughed. He wondered why she sounded surprised, then he smiled at the way she could now feel sufficiently relaxed to display an array of emotion. He was surprised too. He couldn't believe that Ronnie hadn't mentioned the goats and the giraffes and the cartoons.

'I'd like to see them,' Pam said without any hint of passion. 'I'd like to draw. Landscapes. I've always thought I could do it. Never had the time. Never likely to get it either. I crochet. It's a sort of step up from this. I do quilts and things.'

'You sell them?'

'Yeh,' Pam nodded. There wasn't a hint of pride or a flush of success. It seemed to leave her cold. 'I sell them. I get ripped off. I take things to this gallery in San Antonio and he pays me peanuts. Puts the price up a hundred and fifty per cent. Then he sends me letters. Says he wants more, that he can sell them. So I say you pay me more. He never does that. And it's finding the time. With the kids it's difficult.'

'You should find the time,' said Francis.

The words made Pam smile. 'Yeh, you're right. I should find time. Why not?'

'Course you should,' said Francis, feeling he had found something he could exploit. He listened to her laugh at some thought and watched her put down the knitting. She looked up at him. She took in his scruffiness and the wild hair over his serious, rather hard, gaunt face, the thinness of all his features. 'You wanna drink?' she asked, warming more and more to Francis. 'Coffee?' she hurriedly added. 'There's one on the stove. Help yourself.'

When Francis returned, Pam was cradling a cup of coffee, looking straight out towards the tower. 'You like it there?' she asked. 'Bit primitive, ain't it?'

Francis nodded, taking his first sip of coffee. He sat on the lip of the veranda and turned side on to face her, realising he wasn't sure which question he was answering.

'Ronnie likes the tower. Mind you I think it's you. You're the attraction. I guess she got used to going there. She used to visit Brad. Hey perhaps she likes getting away from me. I nag her. Brad's good with the kids. Better than me.'

'Go on.'

'No. He is. He's a good father. Got lots of faults, but he's a good father. I'll say that for him. I find them more difficult. You understand?' She turned towards Francis and bit her lip, smiling throughout. A shrug of her shoulders increased her vulnerability. 'I shouldn't say this,' she said, 'but they get in the way. I mean I love them. Shit I worship them. But sometimes you need space, yeh?' Again she looked for some expression on Francis' face that would offer support. He nodded. 'Brad seems to be happy with them. That's all he wants. I mean kids sort of fit in with his religion. Kind of the fruit of God. So he's happy to have them night an' day. He never turns them away. I would.' She shook her head thinking how such a confession seemed almost criminal. 'Perhaps your father felt like me,' she suggested, trying to draw Francis back into the conversation.

'No.' Francis said the word with certainty. A slight shake of his head compounded the effect. 'It wasn't time. It wasn't anything to do with wanting things for himself. He didn't have the ambition. No, it wasn't that. He just got it wrong. I mean whatever you say, you and Brad seem to have got it right. The kids are happy. They're alive.'

'Oh yeh?'

'Yes,' said Francis persuasively. It made Pam believe he was being sincere. She smiled, then laughed. Francis watched intently. He enjoyed seeing the amused look on Pam's face. It made her attractive. Then he looked away and joined her silence. He thought of his father again. He thought of the way everything was continually assessed, how his father's looks and words were like ticks and crosses. They were like an assault, battering away, forcing Francis into a shell. He remembered practising words and actions, never thinking for himself. He remembered constantly trying to please his father. While he thought, Pam said failure was like a weight. She said you can feel it falling. Francis thought that that was it. It was certainly what he had felt. It was like a bully, pinning him down, interrogating him.

Francis came to think that Pam had got it right. He began to believe that she knew the exactness of the pain, that she, too, had felt it. He thought back to previous conversations with her and remembered how she had laughed away the idea that her father had hit her. Now Francis didn't believe her. Instead he believed she too had struggled with her father, that she was a kindred spirit. It made him view their association as something of a club. Fellow sufferers, he would think. It also made her more attractive. He began to enjoy exploring the elaborate gestures that accompanied her words and the brilliance of her yellow tumbling curls. Mostly he liked her eyes, the way they would flicker enthusiasm. He liked her shoulders too. The way they would nudge when she was embarrassed or emotional.

He was thinking of that one evening when he called for the milk. He called once every three days for the milk. He took no milk in his tea or coffee, so he used milk sparingly – only on his cereal. A pint would last him three or four days.

'Hello,' he shouted at the kitchen door.

'Hi. Come in.'

Francis could hear Pam's voice blaring over the sound of the television. He stopped for a second and tuned into the television show. A police programme. Old cops. *Starsky and Hutch*, he thought.

'I've come for the milk.'

'You got a minute? Get a coffee. Come on in.' Pam was lying on the floor. There was no-one else to be seen. From the kitchen Francis asked where everyone was. He returned with a cup of coffee in his hand.

'Family reunion,' explained Pam. 'In town....Brad's brother's in town...they try to do it once a year....here or there...'

'You don't go?' Francis stood by the door as if he was afraid to encroach on what seemed a very private scene.

'Didn't feel well,' said Pam who had moved from the floor to the sofa while Francis was making himself a cup of coffee. She was lying out on the sofa, looking over her shoulder at him. 'Come in and sit down. This has nearly finished.'

Francis looked at the two chairs. Both had washing stacked high upon them. He considered moving a pile, but thought it presumptuous. He decided to sit on the floor.

'He's robbed a bank, killed a guy, point blank, though he didn't mean to kill him. At least that's how it looked. I mean the guy was stupid. But Hutch has tracked him down and now he's got Hutch and ...' Pam broke off as the film rose to a climax. She watched it through saying, 'My God! My God! Aren't they the cleverest?' she added when Starsky arrested the men. 'Ssh!' she shouted when the jokey bit came on at the end.

'You comfortable there?' she asked, turning off the television with the handset. 'Put your back against the chair. That's what I do. Yeh. There.'

Francis shuddered. He felt her hand on his shoulder.

'Hey you need to relax. Perhaps we should put some smoochy music on and get a drink. What do you think?' She took in the lost look on Francis' face. It was like a face behind a window watching a scene but not part of it. 'Just kidding' she said, laughing as Francis looked her way.

'When's Brad back?' he asked.

'Oh forget him. They may not be back until morning. Normally he gets too drunk to drive –'

'So you don't go?'

'Sometimes. Bores me silly.' Pam lay back and stared at the ceiling. 'His brother whistles. He comes all the way from Mobile and just whistles. His little boy does it too. And he likes Jerry Lewis. You know that guy with the daft voice.'

'You should have gone.'

'God you sound like your father,' laughed Pam. She began to stroke Francis' shoulder again. 'That good?' she asked.

'Yes.'

'But you're so tense. Relax. That's it. Yeh that's neat.'

'You're good at this.'

'Did a course,' explained Pam. 'I've got all the oils in the bedroom. Shall I get them?'

'No,' said Francis quickly. 'I should go.'

'Not again. Hey you're always going. We've had all that before. Don't worry. Brad and the kids won't be back for hours. Relax. There.' Her hand worked on Francis' shoulder muscles, feeling its way around to his chest. 'Hey you're neat,' she said, liking the feel of his body. 'You're in good shape.'

'Farm work,' said Francis. He was enjoying it now, letting his body respond in a way that seemed flabby like a fat stomach. There was no tautness.

'Good,' said Pam. 'Now look this way.' When Francis turned around she kissed him full on the lips with all the passion Francis had only dreamed of. She took his hand and placed it on her breast, then brought it down to the clasp of the belt of her jeans. 'You like that,' she said, sensing him return the passion. 'Go on then Francis. Go on.'

Francis played with the belt. He wanted to undo it. He thought of her lying naked. He thought of lovemaking on the sofa and the floor, but something held him back. 'No!' he suddenly shouted, edging away. He stared at Pam for a few seconds, then closed his eyes.

She started to cry. 'What's wrong?' she said. 'You've done it before, haven't you? What's wrong then? It's only a bit of fun.' She saw him shake. His eyes reopened. He shook his head. He saw the light shining on her hair. Her curls were on her forehead now, falling into her eyes. Her eyes laughing after the tears. He thought how his world was spanning out, broadening, accommodating so much more. This was why he had moved away from Brynlas, but he was rejecting it, saying no. It seemed he wasn't ready for it, that he may never be ready for it. As he thought, Francis stayed staring down at the carpet. He knew he should move, that he had made his point, perhaps not convincingly, but a further movement away would do that. He should move, he told himself.

'Look Francis,' Pam was saying. He suddenly heard her. 'Look.' The softness of her voice covered a rustle. He sensed she was sitting up. He thought of Brynlas, of the way life had been, of the predictability, of the certainty. He thought of the excitement now. He looked up. Pam was smiling. He crawled across and kissed her.

It was Sunday when Francis next stared at the calendar. He was reading over the entry for June 22nd. *Taking Ronnie to the Pictures*, it said. In capitals. In red. It was important. So important that Davison had agreed to give him an afternoon off and Fritz was lending him the van.

While he stared at the calendar, he wanted to draw. He picked up a pad and shaded the line in charcoal that would normally start him off. But then nothing happened. Instead he sat poised, thinking how for a day or two he hadn't once thought about Wales, how Fritz's admission had let him dwell on Pam. She had shocked him. It wasn't so much what she had done, but the way he had missed things. He couldn't believe the way he had missed the coolness between her and Brad and the signs that she needed closeness. He cursed himself, believing he should have interpreted reactions and realised the consequences of conversations. Yet somehow the past seemed rather murky. It hid the miserable, quite morbid side of Pam's life. Rather, his perspective had adopted qualities of verve and excitement and the implications of his submission made it seem almost celebratory. Certainly he had enjoyed her lovemaking. He hadn't expected to. Throughout childhood, he had been surrounded by sex. Animal sex. In the fields. In the barn. On the tracks. Place didn't matter. He had learnt that instinct could strike at any time and in any place. It made him think how humans were too controlled and how control developed repression and repression developed all sorts of psychoses. He was sure he had hang ups. After all, before Pam, the closest he had been to sex was in the car park at the youth club when, one night escaping talk of pop groups and girlfriends, he had watched the stars and the outline of the hill. It was a silent night. For once no wind. It made him stand still. He knew what the noise was, but that didn't stop him peeping around the corner. Gerallt, one of his school friends, was tangled with a girl. The sounds told him it was pleasurable, different from animal sex, more imaginative, more passionate, more adventurous.

He thought too of Fritz. Fritz had surprised him. His admission had come so easily. It was as if he was proud of his adultery. Francis sensed then that it wasn't so much the content of the admission that shocked him but the fact it was made, the fact that Fritz could allow himself to be seen to be so vulnerable. It didn't fit his image. But images to Francis now seemed more like screens, covers for what was really going on. What to believe? That was the question. He wondered whether it was a feature of adult life or modern life. Modernity would restrict it, he thought. It would keep it contained in the present, keep it with Texas and Brad and Pam, but if it could be applied to adult life, then it would be drawn into all his interpretations of Wales.

It was then he had his first thoughts of Brynlas for some time. He tried to consider them in the context of images and screens. He wanted to try to take away the filters, but he learnt quickly the retrospection wouldn't allow that, that he saw the scenes as he had responded to them. This time it was his father reciting names. 'Sarn, Hafren, Pantygog, Farngoch, Carn, Brynteg, Blaengarw...' The names were of the old farms that surrounded Brynlas. His father was at his best showing off his local knowledge. He was in the dining room. In his chair. The history dripping out of him. His arms limp, bolstered by the table. The sun coming in. A dog barking in the background.

He would talk of the present too. The new hopes. 'Good luck to them. That's change isn't it? Century ago it was lead. That was the bloody dream. Now it's heritage bloody centres and long haired bloody goats. Fair enough.'

'Aye,' said the man alongside him. It was shearing day. The shearers were enjoying their lunch.

'Bloody harder every year,' said Francis' father. He was referring to pitching the sheep. It made Francis picture the sheep turning white, their feet suddenly black, the blotches of red from cuts. 'Next year I'll bag up,' said his father. 'Always preferred bagging up.'

'That's harder,' said Gwyn who had spent the morning folding the fleece up like a sleeping bag and packing it away. 'Still this is what it's all about,' he added, surveying the food. 'Always a good spread with Mairwen.'

'Used to have a big roast dinner and a huge steamed pudding. Spotted bloody Dick,' said Francis' father.'Boiled in the biggest bloody saucepan you could find... Still, not bad,' he added, glancing across the table. 'Could have done with more fruit on the table. None of you buggers will eat fruit. I've always liked my fruit.'

'I like fruit,' said one of the shearers.

The other shearer nodded. 'Used to go down the pub,' he remarked.

'You used to stay,' added Francis' father. 'Used to bring the sheep here. From the other farms, that is. You used to stay overnight. In that bloody hut by the shearing shed. Cold in there mun. You couldn't do it now,' he said, laughing. 'Yes, yes. Down the pub by tractor at night, remember?... Three pints and a game of dominoes. You were bloody good at dominoes. And we'd have a bet on how many sheep you'd do the following day.... Pass me the fruit bowl Gwyn,' he shouted, shaking the nostalgia away. 'Swop this.'

'What the bread?'

'Aye don't like bread. Never have. Prefer fruit.'

'With soup,' laughed Gwyn.

Francis' father gave Gwyn a look. It said pass it here. Gwyn obliged. One of the shearers looked up. The look also took Francis' father's gaze across the table. 'Why's that there then?' he said nodding at a place set alongside the shearers. 'Mairwen,' he shouted, 'you bloody miscounted? One, two, three, four, five,' he counted, pointing in turn at the shearers, Gethin, Gwyn and finally himself. 'Bloody women,' he whispered. 'Women can't bloody count. Can't bloody count.'

'For Francis,' explained Francis' mother. She appeared at the door that led through to the kitchen.

'For Francis? What do you mean, for Francis?'

'He can eat with you,' said Francis' mother.

'Eat with us? Since when?'

'I thought –'

'You thought wrong. He's too bloody young.'

'Too young? He's fourteen going on fifteen.'

'Exactly, he's a bloody boy.'

'He isn't,' protested Francis' mother.

'Listen. there'll be a lot of man's talk going on here. Bloody boy,' cursed Francis' father. 'I told him yesterday, I said remember this now son, roll it don't tie it, that's the bloody directive this year.'

'Directive?' asked one of the shearers.

'From the bloody Wool Board. Changes every year. And what happens this morning? I look around and he's bloody tieing it. Bloody boy. He's in a world of his own. So he can eat where he always eats when you boys are here. In the kitchen, in the bloody kitchen.'

Francis' father stood up and moved around the end of the table towards the shearers. He picked up the extra cutlery. 'There. Much better for you two,' he remarked. 'You've got bloody room now.... Setting a place for the bloody boy,' he said to himself, returning to his seat. 'He gets a place when I say so. Understand?' he added sharply to Francis' mother. 'When I say so.'

★

Francis tried phoning Zelda just to check arrangements. When there was no answer, he decided to walk over. Call on spec, he thought. She had said that would be alright. She had said it at the funeral. Just blend it into the walk, he thought. Make it natural.

Zelda was in, Ronnie was out. 'You're jinxed,' said Zelda, laughing lightly. 'Still you'll see her soon.'

'Wednesday,' said Francis.

'Yeh Wednesday. You want a coffee? I could kill one. Sunday's a hell of a day. I work more on Sunday than Monday, you know that? Hey you like the music?' She walked across the room towards the kitchen.'

'The music?' mused Francis, listening.

'Yeh. Is it familiar?'

Francis listened again. Another test, he thought. Why should it be familiar? Piano. An orchestra. A piano concerto, thought Francis. He got no further.

'God you Brits. Saw you coming up the drive and I thought make him at home. You don't get it do you?'

Francis thought quickly again. Home, he thought, Wales. Pianos. Concertos. Nothing came to mind.

'*Brief Encounter*,' Zelda shouted from the kitchen. 'That great British movie. That great British middle class movie. You know, railway stations and Trevor Howard. So smooth. You like movies?'

'Yes.' As he shouted he saw that Halliwell's was still on the table. A cup stood on it now. Francis stared at it, at its yellow colour. A strange colour, he thought. Certainly not most people's favourite colour. So why yellow? Star coloured, perhaps; though he couldn't make up his mind whether stars were yellow or orange. Whatever, there was a link. Stars. Hollywood stars. Heavenly stars. Yellow. He couldn't piece it together.

He laughed, making a move. He leant across, moved the coffee cup and then nervously wondered whether it would leave a mark on the table. He moved it from hand to hand, looking for something to place it on. The videos were too far away. There was nothing else. Hold it, he thought, gripping the cup handle with his left hand. Halliwell's was too heavy to move with just his right-hand, so he tutted and replaced the coffee cup.

'Put it on the table,' urged Zelda, coming in through the door. 'My fault. I should have put it away. Kind of got a bit carried away with it earlier. Christ,' she shook her head. 'Sunday.' She watched Francis pick up the book. 'So what you looking for?' she asked, accepting the cup and moving away again towards the door that led to the hall and kitchen.

'*Blade Runner.*'

'Oh yeh. What a film! You like it?'

Francis put on a puzzled look. It was for himself rather than Zelda. She's forgotten, he thought. He made it seem like a crime, but it told him how important he was to her. It made him feel on his own; self contained, self referenced, he thought, establishing how often he felt such a feeling. Disenchantment seemed at the heart of it. It made people revolt. They forgot what they said like Zelda or lied like Brad or fell silent like Pam. All of that weakened links and trust. It obscured reality. She had said it, he thought. *Blade Runner.* She had admitted it here, in this room.

'Wasn't you I said it to recently, was it? Said it to someone. Thought it was Dolly in the office. Oh shit it was you, yeh I remember now. Halliwells.' She pointed at the book. 'You have a read.'

Francis read. It wasn't what he expected. Sci-fi. Bleak. Gloomy. Like a firework display seen through some fog, said Halliwells. Somehow that didn't go with Zelda. Zelda was never associated with fog. Where's the glamour? he thought.

'It's not you,' he said, looking up.

'Not me. Thank God,' she laughed. The smile left her quickly. It went with some thought. She sat down alongside Francis. 'Hey can I have a look then?' She read the write up. 'Oh shucks it's better than that. Yeh. And it's grimmer than that. All that urban decay stuff.' She shook her head. 'You know I wake up now and look outside, just to see if it's like it is. I mean how does it arrive? You know what I mean? All that decay.' She shook her head again and turned her attention back to the words. Francis watched her lips move with the words. 'He's gotten it all wrong. Shit.' While he watched he thought how she believed the image, how she saw capitalism eroding itself around her.

'You ever feel sort of threatened?' she asked. She finished reading and sat back. She tilted her head and looked into the ceiling.

'Yes.' Francis wondered how much he should say.

'So you know.'

'Know?'

'What it's like. I trust no one. It's real scary sometimes. You're there – in the office, I mean – thinking now do I trust you? Can I believe what I see? Shit, that's scary.'

'So you think that with me?'

'I think it with everybody, don't you?'

Francis had to think about that. 'No,' would have been his response back in Brynlas. Everything was clear there; everything was open. He would say no now. Brynlas' sensibilities had travelled with him. He expected definitions, not vague statements. He was confusing them. Brynlas conditioned him to do that. There was nothing he could do about it. He just worked in that way. 'No,' he said, trying to express his thoughts. 'A cultural difference, I think. Different perspectives.'

'Why? You heard of the global village?'

'I've heard of the village. I'm still very local.'

Zelda laughed. She lowered her head and looked at him. She let the laugh extend. 'Shame,' she said.

'Shame! Doesn't sound like a shame to me.'

'You'll change.'

Yes, thought Francis, he would change. He knew that. He felt it happening. The awareness beginning to infiltrate, to change perspective, to question. He was fighting that. He thought it strange. It was like preserving Brynlas. A touch of shock accompanied the thought, shock at the realisation he had found something worthy in Brynlas, something that he valued and wanted to maintain.

'You're surprised, aren't you? I guess it's not very predictable.'

'What?'

'Me liking *Blade Runner*. You'd have expected *Dynasty* or *Dallas*, something glitzy.'

'Something that goes with your shades,' laughed Francis.

Zelda laughed too. 'Yeh something that goes with my shades,' she said, standing up and moving to the window. She looked out. Another check, thought Francis. She looked up and down the road. He shook his head, thinking she had got it wrong, that areas like this were secure, that they would stay smiling and green.

In the evening Francis went for a walk. It was really more of an inspection, a review of the vegetables, the scarecrow and the tree house. Brynlas stayed with him. He thought how at home in Wales the outside was moorland. Grass tufting up. Water bedding the land. It was open. It allowed him to stand and think and find something almost religious, certainly remote from life. In Texas he never had the sense of being inside and protected. Rather, he was exposed. It was like being permanently young and keen-eyed. He was ridiculed and ridiculing, always finding something vast and bewildering.

For now, the focus of all that was Pam. By the storehouse he thought that she seemed so lost, that she needed direction, that clinging to him and Fritz had been a cry for help and that it had been futile, that the influence of Brad had held on. It had been a strong grip. Even with few words and no intimacy, Brad had exerted control. Francis wondered whether it would have continued, whether Brad's love of the children would have been enough. He wondered about the children too, how they would have reacted in time. The division must have become apparent, he thought. It would have become obvious in the way that evenings were spent in different rooms and activities were arranged in separate groups. But then they had been brought up like that and it may have seemed normal, as normal as his own father's aversion to family trips. He remembered August Bank Holidays in New Quay and his father's itchiness amongst people, the aggression it quickly developed in him.

Walking back to the tree house he felt sure Pam would have endured the situation until the children left home, but then he considered the possibility the boys may have stayed. After all, rural lines tended to be clear; rural families tended to become extended when there were no great choices. He thought how Pam would have reacted to that, how it would have gradually clawed at her and made her feel there was no way out, but then she may have already felt that. Francis thought it likely that she probably lacked the confidence to move away, that all she could do was snarl in a corner and hope that it was enough to let Brad feel it was necessary to keep his distance and allow her space.

After the walk, Francis drew. For once he was fluent. He drew giraffes for Ronnie, extravagant giraffes with jungles for eyelashes and roller coasters for necks. Giraffes in Texas, dwarfing the nodding donkeys, one looking into the water tower from above, smiling at Francis. More than anything he liked the caricature of himself: a needle with a nose and two eyes rather than one.

After the giraffes he took out his Fred sketch pad. He laughed at the old cartoons and looked at the months that were left: August, November, December, March. November was easy. He drew Fred lighting a long fuse. He was in his own front room and the caption

116

read: Fred decided to work out what went wrong with the gunpowder plot.

Francis laughed at that. He looked at the cartoon and laughed again. It was such a lovely sound. He climbed the ladder and let it invade the desolation that the charred cottage held. Then he stopped. Looking out, he realised what a lovely night it was. He watched the moon pale things, colouring them the shade of his breath. So quiet, he thought, the cottage, the veranda, the garage, the storehouse. He moved quickly. To linger would be to release events. He dwelt on the woods. It seemed so shadowy and vast. Occasionally it gleamed, like a stocking in the light. Even in the dark he found he could trace the paths that ran in lines and the tree house and the vegetable patch and the place where he had last seen Pam. He recalled the note he had written to her, saying how they should talk, be adult. He had wondered why she seemed embarrassed, whether she wanted to go back to being an acquaintance. All he wanted to know was whether they should move on or go back. The alternatives were so clear to Francis, yet Pam seemed to squirm away, to avoid him and leave him in nothing but confusion and sadness. Let's stop this, Francis had written.

When they met on the path that led to the road she was picking mushrooms; he was coming back from Davison's. 'Hi,' he said, surprising her.

'Mushrooms,' she said, showing him the basket. 'Not exactly picked at dawn by a vestal virgin, but they're fresh enough. You like paté?' She waited for Francis to nod a reply. 'Then I'll save you some.'

Francis smiled. He was enjoying the unforced pleasantness of her words. He felt surprisingly at ease. But nothing followed. He watched Pam turn her back on him and return to the mushrooms. Suddenly the freedom had gone. Suspicion returned. Francis began to move on. He felt he had nothing to say. He understood her response. He had seen it before. It was the bitterness that accompanied all her words with Brad. It held a simple message: no way back.

'Francis!' Pam called out. A warmth returned for a second. Pam knew how to use it, how important it was to let words linger and then provide an expectant smile. It worked on Francis. He stopped and turned. He smiled. He enjoyed her passion. He was willing to give it a chance, to let it thrive.

'What is this?' Pam's mood changed. She pulled the note he had sent her from her blouse. 'I mean what's all this about moving forward or going back? What the hell does it mean?'

'Options,' said Francis, feeling awkward. 'I mean it's what we could do. I mean after doing what we did.'

'Francis it was sex. We had sex for chrissakes. It was fun.'

Francis stared at her. She was denying everything now, turning it into a night of television, a night when she didn't even answer the door.

'What does it mean to you?' she asked. 'I mean let's spell it out. We did it, yeh? Ok. Let's not turn it into something else.'

'It was good –'

'Oh come on, mushroom paté's good.'

Francis nodded. He walked on. There were no more words. He looked back once. Pam was bent over, picking again. He stopped and almost called out, but the inclination to sort out the complications had gone. He paused for a second and wondered what was overwhelming her, why he had disturbed her, why their lovemaking was worth so little.

'Hey I've been waiting.' Fritz's smile greeted Francis' return from work. 'Where you been?'

'Walking.'

'Walking? I called at Davison's. Thought I'd see you there, but no way. He's gone, they said. So where you been?'

'Here and there.'

'What d'ya mean? Walking. Here and there,' he said in a mocking way. 'That means somewhere. Tell me. Come on I need to know where to look next time.'

'The woods.' The answer was enough to allow Francis his moment of deviousness. He covered his relationship with Pam and simply talked in terms of trying to sort out what he knew and understood of Pam and Brad. He never let on what he really knew and that let Fritz seem to be equally troubled. It made him feel he had to offer some ideas, some insights. More than anything he wanted to try to ease the level of concern.

'They were just screwed up. I mean Brad screwed up. He got it wrong –'

'But why? I mean people point to the evil, what he did, but with me he was fine. In fact he was very kind.'

'He could be. But he could also be fuckin' wild. You've seen him. You saw him with Jim, remember? At Oscar's. No fuckin' control.'

'But with the kids. With you. With me.'

Fritz smiled. He couldn't disagree. He told Francis of the way Brad had appealed to him to help with the wall he had been building.

'You,' laughed Francis.

'Yeh. He wanted me to wear a fuckin' tee shirt and shorts and join in. More hands the better, he said. He was rushing see. Running out of time. Some politician was coming to open it. He did everything. So it was buy me this and bring me that. He even offered me tickets for the big game. Yeh. He even offered me that. Just to get me working on the fuckin' wall.'

'You help?'

'Oh yeh,' smiled Fritz. 'Listen you got a beer handy? All this talking makes me dry.'

Francis laughed. He vacated the chair and let Fritz sink into it. He watched him and thought how he did it well. It was as if his body was meant to fold up or crumple into relaxation. 'Any cookies?' he added when Francis was half way up the ladder.

'I'll have a look,' replied Francis.

'Yeh, you do that. Me, I'll stay here. Hey you weren't shocked at what I said the other day, were you?'

'About what?' said Francis, climbing down the ladder. He threw Fritz a beer. 'No biscuits, I'm afraid.'

'No biscuits!' mocked Fritz. He pulled on the ring of the can of beer. 'Now what should I be shocked about?'

'About Pam. You weren't,' said Fritz watching Francis shake his head. 'I'd have been. I mean if you said you and Pam had, well you know. Gee that would have shaken me. I mean I know it shouldn't have.'

'Why?'

'Well Pam sort of became a bit liberal.'

Francis laughed. He shouldn't have, but it was inadvertent, picking up Fritz's surprising shyness when it came to sexuality. Francis' laughter made it worse. 'You know what I mean,' he said, fumbling even more. He put down the beer and became more deliberate. 'I mean she slept around. She had a few men. Nothing wrong with that. I mean she enjoyed men. She was a passionate woman. She needed closeness. She was afraid of Brad. I mean after he hit her.'

'Did it change her?'

'Brad beating her? Yeh. Yeh, it did. I mean in that way it did. I think in other ways too. You know she was quite a Christian girl when I first met her. She was a church-goer. Used to go to St. Martin's. In town. Used to take the boys. Dragged Brad along too. Turned him into a Christian. Then he beat the Christianity out of her. So in the end she stayed home, making jam, picking mushrooms. He took the boys to Church. God's country. God's fucking country,' said Fritz, imitating Brad.

119

'Did Brad know? I mean when she started seeing other men.'

For once Fritz was thoughtful. He took in Francis' question and said he didn't really know the answer, that Brad had become distant, never talking to him about the family. 'Doubt if he knew,' he added slowly. 'I mean she was careful. I know that. You know I don't really know...' Francis listened closely, thinking that Brad would have cared, deeply cared. 'He'd have had her back,' remarked Fritz. 'I don't think he ever thought of her as distant.'

Francis nodded an agreement. 'I think you're right,' he said moving over to an old stone. He sat on it and thought how he and Brad had sat in the same position only weeks ago, how they had talked over work and Davison's plans. They talked about the children too, about Denny's lack of discipline, about Paul and computers. Less was said about Ronnie. 'She's great,' Brad had said. He left it at that. He didn't expand. No reasons were offered. He simply smiled. Perhaps the warmth of the smile said much more. Certainly the love for his children was obvious. Pam, though, was never mentioned.

'He said so little to me about Pam,' remarked Francis.

'He didn't want to hurt himself,' added Fritz 'He was nuts about her. She was sort of luke warm for a while. Then she hated him. She stayed for the kids. And that was kind of ironic cause it was Brad who wanted the kids. Pam wanted freedom.'

'Did she think about going?'

'Yeh. She considered it. But where would she fuckin' go? That's a big question for a girl who's a housewife. She didn't have the confidence.'

Francis wasn't so sure about that. He considered it. Sexually she was pushy, he thought. In other respects though he considered her naive, even nervous.

'She didn't get out enough,' continued Fritz. 'I told her to join the clubs. Act. If that's what she wanted. She had no go, no self belief. She didn't even realise what a good looking woman she was. I mean no-one fuckin' told her. Most of the time there wasn't anyone to tell her. Only Brad. And he'd fucked up. She never believed him.'

Francis nodded. Fritz was right. His analysis was persuasive. It made Pam seem terribly delicate, as though she was on the point of breaking. For all the accuracy, that didn't seem right, but then Francis had only seen her from one dimension. He began to believe that dimension was her last hope, that he had witnessed something equivalent to a last stand.

Fritz burped. 'Lovely,' he said, moving the can back to his mouth;. 'You speak to Zelda?' he added. It broke Francis' concentration.

'Zelda? No,' said Francis. 'I'm phoning her tomorrow. She wants to know what time I'll get to pick up Ronnie. She wants to know where we're going, what time we'll be back –'

'A real fuckin' mother,' quipped Fritz.

'Yes. I thought that –'

'Good though.' Fritz nodded his approval. 'I mean the kid could have ended up in a home. God knows where.'

'True. She's alright,' said Francis, meaning Zelda. 'A bit wild perhaps. But she loves Ronnie. That's the main thing.'

'So what time?' Fritz remembered the reason for his calling. He waited for a reply, but nothing came. 'I thought if I get there at three. You can drop me back, so Betty can sort me out for dancing. You keep the car, bring it back to me after the dancing. Say eleven. That Ok?'

'Eleven? Yes, fine.'

'Well any time after ten. Ten will do. We're back by then,' said Fritz, finishing off his beer.

On Wednesday Francis kept to his routine – thinking of Brad on the way to work and Pam on his way home – only this time he left work just after noon and spent an afternoon washing and combing his hair, preparing himself for Ronnie. He looked in the mirror at his sallow skin and boney face and then at the calendar: Wednesday, June 22nd, *Taking Ronnie to the Pictures*. In capitals. In red.

'Ready?' shouted Fritz, disturbing him.

Francis emerged in jacket and tie.

'Oh yeh,' shouted Fritz, watching Francis climb down the ladder. 'You look as though you're on your first date,' laughed Fritz. 'Where'd ya get the jacket?'

'Brad's,' said Francis.

'And it fits. Hey you're bigger than you look. But won't Ronnie recognise it?'

'He told me he never wore it. Didn't like it, so he said. He gave it to me to wear to meet Davison. Impress him, he said. He's the boss.'

Fritz took Francis back to his house. It was exactly as Francis had expected it to be: open plan with a long front garden with one big tree spraying shade onto the lawn.

'Nice,' said Francis.

'No. Zelda's is nice,' said Fritz. 'This is Ok. The back's better. Sprinklers and shade round there. A sort of bog garden. You like gardens?'

It was a twenty minute drive back to Zelda's. While driving, Francis was surprised by his thoughts. He suddenly focused on Brad. He recalled his morning's thoughts. He had been considering their first meeting in town, the conversation on the way to the wood, how Brad had immediately taken to Francis because he was from Europe. Brad had thought that made him different.

'My family came over from there, 'Brad said. 'My great great grandfather came over in the 1820's or 30's. Don't know anything about him 'cept he had two sons. I guess he was English, always thought he was.'

'Why?' asked Francis.

'Oh the name. Stubbs. John Stubbs. Now that must be English'

'You called Stubbs?'

'That's me boy. Brad Stubbs.'

Francis shook his head.

'See it's just gotta be English.' Brad smiled. It was as though he was finding himself. The smile seemed to bolster his confidence. It egged him on. 'It's not from Wales then?'.

'It's not one of the common Welsh names. No.'

'Could it be Scottish?'

Francis ran the name through his mind, trying to think of actors or sportsmen or politicians. Nothing came to mind.

'Anyhow he came over and had a son. Now he would be my great grandfather. I know a bit about him. Hey, isn't this boring you? I mean you're from England. All I'm doing is taking you back there.'

Francis smiled. He thought how big movements created interest, how in years to come his trip to Texas would have put him into the sort of category Brad's great great grandfather had carved out for himself.

'You're not bothered?'

'Of course he isn't,' said Pam. It was the first time she had spoken during the journey. 'Would you be bothered? Would you want this? I guess he'd prefer to be in San Antonio, in some little hotel, minding his business.'

'Who needs a hotel?' snapped Brad, looking back her way. The vitriol was obvious. It set her up. She tutted and scowled. The sounds under the growl of the old engine were contained. Francis picked them up once, but made no connection. He imagined she was doing the crossword and had missed a clue or was knitting and had dropped a stitch. All he could see was that she was head down looking at something.

'Hey compatriot!' laughed Brad. The outburst shocked Francis. It followed a period of calm and issued in another period of talk about the past. It left Francis thinking that he had connected Brad to all the excitement and expectation of exile. He began to imagine that Brad was seeing Francis as his great great grandfather arriving somewhere in the States in the 1830s.

The thoughts had passed by the time Francis reached Zelda's. He waited outside for a minute or two, half expecting Zelda and Ronnie to come running out to greet him. While he waited he organised the book he had brought and the drawings he had placed inside. They were in a specific sequence. He checked the sequence and smiled.

'Ok,' he said, getting out of the car. He tugged on his trousers to get them to sit on his hips. He raised his shoulders to straighten out his jacket. He felt smart, more tidy than he had been in years, though he wondered what Zelda would make of it.

There was no sound in the house. He rang the bell twice, knocked on the wood of the door and called out. Then he waited, thinking he was early and Zelda was preparing Ronnie. He tried again. 'Hello,' he shouted. He walked to the side of the house, saw the area where the bar had been during the funeral. It had been regrassed now, everything was back in place. It looked unlived in. 'Zelda,' he called, staring in through the lounge window. Only Chatfield's sculpture stared back at him. He looked and listened. He heard nothing. He knew then there was no-one at home.

He spent the afternoon at a roadside diner. He drank coffee after coffee, took off his jacket and looked out at the road. Someone spoke to him and he smiled.

'Gonna rain,' said a voice.

'Yes,' said Francis.

He returned to Zelda's two hours later, hoping there had been a mix up of times or days. 'Wednesday,' his mind kept saying, 'June 22nd. Taking Ronnie to the pictures.' He repeated the phrase time after time. His mind was saying it as he called out 'Zelda!'

'Hey you alright?' a man cried from the sidewalk.

'You seen her?' asked Francis, turning around. The man had stopped walking. A small dog was sniffing at his side.

'You know her?' the man asked.

'Yeh. I'm a friend,' said Francis.

'Never seen you before,' remarked the man.

'Look I'm a friend.'

'Ok. Ok.' The man sensed Francis' edginess. 'I'm Jack Dellmot. Zelda's neighbour, live next door.'

'Hello,' said Francis wondering what the etiquette was and why, under the circumstances, he was trying to abide by it. 'I'm Francis. Francis Williams. I was supposed to take her niece out –'

'Ronnie?'

'Yes, Ronnie.' Francis had begun to walk towards the man. He stopped once when he thought he heard a clicking noise behind him. He had thought Zelda was opening a door. 'Did she say when she'd be back? I mean I'll wait if she's only going to be a few minutes. Is she picking Ronnie up from school?'

Jack Dellmot laughed. He shook his head and pulled hard on the lead to control the dog. It had begun to show an interest in Francis who was encroaching on their space. The dog calmed down. 'You don't know?' the man said slowly. 'She must have forgotten you were coming over. Did you tell her?'

'She told me,' said Francis. 'We arranged a time.'

'Well she's gone and forgotten all about it –'

'What do you mean?'

'I mean she's not here. She's gone. Went this morning.'

'Where?' Francis was hurried now. The shock on his face somehow was illuminated by the force of his words. He seemed breathless.

'Gone to Mobile. To her brother's, took Ronnie with her. Didn't mention anything about you. Strange that,' said the man thinking aloud.

All the way to Fritz's, Francis shook his head. He missed gears, took a wrong turning, stopped at the edge of the woods. He convinced himself Zelda's mistake was elementary, a confusion of times and dates. Nothing more. It was the sort of thing his father would have done with men from the ministry or with forms he was meant to fill in and return. Zelda got it wrong, he kept saying, convincing himself she had meant Tuesday. Perhaps yesterday they had been waiting for him, saying the same sort of things he was now contemplating.

Fritz backed up Francis' thoughts. 'Mistake,' he said. 'Couldn't be anything else. I mean they've had a shock. Guess Ronnie's uncle phoned up and said, come on down. Zelda'd be glad of that, I guess. Takes the pressure off.'

Francis agreed politely. 'Expect so,' he said.

'Yeh. Come on. Sure to be. You wait. They'll call when they get

124

back.' A silence greeted Fritz's words. 'You didn't fuckin' ask, did you? Hey shit brain what the fuck's up with you? You didn't fuckin' ask when they're getting back.'

Francis laughed. The confusion had left him bewildered, conducting more of a conversation with himself than with the man he had met on the sidewalk. It meant he would have to wait. But it wasn't that that bothered him. It was the fact he wasn't sure how long he would have to wait that stuck in his mind.

'I'd drop her a line,' said Fritz, stopping to let Francis out. 'Tell her that you called, that there's been a mistake. Just let her know that you'd been there, that you went to see Ronnie. She'll understand that. That guy Dellmot said he had a key didn't he? He'll put it in for you. Or post it. Yeh why not just fuckin' post it?'

Francis thought how the conversation with Dellmot ended with Dellmot saying he was looking after the house while Zelda and Ronnie were away. 'Good idea,' Francis said suddenly, seeing the sense of what Fritz was suggesting. He smiled as he watched his friend drive away.

Francis started to write the letter as soon as he returned to the water tower. He sat back on Ronnie's stool, thinking of a start. Dear Zelda, he wrote, I called today, I met a Mr. Dellmot. Then he crossed it all out. Dear Zelda and Ronnie, he wrote on a second sheet.

The words came slowly. He told himself to keep it simple, to say just what had happened. Nothing else. There was no need to mention anything else. But somehow that seemed difficult. It proved impossible. He allowed himself to be side-tracked onto Toggie and Zoon and then giraffes and drawings, even Fritz at one stage, then he censured himself and ended the letter quickly, perhaps even abruptly.

He sighed when he signed and sealed it. Then he turned it over and let it lie in front of him. He stared at it for ten minutes, his mind running over times with Ronnie and Brad. He thought again of his introduction to the tower, of the way he and Brad had talked farming as though Francis had been ranching all his life. He remembered the drink they had had. The concealed bottle of Rebel Yell.

'Hey look at this,' Brad had said, taking it from behind a chair.

'Rebel Yell?'

'Yeh. You heard it?'

Francis shrugged. He jumped when Brad yelled, then smiled when he laughed. 'I guess that's it. Nobody really knows.'

'What do you mean?' asked Francis, anticipating a reply that would identify some local type of coyote that bayed in the moon at midnight.

'It's the rebel yell. Hey come on.'

'The rebel yell?'

'Yeh.'

Francis played for time. He thought over the words, linked them with what he knew about Brad. He could see they meant something to Brad, something special. They had lit up his eyes. They had made him smile. Suddenly Francis remembered the way Brad's eyes had smiled when Francis had first seen the maps in the water tower. The look was identical to the one that was confronting him now. It made him sense the answer. 'The confederates,' he said.

'Yeh,' said Brad warmly. 'The union used to cry hurrah or something. Sounds crazy, doesn't it?'

'Probably English,' suggested Francis.

'Yeh, that's it.' It was Brad's turn to nod. He stopped to take another sip. 'Of course they had nothing like this. They used to make their own brew –'

'They?' asked Francis.

'The soldiers. Used a drop of alcohol and just about anything else. Used to call it "Knock em stiff" and "Oh be joyful"–'

'Oh be joyful,' laughed Francis.

'You bet,' said Brad.

It was a couple of days after their first slug of Rebel Yell together that Brad showed Francis the storeroom. It seemed a strange name for a room that was so large. Francis wondered what it had originally been. It was detached from the house. A few paces away from the veranda. It looked exactly like the house. The same wood, the same windows, but no partition. Inside it was one large room. Half of it held stores of wood and gas, half of it was Brad's.

'This used to be up the tower,' Brad admitted. 'Don't know why I moved it. Guess the kids wanted the tower. Ronnie loves it. She gets up there all by herself now. She's eight. You'll see her. She'll appear.' Brad laughed. 'She'll have a hell of a fright...' The image of the first meeting between Francis and Ronnie made Brad laugh. The small laugh. The snigger. Puffs of air pushed out of his nose.

'So what is it?' Francis was looking down on a large central table that was the focus. Around it, flanking the walls were cupboards, some open, some closed. They were stacked with books and pots of paint and models of ships and frames and photographs. Somehow all of that seemed subsidiary, almost feeding off the table that was holding a three dimensional model.

'That's silly,' said Brad. He looked away from Francis and let his eyes run over the material on the table. He was checking it was all in place. 'Those boys come in here,' he said. 'They play with it. They pretend they're there –'

'Where?' asked Francis.

'Shiloh. It's a Hebrew word. Means place of peace.' Brad scoffed at that. Francis wondered why. He wished Brad would get on with the explanation rather than drawing out his thoughts. He watched Brad move around the table. Throughout, his eyes were down. They were looking at the colours, taking in the terrain. Francis had never seen Brad so focused.

'It's a battle, right?' said Francis.

'Yeh boy. Left two thousand, four hundred and seventy seven dead and twenty three thousand wounded.' Brad kept walking. His eyes stayed fixed on the table. 'And there it is.' He suddenly pointed to a model of a log-built Methodist chapel. It was near a papier mache hill. Francis moved closer and took in the details. The model was a mix of materials, a mix of the home-made and the bought. The trees looked bought. Francis imagined Brad stealing them from one of his children's toys. A farm set, perhaps. The soldiers were bought too.

'One good southerner worth ten Yankees,' Brad was saying, talking to himself. Francis could see he was annoyed. 'Why did they wait? Had them licked. Look at it. Who'd have won? Who'd you think?' He turned towards Francis. 'Go on. Take your time,' he said. 'Take your time.' He sat down. Francis could see there was an impatience about him. He coughed and fidgeted. He wetted his lips, scratched his left eye and smiled.

Francis moved around the table. 'Blue's union, right?'

'Yeh, yeh,' said Brad, nodding with the words.

'Right...' A coldness spread through Francis. It felt like the effect his father would have when he had placed him on the spot. Francis knew he would falter next. He told himself how silly it was, how this was Brad, a friend, someone who was lighter, more quirky than his father could ever have been. This was someone he got on with.

'The confederates,' he said, forming some sort of reasoned judgement from what he saw in front of him.

'Yeh. Of course. That front you're looking at is three miles long,' Brad moved closer to Francis. He swept a finger along the line. 'Worst fighting was at the centre. Twelve assaults there –'

'So they pushed them back,' added Francis, interpreting the events.

'Sure. Oh yeh boy they pushed them right back, but they didn't finish them off. They left them there.' Brad stared down at the table. Francis looked at his face. He thought it was a look that should have been attending a grave. It was dark, severe, forebidding. It stopped Francis. It interfered with his thoughts. It made him realise he was becoming aware of the subtle currents that changed Brad's mood. He looked away when he sensed words coming.

'Must have been a hell of a night. I mean men everywhere. The water in that stream was red with blood. There were calls crying out for momma and Jesus. There was rain and lightning. There were animals feeding on the dead. I've read about it,' he added, sensing that Francis was about to ask how he knew.

'So what changed it round?' asked Francis.

'Reinforcements. Grant licked them. Son of a bitch. Seventy thousand against thirty thousand. He just licked them.'

'So what did he say?' asked Fritz, cradling a can of beer as he sat in the water tower. Beads of perspiration greeted the coolness of the liquid.

'Dellmot? He said fine. What could he say?'

Fritz nodded. He smiled at the beer. Francis smiled at him. He liked the simple recognition. The transparency. 'Ok. Ok. So he's taken the letter. Now we wait –'

'We,' laughed Francis.

'I mean you. You wait. She gets back. She reads your letter. How does she get to see you? You thought of that? God you got to think of everything. It's like a campaign.' Fritz paused for another swig of beer. He shook the can.

'I'll get you another –'

'Hey that's real good of you. This ain't bad.' Fritz sat at the desk eyeing Francis as he stood up and left the bean bag and turned to go to the fridge. 'Hey, how's work? How's it going? How's Davison?'

'What d'you mean?' asked Francis still bending down trying to locate a drink. 'You know Davison?'

'Know Davison. I've worked there, remember? No. How can you? I mean you're new. Davison had the biggest fuckin' rats you ever saw. He had the albatrosses of the rat world. That size.' Fritz measured out an expanse between his hands and then cut what he had measured by half. 'Black rats. Rats so fuckin' fat I could have caught them.' Fritz took a long swig and smiled as the beer took effect. 'You get talking to people when you're ratting –'

'What about? The weather? The economy?' laughed Francis.

'No. Men's things. Football and horses and women –'

'Interesting.'

'Yeh. And Brad. Davison told me about Brad.' Fritz paused. He wondered whether he should go on. He recognised a trait of his, the way his mouth cornered him and put him on the spot. Francis smiled and shook his head. He knew what Fritz was thinking.

'Why do you do that? You get yourself into some situations.' Francis was shaking his head as he slumped back onto the bean bag. He bounced about, pushing and prodding the bag until he found a comfortable position. 'Come on,' he said. 'You'll have to tell me now.'

'Will I?' said Fritz contemplatively.

'Yes. Remember? No secrets.'

'God yes.' Fritz sounded serious. His smile continued, though he wanted to pull back. He could see Francis was looking smug. He saw him as a predator hounding him. 'Oh gee I guess it's nothing really. Just one of those personal things.'

'Personal things?' The phrase sounded clumsy to Francis. He wondered why Fritz had chosen such words. He waited for an explanation.

Fritz saw the look on Francis' face. He thought it so beguiling he almost wished he had seen nothing but a rather neutral attention. It almost sidetracked him. He overcame the urge to inquire about the interest.

'Davison knew Brad's father,' Fritz said rather hurriedly.

'Davison did. When?'

'In New Orleans. Brad was born there.'

'He never said.'

Francis raised his eyebrows. He tried to recall whether it was the sort of detail Brad let slip. He thought it was. One, two, at least three conversations he recalled with New Orleans and childhood as central themes. 'Lived there till he was seven. Then his father got a proper job. Became a salesman. Served Texas and Louisiana. They were his areas,' laughed Fritz. 'Man, the fuckin' world. Where else would you wanna go?'

Francis joined in the laughter, though his mind was searching back through Brad's words making links with New Orleans, the Big Easy as Brad called it. Francis remembered more detail. 'His father was a trumpeter,' he recalled.

'Yeh. Had a residency. Big friend of Buddy Bolder. You heard of Buddy?' Fritz watched Francis shake his head. 'One of the greats. Brad mixed with them all. He used to sit on the edge of the stage. Heard Jelly Roll Morton and Louis Armstrong, all the greats. Surprised he didn't mention it. Didn't you see the photos?'

'Yes, yes I did.' Francis remembered the photographs on top of the television set and on the living room cabinet. He remembered Bourbon Street full of revellers and laughing faces. He saw it in colour, though the photographs were in black and white.

'He had some fuckin' great photos. Saw one of the club. Can't think of its name. Shit. Some characters on that. All half stoned. It was in the Storyville district. Bordellos and clubs. What a start in life.'

'He liked it?'

'Brad? Course he fuckin' liked it. He worshipped his father. Well he was a name. Lou Stubbs. Got a sort of roll, hasn't it? Makes you sit up.'

Francis wondered why Brad had kept quiet about his father. Perhaps the hero-worship Brad had adopted may have shifted from figure to figure; perhaps he had discovered his great grandfather, the civil war photographer, later.

'Come to think of it, it's a long time since he mentioned his old dad.'

'He's dead, is he?' asked Francis.

'Yeh. Died a sad man.'

'Why?'

'He was let down. He wouldn't go back for mardi gras. He was invited, but said the fuckin' southern Protestants were taking over New Orleans. Something about spirit,' mused Fritz. 'Lou reckoned it was being shaken away by quirky fuckin' protestants. Miserable shits. So he wouldn't go back. Wanted to remember it as it was.'

'So?'

'So he accepted an invitation to play at a club up north, in Chicago. With the band he used to play with. They had some dates, so he went up. The one time he visited the north. He never came back. Got some chill that turned to pneumonia.'

'Brad miss him?'

'Guess so. The old man worshipped the kids and Pam. It was sort of solid. Or that's how he saw it. Something he never had.'

Francis listened to the words and saw the implications. He began to believe it was no accident that the photograph of Brad's father had disappeared. He believed Brad knew that his father would have been hurt by the family split. Such understanding played scenes in Francis' imagination. Father and father, he thought, finding common ground. The association seemed to dissipate any tension and that made it unsatisfactory, which Francis realised. Yet he still enjoyed it. He liked the huffing and puffing, the immediacy of discovery; he liked fixing it into what he knew and settling back to consider the implications. Any complications were dwelt on, the exactness of their nature considered;

reactions were deciphered from what he knew. But what he knew of Brad's father was limited to Fritz's few words. A musician – that made him an artist. He seemed outspoken and opinionated. He seemed interesting, but hard and certainly difficult. He tried to pick out the qualities genes had transferred. But that was a game. More interesting was the question raised by Fritz and the way the knowledge gained supported all that Francis suspected: glorification of the past; a liking for the larger than life. He thought his way through them one by one and wondered how they had affected Brad.

Fritz didn't stay long. He had groceries to buy and clothes to collect and children to pick up. He left Francis thinking over New Orleans and jazz and Brad's environment for growing up. It seemed so far from the openness of the hills. He wondered whether, had he been brought up in the American south, he would have wanted to leave New Orleans. He wanted to think that all young people behaved the way he had, that some desire to see more and do more packed them off elsewhere. Perhaps Brad would have wandered into the country-side to test tranquillity, perhaps that was why he was living in a wood-land and working on a farm.

The evaluation made Francis think again of his own reasons for leaving. 'Everyone's reasons,' he said, trying to make sense of it. More than anything he decided it was variability that moved him on. He had wanted something to intercept him, to make him tangential. He had wanted to be part of a group. He saw that now. He saw that he had been tired of everyone being a driving force. He had wanted to rest, to be carried along.

He tried to fit such feelings to Brad and then to Brad's father. It became a model. He kept saying, 'That's why' and laughing. 'That's why Brad worked for Davison... That's why he fell out with Pam.... That's why he made up the battles.' For much of the time he was fixing events. Large holes remained. He searched for evidence. That was difficult. The fire had burned away all their belongings. And they couldn't be interrogated. He decided the only evidence he had was in his head. He sat back, focused on memories, on sights and sounds, on conversations. Again he thought of Brad's fascination with the past. He thought of his laughter the day he walked into the tower with the photographs his father had given him. They were treasured posses-sions, cherished. His great-grandfather had taken them.

'Here they are,' Brad had said. 'All that's left boy. All that's left. Now you remember how primitive it all was. I mean they don't look

131

much, but all they had were huge box cameras on tripods and slow
shutters –'

'So?'

'So they rarely took action shots. Mostly stills. Poses mainly. And
lots of scenes after the battle –'

'After the battle? What corpses?'

'Yeh.' For some reason Brad had laughed. He turned over the photographs to check the detail he was about to reveal. 'You know it's
really odd, what they were up to.'

'What do you mean?' asked Francis.

'Well those guys. The photographers. I mean they weren't attached
to the force. They weren't hacks or anything.'

'So what were they there for?' Francis found the conversation interesting. The deftness of history was confronting him.

'Well they were like wedding photographs, I guess. The war was the
wedding. The men were the guests.'

Francis nodded. He understood what was being said, that the photographers were largely there to take shots of the combatants, to send
them back home to loved ones. Mementoes, he thought, reassurances.

'I've seen photos,' said Brad, continuing. 'They'd work in tents.
Half the side of the tent would be open, welcoming men in. And the
men would come, captains to privates. I've seen the photos. Captains
with pistols on their laps, always sitting down. Corporals standing with
their hats on and rifles raised over a shoulder, bayonets attached.'

'And that's what's on these,' said Francis, sensing Brad was about
to issue a list of ranks and poses.

'Sort of. Well this one is. Remember these are confederates.' He
turned over the first photograph and showed it to Francis. Silence
came with the viewing.

'God,' said Francis. He accepted it from Brad and felt its texture.
It seemed thin, delicate. Its colour was an appropriate khaki. 'This is
marvellous.'

'Good quality,' suggested Brad.

'Oh yes. I mean considering what you said about the equipment.
They must be worth something.'

'Oh I guess they are boy, but I wouldn't sell them. Couldn't.'

Given what he knew about Brad, Francis' mention of value was
insensitive. He bit his lip and tried to think of something that would
redress his indiscretion. All his concentration was placed on the boy
in the photograph. He was taken by the darkness of the face. 'That
sun tan?' he asked, pointing at the boy's skin.

'Mud,' answered Brad. 'It sort of goes with war.'

Again Francis felt inadequate. The compensation had backfired. He had tried too hard. Deciding to relax, he allowed himself time. He took in the boy's features. The face was flat. The eyes dull. An old man's eyes, thought Francis. It made the face serious. He began to consider the reasons for that – low morale, nervousness, bewilderment. 'I wonder who he was,' said Francis, more to himself than Brad.

'Those caps are back,' said Brad, looking at the boy's flat peaked, flat topped cap. It was as flat as the face, thought Francis.

The second photograph was as brown as the first. There was only one person to be seen and he was in the distance clinging to the top of a straight pole.

'You've spotted him,' said Brad. 'He's an observer. He'd spot troop movements. Find targets for the guns.'

'And the bridge?' Francis was referring to the photograph's main feature: a bridge. It was like a collapsed table with legs splintering out. Beneath it a slow flowing river was holding reflections. There was wood everywhere, bits of timber professionally cut, lying like a half made pontoon across the surface of the still water.

'Even the river's dead-legged.' said Brad, describing its sluggish look.

'And you don't know which bridge this is?'

'No.'

'It could be important. You know the only photograph or something. Which river's that?'

'Probably the Tennessee. I've worked that out by his movements. Where the battles were. But the Tennessee's a long river. Could be anywhere.' Brad leant across to take another look. He smiled at it as though he were greeting a friend. Francis saw the smile and thought how he was touched by the way Brad handled the photographs. He took such care. He was precise in his movements, holding them by the edge, blowing the dust on them away. He wanted them to be seen at their best. There was no doubting their value to him. They were identity. Something Americans craved. Brad had it in his hands. He was holding something his great grandfather had produced and touched. More than that it was something his great-grandfather's mind had conceived.

'No self portrait?' asked Francis, as he started to look at the third photograph.

Brad shook his head. 'I hope not,' he said. 'I mean the boy could be him. This could be him.' Brad leant across to look at the figure in the third photograph.

'Not good looking enough,' said Francis whimsically.

133

'Hey that's right boy. Hey look at his jaw. He's got the jaw of a horse. He could be chewing grass.' Brad enjoyed the re-evaluation. He did a little mime and smiled. He looked ridiculous, but Francis smiled back. He was more intent on taking in the man in the photo who was washing clothes. He held a washboard between his knees; he was rubbing a vest. Francis spotted a drop of water falling into a barrel. He thought of the moment.

'Too scruffy,' added Brad, looking at the man's collarless shirt and bracers. The man's trousers were up over his waist to just below the chest. 'He's a fat horse,' laughed Brad. 'Too fat to fight. No wonder we lost the war.'

Three days later Fritz called to see if a letter had arrived from Zelda. He sat with Francis under the water tower. Francis found himself listening to talk of temperament, in particular Brad's temperament. Fritz talked of the battles Brad had gone through. Somehow it was obvious to Fritz that Brad would have struggled through life. It made him think there was something in an early death. Avoidance of heartache and disappointment made it seem almost worthy. Francis disagreed with that. He spoke of change, of his experience. The way leaving Wales had let him almost shed a skin. That baffled Fritz. 'But you're still the same,' he kept saying, confused by the picture Francis was creating. 'You're just older,' Fritz said, making his point.

'No, it's place. It's where you are. How you fit in. What's taken for granted. I could have been forty or sixty, I'd still have been the same coming here.' Francis tried to stress how it was environment that made him nervous and diffident, how he had always been emotional, how there were always issues that made him angry or sad. He told Fritz how in Wales he had formed opinions, but they had stayed within him. 'Places see,' he said.

'So you change,' Fritz said, shrugging his shoulders. 'You'll be different when you're sixty. You'll be different when you're eighty. Different ages, different people.'

'But it's place, it's people. As much as anything it's those things. They cause change. I've lived through that.'

'Yeh, yeh, so you said.'

Francis sighed. He knew the way Fritz cut off people and drew lines under conversations. He expected the subject to change.

'So what about Brad?' Fritz said slowly.

'What about him?'

'He changed, didn't he? Same place though. And the same people.'

Francis nodded an acknowledgement of the point. He realised he should have challenged Fritz, but wondered what grounds he had. The silence made Fritz smile. 'He got frustrated that's what happened to Brad. He sensed time was moving on. The trouble was he wasn't. He was stuck. They were all fuckin' stuck.'

Again Francis nodded. Their agreement was surprising. Francis thought over the conversation, wondering how they had moved from division to consensus. 'So how would you describe him?' Fritz asked, a slight smirk on his face suggested he was looking to return to division.

'Brad? Detached.'

'But sometimes he was gregarious.'

'And sometimes he was calculating.'

'You think?' Fritz nodded his head slowly. Reflectively thought Francis, as though he were replaying occasions, matching the man to the description. 'I can see what you mean, but sometimes he was fuckin' stupid. I mean he did some dumb fuckin' things.'

'Sometimes he was happy. I mean with the boys.'

'Yeh...'·

The pause allowed Francis to join Fritz in recollections. Images followed each characteristic that was considered. They made the adjectives come to life, punctuating them with a vivacity that confirmed they were appropriate.

'And sometimes he was wild –'

'Explosive,' said Francis, describing exactly what Fritz meant.

'Yeh. With me. And with others. So he was tough and tender, eh? Makes him sound like a fuckin' steak,' commented Fritz, laughing loudly.

With all the analysis one particular memory came to Francis. He remembered roaming the wood, looking for Brad. Pam had said he was moving a tree that had fallen east of the house, but Francis had found the tree spread out on the path chopped into small pieces. There was no sign of Brad.

Then he heard him. Francis cut through the trees between the paths, following the sound. He was hurrying, somehow sensing that the sound was moving further away. That was a deception. The sounds came and went as the density of vegetation changed. Quite near, a wall of low growing bramble in a gap in the woods made Brad whisper.

A foot on a twig alerted Brad to Francis' presence.

'God! What the hell!' exclaimed Brad, turning around to face the direction of the noise. 'What you doing boy?'

'Only me,' said Francis, smiling. Brad was laughing now, staring at the out of breath Francis. A drop of blood was running down Francis' face. Francis stuck out his tongue, swept it to the right and licked the blood away.

'How'd you do that boy?'

'Bramble,' said Francis still licking away the blood. 'I've only come to say that Davison said report to Lock's Field tomorrow. He wants to see you there. Nine o'clock. He forgot to tell you. And I thought I'd forget if I left it till the morning.'

'You forgetful then boy?'

'Not really.' Francis' lack of logic made Brad smile. He shook his head recognising his visitor's nervousness. He moved his jacket off a tree trunk and gestured to Francis to sit down. Francis' face twitched as a drop of perspiration found the scratch on his face.

'So what you doing?' Francis asked, settling on the trunk.

'Helping the boys. They're picking up these branches and taking them up there.'

'The tree house?'

Brad nodded. 'They sort of got carried away. I mean they should be in bed now, but what the hell. They can't wait now they've built it. They want to camouflage it –'

'Pa.' Denny rushed on to the scene, panting and smiling. 'It's working. It's turning green.'

'That's the idea son. But remember it's dead so the leaves will drop off –'

'So we'll get some more leaves.'

'Yeh. Of course.'

'This one ready?' The boy pointed to a branch. He was about to drag it away when he suddenly stopped. It was a movement Francis recognised. It told him the boy had remembered something.

'Oh pa.'

'Yeh?'

'Paul says when we're finished will you do something for us.'

'If I can son.'

'Well he wants to sort of try it out.'

'You've done that, haven't you?' said Francis, moving into the conversation.

'What do you mean son?'

'Try to see if anyone'll spot it.'

'Ah..' Brad smiled now. He turned to Francis and raised his eyebrows. He thought quickly, trying to establish how the tree house's camouflage could be tested. 'Well son, that may be difficult –'

'Fritz pa.'

'Fritz?'

'Yeh. He's not seen it. He wouldn't know where it was.'

'No. That's right son –'

'So you'll ask him.'

'Yes son. Yeh, I'll ask him.' Brad watched Denny carry the small branch away towards the tree house. 'Great pa,' Brad heard him say. 'Fritz'll just love that,' laughed Brad. 'Fritz in a wood. Gee it's like a gorilla in a desert. Those boys,' he added, shaking his head. 'They've got some ideas. They're gonna make it. No doubt about it. They'll be there.'

Francis woke up wondering what that meant. 'They'll be there,' he said, turning over in bed. He opened his eyes and looked at the alarm clock. 'Half past ten. Time to open up.' He liked such moments. He liked opening the tarpaulin and watching the clouds. He liked just lying there. It made him wonder about the pleasure of lying in. In Brynlas it wasn't allowed. The work principle, he always thought. Perhaps habit. Now he thought it may have had a much deeper base. In many respects, watching the clouds and imagining shapes and thinking of the weather or of something much more simple like the colour blue, the colour of the weather, was a little like returning to infancy. It was the pleasure principle reborn, resurrected because Francis had actually slipped away from rules and duties. This was instinct ruling. Ok it could only happen on the days when Davison didn't want him, but on those days the regularity of reality was swept away and he did what he wanted.

And what he wanted on this particular morning was to think over all Fritz had said. He thought of the way their words and thoughts had put together a picture of Brad that was similar to the mixed up features of a police identikit image. Brad was the wanted man. The profile was unbelievable. Yet that was Brad. It made him wonder what had drawn Fritz and himself to Brad, what he had found interesting on that first meeting in San Antonio.

He searched through the evidence of that meeting. The words. The looks. The laughter. The misinterpretations. Got it, he thought, realising it was spontaneity that had drawn him. The impulse of an offer of a home. The no going back. The way it had all worked. It seemed like a challenge to the rational. Reality should have stifled such an impulse. It should have seeded doubts, created tensions. But there had been none of that. Instead there was an openness and it was through such openness that Francis glimpsed the other qualities of Brad. He saw he was an enthusiast. That again made him wonder about the attraction. Enthusiasts had always worried Francis. He hadn't met many, but those he had met tended to agitate him. There was something about them – anti-conformity, loss of perspective – something Francis found difficult to deal with. They made him nervous. John Rees in secondary school did that. He was a butterfly collector. The way that took over his life disturbed Francis. At first he applauded it. He thought it was the pleasure principle in its most refined form but when he met it again in his father's friend Dave – a builders' merchant who specialised in gravels and spent his holidays touring quarries – he saw that pleasure in this form could develop frustration and frustration could develop aggression. Still, Brad had always concealed that from Francis. It was there, but it was reserved for Pam. It was the positive, pushy side that he had left open.

Francis wondered whether Fritz had seen that. He guessed he had. He guessed too that Brad's enthusiasm would have similarly worried Fritz. It certainly would have been alien to his own nature. Fritz was a cynic who couldn't accommodate all the bonhomie and solidarity that came with a cause. Fritz had no great cause. He had just wanted to get through life, to take it as it came and hope that it came easily. The focus Brad possessed would have disturbed Fritz. Yet Francis knew they were drawn to each other. Fritz's wit and humour, he thought, easily understanding what it was that Brad liked. The natural obstacles the other way made it difficult interpreting Fritz's liking of Brad, but then Francis thought of the scrapes and conversations and the way events threw them together. There had been a strong bonding. Francis knew that. He knew they were good together. He knew that they gave each other stability, that they provided structure. He also knew that, more than that, it was the loyalty of Brad that Fritz would have liked. Loyalty was the sort of quality that lurked in the southern states. Brad had it. Fritz had it. To a degree, Pam had it. It was a quality that blocked imagination and progression. It was a quality that kept a sense of order. Fritz liked it. He needed it. And Brad became an integral part of it.

The following day at work Davison drove over to the fence Francis was working on and called him over. 'Something for you,' he shouted, winding down the window. It was a letter marked Mobile, Tennessee. There was no sender's name and address.

Francis read the letter over and over. By the end of the evening he could have recited it. How Ronnie liked her uncle Paul, how Zelda liked Mobile. He wondered why she hadn't mentioned any disappointment at missing him. More crucially, he looked for the intimacies he would have expected. That was the strangest thing. There was no mention of giraffes or the goats, the things Ronnie had loved. Most surprising was the way that apart from telling him that she liked her uncle Paul there was no other mention of Ronnie.

He shook his head at that and moved to the desk. He decided to leave the thoughts of the letter. To do that he took out his sketch pads. He laughed at some of the ideas that emerged as he flicked through the pages. There was so much to show Ronnie. 'See me next Tuesday, call at ten,' Zelda had said in the letter. It meant they were coming back, that they were returning from Mobile. Francis couldn't get away from the prospect of that. He assumed Ronnie would be there and that they would swop drawings and stories. That calmed him. All the omissions he had thought of in the letter suddenly seemed insignificant. He put them down to Zelda's economy. She wasn't a writer. He could sense that. The letter's tone was clipped, perhaps forced, as though it had almost hurt Zelda to put pen to paper; its organisation was too loose. It was written as though her mind was elsewhere. There was something perfunctory about it. Francis laughed at that. He thought how the pace of her life must have made it difficult accommodating such a slow activity. The precision would aggravate her. He imagined her cursing her way through the lines. He sensed her relief when the letter was finished.

The thoughts returned him to the letter, though its familiarity now left nothing new to be discovered. Quickly he was sidetracked. He found himself thinking of Brynlas, of his father standing over him, regulating, overseeing. He remembered the sheep dip. The smell of chemicals. His father standing by a sheep, one hand under the sheep's chin. He was pulling it along, holding it by the fleece above the neck. Its front legs were bent; its back legs were loose. 'You,' his father would curse as though it helped him summon the energy to throw the sheep into the dip. Francis remembered the way only their heads would be above the milky water, the way they would point automatically towards the grill that kept them in. His father would be watching then. One arm would be outstretched towards the wall, propping him up. He would scratch his head, his eyes watching only the sheep as its nose would be edging at the metal grill, trying to raise it and escape. That would be a sign. 'Right,' Francis' father would say, requiring Francis to raise the grill. 'Silly bugger. Come on,' he'd add if the sheep stayed. He would prompt it by placing his wellington boot on its back, pressing it forward. 'You bloody blind? Go on!' Francis recalled the water flooding off the sheep's back when it ran out and its head twitching at the burn of chemicals and his father moaning, scratching the back of his head under his pork pie hat.

Francis stayed home the following day. He felt agitated. There were so many thoughts and considerations that he went for a walk around the wood, staring in down the walkways and tracks. He had never seen such views. They made the water tower prominent, standing out over the trees, the ones planted by Pam. He saw the place where Pam had picked mushrooms, the tree house which he had helped the boys build. The memories were clear, as was the significance of the location, but the glances gave no happiness and together the images were like a spent force. They left a kind of unease. They made domesticity seem unsafe.

The feeling made Francis hide himself away. He drew a giraffe and read a paper. The slackness was welcome. It took the tension away. It let him lose the predilection to inhabit characters. Instead he tried to think of himself, of what he had gained. He examined it like an anthropologist, adopting logic and reference, setting it back against what he knew and what was different. Part of it was defamiliarisation, it placed him back in Brynlas, put him into situations and tested them rather than him. They seemed somehow flat. They certainly couldn't correspond with the energetic enthusiasm that his new life gave him. They made him see the sense of leaving Brynlas and the way the decision had hardened him. That must have shocked his family. They must have seen him as compliant, as a name in the family Bible that would stay and flourish in a traditional way. Instead he had wondered what the beauty was of going down the same path. 'No, no, no. No!' he had said, coming to a decision. His announcement followed. He remembered the reaction too. 'Why should I talk to him? He's bloody daft. Always has been.' His father's words replayed in his mind. He remembered listening from upstairs, hearing his mother's tears and his father refusing to try to talk. 'Talk some sense into him dad'. His mother's voice seemed softer, more caring. His father's pride found it difficult to cope with that.

He thought too how those memories of Brynlas now seemed somehow unreal. They seemed like an excursion, a trip into another life. He liked them being like that. They provided relief; they let him store energy. He saw such a relationship as useful. It was a desirable combination, playing one off against the other and realising where the focus must lay. It had to lay in Texas, in the present. At that moment

140

it lay on Brad. Francis was recalling an evening in the storeroom when he had been looking for Brad. He was looking to thank him, to show how grateful he was for Brad's efforts to get him a job. He remembered the look on Brad's face. The intensity. The commitment frightened Francis. He listened to Brad talking about command structures and leadership.

'In the end it's down to the leader. The man in charge boy. The authority. Gee it must be fine having all that power.'

'You'd like that?' Francis asked, standing still near the door.

'Oh yeh,' said Brad emphatically. He was polishing soldiers, shining them up and replacing them in the battle scene. Francis thought how the shine contrasted with the mud of the real battle. He remembered the photograph Brad's great grandfather had taken of the young boy. 'Lee was good, Lincoln was great,' remarked Brad. 'He came through it.'

Francis just listened. He thought how it was like being with his dad, how he felt like a prop. He began to dislike that. He felt he had to talk, to impress his presence on Brad, but there was no opportunity to enter the conversation.

'I mean he had a lot to put up with boy. His wife was mad. See his son died. That turned her mind. I mean gee that's a blow. If one of my kids died, well –'

'What did he die of?'

'Some sort of fever. Wife turned to ouija boards and tarot cards. Jesus,' he laughed. 'I mean he was a regular guy, he couldn't cope. I mean there was so much there. No wonder Lincoln had all the great quotes. The bottom's out of the tub, what shall I do? That's one of his. Hey he had this general, called McClelland. A general who wouldn't attack. Get that. A general who wouldn't attack. So what does he do?' Brad paused. He shook his head and looked as though he had considered the point many times before. He waited for inspiration. But he had waited at this point before. And he knew nothing ever came. He shook his head, put down a polished soldier and picked up one that was unpolished. He stood motionless, cherishing the soldier, laughing occasionally at his thoughts. 'Hey this one's half dead,' he said , looking at the detail. 'Lost half his arm.' He put the soldier in a safe place, back from the assault that was under way. 'Hey where's the field hospital?' he said, laughing again.

'So what did he do?' asked Francis, irritated by the sneering laugh.

'Oh yeh. I was coming to that boy. Lincoln sends a message to the dummy –'

'McClelland?'

'Yeh. Who else boy?' Brad dismissed the intervention. 'He says if you don't want to use the army, can I borrow it for a while? Get it boy?' Brad laughed wildly. The humour he found in the quote far outweighed its impact. 'McClelland said Lincoln was the original gorilla.' He shook his head and laughed again. Francis laughed too. It brought a nod from Brad and a long smile.

'You mean guerilla, as in terrorist?' asked Francis.

Brad stopped sniggering, took some time to think and then started to laugh again. 'You know boy, I don't know. Ain't never thought about it. Guerilla? Yeh,' he said warmly. 'Hey I'm not sure. I mean he looked like a damn gorilla. You know the one that eats bananas. You seen a photo of him?' More thoughts followed the words.

'So why'd you like him?' asked Francis. 'I mean he's on the other side −'

'Oh that's simple. He's a winner.'

'But you wouldn't have known that at the time. Your great grandfather wouldn't have known it, would he?'

Again the words made Brad think. He picked up a soldier. He held it like a child. Then he put it down on the battlefield. Anywhere on the field would do. He stared at the trees and the houses, at the terrain. 'I guess...' he said, talking over his thoughts. Another pause followed.

'I mean you might have thought McClelland's caution was Lincoln's, don't you see?' Francis tried to help Brad to imagine what it may have been like. 'You might have thought he wasn't up to it.'

'Wendall Phillips, the abolitionist, called Lincoln a prostrate, second rate man.'

'What are you saying?' Francis was a little bemused.

'I'm saying you may be right boy. But in the end he won. Americans like winners. I like winners. It's like having the last word. Whatever they called him, whatever they thought of him, he had the last word. I respect him for that,' said Brad, putting his duster on the table and moving away.

Fritz turned up on Saturday. He found Francis in the vegetable patch, weeding and feeding the plants.

'There you are.' Fritz's voice boomed from behind Francis. It made Francis jump. He turned and glared at Fritz.

'Sorry, sorry. I'm always doing that. Betty's warned me. I make her drop things. At least you kept hold of that.' Fritz pointed at the fork Francis was holding and nodded. 'So how you doing? You Ok?'

Francis put down the fork and edged his way through the vegetables. 'I'm fine,' he said as he moved. 'Had a day off today. Couldn't face going in, but I'm better now.'

'You ill?'

'No.' He gestured to Fritz to sit on the old deck chair that was permanently placed by the vegetable patch. 'Go on,' he said encouragingly. 'You look as if you could use it.'

'Yeh I could. I'm bushed.' Fritz sat down. He settled himself. 'Know what I've been doing today?'

Francis shook his head.

'I've been killing rats.'

'But it's your day off,' laughed Francis.

'Hey, see. You know that. I know it. Does Betty fuckin' know it? No sir, she tells her friend, Meg, Oh don't worry Fritz'll sort it out. When you in? Fuckin' Saturday, that's when she's in —'

'And it's when you're off.'

'Exactly.' Fritz paused and looked at the vegetables for a second or two. There was silence. Francis thought how it was so unlike Fritz to pause. He looked his way and thought he saw a confused look on Fritz's face. Sensing the attention, Fritz pulled a face. 'What the hell was I saying?' he said.

'Just now?'

'When I arrived. Or was it something you said? Oh yeh, I remember now. Your day off. Why? No work?'

Francis told Fritz of the letter, of the way it had arrived, of his conjecture.

'Ah it's nothing,' said Fritz. 'Absolutely nothing. You'll go there. She'll say sorry and explain it all. You'll have a drink and Ronnie'll come in.'

'You think.' Francis felt positive. He would have settled for Fritz's version of events. He shook his head.

'Why the doubts?' asked Fritz. 'I mean there's nothing there to give you any cause to doubt what will happen.'

Francis thought how that was exactly the problem, how the brevity of the letter left so much unanswered. He wondered why they had gone, why there had been a mix up. He was sure Fritz was right, but, at the same time, something in the run of events smacked of a crisis and a reaction. It seemed to him Zelda had needed support. He wondered why.

Davison gave Francis a day off on Tuesday. Fritz, who had agreed to pick him up and take him in, was five minutes late. 'Fuckin' cow run down back there. Some woman said she didn't fuckin' see it. I said, can you see me? She said, yeh. I said well the cow's three times the fuckin' size of me.' Fritz laughed and laughed. Francis laughed too, but in a perfunctory sort of way.

'You ready for this?' asked Fritz, as he began to drive away.

'Oh yes. I've been waiting for this,' replied Francis. He sounded cool, collected even. 'All those false alarms. Poor kid –'

'Yeh. Give her the best from me. That's if she remembers me.'

Francis nodded. He settled back in the passenger's seat, smiling to himself, doubting whether anyone could ever forget Fritz. He shook his head and looked towards Fritz. A sad look ebbed away off Fritz's face. Out of the blankness came a smile.

'You know what she said?' said Fritz, about to explain the smile. 'That woman back there. Is it dead? she asked. Is it dead? Its fuckin' head was chopped off. I mean what do you say? I mean do I sound optimistic? You know, full of beans. Oh yeh maam, it's fine. Look it's lost its head, but it's still fuckin' mooing away. I mean what do I say?'

Bewildered, Francis shook his head.

'Here we go. You fuckin' English. Diplomacy, the great skill. That's the one thing you've got left.'

Francis laughed now. As long and as heartily as Fritz had before. Again he glanced towards Fritz.

'So what are you going to say to her?' asked Fritz.

'Who?'

'Zelda. You know, the woman you're gonna see. That is where we're going, yeh?'

'I think I'll leave it to her. She should say things to me. To be honest I don't really care. I just want to see Ronnie.'

Zelda was in the kitchen making coffee when Francis arrived. She left him in the main room staring at the sculpture. He listened to the strange mix of the machine's coffee-making sounds and the soft sweep of a symphony on the CD player. He was surprised by the choice of music. Punk rock or folky protest songs would have been more in character, he thought, but these sounds were soft and soothing. They helped him feel less awkward. They turned the agitation into a restlessness. He began to wonder where Ronnie was. The symphony and the coffee making somehow told him she wasn't at home.

'You seen my shoes?' asked Zelda, bending down to look under a chair. 'Brown. You know those fashionable things. Boots. God I don't feel dressed without my shoes –'

'Don't look for me,' said Francis uncomfortably. He tried to keep his hands on his lap, to appear relaxed.

'It's not for you,' laughed Zelda, standing up again. 'It's for me. God I'm only five feet two.' Again she bent down. This time to feel her way around the base of the chair. She smiled as her fingers touched the heel of a shoe. Francis watched the delight on her face as she slipped it onto her foot. 'You must have heard about our complexes,' she laughed. 'All American women have got them. Food, sex, shoes. You name it. Mostly it's about how we look.' She sat down in the chair opposite Francis. He watched her cross her legs and sit back. 'Boobs, bum, you name it. There's a complex there, just waiting to emerge. Well I've got a nice bum. You noticed?' Zelda gave a look that was an apology. She hadn't meant to embarrass Francis. She waved her hand to try to take back her words. 'Sorry,' she said, moving on. 'It's my height that gets me. I mean ol' Brad was so tall. He followed my dad. I followed my mum. I need to be tall,' she remarked, slipping on a second shoe. 'There. How about you?'

'Me?' Francis was taken by surprise. He had assumed being male would exclude him from the conversation.

'Yeh. How tall are you?'

'Oh.' Francis felt too relieved to think deeply about the question. 'I'm not sure,' he said. Again he shook his hands nervously. 'About five eleven.'

'So you're alright.' Zelda started to look away, then stopped. 'You know why?'

'Why what?'

'My complex. Why I've got it?'

Francis shook his head.

'My father. I wanted to be a ballet dancer when I was seven or eight. I even went to lessons. Then I stopped, or rather my father stopped me. He said I was going to be too tall. I was big for my age. Well I guess he thought I was going to be like Brad and Paul and himself. He was six two. So he sent me to piano the following week. It's been with me ever since.'

'With you?'

'The complex. Hate tall people. Particularly tall women. Anything over five eleven and a half makes me scowl. You're alright,' she smiled. 'Just!'

When she brought in the coffee, smiles were exchanged in such a way that Francis knew they were both hiding behind screens, covering over something.

'Cream?' said Zelda.

145

'No,' said Francis.

'Sugar?'

'No.'

'Cookie?'

'No.' Francis sipped on his coffee, fretting over how he should approach the subject he had convinced himself they were both thinking of. He felt the frustration mounting by the sip, but silence somehow drifted in out of control. He smiled at her. She smiled back.

'Nice coffee.'

'Yeh,' she said, sitting back. She uncrossed her legs and placed the coffee cup and saucer in her lap. Suddenly she laughed.

'What's wrong?' asked Francis.

'This is so English –'

'You playing games?' asked Francis sounding serious.

'Ok. I'm just seeing how long it takes. You English! Why hide away? Say it –'

'What?' said an exasperated Francis.

'Where's Ronnie? Where the fuck is Ronnie?'

Francis was shocked by the expletive. Momentarily he wondered why. He had heard it much more often in America, but not from Zelda. He associated some sort of sophistication with her. He listened to the symphony. He recognised it now. Tchaikovsky. *Winter Dreams.* It reminded him of his mother. She played the piano and liked the Russians. Shostakovitch particularly. He thought of her playing her music while his father was out. He thought of her leaving the piano when his father came in.

'Ok I guess the game's up. Ronnie's not here.' Zelda said the words directly at Francis. She watched a cool look come over his face. His eyes narrowed as he took in her words. She wondered what controlled such emotion.

'So where is she?' asked Francis.

'Now you won't be too disappointed. You will see her,' assured Zelda. 'Ok. She's in Mobile. I left her there. She likes her Uncle Paul and he has a vacation coming up, so, anyway, we thought it made sense to let her stay on. He's taking her to Epcot. She'll be home in a couple of weeks.'

'I see.' Francis could hardly hide his disappointment. He looked down at his coffee, then, regaining control, glanced a smile Zelda's way. 'Good. She'll enjoy that. She deserves it.'

His reaction made Zelda stare more intently at him. She was surprised. Francis' magnanimity shocked her. She tried to assess it, to see behind its cover.

'So I'll have to wait until she gets back –'

'You'll see her then.'

'I was going to take her to the pictures.'

'I know.'

'The drive-in. I've got more drawings too.'

'Great,' said Zelda, genuinely impressed by Francis' show of interest. She smiled warmly and kept her gaze on him, expecting to see through the cover. He sensed the scrutiny and maintained the smile, though he began to feel the disappointment more profoundly. The implications were more clear now. A couple of weeks. He would have to go two to three weeks before he took Ronnie to the pictures. After all that had happened that seemed like a lifetime. Francis thought of the fire and the funeral. He thought too of the mad vigour that had pushed him to draw and draw and speculate about his meeting with Ronnie and how now he would have to wait and wait. Dropping his guard, a look of contempt came over his face. Surely Zelda could sense his pain.

'Listen, you'll see her. I promise you that. Yeh?' She waited for a response, but Francis' face didn't move. He kept staring her way, taking in her words. 'She says she's missing you,' Zelda said quickly trying to retrieve Francis' smile. 'She keeps the photo of the goats with her. Night and day. It never leaves her side. She likes them so much that Paul bought her a toy milking parlour. She makes the noises. You know, switching on the milking machine.'

The words cheered Francis' face. He smiled deeply.

'Paul's got a friend with a farm,' explained Zelda. 'Dairy cows. He took Ronnie to the dairy. She remembered all the sounds. You'll have all this,' said Zelda, playing with a shoe that was swinging on her toes.

'Good,' said Francis, wondering what to say.

'Hey, I haven't told you my news –'

'Your news?

'Yeh, I'm changing jobs. Promotion.'

'Really?'

'Yeh. Isn't it great? More money. More shoes,' laughed Zelda, pouring Francis a second cup of coffee.

Later, Francis sat beneath the water tower. He lit a fire and stared at the streaks of rising yellow and orange. He felt the breeze on his back fan the flames. All the time he thought of the calm of Brynlas, how his brushes with his father's authority were swept away easily because he never really confronted them. He remembered the uneasiness and the anxiety that he kept within. It affected his outlook. It threatened an aggression that, had he not travelled, would certainly have inched its way to the surface. He thought how occasionally he had had to bite his tongue, how his mind had to stay alert to remind him of his father's bigotry. Not once did he argue in a serious way. Instead he accepted and, in the process, the malaise and the disenchantment accumulated.

By contrast his Texan life was riven by crises. He decided there were crises everywhere, at all scales. Ronnie staying on at Mobile was a crisis of the minor scale. He thought of it again. Once more it was Zelda's delivery that surprised him. Why wait? All the coffee making. All the banter. To Francis it smacked of a preoccupation with control. But, in this case, it seemed ill judged, misguided even. She must have known the significance, thought Francis. But then, perhaps, she fully understood the significance and was afraid of it.

He settled for that. The explanation worked. It fitted the facts. It contained nothing preposterous. The only thing that surprised Francis was the way it seemed so calculated. When he considered Zelda's character it seemed so unlikely. It made him shake his head and throw a twig into the fire and think how something was missing, how the mystery of their trip to Mobile and Ronnie staying on had seemed too easy to explain. There was something more. He convinced himself of that. He tried to work out what it was. The effort of that concentrated sounds. He heard a crackle of vegetation. Words followed. 'You there? Hey blockhead, you in? Ah.' The voice was Fritz's. It came from behind Francis who shook himself. 'You asleep? Very cosy. Room for me?' asked Fritz, looking down. He put an arm to the ground and eased himself down. 'You sit out often?' Francis nodded a reply. 'No kidding? Brad used to do this sort of thing. With the boys. Fuckin' treehuggers. So you just sit here?'

'Why not?'

'No reason. Just seems a little wild.'

'I like it –'

Yeh, I can see the attraction. I mean it's a bit like a camp fire. Playing cowboys eh? The ol' coyotes should be calling now. There should be indians out there. You should be having a bowl of beans.'

Francis laughed. He sat himself up and smiled at Fritz.

'So you saw her, yeh? And how'd it go?'

'That's why you called?'

'Yeh.'

Francis shook his head. He wondered if Zelda had any inclination of the depth of concern the family's old friends carried.

'What's wrong?' asked Fritz, shuffling to find a more comfortable position.

'You should be at home. You've a wife and kids –'

'And don't I fuckin' know it.'

Again Francis laughed. This time it wasn't the content of the words, but the despair that pervaded the delivery. He thought how colourful Fritz's expressions could be, how they brought with them images that were persuasive. This time they made Francis feel that it was time to call it a day, to accept the worst.

'You laugh a hell of a lot. Anyone told you?'

'You should be at home,' said Francis, almost bluntly

'Hey don't lecture me. I've come out for some fresh air. Always do that this time of day –'

'You do?'

'Yeh. I walk the fuckin' dog. Take it round the block. It meets its friends. So tonight I thought I'd treat myself, thought I'd meet my friends.'

'So where's the dog?'

'In the van. Guarding it. Eating its way through a packet of dog biscuits.' As Fritz talked he examined the atmosphere. Gradually he sensed a looseness. Everything suddenly seemed relaxed. The impatience had gone. Francis was smiling again. 'So come on. I've got five minutes. What happened eh?'

Francis told Fritz the full story: the coffee making and the diversions and then the news of Ronnie. It shocked Fritz as much as Francis. That surprised Francis: he had expected Fritz to find the logic immediately and explain it all away. Instead a silence extended itself. It was eventually broken by Fritz saying, 'I see.' For a minute or two, they both stared into the fire, lobbing twigs into its heart. They waited for the flames to grow.

'I think it's strange,' Fritz said finally. 'I mean is she disorganised or what? Telling you to call on such and such a day and then being a thousand miles away. Then writing to you and saying meet me here. And when you go – I mean dragging you all that way – you find Ronnie's in fuckin' Mobile, Tennessee. I mean what's going on here?'

Francis shrugged. For all his analysis, he could contribute little. He thought it best to let Fritz develop the issues. 'So what should I do?' he asked, prompting Fritz.

'You accept it. You have to. You have to fuckin' trust her.'

'I guess you're right. I suppose there's no alternative.'

'Oh there's always an alternative.' Fritz's smile somehow pleased Francis. He associated it with scheming. He knew that behind the conversation Fritz had been working things out, seeing a way forward. Now some defining moment had arrived. It had told Fritz what to do.

'I'll go and see her,' he said.

'You?'

'Yeh. Why not?' She knows me. I know her. I'm a friend of Ronnie's. Like you. You went to see her. So why not me? I'll just call in. See what's what.'

Francis stayed by the fire. He watched the shape of Fritz blend with the night. He waved knowing that Fritz would still see him in the light of the flames. 'Bye,' he shouted, then he thought of the last time he had sat by a fire, how it was with Brad and the boys, how they had been laughing at the way Fritz had missed the tree house.

'Why once he stood under the tree,' said Brad, who had trailed Fritz around the wood. 'He stood still and scratched his head and one of you guys whistled like a bird.'

'That was me,' said Denny, practising his bird whistle. Francis sat back and listened and nodded an acknowledgement.

Brad shook his head as he considered Fritz's plight. 'Then he thought he saw you up a tree. He started talking to the branches.'

'We were good pa.'

'You were,' said Brad, answering Denny. Paul stayed silent, smiling.

'We deserve something, don't we?'

'Hey you guys, remember what I said? There's no medals in the confederacy. We're all heroes.'

'Yeh,' said Denny enthusiastically. The boy looked serious. 'We'll be mentioned in dispatches.'

'You sure will. Yeh. You run in and tell your ma what happened. Go on.' Brad laughed and shook his head again as he watched them go. 'Those guys. You know all the wealth in the world and the only thing that makes me happy is those kids. Aren't they great?'

'They know all about the war,' remarked Francis.

'Oh yeh. You ask them about Lincoln. They know his dates, where he lived, what his wife was called. You name it, they know it. Hey they even know some of his quotes. "In giving freedom to the slaves, we assure freedom for the free." Paul knows that one. Paul knows several of them. Even Denny knows one.' Brad shook his head as some thought came with the realisation. 'He had to learn one just so he could be like his brother. "So corrupt the only thing he would not steal is a red hot stove." That's Denny's.' Brad kept shaking his head. Another thought came and went. 'He doesn't know what it means and he gets it wrong most of the time, but who cares? At least he has a go.'

'They're fine lads,' remarked Francis.

'Fine? They're great. I'm a proud father, you know that? Hey I bet your father was proud of you, yeh?'

Francis was struck by the question. The way it redirected the conversation surprised him. He withheld thoughts and tried to think positively, but he knew his responses wouldn't fool Brad. He knew he couldn't be believable. He opted for the truth. 'No,' he said slowly.

'Mine neither,' said Brad, releasing the pressure on Francis. It was the first time Francis had heard Brad mention his father in a negative way. He wanted to ask why, to develop the issue and swop thoughts on what went wrong in childhood, to discuss the problems their fathers had. Francis was sure the problem lay with Brad's father. He couldn't see it any other way. The focus had to be on the father, not the son, the son always had to be innocent. Like him.

'But I was proud of him,' said Brad thoughtfully. 'God was I proud of him.'

The following day Francis felt much more alone. He believed the feeling came with the loss of control. By allowing Fritz to take an initiative, albeit an initiative that he had welcomed, he felt ashamed. Like a wounded soldier, he thought, or an injured sportsman. It was the fact he allowed Fritz to go away with no sense of strategy that worried him. He felt he should have intervened and thought of goals, of what was to be achieved.

Such questions disturbed his concentration. He thought how they hadn't really worked out what was achievable. Perhaps it was simply a case of Fritz assessing whether Zelda was being straight. Fritz would sense that better than Francis; and Francis knew that. He knew that the one thing he had learnt in Texas was that he was unable to read situations. He was too trusting. He believed. The events over the last few weeks, particularly the recent revelations, taught him to trust no-one and to doubt his inclinations.

Over lunch he played with such thoughts, wondering when Fritz would call on Zelda, what he would say and whether Fritz would report back. Francis hoped he would. He hoped Fritz would call today. It would eradicate uncertainty, he thought. Then he thought how he'd react if Zelda was hiding something. That told him a lot. It made him see how determined he had become, how his confidence had grown, how he wouldn't back away.

A flutter of panic overcame him when he realised someone was speaking. He was staring at an orange, smiling when he became aware of the words.

'You gonna eat that?'

Francis looked up to see Davison standing over him.

'It looks good. Just what you need on a day like today.'

'Oh hello I was just....'

'Thinking,' laughed Davison. 'Nice thoughts I hope. You've had a rough time.'

Francis smiled. He thought of the way the men on the ranch were in awe of Davison. Tales of ruthlessness abounded. They thought him dangerous, untrustworthy. Francis had always fought such views. He stood up for Davison. He told them of his kindness, of his concern. Again he was impressed by Davison's interest. He watched the man take off his hat and scratch his head before sweeping back his grey hair. He returned Francis' smile.

'Anything you need?' he asked. 'You thought about the cottage? I mean I understand you liking the tower and all the stuff about memories and things, but you'd be more comfortable. You think about it. It's there if you want it.' He smiled again as he began to move away. Francis saw the slight stiffness in his movements and remembered the story of a riding accident and a twisted knee. He watched the movement, the stiffness being exaggerated by the clicking of his leather boots as he walked away. Then the clicking stopped. Davison looked around. His left hand wiped his mouth. Words followed. 'How's the girl?' he asked, quite unselfconsciously.

'Ronnie?'

'Is that the daughter?'

'Yes. She's alright. Thank God. A little shaken. I'm hoping to see her soon.'

'Good,' said Davison, walking away.

In the evening Francis tried to write home. He wrote once a fortnight. Most letters were brief. He kept back the main details of his life. All his parents learnt was that he was well and working and settling for a time in Texas somewhere near San Antonio. Sometimes he described the ranch and his work. He knew that would interest his father. It would make him read the letter. The human side though – relationships, friends, the American way of life – was disregarded. He knew his parents couldn't consider that, that they couldn't associate it with Francis.

He found it surprisingly easy to write. The words always seemed to flow. The immediacy surprised him, particularly as the focus of his mother and father made him think more of Brynlas than the water tower. The images that came and went sidetracked him. Tonight it was markets. He thought how the topics were linked to the time of the year, how they reminded him of what was happening in Wales. With the thoughts he sensed the weather and the words that would go with occasions. With the market, he thought of the pens on the hills, of his father at the end of the passageways selecting sheep. One glance told him which sheep to keep. His father's intense face, stubborn-eyed and stern-mouthed, filled his mind. He knew his voice. 'Go on! Go on! Go on! Work down there!' And he saw the handclapping and waving that went with the words that directed the selected sheep down to the valley floor and the waiting lorry. He saw the sheep too. The faces, black nosed, black eyed, horns developing. Then he would put them together – the men, dogs and sheep – making his father the general, developing and reconsidering strategies as the sheep failed and the sheep misbehaved. He saw lambs running to the right, all at once and in the same direction. The dogs were sitting down and staring, responding to the sounds. 'Shut that bloody gate!' his father was shouting. Mostly he remembered the conversations: his father saying the sheep were 'all to hell. Never seen them so bad. But they can't look their best see. Not when it's like this. Bloody wet. Bloody cold. Bloody windy. Look at that one down there. Poor sod. I mean none of us look our best when it's like this.'

The moan was typical. It was his natural state. It went with the sighs and shakes that controlled his head. Smiles were sly, controlled and surreptitious, somehow timed to coincide with a glance away. There was something rather roguish about the whole demeanour, about the way he would settle his hat straight and put pressure on a conversation. He did that more and more. Somehow the stoop he had gained with age had helped. It bent him forward, gave him an air of unsympathetic indifference. It put people off. And he knew it.

Francis heard the moans in different situations, mostly difficult ones like when the government inspector came to evaluate the quota allowance. The official would click the counting machine he held in the palm of his hand as the sheep passed. Francis' father would stand alongside him, moaning. On such occasions he would be at his most talkative. Francis knew he stored topics and used them to distract the official. It was a ploy to cover the inaccuracy of the claim. Too few sheep and Francis' father would be making up losses and remembering unrecorded sales. 'Christ I forgot that mart,' he'd say. 'Yes. God yes, I was over there the other day, wasn't I Geth? Remember? The bloody rain. It was the day the lorry's tyre went and we were nearly late. Christ we thought they'd jack it up before we got there. But it went ahead. Remember? Oh aye. Good sale.'

'She's fine, I'm fine. How are you?' Zelda couldn't hide the the tone of surprise that greeted Francis' call. Somehow he had found it necessary to call. The domesticity of his thoughts had provoked it. They had left him thinking of Ronnie and Brad and the way their existence had been so fragile. The fragility also told him that things can change quickly. Ronnie could come home before time. An illness, a call from a friend, Zelda wanting to take her somewhere. She might even decide that it would be nice to see Francis. He smiled at that. It urged him on. It led him to the road and the phone box. It led him to dial Zelda's number.

'So what you doin'?' asked Zelda.

'Me? I'm taking a walk. I do that sometimes. It's a lovely night. Very clear.'

'I see.'

Francis knew that Zelda didn't see, that she could not comprehend such activity. 'And what are you doing?'

'Me? Oh I'm planning spaces.'

'Planning spaces?'

'Yeh I'm always doing that.' She laughed more to herself than Francis. Some thought struck her. 'I see something and then I've got to change things. It sort of spurs me on. I do crazy things. I saw *Basic Instinct* the other day. You seen it?'

'No,' admitted Francis.

'Don't bother,' Zelda almost scowled her dislike of the film. 'But Sharon Stone's house by the sea is really something. Oh my God I saw it and I thought yeh that's what I want.' She paused. Francis pictured her shaking her head at what she was saying. 'Still I saw *Citizen Kane* last night at the art house. What a staircase! What a fireplace! Huge. Oh my God I've got to have them I came away saying. So I'm sort of getting myself together now, considering what I can do. And tomorrow I'm taking a morning off.'

'That's nice,' commented Francis.

'Oh it's not really. I'm going to school.'

'School?'

'Ronnie's school. It's one of those things that needs doing.' She laughed. Organising a life, settling it into a new system was more

154

demanding than she realised. 'God I never understood school. Did you?'

'No,' said Francis thinking how there was little to understand, how you turned up each day and were taught, how nobody really questioned what was offered and received.

'I mean what's it preparing you for? School,' she said derisively. 'I mean we all know what's out there. Morality or no morality. It's as simple as that. Even kids know that. I mean they see their father skulking around, their mothers cutting corners. They see Church on Sunday and all the real shit from week to week. Hey we used to have a pupil of the week. Did you have that?' She waited a moment for a response. Nothing came. 'You'd have your photo up in the hall or the entrance. Pupil of the week, Zelda. You'd do anything for that. Lie, cheat, steal, copy work, tell tales. I got it once, yeh I did,' she said responding to a little giggle from Francis. 'April's pupil of the month. Yeh, the month! Zelda Stubbs. God it was good. I went into the hall every day and there I was, hanging up. My best photo too. Pretty darned pretty. My mother took it the month before, at Easter.' She paused again to picture herself in the photo. 'God my hair. So damn shiny.' She pictured it. The glint. The reflection. More like teeth in sunshine. Not hair. 'Coconut oil,' she said.

'What?'

'Coconut oil. That's what my mother would put on it. Tubs of it. When I was young she'd wave it with pins and things. And it worked. I had the waviest hair in the class. God I had real nice hair, real nice.' Again she was contemplative, then she laughed loudly. 'God and they'd say what your interests were in the school magazine. Ambition. That was one section. Ambition. You know what I said?'

Francis didn't like to interfere. 'No,' he simply said.

'I want to have a yard –'

'A yard?'

'You know. The thing you were admiring at the funeral.'

'Oh the garden.'

'Yeh a yard. That was my ambition. A yard with some dirt.'

'Dirt?'

'Yeh dirt.'

Francis was drawing when Fritz called. He had settled by his Fred calendar. He was thinking of March. Daffodils, leeks, St. David's Day, wind, rain. All his thoughts were of Wales. They dressed Fred in a bobble hat and scarf, both coloured red. Francis was surrounding Fred with daffodils when Fritz reappeared. 'Anyone home?' he said, pulling back the tarpaulin. 'Oh you working? Listen I won't disturb you. I know how seriously you take your drawing.'

'Go on,' said Francis as Fritz climbed down the steps into the tower. 'Have a beer.'

'You sure? I mean this can wait. You got time?'

'I can do this anytime,' laughed Francis.

'Oh come on, you don't mean that. I mean I always thought there was more to it than that. Gee that's disappointing. I mean what's with inspiration? Isn't it something that sort of zaps you? Hey you look as if you've been zapped.' Fritz was smiling at the sight of Francis at the desk with the sheets spread out. He looked at the figure materialising on the paper. 'So what's he doin'?'

'Don't know.'

'So he's sort of waiting for April,' laughed Fritz, looking again at the inactive Fred who was standing on top of the large letters that spelt March. 'Know the feeling,' added Fritz. 'Well March is a fuckin' mopey old month. Know what I mean? Sort of cold some years, warm others. It's sort of mixed up.'

Francis nodded. He recalled how March this year had been cold. He remembered Brad standing where Fritz stood now saying how the boys had started to build a tree house and how cold it was to be out putting strips of wood together.

'Good beer.' Fritz was already drinking. He watched Francis put down the pencil and look his way. 'Hey don't give me the long looks. You don't know if I've been yet –'

'Have you?'

'Yeh. I have, but don't get excited. There's not much to tell.'

'Oh.' Francis' disappointment was immediate and transparent. Its suddenness seemed to surprise Fritz. He watched the expectancy drain out of the face. He took in the coldness that remained.

'But that's good, isn't it? I mean it means everything's Ok, that you've got nothing to fear.'

'Fear?' Francis was surprised at Fritz's choice of words.

'You know what I fuckin' mean.' Fritz shook his head. Francis' use of English annoyed him. It placed more emphasis on structure than content. He had never met anyone so concerned with structure, but, then, Francis was the only European he had ever met. Fritz shook his head. 'Your fuckin' precision. It's all pretty pretty. It's the meaning that counts. The impact –'

'Ok, Ok.' Francis was willing to concede everything to hear what Zelda had said. 'Come on, what did she say? I want to know everything.'

Fritz could tell from the look on Francis' face that he meant those words. He waited for a smile to come, for a looseness to arrive. Nothing came.

'Well what do you want to know? What she was fuckin' wearing?' He tried to lighten the situation, but seemed a little lost when Francis didn't reply.

'Ok. I'll tell you what she was cooking and what she was writing when I arrived and what her new job's all about and about Ronnie phoning –'

'Ronnie phoning?' Francis was suddenly more alert. 'When?'

'When we were talking.'

'In the afternoon?'

'Yeh. It was afternoon. She was out, at Epcot or somewhere. She was excited, wanted to tell Zelda, so she did.'

'And what did she say?'

'Hey how do I know? I was fuckin' sitting ten yards away. All I could hear were responses. How's Paul? What's the weather like? Good food there?'

'But she seemed Ok?'

'Yeh, she seemed Ok. Now can I get a word in....' Fritz told Francis how he had arrived early and had caught Zelda writing an article, how it was on modern relationships, how she was really writing about Brad and Pam and her relationship with Ronnie. He told him too how she had seemed so sad. 'She's missing her,' said Fritz. 'I can tell.'

'Go on,' urged Francis when Fritz paused to think.

'Well,' he said, starting again. He began to tell Francis how Zelda had said the same thing to him, how it was all coincidence. She had mixed up dates. She had gone to Mobile. He was sure of that. 'She's telling the truth,' he said.

'You sure?'

'Oh yeh, fuckin' sure. She was straight with me. I believe her. She's a classy lady. Why should she hide anything away?'

April. Francis thought of the Boat Race and the Grand National. He drew daffodils and Fred before tearing out the page and starting again. He kept the brilliant carpet of yellow, but tried to get Fred to match its exuberance. He made him lamb-like, kicking his legs up well above the level of daffodil heads. He tensed some of Fred's muscles, slackened others. He made it seem that Fred was enjoying himself. There was something in his eyes. A smile on his face. The caption read:

'Fred was partial to a gambol on the day of the Grand National'.

Francis laughed at that. He liked it. 'One of the best,' he said, beginning to doodle, surrounding Fred with sketches of torsos. Female torsos. Thin hips and large breasts, women bending and crawling. Strong women staring. They were encapsulating all Francis' thoughts about Pam and Zelda. He was wondering about power and place and how women fitted in. Zelda would certainly have scoffed at any irrational consideration of gender. She seemed strong, independent in terms of her work and the way she organised her relationships. It was she rather than her brother Paul who had come to the fore after Brad's death. Yet she was younger than Paul and quite deferential to him on the day of Brad's funeral – Francis remembered how she had waited for him to lead the way coming out of Church and the way she had prompted him to say words at the house. But such incidents were isolated. Most of the time she was stronger; more alert, he thought, better organised.

More baffling was Pam. He saw her now as a protester, but he wondered what she was protesting about. He was annoyed by that because he knew of the need to take on the hierarchies. And gender was one of the hierarchies. He doubted whether Pam by staying with Brad could have effectively challenged. She had needed to pull away, to take Paul and Denny and Ronnie and make the point that they could survive without Brad. Francis thought, by staying, she showed a lack of self belief. He overlooked love and concern. Brad's violence obliterated that. He couldn't believe love could endure such attacks. He was probably right, but he still overlooked the day to day reality of everyday life, the way the web of interrelationships between mother and father and children would have been broken.

He shook his head at that. It made him look around. He thought how he enjoyed such lunch times when he sat with his sketchbook and a sandwich on the banks of the ditch he was clearing. There was little cover in the bare fields, so he wore a large hat and turned his back to the sun. Thoughts of rain would bring thoughts of Brynlas. He was thinking of market day when Fritz called from the nearby track. Four thousand lambs were bleating, hating the rain, looking bedraggled in pens. He was remembering how they were graded by size, how some were tossed over railings into the correct pen. He practised the throwing position – the arms under the front legs, the legs in the air.

'Francis!' Fritz was calling. Francis was recalling the auction ring. His father telling him to move them round, using a stick. He would wave it to the rhythm of the auctioneer calling out prices. 'Thank you. And on we go. Next in please,' the auctioneer would say, finishing.

'Francis!'

Francis suddenly heard the call. He acknowledged Fritz, waving almost violently. He left his lunch and walked over to Fritz who was standing by his van.

'Hey this is handy,' said Fritz, referring to the way the work was being carried out in the field alongside the wood and the water tower.

'Ten more minutes in bed every morning,' said Francis.

'And home for lunch,' laughed Fritz. 'Fuckin' hot, ain't it?'

Francis nodded and pulled the brim of his hat further down his forehead. He wiped his chin. 'You got a drink?' he asked, thinking of the heat.

Fritz shook his head. 'Had a milk shake back in town. Black cow flavoured whatever that is. Hey a milk flavoured milk shake, ain't that a fuckin' rip off.' He laughed again. He seemed somehow happier in the heat.

'So why you here?' asked Francis, sitting down.

'I was gonna ask you that. What you doing?'

'Cleaning the ditch,' replied Francis, not realising that from the road the ditch wasn't visible. He watched Fritz stand on tiptoe. 'It's in a little dip. The land falls away,' explained Francis. 'But all the heat reduces the stream to a trickle, so I clean it out, prepare it for the rain. Now what about you?'

'Lunch,' said Fritz. 'Thought I'd see how you are, whether you'd heard anything. I can't stay long. I've got a job in a school.' He laughed loudly. Francis smiled. He liked the way all of Fritz's features responded to the laughter, the way they never agitated into a looseness that suggested a loss of control. The jolly smile suited the round face, he thought.

'Hey listen, that school. I went out yesterday and the smell was high. Soda and dead rat, I thought. So the kids are sent home and I'm putting down poison. And the fuckin' janitor says there's nothing there. So I tell him his sense of smell has gone and he gets a teacher, says I've insulted him. And the teacher takes me to one side and says the janitor's taken it personally. And I said judging by the smell so has the fuckin' rat.'

Francis imagined the exchanges. A meeting of enthusiasts, he thought, a battle of pride. Who is this upstart? he imagined Fritz and the janitor thinking simultaneously.

'So I've got to go back and see this arsehole and tell him the smell will get worse.' Fritz paused. A shake of the head told Francis how much the janitor had annoyed Fritz. 'You know he took me in a room and asked me time after time if I was sure it was a rat. Then he made me a coffee and left me to think it over. Think it over! What was there to fuckin' think of? A rat is a rat. He left me there so long I had to use his john. And you know what I thought while I was sitting there? I thought if I find this fuckin' rat I'll nip back in and put it in the john. Then he could find it when he goes to sit on the john and, when he tells me about it, I could be all concerned and serious and I could ask to examine it and come back saying it had died of shock. Died of shock, get it?' Fritz shook his head and looked menacing. He listened to Francis' laughter and warmed. 'So how are you?' he said, continuing.

'I'm fine. I'm working hard.'

'I can see that,' laughed Fritz. 'So no word then?'

Francis shook his head. A week had passed since he had seen Fritz. He had half expected Davison to call him over to give him a letter. But nothing had happened and on the days he normally checked his mail, the expectancy had quickly turned into disappointment. 'I almost rang her,' he admitted.

'Who? Zelda?' said Fritz in a concerned sort of way.

'Yes. I thought I'd check, pre-empt the mail, I suppose. I mean I thought there was a chance she'd turned up that day and Zelda hadn't found the time to put pen to paper. I mean it's a possibility.'

'S'pose it is.' Fritz tried to sound supportive. Francis knew him well enough now to work out when Fritz lacked wholehearted commitment. This was one of those occasions.

'So you think I shouldn't.'

'What phone? No. Only because it's unnecessary. She said she'd contact you when Ronnie returned. Trust her. Besides she'll probably phone Davison –'

'You don't think she'll write?'

'You fuckin' English may write. We Americans phone.' The intensity on Fritz's face suggested a certainty. Again Francis' knowledge of Fritz told him there was no room to argue. There was no point, either.

'Ok. I won't.'

'Well you knew it would be a week. She told you that. She fuckin' said so –'

'A fortnight –'

'Well there.'

'I know.' Francis fell silent. He wondered why the conversation was taking place at all. After all they had both known the situation, that Ronnie would be away with Paul for up to a fortnight. Zelda had made that clear. So why was Fritz around asking if there had been any developments? That concerned Francis for a moment, but then he realised he had accepted the obvious, that Fritz was being neighbourly, just showing concern.

'Look I've got to go –'

'See the janitor?'

'Yeh. See ol' rat face.' Fritz laughed again. 'Hey I'm sorry I've not been over but Betty's been ill –'

'Ill?'

'Yeh, some bug got her. Probably something I tried to kill getting its own back.' He sniggered and shook his head. 'So I've had the kids and work.' Fritz paused and watched Francis nodding his understanding. 'But how about a drink tonight? I'll pick you up.'

'Eight?'

'Yeh. That's great.'

All the way to the bar they spoke about Brad, about his love for the boys and Ronnie, about his abuse of Pam, about his hero, Lincoln, and his love of the Civil War and mostly about his regard for his great grandfather.

'Did he show you the photo of his grave?' asked Fritz as he drove.

'No.'

'He went there and found it.'

'He found the grave?'

'Yeh. He showed me a photo. His great grandfather's name on a big badge carved out of stone. Had a semi-circle above the name which was normally for the rank and army number. His great grandfather just had "photographer". Quite a lot of letters that.'

'He told me about the battle,' remarked Francis.

'Shiloh? Oh yeh. Well he had that reconstructed. He'd play it through. Turned his great grandfather into a toy soldier. Always thought that strange. I mean the fuckin' thing was a disorganised fist fight –'

'And he'd been there?'

'Yeh. It's up on the Mississippi-Alabama border somewhere. He was planning to take the kids there.'

'All of them?'

'God who'd want to go on vacation with Brad? Where you going this year Fritz?' He imitated an inquiring voice. 'Actually we're going to Shiloh. It's got a log chapel and meandering lanes. And two thousand four hundred and seventy seven graves.'

'Sounds fun.'

'Oh yeh. So does going back to Vietnam.'

161

While drinking they played games, Scenarios, Francis called it. A simple game. It involved Zelda and Ronnie and the way Francis was to make progress. Fritz still favoured the simple outlook that Ronnie would return and Francis would be able to resume the sort of relationship they had when Pam and Brad had been alive, that little would change.

'And they all lived happily ever after,' smirked Francis, some sense of the unlikely gripping him. It seemed so distant; and the relationships and the deaths and events of late seemed so prominent. More crucially the explosion linked them more successfully than any of the previous warmth they had enjoyed. Francis remembered the smoke, the smell, the sound of burning, the bewilderment on the little girl's face. He heard her answer his question. 'Who's home, Ronnie? Who's at home?' Her odd expression. Her terror. He wondered if she realised what was happening or whether his urgency shocked her.

'So what's your version of it?' asked Fritz, returning with two cans of beer. 'What would you want?'

'I'd want what you suggested.'

'There, see?'

'But that's not my version of it.'

'So?' Fritz waited. He sipped on the beer and settled back, reflectively trying to tune into the subtleties that he suspected Francis used to convey meaning.

'Well...'

'What? You think she'll have forgotten you? That's fuckin' stupid. You told me Zelda said her room was a shrine to you –'

'To the goats.'

'Ok the goats. Same thing.'

'Anyway I don't think that. I think she may want to forget me. I mean she may want to forget the past. And that's where I come in. I was there, remember?'

'We were all there. I was there,' scoffed Fritz. He saw Francis snap the features of his face. He knew that meant Francis was dissatisfied with his words. He waited for Francis to try again.

'I meant I was with her. I got her down. I put her in the wood. I tied her to a tree. I asked her who was home.'

'So?' Fritz somehow played down the relevance. He shook his head. 'She'll be thankful for that.'

'Fritz, she's eight –'

'Ok, Ok.'

162

'No. Look. I was with her. She'll think of her father and mother, how they died, how she was with me.'

'You're saying you'll remind her of it, yeh?' Fritz waited for a response from Francis. It came in a nod. Fritz smiled. It was a smile of recognition. A smile of comfort too, thought Francis, imagining that Fritz was going to play down the relevance. He watched him sip on the beer. 'I still think she'll want to see you,' he said.

It was after an update on the rats and the school and the janitor that Fritz got back to the game. Francis decided it was his turn to initiate an interpretation of events passed or of what may happen in the future. 'So what if she's lying?' he said, trying hard not to slur his words.

'To us both?'

'Yeh. What if she's leading us on, you know?'

'Go on,' said Fritz seeming interested in this perspective.

'What if Ronnie's gone for good?' As he spoke Francis shook his head. He thought quickly back to a conversation he had with Zelda in the room with the sculpture. It was their first meeting after the funeral. She was talking about Ronnie. He was listening, just sitting and assessing what was being said. He remembered the revelations about image and fashion and the publishing world. Zelda was saying how unusual it was for a woman to be successful in publishing. Francis said nothing. 'You're not missing much,' Zelda had said. She talked of image, of being fashionable, how she prided herself on setting standards. Even while she spoke, there was an air of superiority, a benign air. It somehow came over her. He imagined it dominant in the office, helping her. When she smiled it left her.

'Now what you thinking?' Fritz had seen the abstraction.

'I was thinking of Zelda. Something she said.' Francis again thought of her that day. He remembered how she said she stayed fashionable, that she stayed one step behind. It made her stand out. Last year's colours, familiar and warmed to, were used spectacularly. They stood out in the swathe of blues or greens or whatever it was that was in. Francis told Fritz of the outlook. 'Can't see Ronnie amongst all that. Can you?'

'Could set a trend –'

'Yes. But trends change. They come and go –'

'Well there. Perhaps she won't come back.'

'So where does she go? I mean she's eight.'

'Mobile, Tennessee. She stays there.'

'Then I'll go to Paul's.'

Fritz nodded his head. Here was the answer to all the possibilities: Francis would follow; he would find her and try to give a little comfort, if only the once. Francis considered the strategy too. He wasn't sure of the sense behind it. He wondered how many different scenarios could demand the same response. It made him think it wasn't dynamic enough. An exuberance was missing.

'Where else could she go?' asked Francis.

'I don't know. Friends, family?' Fritz shook his head. 'I don't know. What if Zelda takes her away?'

The thought was like a knife sticking into Francis. He hadn't considered the possibility. He let the idea extend. He built his last meeting with Zelda onto it, the trip to Mobile, the change of job. It was that that stopped him.

'She's changing her job,' Francis said.

'Yeh.'

'Well would she do it?'

'Do what?'

'Go off. Take Ronnie without saying.'

'Disappear you mean?' Fritz laughed.

'Why you laughing?'

'Cause she couldn't do it. Nobody could do it. This is America, small town America. You try disappearing.'

Back in the tower, Francis lay on the bed. He wondered how Fritz managed to drive, how he had fallen asleep, how Fritz had opened the car door and dragged him out. Now he was comfortable. Warm. He had left the tarpaulin off. The warmth of the night crept in. Now and then it touched him and reminded him of where he was. In the interim when he imagined he was in Wales, he recalled his father down valley for a night with the boys. His father would take the tractor. He remembered seeing its lights from his bedroom, the lights wandering and searching through the countryside. At one point they would fall on his face and he would duck away and hide.

'Gafr wen, wen, wen....' Francis began to sing some of the songs that would become clear as the tractor approached and parked. His mother would moan from the bedroom saying, 'It's just as well we haven't got neighbours...' She would make Francis laugh and, on hearing the giggles, she would screech that it was time for him to get to sleep.

He laughed intermittently as his mind tracked the memories, then he thought of his night out. No dominoes or cards like his father, just considerations. That surprised him. He seemed so confident now. Just being an outsider did that. He realised what he had to offer. Days in the old world. A life of old ways and traditions. A life set in custom. It seemed so different to the men on the ranch or the men in the township and the men in San Antonio. He had a different perspective. It was that that gave him confidence. He could talk now, challenge people, make up his mind. He seemed to understand things better too. He could see Zelda's point about fashion. The need to be different was in a way its essence. Setting a trend, people called it. Then people followed. Zelda was using the cycle. But he doubted how Ronnie fitted in. Unless it was a trend. Perhaps it was fashionable to have children. That made Ronnie seem like a necklace or a car. It made her a commodity. Francis cursed that. Yet he sensed too a genuine love, something that was outside the world of fad and trend, something that was permanent and meaningful. It was that that made him believe Ronnie would stay, that she wouldn't be hiding away.

Two days later Francis made up his mind to go to Zelda's. He went after work, taking up the offer of a lift from Kevin, one of the men who worked on the ditches.

He waved goodbye to Kevin a block away from Zelda's at the corner of a street. He wasn't sure why he hadn't shown Kevin Zelda's house or why he had changed Zelda's identity into an old cousin of Brad's who had wanted to show him some old photos of the family. Whatever, the application of imagination had calmed him and made his arrival at Zelda's seem thoroughly normal.

Zelda wasn't in. He could tell by the curtains in the front room windows. When he reached the door at the back he sensed the house was like it was the previous time he had called and found her out. It was the quietness that did it. Zelda was always playing music. She played it loudly, turning it down only for guests.

When Francis turned the corner of the house to confront the sight of the green grassed bank and the road, he sensed a touch of deja vu. It was the sight of the man with the dog that did it, the neighbour who had looked after Zelda's home while she was away. He was by the hedge bordering Zelda's property when Francis appeared.

'Hey you haunting me?' said the man, recognising Francis.

'Mr. Dellmot,' said Francis, who was now striding down the bank towards the man.

The man smiled. 'Thought it was you. You know I walk this way with ol' Barney once every two weeks. Go out of the house and turn left most days. The last time I walked him this way you were here. This time I walk him an' again you're here.' He shook his head. 'Ain't that strange? You always here?' he laughed.

'No,' said Francis, smiling back now. He decided he liked the man and needed to let the man sense he liked him. He could be important in tracking Zelda. That thought disturbed Francis. It made him see how quickly the idea of Zelda going had taken root. He thought how it was based on the flimsiest evidence.

'She's away again, isn't she?'

'Yep. Gone back to Mobile.'

'I see.'

'Yeh. Strange her going –'

'To Mobile?'

'No. Her job. My wife thinks she's nuts. She blames it on the pressure. She blames everything on the pressure. I'm overworked, she's overworked, ol' Barney here, he's overworked. Me, I blame it on the weather. It's too darn hot. People do bum things when it's hot.'

'Has she said anything to you about it?' asked Francis, watching the man bend down to attend to his dog. He lengthened the lead and it showed interest in Zelda's hedge.

'She's mentioned the house. Says she wants to let it out. I told her to sell up, to get out, but she wants to hold onto it.' The man scratched his head. Francis waited for more. It seemed an unnatural break.

'God she'll have a lot to tell me when I see her,' Francis tried to prompt the man.

'Didn't she say goodbye?' he asked. He watched Francis shake his head. 'She had a dinner party the other night. One or two friends. Work friends I think. My wife knows them all by sight. We were passing in the car when they arrived. The little girl was there. She was messing around on the grass –'

'What? What little girl? Ronnie?'

'Yeh.' The man's flow of words dried up as he looked for the dog. He missed Francis' shock. A raising of the eyebrows. An opening of the mouth.

'So she's gone to Mobile?' said Francis, cutting into the man's flow.

'As I understand it,' he replied. 'That's what she said. I've got the key till she sorts out an agency.'

'How long for?'

'Didn't say.'

'When did she leave?'

'Today. Ten o'clock. You want me to give her a message. She said she'd phone some time.'

Francis shook his head and looked disconsolate. He couldn't think what he could say in a message to change things. It needed more than that. It needed contact, face to face, and an openness. He began to hope the man would forget him and not mention the conversation. Then, when he thought there was little chance of that, he hoped Zelda wouldn't phone for a few days.

There was a temptation to run. It was that sort of situation. Instead Francis remembered Zelda mentioning a park two blocks away where she had taken Ronnie. Somehow Francis found it. He walked east and into it. Then he found a bench and sat in the shade and thought of Fritz and the game of scenario they had played while drinking and how the idea of Zelda disappearing had been deemed impossible. The realisation she had gone to Mobile had made Francis wish he had wheedled more information from the man with the dog, though he knew the man had little more to tell, that he was a convenient neighbour and nothing more to Zelda. He wondered whom she talked to. Something about her told him there would be somebody. He wondered who. He thought how she was too open and needful of company to cope by herself. She would need to play off ideas, to consider consequences and dangers.

Francis also wondered where he fitted in. Whether he was inconsequential. It seemed to him his relationship with Ronnie was more peripheral than he imagined. To place himself at the heart of things, as a reason for her movement seemed ridiculous. The good thing that came from that was that Zelda wouldn't have even considered how he would react, whether he would simply forget them or track them. Either of the range of reactions wouldn't have mattered to Zelda and Ronnie. And there was comfort in that. He began to believe the reasons for moving were simple. A new start. That was all it was. He understood that.

Outside Fritz's, Francis pulled at his shirt, straightening it. He wiped it with a hand, coughed and marched forward. He knocked on the door. There was music inside. A Latin American tune was pumping out a beat that drowned the melody. A woman moved with the music. Francis could see her through the glass.

'Hey. Hello. How are you?'

'I'm fine,' said Francis a little mystified by the show of friendliness. He assumed he was talking to Betty, Fritz's wife. He compared his image of her with the woman who confronted him. It was that that made him smile. He was expecting her to be frumpy. Fritz painted her as downcast, dissatisfied with him and her life.

'Hey don't tell me. You're that Englishman. The one who's living in the tower. You are, aren't you? Gee Fritz described you perfectly.' Betty took a step back and looked Francis up and down. It made him edgy. 'Come in. Come in,' she said. 'Have a drink.' She walked into the room where the music was coming from and pointed to a drinks cabinet in the corner. 'Help yourself,' she said.

'No. I'm fine, really. Thanks all the same.' Francis smiled. His eyes swept round the room. It was remarkable only for its mismatch of colours. He thought how Betty was like another colour, out of place, like one of the trinkets that filled the room.

'Golf memorabilia,' she said, moving again to the music. 'Hey do you mind if I do this? It's sort of work out time. Do this every day. Love South American salsa.' Her words found the rhythm and settled neatly. She smiled and shook back her hair. 'You dance?' she asked.

'No,' said Francis who had settled into a chair. 'You're good,' he added, tapping his foot to the rhythm and watching her.

'You should try it. Of course Fritz doesn't. He goes with me to lessons. But only for the company. That's what gets my goat, all those handsome men who don't dance. Ah,' she said sounding disappointed as the music finished. 'I always think it's a shame,' she remarked sitting in an easy chair opposite Francis. 'I mean Fritz can do most anything, except dance. Mind you I secretly think he can do that. He just doesn't want to show me.' She shook her head and sipped on her drink. While the liquid went down, Francis thought how she was more attractive than he would have imagined. His eyes rolled over her tall and slender shape, at her golden skin. He thought all the time how he particularly liked her voice. It was serene, soothing but also disturbing. Its occasional burst of excitement did that. Francis imagined thoughts arriving and the voice reacting, letting loose its power.

'Of course you'll have to excuse the clutter.' Betty looked around the room. The look on her face told Francis she had grown used to the pots and postcards and trophies. 'You must play?' she said.

'No,' said Francis. 'Where do you play?' he asked, assuming somehow that the golf memorabilia belonged to her.

'Me!' she laughed, her voice acquiring its power again. 'Me play golf! Oh you've got it wrong. You've got it all wrong. It's Fritz who plays golf. I'm a golf widow.'

'He never said –'

'God I wish I was you. He's never said! God.' She shook her head. 'If Fritz never mentioned golf again we'd have a normal relationship. You mean to say he's never mentioned caddies or links or shanks. That sounds like bliss.' She exhaled and stared towards the ceiling, still shaking her head. 'Hey where d'ya think he is now? Yeh, playing golf. That's where he is. Still, he probably wishes I could play. Me, I wish he could dance. Cha, cha, cha.' She made up a rhythm and moved in the chair.

'So when will he be in?'

'Let's see.' She looked at a clock on the wall. 'Anytime between now and six. You wait and talk to me. I'm enjoying it.'

Francis smiled. He was trying to assimilate a vision of Fritz at the golf club, the mix of etiquette and decorum defeated him. He could not imagine it. Somehow the sharp tongued looseness of Fritz and his wild ideas didn't fit the staid image he had of golf clubs. Not that Francis had been to a golf club. All he had to go on were P.G. Wodehouse stories on Radio 4. 'The Oldest Member' he thought, remembering the title and their representation of hierarchies. He was appalled by the thought of Fritz mixing in such circles. More worrying was the fact it was kept secret, though Francis began to think that it was something of a cover up. Golf would be the perfect alibi for a multitude of Fritz's sins.

'So what do you think of him?'

'Fritz?' Francis was surprised by the directness of the question. Fritz would have noticed the tell tale jolt of his features. Betty saw no such change, though she knew the long deliberate uttering of her husband's name was nothing more than a play for time.

'He's smart. You must have noticed that. And to him everything is important. That's why he's here, there and everywhere. At home he only drinks white wine. Hey you're laughing –'

Francis shook his head. He couldn't contemplate the domestic Fritz with his slippers and golf clubs and white wine.

'You know he's got a sister called Bella. Isn't that the damnedest name? Bella.' Betty shook her head and let her voice find its smoky lowness again. 'Oh and he says I holler. He must have told you that. He tells everyone that. His hollering wife. That's me.' She stopped and leant forward and poured Francis another drink.

'He's a character,' said Francis, pushing out his glass.

'He's a lunatic. He talks too much. And about anything. And to anyone. He don't hold back.' She put down the bottle and sat back, swirling the liquid around in her glass. 'And now it's this Zelda. Zelda

169

says this. Zelda says that. I say to him, hey hold on, remember I ain't seen this woman. And all he says is, Oh you'd like her. As if that matters.' Betty shook her head. 'You met this Zelda?' she asked. Francis nodded. 'You like her?'

Francis paused. He had never thought of Zelda in terms of like or dislike. He thought of her only in terms of Brad's sister or Ronnie's aunt. His perspective was functional. 'I suppose,' he said finally.

'Hey you had to think. You don't have to think if you like someone. It kinda makes me think you might be a little cool on her.'

'No. I like her.'

'Ok. I get you.' Betty smiled. It bewildered Francis. He smiled back, laughed and looked away. It was a nervous laugh.

'Fritz said you laughed.'

'Did he?'

'Yeh. He said you laughed real good. And you do. He said you were worried about Ronnie.'

'You know about Ronnie?' Francis waited for a nod before admitting to being worried.

'Oh she'll be alright. She'll be fine in Mobile.' Betty suddenly spoke slowly. She stared into her glass, swirling around the remains of the liquid. Francis was looking directly at her again, contemplating her last statement. She knows about Mobile? What does she know? his mind was saying. He needed to ask.

'Fritz says she's a fine girl. He was surprised by her. Thought she had coped with it all well. Me, I'm not so certain. I mean girls cover up. Kids do. I mean there's no-one left close to her.'

Francis' mouth almost opened. He couldn't believe what he was hearing. For a second he shut it out, then he listened and considered interpretations, then he confronted what she had said. 'Are you saying Fritz has seen Ronnie?'

'Didn't you know?' Betty looked shocked now. 'Oh my dear, he saw her, but only for a minute or two, I mean he wasn't close to her. Now the boys he knew. That would have been different, but Ronnie, well no, he didn't really know her –'

'But he saw her?'

'Yeh. Couple of days ago, I guess. Let me see.' She tried to work out the day.

'But I saw him Tuesday. He didn't say anything.'

'You sure? I'm sure he said he told you. He said he'd seen you. In the field, yeh?'

Francis stood up and marched to the door. He felt he was losing control, losing a sense of perspective that only quiet contemplation could assist. He made some attempt to apologise as he walked away. 'Nice meeting you,' he said. 'Tell Fritz I called. Say I'll see him soon. Nice drink and a nice tune. Thanks.'

He walked along the avenue without seeing faces or cars. All he did was think. He recognised the intensity of the moment, the way it threatened him. To date he had coped. He was proud of that. Rightly proud. Now all that could change. He thought how it was all to do with trust, about not being let down. He recognised the need to have expectations and the need for compliance. It was the application of that that hurt. He believed in Fritz. He had thought him open, predictable. He liked that. He needed it. It gave him support. It gave him an outlet. To think of that being abused was difficult to take.

He kicked a stone that was sitting on the sidewalk. He followed it into the road and kicked it again. It bounced several times. The last bounce took it back onto the sidewalk. He thought of Owain and the club, the way he had tried to go along but had failed. He thought of his father; he thought of his maps. He thought of all the broken relationships and the way they had carried on. He thought how he had stayed with them.

He tried to kick the stone again, but missed. He yelped and turned around and picked it up and threw it against a tree in a garden. As he watched it, he thought how Fritz was different, how he had seen the others drift away, how he had understood that motivation. He suspected nothing with Fritz. He checked that. He thought back to the field, how Fritz had called. It reminded him of his excuses, of how he should have asked Betty if she had been ill. Nothing had been mentioned. And she seemed fine. And Tuesday was the day Zelda had left. He saw it all now. The complicity. The arrangement. Why else had Fritz stayed away a week? But he still didn't understand why Zelda had moved on and why Fritz had helped. He stopped there. He tried to remind himself that all Betty had said was that Fritz had seen Ronnie. But it must have been more. He must have helped, thought Francis, moving his understanding on a stage. Just keeping quiet seemed like helping. But why? He could only believe that Ronnie had somehow drawn Zelda and Fritz together. That was always a possibility, but what had triggered it? A request? Something as simple as a word, a statement of allegiance. Francis couldn't believe that because his allegiance with Fritz was far more solid. He knew sympathy may play a role, but he couldn't believe it would sideline him. Why had he been cut out? Why had Ronnie favoured Fritz?

As much as he tried, he couldn't work it out. And mixed with it all was the other revelation. Francis pictured the room and imagined some of the postcards, particularly the one he had wanted to remark on but had never had the chance, the one of the stained glass window at Gloucester Cathedral. 'Gloucester, England?' he had wanted to say, but there had never been a way in. Betty had always moved on, guiding him away. Now all he could think was that golf seemed such an unlikely game for Fritz. Somehow he wasn't phlegmatic enough. Francis thought he could never have been in control long enough to last a round. But then this was an undiscovered dimension of Fritz. He wondered what else lay under wraps.

As much as that concerned him, more and more, as he walked and thought, Francis began to believe the complexity of Fritz meeting Zelda and Ronnie and keeping Zelda's departure a secret was down to eccentricity. Nothing more than that. It was simply down to Zelda talking him into helping. Francis imagined their conversations. Zelda saying Ronnie needed to get away, to start afresh and Fritz saying he understood and that he would help. They probably needed help. The organisation of the move would have been quite demanding and there were all sorts of circumstances that would have drawn Fritz in. The slightest sign of female vulnerability would have done that. And Francis knew that Zelda, for all her eco-feminism and trendy ways, would have used such ploys to get her way. She could have made things up, thought Francis, said Ronnie was hallucinating or that Ronnie's friends were talking, anything would have convinced Fritz he should help. And he would have pledged himself wholeheartedly. Francis knew that. He knew that Fritz would have always been faithful and, more importantly, efficient. But why choose Fritz? Why not him? What was the difference? Perhaps it was something to do with numbers. That it could work with three but not four. Perhaps it was something to do with his foreignness. His not knowing America and the way it worked could have been crucial. That seemed plausible. Just. Though it didn't seem strong enough. He really believed there was a more substantial reason, that something was hidden away, something that Fritz knew.

It was a long walk back. When he reached the wood, Francis stopped. He sat on a tree trunk. It had cleared a gap in the wood. He looked up to the stars. A plane sliced across the sky. It reminded him of his arrival, of those nervous moments at Newark when they opened bags and he became edgy. He remembered the small man at immigration ignoring him, showing interest only in his passport and firing out questions. Questions he couldn't answer. Where you staying? Why you here? He thought too of the way he had gained confidence, of the way such experience as his arrival gave him an armoury he could use. More than that everyone wanted to know where he was from and what it was like. And in answering them, he gained a fluency and found he could consider and develop ideas and even make comparisons. They want to know, they're interested, he told himself. The confidence that gave him made it difficult imagining a crisis had developed. Something had gone against him. He knew that. The wood made it seem it would always go away. It was like a late night story to a seven year old. But he knew there was something wrong. So he tried to calm himself. The wood helped. Its smells and breezes soothed. In some ways he wished it was all detestable and threatening, that it was keeping him alert. He believed he needed that. Instead he found himself being frivolous, thinking of all the silly things he couldn't do. Reciting the alphabet was one such thing. He was alright to r, but after r the letters became a little random. 'U, s, v,' he whispered through the wood. Pronouncing r was another problem. He said vicar and vicar over and over trying not to let it sound like 'ricar'. He knew, when he was lazy, it would just slip out. 'Ricar'. With the exercise came the therapy of memories. 'Vicar,' he would say, deliberating over the first syllable. 'Vvvicar.' And he would remember how his mother had taken him to see the head teacher of his primary school to ask about his diction, how she had marched him into the head's room and sat him down. 'Now what's the trouble?' asked the headmaster. 'He has trouble with his r's,' said this mother, making it sound like arse. He remembered the head and his mother laughing.

Now he was laughing. The breeze carried the sound around the wood. He sensed the slight echo and listened. Normality returned. It told him faith had been broken. Fritz had lied. It was important that he now knew the price of lying, that he knew what it was that had persuaded Fritz to ally himself with Zelda and work against him. To Francis the shift in allegiance was a little like spying. It was the way Fritz had carried on as though everything was normal that upset him. He told himself he couldn't have done that, that he would have refused Zelda. Yet it wasn't that that worried him. It was how he would react that worried him. He knew that he couldn't stay in the wood and hide forever, that soon he would have to go out. The problem was facing it. He wondered if he would shut up and take it, whether it would be oppressive, whether it would stifle all he had acquired.

Such appreciation became academic. He heard shouting. He

thought at first the shouts were echoes, but then he saw a torch and heard the call again. It was clearer this time. 'Francis!' it was calling. There were grumbles too. Mumbled expletives. And a stumble. 'Over here!' Francis shouted. He had recognised the voice. 'Fritz!' he called. 'Over here!'

He could see Fritz didn't know what to expect. He was slow approaching. He used the night as an excuse. The reality was he did not know what to say or how to behave. Francis stood still. He watched him carefully. When they were close, he smiled. 'How's Ronnie?' he asked.

'Ronnie? She's fine,' Fritz replied. He was careful with his expressions, though the relief inside must have been immense. It allowed him to behave normally. He sat down alongside Francis. He looked his way, seeing the redness of Francis' eyes. 'Hey you know what? She draws now. She got that from you. She's got all the pens. And all the ideas. She draws animals –'

'Goats?'

'Yeh. Sometimes.'

Francis smiled. Fritz managed to catch a glimpse of the look as a little light from the full moon caught the side of Francis' face.

'She's growing too. I was surprised. She's gonna be a fine girl. Brad would be proud of her.'

A silence followed. It allowed the smile to linger on Francis' face, though he hid it by turning away and looking into the wood. The stillness amplified the effect. It made Fritz edgy. He seemed to be trying to think of what he should say, how the conversation should progress.

'Did she mention me?' Francis asked, turning back towards Fritz. For the first time their eyes met. It was a sign that Francis wanted to check the truth on Fritz's face. He needed to be sure.

'No,' said Fritz, resisting the temptation to lie. 'I mean she didn't say anything, but I only saw her for a few minutes. I was talking to Zelda and she just came in. I didn't know she was there. Said her dress was wet. She'd been playing with the tap outside.'

Francis nodded. As Fritz spoke, he pictured Ronnie. He draped her on a chair, then against a wall. He made her laugh and smile and disagree and try to get her own way. He made her demand attention. She was in charge. 'You didn't tell me,' Francis said softly over his thoughts.

'Never came up –'

'Never came up,' laughed Francis, making his disgust obvious. For a moment he feigned languor. It helped him think of the questions he should ask, the anger he should feel. As he spoke, he watched Fritz nervously interweave his fingers. It stopped his hands moving, gesturing, saying more than his words. The movement made Francis sense Fritz was in no position to fight back. He would just accede, allow Francis to say his piece. Fritz waited, but nothing came. He must have sensed Francis was waiting for him. He smiled and spoke. 'Ok. I went round. I hadn't planned to. I was passing. Some job down that way. Strange sounds coming from a bedroom someone said. Strange fuckin' sounds. Like monkeys.' Fritz shook his head. 'So I was passing and I saw her, so I stopped. I said I'd call in if I was that way. Why not, I thought.'

'Go on,' urged Francis, not at all taken in by the idea of spontaneity. It seemed too planned to him.

'So I knocked on the fuckin' door and she let me in. And Ronnie came in – as I said. She came in just after I got there. Hey you knew I was going there. I told you. You said yeh.' Fritz waited for Francis to nod.

'And Ronnie was there?'

'Yeh. She hadn't stayed on.'

'Zelda lied,' said Francis quickly.

'To protect Ronnie.'

'Protect her? What do you mean protect her?'

Fritz knew it was what Francis had been wanting to ask. He saw the fury on Francis' face. The passivity had gone, moved on by an urgency that had built up. Fritz also took in the control that came in a gaze his way. 'When I got there Zelda said she was moving on. And she told me why –'

'It's the past, isn't it? Like I said before, I remind her of the past. That night. The fire. The smoke. The smell. I remind her of the smell.'

Fritz was shaking his head, disagreeing with the interpretation Francis was offering. He had to wait to find a moment to make the point. 'No,' he said quickly, finding a way back in. 'I'd like to say yes. I fuckin' would, but it's nothing to do with that...' A silence followed. Francis watched Fritz bite his lip. He seemed to be suffering, as though the truth was thoroughly abhorrent. He waited for the worst. He could see it would be bad, though he had no idea what it was.

'Ronnie was abused,' said Fritz softly. He delivered the words without any movement apart from his lips. He was trance-like, returning to the worry of not knowing how Francis would react.

'Ronnie was abused?'

'Yeh.'

'When?'

'Recently.'

'Why?'

'What d'ya mean why? Why are kids abused?'

'You mean physically abused?' Francis' tone made the option sound bearable. The relief in his voice somehow took the darkness out of it. It couldn't be as bad as mental abuse, it just couldn't. He couldn't imagine anything worse. I'd have detected it, he thought. I'd have seen it. So he assumed the abuse wasn't mental, that it wasn't like his, that it didn't repress or patronise or overrule or ignore or ridicule. It wouldn't have cornered her with words that would echo and echo and prey on her time and time again, he thought. He pictured his father watching; his father sneering and shaking. Ronnie was abused, he thought, returning his attention to Fritz. He replayed the words. Was, thought Francis, was.

'We don't know much about it. Only what she's said. Zelda doesn't want to frighten her. She doesn't want to remind her of it. She thinks it will go away.'

Francis thought of his childhood. He resisted the temptation of telling Fritz, of explaining why he was here and how everything that had happened in a strange way had helped. He saw that Ronnie now needed such help. 'She needs help. Is she getting help? What's Zelda done?' The storm on Francis' face had now evolved into a look of panic. Fritz sensed the need to enlighten him more quickly.

'Zelda thinks she's young enough to forget it.'

'It doesn't work that way,' said Francis shaking his head angrily. 'She's got to act. She's got to understand.'

'Zelda thinks she's recovering. Ronnie doesn't mention it.'

'She wouldn't.'

'But she never seems strained.'

Francis shook his head again. He made up his mind to see Zelda to explain the effects, to tell her of his father, of how it had been, of the way he had fought and lost, of the long days and hard nights, of the pain. They had to stop that, to intervene. He thought of the abuser too, how his father had needed help, how he could have enjoyed his son much more. 'You should help whoever did it too.'

'So what do we do? Get the police? Call in the fuckin' authorities?' Fritz made the point as succinctly as he could. It was suddenly a much more difficult problem than it seemed. 'We agree with you,' continued Fritz, calming down. 'We feel the abuser needs help.'

'We?' asked Francis.

'Well Zelda and I.'

Francis shook his head. He began to want to make a commotion over their inaction, to demand something more positive.

'Still it's Ronnie that matters,' said Fritz. 'And she seems Ok. Zelda thinks bringing in the police will make it worse for her. Why do that when she's Ok? I don't know. I suppose she's fuckin' right.'

'And that's why they're moving. To get away from the memory.'

'Yeh.'

'I see...' Francis considered the rest of the jigsaw. He tried to fit the pieces together. There were only a few gaps left. 'But what about me?' he asked. 'Why doesn't she want to see me? You said it wasn't the past. So it's not the fire?'

'No,' said Fritz, too seriously for Francis' liking. 'It's not just that.'

Francis wondered what that meant. Not just that. How could there be more? And how could it fit into Fritz's revelation?

'Go on then. Tell me,' demanded Francis.

'What?' said Fritz, trying to appear innocent.

'All you know. You're holding back. Remember what you said. No secrets, you said. No fucking secrets. So come on. Let's have it. Let's have the truth.'

The look on Fritz's face told Francis he sensed the passion. It was the first time he had heard Francis really swear. It was the first time he had sensed a lack of control. That clearly worried him. He must have been thinking of reactions, of what may occur, but something seemed to override that. Francis sensed that some crucial words were arriving. Fritz spoke them quickly. 'Zelda thinks it's you.'

'What d'you mean me?'

'You. She thinks you abused Ronnie.'

Francis shook his head and stayed silent for a second or two. 'Me?' he said softly. 'Me?' The tears that came ran quickly. He thought of injustice, of cruelty, of all the things he had believed he had left back in Wales. He couldn't believe the new form that now confronted him. It was equally malicious. He laughed. He couldn't believe the words. He checked Fritz's face, expecting to see a grin and a laugh. He couldn't believe Zelda would see him as an abuser. He couldn't believe Ronnie had accused him. He couldn't believe Fritz had gone along with Ronnie. The silence accompanying the thoughts over-whelmed Fritz. He shuffled about, stretching his legs, folding his arms as though he was trying desperately to think of something to say, something to change the subject or ease the intensity of the moment. Instead Fritz found himself giving up on that and adding to the silence by falling into deep thought himself. What? thought Francis. What? What's going through his mind? His position? How his friendship had been compromised? How something about Zelda had been persua-sive? After all, Fritz seemed to believe her. Zelda at her best, thought

Francis, imagining she was using all her marketing skills to sell a scenario. Francis abusing Ronnie. Ridiculous!

'Did Ronnie say I touched her?' Francis waited for Fritz's reaction. He needed to know now what he was up against. Fritz shook his head. 'So why me? Why does Zelda think that I abused Ronnie?' Francis gasped. 'I mean if Ronnie said I had, then Ok, perhaps. But if Ronnie said nothing –'

'She has –'

'What do you mean she has? You just said.... Look, what are you saying?' Francis seemed exasperated. He slumped backwards, forgetting there was nothing behind him. A nervous jerk brought him back into an upright posture. 'So come on. No secrets. Come on.'

Fritz tried to compose himself. He moved his shoulders, raised his head. He seemed to be trying to remember precisely what had been said. 'She said it happened in the water tower.'

'So? Is that it?'

'It's enough, isn't it?' responded Fritz.

'Oh come on.'

'You live there.'

'Now I do, yes. But when did this happen? Did she say? Did Zelda ask?'

'I don't know.' Fritz sounded angry now. A confession would have satisfied him, but to turn it all around, which it appeared Francis was trying to do, infuriated him. He took a deep breath.

'So she didn't say me?' asked Francis, confirming what had been said.

'No.'

'And you thought it was me?' Francis sounded disgusted now. He let Fritz know that the evidence was too flimsy to be conclusive, that anyone could have access to the water tower, particularly before his occupation. It was that that drew Francis. He knew the odds were stacked against him, that they would assume it had happened recently, that a child would forget anything more than a few months away, but he would have remembered. He told himself that. He reminded himself. It gave him strength. That showed in the outrage of his words and the purpose of the expression on his face. It all surprised Fritz. He would have expected contrition. Instead the anger Francis felt had stoked up aggression. 'You don't know when it happened. You think recently. Nothing she said intimates that. Come on. Ok I live there. I've lived there for nine months. Nine months. Ronnie only came to the tower to see me over the last five months. For the first four months all we said was 'hi'. But she visited the tower before I came to live there. So this could have happened before I arrived. You considered that?'

'Brad?'

'Why not?'

Fritz's face told Francis that Brad seemed an even less likely suspect. 'He loved his kids. He wouldn't harm them –'

'You sure? You said yourself he was wild –'

'He is. With everyone 'cept his kids.' Fritz tried to oppose what Francis was suggesting, but there seemed a certain logic. 'He wouldn't have touched her,' he said rather unconvincingly. 'No way. And what about the tower?'

'What about it?'

'Well she wouldn't have gone there.'

Francis was annoyed by the use of assumptions. Some of the deductions being made were poor too. He had wanted to point that out to Fritz, but he decided to maintain his concentration, to point out the obvious. He decided to tell Fritz how Ronnie first came to the tower.

'She used to knit there. You know that? I knew it. One day when I was taking a break from sorting out the tower, she came in. Must have been two, three months after I moved in there. I couldn't get over it. I mean I thought it was dangerous. It wasn't really, but it took courage. I somehow assumed it would be too much for an eight year old.'

'She came in by herself?' said Fritz in disbelief.

'Yeh. She'd learnt how to use the ladder. Brad used to encourage her to come up. While he played soldiers, she learnt to knit –'

'So you're saying it was Brad?' said Fritz.

'No. No, I'm not saying that. I don't know. I'm just saying it could have been him as much as me. And it certainly wasn't me.'

Fritz shook his head.

Francis felt isolated when Fritz left. The situation seemed hopeless. He couldn't think of that. But he did think of Ronnie and Zelda and Fritz. He considered their roles. It surprised him that the greatest sense of despair came not from the tragedy, but from the way Fritz had so quickly condemned him. What happened to loyalty? Francis thought, the loyalty that had been so crucial to Fritz. Its disappearance shocked Francis. He wondered why Fritz didn't take a step back and say 'Francis wouldn't do that.' But then perhaps nine months wasn't long enough to bond them sufficiently. More crucially, if it wasn't Francis, it was Brad. No-one else had spent sufficient time in the water tower or knew their way around it. Surprisingly that eased Francis' pain. It made him realise that Fritz had made a choice. He had backed Brad. Francis could see the logic of that, though he disliked the way it left him alone. It made him feel extremely vulnerable.

'If only they were alive,' said Francis, meaning Brad and Pam. They would provide answers. As it was there was only Ronnie and himself. More and more the realisation made Francis wonder what Ronnie had said. Fritz hadn't seemed sure. Perhaps he was being kind, taking the pressure off Ronnie. Perhaps she had named Francis. He found it difficult to believe that, though, as he considered what he should do, periodically he would think of the funeral, of all the words eulogising Brad. They made him almost saintly. He imagined Zelda telling Ronnie of the priest talking of the building of the wall, of the way it portrayed Brad as a carer, as a supporter of the community. All the good things would have been relayed and Ronnie would have taken them in. That would have impressed her. She would remember the good things. Her father giving her treats in the tower. The way he swore her to secrecy. The things he did. But there was potential for conflict there and Francis wasn't surprised there had been a discharge of emotion. He was surprised it had come so quickly and that it had chosen to direct itself at him. But, then, he thought that it hadn't really, that it was his association with the water tower that had linked it with him. Not Ronnie. Ronnie's mind hadn't worked in such a way. It couldn't. She was eight. He thought of Ronnie's constant switching of attention, of her inability to develop consecutive thought.

It was those inadequacies that made Francis see it was all up to himself. He had to be persuasive. He had to plan. That was the difficult bit. It was also difficult focusing. More and more, his mind kept thinking of the way something random had disturbed his life. He found no reassurance in that. It made him think of childhood, of the way his father always did something to make him feel small and threatened. He hated that. He hated the way it undermined confidence. He hated the way it left him paranoid. Now it was happening again. In a new form. With a different focus. But the effect was the same. He felt in a corner. He felt everyone closing in.

He thought too of Brad, of the day when Shiloh was recreated and they sat and talked of what his great grandfather would regret.

'Nothing,' said Brad.

'Everyone regrets something,' suggested Francis.

'Not him. And not you. If you dominate, make the most of it.' Brad stayed head down over the battlefield. He reached out and moved a man on a horse forward. He turned it slightly to the right. 'He knew what he was doing. He knew there was no way back. It's when you spend all your time wanting to change things. You know what I mean?'

Francis nodded. He knew the feeling of lost chances, though he also knew that they were no longer there and that there was no way back.

'See? If you just forget about it, then it's easy. My great-grandfather did. I'm sure of it.'

'How do you know?' asked Francis.

'I just feel it.' Brad smiled. He seemed to understand that words weren't an adequate medium for what he was trying to say. 'I can't do it. I'm always thinking if this and if that. I stay in places. I stay in jobs. If it's all going well, fine. There's nothing wrong with that. But sometimes it's just not healthy.' Again he looked at the battlefield, he moved two pieces into the woodland and sighed. 'What it is is control,' he said. 'My father had it. I haven't –'

'Why?'

'Oh kids, marriage. I don't know.'

'But you moved into that because you wanted it.'

'Perhaps. Some people do. Maybe you will. Make sure you do.'

Francis spent the morning tidying the water tower. He packed certain things – the better clothes, the sketch pads, the map, the ceramic pig. Before he placed them in his bag he stood for a second, inspecting them, thinking how it all seemed meagre. A feeling of failure followed, but then the slim trimmings suggested an organisation and control that was desirable. It made him remember Brad's words about control, about environment or relationships or society – something – taking over.

He left then. There was no last look or thought, no rush of memories. He simply climbed to the tower's rim and descended the ladder. He was surprised by that. He was surprised by the lack of sentiment. He expected flashbacks. Like when he left Brynlas. Instead he kept moving. As he walked there was a certain sense of enchantment, disbelief almost at the way he had lived and at what he had done, but there was also a souring that came from the accusations, from the way the tranquillity had been eclipsed. That was it. Nothing more. He simply lifted up the rucksack and turned his back on the tower.

At Fritz's, Betty answered the door. Again she was in leggings and sweat shirt. Again she was dancing. She spoke to him making the square movements of the cha-cha-cha as she spoke.

'You off somewhere?' she asked between big breaths.

'I'm going.'

'Going?' said Betty, as though Francis hadn't said enough. 'Where you going?'

'Home,' said Francis. 'I guess I'm tired.'

'Home's the place then,' said Betty, nodding her head to the rhythm that suddenly ended. 'I'll get Fritz.'

'Is he in?'

'He's out the back. Chopping wood. God knows why. It's ninety degrees for chrissakes. Still he knows best. Something about drying out, preparing it.'

Francis walked behind her. She told him to sit and help himself to a drink. He sighed as he saw her disappear. He was suddenly alarmed, a little shaken by Fritz's presence. He was glad he had called, but he had half expected Fritz to be at work by this time. He thought how much easier it would have been to have left a note.

'Fuckin' woman,' Fritz stormed in, drying himself with a towel. 'She's telling me what to do on my day off again. Remember this, remember that, remember you said you'd go over to so and so and check out this and that. Christ. And all she does is dance about the house all day cha-cha-chaing. And all I want to do is play golf and sit in the bar with the boys and play hell with the fuckin' blacks. You alright? Drink?' He turned and threw the towel into the kitchen and fixed himself a drink. 'You sure?' Francis shook his head. He watched Fritz sit down. Perspiration beaded on his forehead. For once Fritz seemed hesitant as though he was wondering what to say and how to say it.

'So what's up?' he asked, coming to the point. 'You know what gets me is I'm bushed on my fuckin' days off. Work days I can play my tapes, relax, smoke a cigar, gaze at a pretty woman. Now I'm rushing.' He took a quick glance at the clock. It was then he saw the rucksack. It was lying under the clock propped against a small cabinet. 'That yours?' said Fritz looking a little perplexed.

'I'm going,' said Francis quickly. 'I thought I'd better come and say goodbye. There's a note here for Davison.' He scrambled a hand around the inside pocket of his jacket. He found it and smiled, offering it to Fritz.

'Thanks,' said Fritz, seeming a little awkward. He looked at the note in a considered way. Francis sensed he was deciding whether to mount a protest.

'It just says thank you. He's been good to me. You have too. Thanks.'

Fritz put his hands up and opened his palms to Francis. The gesture was meant to say, it's nothing or any time, or it's a pleasure.

'So you'll drop it in?'

'Sure...yeh sure..' Fritz shook the envelope. He looked at its white-ness and tapped it against his empty hand. 'You sure about this?'

Francis nodded.

'I mean Zelda's not going to get the police involved, I've told you that. She said so. She told me.'

'I didn't do anything.'

'Yeh, yeh...' Fritz's protests were unconvincing.

Francis grinned. 'Don't fuckin' yeh, yeh me,' he said. He knew Fritz didn't believe him and he wondered why he was still tolerating him, how tolerance didn't fit with the reactionary Fritz, how his hot-headedness would normally have taken over and shouted and raged. The calmness was un-Fritz like too. It made Francis believe that per-haps all of this had changed him. He hoped it had.

Fritz began to giggle. 'Hey you never swear. You know that? And now you have twice in two days. God I better get Betty in and tell her. Hey we should celebrate.' He took a large swig of whisky. 'You'll have to watch that in Wales. That ol' man of yours. He won't be impressed. No sir he won't like it. His boy swearing. You tell him to fuck off from ol' Fritz. You tell him you deserve better.'

There was little conversation during the journey to the bus terminus. Fritz parked across the road and insisted on coming to see Francis off. That made Francis a little anxious. He said the bus wasn't due for some time and that there was no need, that he hated goodbyes. Fritz compromised. He suggested coming over for a coffee and then leav-ing. Francis knew he had to agree.

Inside the terminal, Fritz left Francis and went in search of coffee. Like most city bus terminals, San Antonio's was in the most seedy and decayed part of the downtown area. Francis stared out at a car park and Fritz's car. He thought how the car park was full of shadows and recesses that no-one wished to claim. In some of the distant shadows steps led up to front doors and down to cellars, in others a mix of sex shops and cinemas were lurking, waiting for their neon to make them leer.

'Don't go out man,' warned a cleaner, sweeping up. 'They'll get you out there. Them winos. Them whores.' The man laughed and tapped a cigarette end away from Francis' heel. Francis smiled at him, but the man never looked up. 'Hey there's a baseball game on,' he said, direct-ing Francis' attention to the slot televisions that were behind him.

'Why don't you join them?' added the cleaner. 'There's one free over there. God's with them,' he remarked, glancing at the row of men staring at the screens. 'He's come in out of the rain.' The cleaner laughed again. 'Where you from man? I know you're European.'

'How do you know that?' asked Francis, quickly comparing himself with the row of men watching the television. He couldn't really see a difference.

'By the sack. American sacks are like the cars in England when someone's just gotten married. They've got all sorts of shit dropping out of them. Haven't you noticed? This your friend?' he asked, without looking up.

Fritz was back in the building, looking flushed and holding tightly onto two cups of coffee. 'Nearly got fuckin' run down,' he said, watching the cleaner push his brush across the hall. 'He troubling you?' he asked quietly.

Francis shook his head and accepted the coffee. He took off the polystyrene lid and sipped at its sweetness. 'You sit down,' he said, gesturing to Fritz.

'Nearly run down.' Fritz was shaking his head. 'Some fuckin' woman. She went through the lights. I said, where'd you get your licence from? Seers?' He shook his head again. 'Why can't women drive? No matter how much you teach them, they fuckin' can't drive. You noticed? You noticed the way they grip the fuckin' wheel and get their nose against the glass? And they're always fuckin' thinking of other things.' He sipped again on the coffee and looked around. 'Shame you're going. I mean I had all sorts of plans. Wanted to show you all sorts of things. Hey you haven't been to the Alamo.' Fritz laughed out loud. 'You must be the first tourist in San Antonio who hasn't been to the Alamo. Man you're unique.' He shook his head and opened another sachet of sugar. He stirred it in. 'So what you gonna do? Back to Wales? Back to the farm?'

Francis nodded a reply. He decided to go along with the scheme Fritz had imagined. He made his face tell Fritz he was less than enthusiastic. He made it seem like rather a necessary chore.

'You know I'm going on a bit, but I'll say it again. You don't have to go. You can stay, see the Alamo and the Governor's Palace. Be a tourist for a week. Why not?'

Francis nodded.

'No I fuckin' mean it. Don't matter if you did it or didn't do it. Zelda's not gonna get the police in. All you'd have to do is leave Ronnie alone. And as she's in Mobile that won't be too difficult.'

'You'll say goodbye to her for me, won't you? I know it will be difficult, but there's a card. It's in with Davison's. There's drawings and things too. Stuff I meant to give her. Open it if you like –'

'Check it out?'

'Yes.' Francis sighed. 'And you take care.'

'Hey come on. We've had some good times.' Fritz laughed. Francis imagined he was replaying episodes in his mind. He watched him drink some more coffee and swirl the remaining fluid around the cup. 'Will you come back? Think about it. Betty and I'll put you up. You think about it. I'd like it. I really would.'

'It was easy finding Ronnie. I traced Paul Stubbs in Mobile. There were only four P. Stubbs in the telephone book. Paul was the first I investigated. I got a room then. A small central hotel with a woman owner who kept having nightmares. I started missing breakfast to miss the detail of the nightmares. Sometimes I'd sit in the bedroom, staring at the ceiling thinking how I'd lied to Fritz. It was a stippled ceiling. Shapes like the end of a rake. A chrome fan swirled slowly.

I wasn't lying really. I convinced myself of that. I was just being economical with the truth. After all I was on my way back to Wales, but I didn't mention the stop-over in Mobile. I couldn't tell Fritz that. I knew he'd tell Zelda, so I kept it quiet. That seems alright, doesn't it? I mean I've learnt that all people lie from time to time. Some more than others.

A taxi took me to Paul's address. It was out in the suburbs. There were big trees between the houses. It looked as though the houses had been built in a wood. I made use of that. I hid behind a tree. The first day at ten a girl came out with Ronnie. They went to the park. The same happened the second day. I'd hired a car by then.

In the park there was a little paddling pool. A sort of lake. Ronnie loved it. She placed her feet in the water and made waves. Sometimes they hired a boat. Her friend couldn't row. Sometimes they went into the reed island in the middle of the lake. The girl would have to stand up then and push the boat out. Ronnie would laugh and laugh. After, Ronnie would play with another little girl called Marty and a boy named Paul. That happened every day. They would play tag and laugh and giggle. The girls who brought the children to the park would sit down together and talk while they watched the children. I found a little spot in the vegetation at the top of the hill and watched and listened.

I went back every day. It was the same routine. On the fourth day the boy brought a ball and threw it at the girls. The girls tried to throw it back even harder. Once the ball nearly went into the lake and the girl who had brought Ronnie shouted at the boy. She told him to be careful, to watch the edge of the water. When he retrieved the ball, she told him to play a little further up the hill.

That brought them much closer to me. So close I could see the expressions on the children's faces. I saw Ronnie smile. I wanted to call out, to say hello, to ask her how she was. I wanted to show her the giraffes I had drawn. I wanted to say, I'm alright, we're still the same.

Then the ball came into the wood. It landed by me. One of the girls down below shouted something. 'Be careful,' I think. I heard Ronnie say 'I'll get it. I've been in there before.' And in she came. She stood by me. I said 'Hello'. And she said 'Francis'. She remembered me. And she smiled. That was the most important thing. It put me at rest. I felt calm. And she didn't cry out. She felt safe. I could see that. I didn't threaten her at all. I knew then Zelda had made nothing of it, that, as Fritz had said, they were leaving things alone. But, even so, the girl was welcoming me. So I said 'Let's go. Let's see a movie'. 'Which one?' she asked. Then she asked if Toggie and Zoon would be in it. And I said yes and that we'd have to move quickly. I scribbled a note. I left it by the ball. I thought it would reassure Zelda. On it I wrote, 'Taking Ronnie to the Pictures.'"

Francis watched the police officer read the statement.

The police officer smiled. 'You happy with that?' he asked.

Francis nodded, though his mind was more with the film and the delight on Ronnie's face. They had found a cinema complex with one screen devoted to children's showings. *Snow White* had absorbed Ronnie. She had relaxed and laughed and cried. Afterwards she had asked Francis where he had been, why he hadn't been to see her and when she would see him again.

It was the clarity of such questioning that touched Francis. It made him realise Ronnie was the only one after the deaths of Pam and Brad who had been straight. Every emotion was clear. It was felt and nothing would stop it. The freshness of that allowed him to relax. No longer did he have to see through things and consider motives, no longer did he have to watch what he said and assess how open he should be.

He felt that from the moment Ronnie had walked out of the clump of trees with him.

'We'd better run,' he said.

'Why?'

186

'To catch the film.'

Ronnie ran alongside him. It was only a short trot to the park gates and his car. Over his shoulder Francis heard Marty say, 'Come on Ronnie. Where's the ball?' The little boy shouted, 'Ronnie's playing games. She's hiding. I'll find her.'

But nobody found her. And Francis drove the car away quickly. He had turned the first corner and relaxed a little when Ronnie spoke.

'I'm not speaking to you,' she said.

'Why?'

'Because of the horse.'

'What horse?'

'The one in the album with Toggie and Zoon. The grey horse. You didn't tell me you had a horse.'

'Didn't I? You sure?'

'What's its name?'

'The horse? Bess.'

'Bess. That's a pretty name.' Ronnie looked out at the sidewalk that was deserted in the mid afternoon heat. 'You're very lucky,' she said. 'Having a horse and two goats.'

Francis thought how his father had fallen from Bess, how he had cried with pain and refused ever again to sit on the back of a horse. He laughed at that. He thought how his father had switched allegiance to a Honda motorbike and how he gently rode the bike around the hills at a pace comfortable for his dogs.

Francis didn't tell Ronnie any of that, though he did mention that he rubbed heads with Bess and the way Bess showed her affection by weeing.

'Weeing!' said Ronnie, pulling a face. It showed her distaste.

'It's like you smiling,' said Francis.

'But it's much more smelly.'

Francis laughed, then agreed. He let Ronnie talk. She mentioned her uncle Paul and her visit to his friend's farm. She said she'd show Francis the photographs of the visit. 'I'd like that,' said Francis, thinking of Bess again, of the way he would brush her down and press the bone at the base of her back where he had found a spot that was like a funny bone. He would watch her head stretch up. If she yawned, he knew she would close her eyes, so he would place a finger in her mouth and she would play at being annoyed.

'Hey you're gonna buy me a goat. You promised. A big goat. Like Toggie.'

Francis smiled. He was used to such demands. After the film Ronnie had asked him to buy her 'Grumpy', her favourite dwarf.

'Grumpy's my favourite, who's yours?' Ronnie had said. Francis replied, 'Dopey.' When Ronnie asked why, he said Dopey reminded him of Toggie. Ronnie laughed at that. While she laughed, he thought how she had never left him with the sense that everything can be commodified. Most Americans did. Fritz did. Zelda did.

It was when he was thinking of that that Zelda walked in. It shocked Francis. He noticed her quick glance around the room. Her nose turned up slightly as she registered the warmth and staleness of the air. Francis wanted to apologise. He too gave the room a long look. He sensed its blankness, its bleached look. It could quickly numb, he thought, taking in Zelda's worried look. He had never seen such concern on her face. That surprised him. He thought how her long oval face and its elegant features – small brown eyes and a snub nose and pencil thin lips could quite easily exaggerate concern.

'Sorry about this,' he said. He tried to smile, but felt an intense awkwardness. The feeling made him wonder why she was visiting, what she had wanted to say.

'You been in here long?' she asked softly. She coughed, clearing her throat.

'Couple of hours,' said Francis. 'I've made a statement. And they made me tea. Seemed like a good deal. They're nice. Not like the films.'

'Good,' said Zelda, taking a long look at Francis. He sensed a little concern.

'I know what you think,' said Francis, thinking it was better to get the preliminaries out of the way.

'You do?'

Francis nodded. 'About Ronnie.'

'Oh Ronnie –'

'Yes. I understand how you see it –'

'You do?'

'Yes.' Francis paused. He was finding it all rather more difficult than he had imagined it would be. She seemed rather uncommunicative, as though she was disturbed or puzzled. Something seemed to be interfering with her thoughts.

'How's Ronnie?' Francis asked, trying to make it easy for her.

'She's fine.' Zelda smiled. Francis sensed how brittle the look was, how it could easily disintegrate or evolve into something else. 'She enjoyed the movie.'

'I did too. I enjoyed seeing her. I was surprised she hadn't seen it before.'

'Pam and Brad didn't have a video,' said Zelda. 'God they must have been the only people in Texas without a video. And they never took her to the movies. It makes Ronnie quite sweet, don't you think?'

'Quite normal, I'd say.'

'Yeh, let's say that.' Again Zelda smiled. This time it seemed stronger, more alert, aware of the way she got on well with Francis. It convinced Francis she was thinking how she liked him, how she had been surprised when Ronnie had pointed the blame for the abuse his way. 'You'll be free soon,' she said. 'I've told them it's all a misunderstanding, that you're a friend, that you called and we weren't in, that you were on your way back to Wales. You'll have to confirm that.'

'I've made a statement.'

'They'll ignore that. Paul's lawyer's quite persuasive.' A knowing laugh followed the words. 'You'll be free to go.' She stood up and began to walk back to the door.

'You believe me then?' asked Francis. He had had to ask.

'Maybe,' she said as her hand fell on the door handle. She began another smile, but checked it. A thought interfered. 'I don't know. I really don't know. I'll probably never know. That's why I'd prefer it if you didn't see Ronnie again. You understand?' She waited for Francis to nod his head. 'You see, Paul's lawyer can be a little indecisive. I'd hate him to change his mind. And Paul thinks Ronnie needs a new start. She's young enough to forget, to start again.'

Francis nodded. Somehow he knew that something had changed, that perhaps Fritz had spoken to her about the water tower and Brad's war games and Ronnie's knitting. He knew Zelda had pieced it together and that she had drawn conclusions based more on Brad's reputation. He also sensed she was using him. He quickly worked out why, thinking that if Ronnie didn't forget, Francis was there to blame. By forcing him out of her life he would always be convenient. If Ronnie forgot, then Francis and Toggie and Zoon and the drawings of Fred and the giraffes would seem like Snow White, a fantasy.

'Hey I nearly forgot.' Zelda stopped and turned back Francis' way. 'I've borrowed this editing machine from work. It's really cute. All the latest technology. Gee it can do all sorts of things.' Zelda shook her head. She walked a few paces towards Francis. He smiled, trying to break the silence, knowing that Zelda was always a little unpredictable. He had expected a rush of ideas to come and explain the introduction of the editing machine. Instead a laugh came and went and a shake of the head followed. Francis used the time to think how she occasionally seemed frivolous, how she liked doing new things without having a reason for doing them.

'Gee,' she said, finding new life. 'That machine. It does everything.

So I'm making a film –'

'Really,' said Francis, feeling it was time he made some sort of contribution, however simple.

'Yeh. Of Brad –'

'Brad?'

'For Ronnie. I thought she'd sort of forget him, so I've scanned my tapes and found some footage. It's not much really. Reunions mostly. Then some guy from the group that built the wall came round. He said they had a film of what went on in the club. Well I was so happy when he left it with me. Gee it was great. There was Brad building the wall and driving the van. He looked great. So tall.' A laugh emphasised the point. It drew Francis to recall a previous conversation with Zelda about height. 'So I added that,' she said.

'Sounds good,' said Francis, a little perplexed. He couldn't work out the motivation for Zelda' confession.

'Yeh, it is. Thought I'd tell you.' She said no more words. She smiled clumsily and left. Francis watched her go. He thought how strange her departure was. It wasn't as though they were saying goodbye forever. It was more like saying good night to a neighbour she would see again tomorrow. It made Francis laugh. He wondered if Zelda heard his laughter as she walked down the corridor and out of the gaol.

Home. He remembered the way they would select lambs for breeding and market in August. Francis' father was on Bess. The lambs were short haired, ears back, alert to the ferns and the valley and the rain and the man on the horse whose calls were rounding them up, bringing them to the pounds of Brynlas. As always the sheep were being difficult, making it all the more obvious that Francis' father wasn't very good at herding. Francis knew his technique, how he would get off Bess and spread himself like a goalkeeper and wave his stick and how the sheep would still drift passed him, somehow assessing where his gaze and balance were. It was the words that went with it that Francis liked. They were drill like. Regimental. Sometimes Francis would listen to them and imagine a military band pumping out a rhythm. 'Come here Blod. Here. Here!' his father would shout, controlling the dogs. 'Blod! Can you come over here? Come 'ere Blod. 'Ere. Ivor 'ere. Where'd he go? Here Ivor. Ivor! Where the hell? Where'd he go? Ivor! Here damn you. Where you bloody going now? Here!'

Francis liked the mistakes: the turns, the twists, the late directions, the misinterpretations. He also liked the way his father would talk of the former complications, the way he said that, when there were more farms, all the farmers would help each other over the busy shearing days and how that involved them all out on horseback rounding up sheep. 'Dogs every bloody where,' his father said, describing what went on. 'Hell of a bloody mess. We all had different ideas see. Different bloody ways.'

Francis laughed at that. Then his father taunted him. 'You have a go,' he said. 'Get up there.' He jumped off Bess and offered Francis a leg up. 'Go on. You'll have to do it one day. Don't be bloody daft. Go on.' It was more of a directive when it was repeated. 'You understand? We're picking the best ewe lambs. That's all.'

Francis was less certain. He was surprised when his father offered something approaching sympathy. 'It's the weather,' he said quickly. 'Cold and wet see. It's squeezed them. You understand? They've lost ground, gone backwards. It's bloody difficult.'

Francis nodded. He didn't know how weather could squeeze sheep, but he didn't want to appear ignorant.

'Bloody pick one then. Go on. Fluff your bloody feathers son. Geth's waiting. You can do it. Surely. One bloody sheep. That's all. One good ewe.' Within a second his father was pointing a stick, shouting at Gethin who was across the other side of the pen. 'Put that one out. That one!' directed Francis' father as Gethin waded through the sheep. Francis watched Gethin trying to follow his directions. 'You bloody looking?' Francis' father shouted. 'That one Geth! That one!'

★

The bus stopped at Pensacola. It was the middle of the night. All the way from Mobile, Francis had sat alone, thinking of Wales, of what he was doing. Now in the terminus a man chewing tobacco sat by him. He spoke to Francis about the sea and New York. They shared a sandwich, then the man fell asleep. Francis sat staring at the jowls on his face. They moved like a concertina as he snored and whistled.

'You OK?' the driver shouted as he walked passed.

'Sure,' said Francis.

'He needs a bed,' the driver joked. 'What the hell?' He took another look at the man. 'Wacky baccy I guess.'

As things settled, strange thoughts moved through Francis' mind. 'Go on. You'll have to do it one day. Don't be bloody daft.' His father's words replayed over and over and the previous talk of New York reminded him of his arrival in the States. He considered how he had thrived in his anonymity, how he was suddenly incognito, lost amongst faces in Macys or Central Park. From the Empire State Building he had looked down and thought how moments earlier he was a face on the street. That was the sort of urban he wanted – the fleeting, the transient. He loved the idea of sampling. It was like dipping a toe in the sea. If he liked it, he would wade in. He liked New York. He stayed for three weeks. The same philosophy had moved him on in L.A., where there had seemed no focus, no reference points, and stopped him in San Antonio.

He thought too of his reasons for travelling. He was selective here. Somehow he found he could link it with his pursuit of Ronnie to Mobile. The link lay in a competition he had won when he was fifteen. The *Geographical Magazine* ran it. It was for children. They had to design a map. It was as simple as that. A map. Of anything. All that was required was a degree of originality and the correct use of basic map-making skills. His Uncle Gwyn helped him. 'You never bloody want to help here, do you?' was his father's reaction when Francis offered him the chance to help. Francis never understood the point his father was making. It seemed personal, selfish even. It was certainly beyond the comprehension of Francis, so it never really bothered him. Instead he dwelt on the delight of his uncle when he was asked to help. 'Who me? You sure? I mean I will. Yes, Ok. Now let's see.'

Gwyn set the rules. Keep it local. Focused too. Find a subject. 'Something distinctive,' he said. It was that that set Francis thinking. 'Uncle Gwyn you know your hobby?' Gwyn nodded, knowing immediately that Francis was referring to bird watching. 'You must have data?' Francis suggested. And Gwyn produced the data: bird species in the woods surrounding Brynlas and in the Brynlas fields. To complete the survey Gwyn carried out an investigation of the species around the farm buildings. That gave the area a total coverage.

From the data Francis produced an isopleth map of bird species diversity on Brynlas Farm. The map took first prize. 'Imaginative,' said the judge. 'Accurate and interesting.' The reward was cash for Francis' school and a small prize for Francis. He choose some books on map making and map skills. To present the prize, a Mr. Wilkins of the *Geographical Magazine* was to attend Francis' school's prize day. It was Francis' first and last school prize, his only venture onto the stage. The prize's distinctiveness made it the highlight of the day. It drew the press and put Francis' photograph on the front page of the *Gazette*, the local paper.

It wasn't so much its importance that Francis reconsidered. It was the promise his mother made that both she and his father would attend, that they would clap and cheer and be so proud. Francis said he wanted them there. Somehow he thought their presence would give him strength. He admitted to his mother that he wasn't really looking forward to it. The walk to the stage, the handshake, the walking away – it filled him with fear, yet, somehow, on the day, it didn't seem too bad. He had arrived early and waited outside the hall. He had glimpsed his mother walking down the aisle in the hall, moving to her seat. He had assumed his father was already there. He tried to look out for them when he walked to the stage. The applause seemed generous. Mr Wilkins said nice things too, all about the skills involved. 'Supremely executed' was his verdict on Francis' map. It made Francis smile. The expression stayed with him as he collected the books and walked back down the steps off the stage. The audience was facing him now. He could look more deeply at them: the fathers, the mothers, the familiar country faces. Everyone was smiling. Then he saw a gap. It was the seat next to his mother's. 'He's not there,' a voice in his head was saying, 'he's not bloody there.' It made him rush out of the hall. It left him feeling betrayed.

The importance of Zelda's film became clear then. Back on the bus, he thought of her visit to the police station, of her lack of subtlety, of the way she was manipulative. Francis hated the conspiracy that went with that. It made deceit seem routine. Perhaps the interview room was a set up. He thought how her words seemed rehearsed. He remembered them. The information. The warnings. The intimacies. She at least made him feel close to Ronnie. It was the talk of the film that did that, though it also annoyed him. He thought how it was unsurprising, how Zelda's marketing expertise fashioned her perspective, how she saw Brad as a product, something that she could package and use imaginatively. His annoyance wasn't directed at the idea of a film or at anything Zelda had said. Rather, it was directed at what went unsaid. He thought of *Last Year at Marienbad, Brief Encounter, Bladerunner, Citizen Kane*. This was different. This was Zelda's film. This was her chance. His thoughts made it seem that Ronnie's image of her father was being constructed. Zelda was designing it, creating something that was nothing more than a facade. Ronnie would see through it, he told himself. He believed she would. She was too bright, too honest, though the power of saying 'this is my father' over the images would be immense. Francis knew that. He knew it would have quite a profound effect, that it could create the attachment he believed Zelda wanted.

Brynlas, Wales

'Well we just had to see you. I said to Nina, I said that boy goes all over America, all over the god damn country, and I mean all over.'

Francis listened. There was nothing else he could do. He had learnt that his aunty dominated conversations and left little places for contributions. Sometimes, when people didn't appreciate the places, she gave a look, a nod perhaps, calling someone on. Like a policeman directing traffic, thought Francis.

'And you went to San Francisco. I always wanted to go there. Alcatraz, you seen that?'

Francis recognised the call. He sat up. 'Yes, fascinating,' he said.

'Fascinating, there. I knew it. One of our neighbours went. To a conference or something. Said it was full of gays and liberals. Well I hate liberals. They really get up my nose. I mean they're just do-gooders. That sort of destroyed it for me.'

Francis laughed. The sound could have been prescribed by some activist, some freedom supporter who was hell bent on loosening conventions.

'And you got to LA, yeh?'

Francis nodded.

'And St. Louis?'

'Oh yes I liked St. Louis. I met someone in Texas who was from St. Louis...'

But Ena wasn't listening. She was deep in thought. A quizzical look came over her face. Francis realised she was imagining America, plotting places and movements. 'You could have called then. Jees yes. Kind of strange you missed us. I mean your mother never mentioned St. Louis. That ain't so far away. Half a day by bus I guess. Yeh you could have called.'

'Only stopped there a day,' said Francis, trying to retrieve the situation. 'Had these five day bus passes see. You buy them in London.'

'Greyhound?'

'Trailways.' Francis watched Ena give a knowing look. The explanation seemed to be satisfying her. Francis tracked her expressions. He saw a look of agreement calm her face.

'It was in the middle of a five day pass. Could only spend one day there, that's all.'

'So what did you do?'

'In St. Louis?' Francis looked puzzled. He wondered about the line of questioning and thought how the content of the day needed to be impressive. 'Went to Kachoria. An old indian settlement. Bit like a city. Very unusual. You been there?' The question drew a blank, though the silence continued. It beckoned Francis on. 'Always been interested in indians.'

'Your father's influence,' laughed Nina. 'Always watching cowboys your father. Used to take your mother when they were courting. Your mother used to say he was more interested in the indians than her.' Ena laughed. It drew Francis into laughter too. He laughed heartily. The sound was like an appeasement. It assuaged. It made Ena believe she hadn't been overlooked. Francis found the manipulation rewarding. He relished the power it gave him.

'Still,' she said, controlling her laughter. 'You should have called. I wrote and said that to your mother. I said, that boy. All the way over here and he can't find his way to see his aunty Ena. Gee I was wondering what I'd done. Hey, why you smiling? You know something, don't you? You thinking why you missed little ol' Scranton?'

He was smiling at his opinion of her. She was fierce, dragon-like almost with her strange adenoidal voice giving her a presence that bound all her history – Wales and America, rural and urban, hard and soft. Soft now, thought Francis. The rough edges worn away. He liked that. He liked her exposure, the fact she hadn't hidden away. His mother had. So had his father. They had stayed. They had chosen comfort. There was nothing of interest there, he thought, nothing to intrigue him or draw him away.

Ena only stayed two days. Francis had been home a week. The cultural sensitivities had clashed and Francis had somehow retained control. That was more than his mother and father had managed. They had objected to the state of his clothes, his weight loss, the way he had given up breakfast and had started picking at food. Most of the objections were from his mother. There had been a day or two's grace when he had slept off jet lag, but after that the real emotions emerged. They hadn't impressed him. He saw them as weak. Inflexible, he thought. It was clear they found it difficult to accept change. They should want to learn, he thought, learning is strength. He knew that now. He knew that accommodating differences, absorbing what goes on elsewhere is important. There was none of that in Brynlas. He realised that now. He knew he would never find an appreciative eye or ear in Brynlas for any analysis of what had gone on in Texas. That troubled him. Worse still, there was insufficient privacy to consider the events. Such contemplation seemed vital to Francis. The events had to stay real. They had to stay fresh. He had to treat them like fresh cut flowers. That made him nervous, edgy to the point of staying in his room in the evening and putting off his return to the fields.

'Work tomorrow?' his mother would ask. Francis would find an excuse, though gradually the strength of persuasion grew. 'Your father could do with a hand. Dipping at the moment. Geth's off tomorrow. Something to do with his mother. Your father'd appreciate it.'

When he started to help on the farm, more than ever he felt the need to be alone. He took to sitting outside on fine evenings. Being in meant making conversation. But when it was fine he could sit outside managing a silence. It was then he would notice the birds, the trees, the sky, the grass. He never focused on the cottage. He sat with his back to it. Sometimes he forgot it was there. Other times it impressed its presence on him. The memories. His childhood. The games. The problems. One by one they emphasised just how much he needed space. He needed the quietness, the contemplation, the serenity. He needed the water tower. That was the conclusion. It always came to him in a smile. The experience was condensed now. Like a feeling. It left him focusing on some moment or event that enveloped happiness and held him in it. Smiling, laughing, grinning. He knew the emotions well. They were a confirmation. An acknowledgement that all was well.

Such moments shifted his mood. They left him uncompromisingly amiable, different from the remoteness he emanated during his previous days at Brynlas. Everyone would wonder then what he was thinking, what he believed in, what he wanted in life. Now there was no need for any such questions. It was obvious, clear. He liked it that way. He wondered if it was permanent or whether it was controlled by environment rather than by some mechanism from within. He laughed thinking of his father's reaction, how he had sensed it when he came up the drive. The big change. The difference. He could hear his father whisper to his mother, 'Bloody hell.' He knew his father would dismiss it, that some new term would be employed to explain away Francis' new demeanour, that it would be put down to confidence or maturity. Something easy, something understandable, thought Francis. He wondered how he could convince them there was more to it than that, that the change was down to something more abstract and more difficult to comprehend, how he could explain what had happened without it becoming unfathomable.

In his mind he began to try out approaches. None of them seemed to work, but they all started from his father's first words on his return to Brynlas. 'Bloody hell.' He'd say the words over and over, realising they were a compliment, that they were saying, yes he'd changed. They may also have reminded his father how he had doubted him. Francis remembered that. He remembered coming home one afternoon just before he left for the States and hearing his mother and father talking.

'We could give him money. Tide him over,' his mother was saying when he came in through the door.

'He'll waste it.'

'How do you know?'

'I know.'

'You don't.' His mother sounded surprised at the element of doubt her husband was intent on creating. 'Come on,' she urged.

Francis' father struggled for a second. He was trying to find the right words, the right stress. He didn't want to condemn the boy, but he did want to point out Francis' deficiencies. In the context they were restrictions, holding him back. They were barriers Francis would have to surmount. Francis' father didn't quite have sufficient faith in Francis to believe he could move from challenge to challenge and cope. Somewhere along the line, quite early on, his father thought something would crop up and Francis would give in and return home. 'You know what he's like,' he finally said, trying to be as evasive as possible. 'You bloody know.' He searched his wife's face for a response. A cool, dispassionate look greeted him. It told him it wasn't enough. 'Turkish Delight,' he said.

'Go on,' said Francis' mother knowing exactly what that meant.

'He is. He's full of bloody eastern promise. I've heard you say it.'

'Only in a joking way.'

'You said it over the logs. He said he'd take over and what did he do, he broke the bloody axe head. First bloody swipe. And he forgot to oil the chainsaw. So he stopped. No bloody logs.'

'Ok.'

'Turkish bloody delight see.' His father became quiet. A pause. He looked contemplative, then he picked up his thoughts and spoke softly. 'Bloody boy. Making plans. Scheming. Where does he get that from, eh?'

Francis had left at that point. It was how he would have behaved as a child, listening in, running away. If it happened now he would walk in and laugh. 'Turkish Delight,' he said to himself, giggling. It was one of his father's favourite phrases. It was one he liked. He had come to use it too. Miss Davies, one of his old teachers was called it. She had promised to take the class to Cardiff to see a play, but they had never gone. So she deserved it. The shock was hearing it being applied to

197

him. It meant non-delivery, unreliability. They were traits he wouldn't have wanted.

The decision to move into the shearers' shed came easily. He needed a water tower, somewhere compact and relaxing, somewhere where he would be comfortable. He thought of it like an old chair. Like his mother's in the kitchen, perhaps. Something that could mould to his needs, something that gave him the feeling of a warm room with some sort of decoration – a fat, purring cat, perhaps. Nothing could purr in the farmhouse. The ludicrous television programmes provided meaningless noise and his parents adopted an annoying habit of looking into his bedroom whenever they wandered about during the adverts. 'Alright?' his mother would ask. His father, less open, would build up some talk about someone he had seen during Francis' absence. 'Asked after you. Bloody shocked when I said Texas. He's in Texas. I could see them imagining you with a ten gallon hat and spurs, you know those things that catch the sun and bullets in westerns. Christ they thought it was wonderful. When's he back? they'd say. He is coming back. Francis, I'd say. Oh Christ aye. He'll be back.'

'I am,' said Francis.

'Course you bloody are.'

'But I have changed.'

'Hell we all change. Even I bloody change.'

'But that means I'm different. You've got to accept that.'

'Ok.'

'So let's try it then.'

'Try it?' His father didn't understand.

'What would you say if I moved into the shearers' shed? You know the room in the courtyard.'

His father looked a little lost.

'I'm going to live there.'

His father laughed. 'The shearers' shed,' he managed to say. Francis stayed serious. It was the look on his face that conveyed this was no game. 'You serious?' asked his father.

'Why not?'

'Why not! Well for one thing it's got no bloody heating. It's damp. It's bloody falling down. There's no bloody windows.'

'I'll fix it.'

'Oh easy as that is it?'

Francis laughed. He pushed the book he was reading away and stared at his father. He felt a little pity for the look that met his eyes.

Confounded, he thought. Lost, totally lost. He imagined the thoughts. America. Bloody America. It took on a new significance now. Its menace was starkly vivid. Like oil on water. It was floating towards his father. It was threatening him, targeting the cosy, compact world he had formulated. Francis will come home, his father's mind would have been saying while he was away. Francis will come home. Since his return, his father would have relished lingering on that. Now it would be saying, Francis is home, the cows are back in the field, the cows are back in the bloody field. Now it was supposed to be the same. As it was. No change.

'Come on son, it's not for living in. I wouldn't put the goats in there. There's no heat. There's no bloody water.'

'I'll sort it out,' emphasised Francis, meeting his father's gaze head on. 'I'll get power. I'll get water.' Francis was prepared to counter everything. His father could see that now. There was something in Francis' face that said this will happen. The look left no leeway. Defamiliarise, change it was saying. To him that was enchanting. To his father it was portentous. He knew he needed to fight it, but the old ways wouldn't work. Francis knew that. It made him think how his father would have to adapt, how he would have to come up with a new strategy. Francis wondered what he would come up with.

'Ok, Ok,' Francis' father said defensively. 'We'll see. We'll see what we can bloody do. Geth'll know. He's good at that. Thank God. Hasn't got a bloody clue with animals. Doesn't communicate. Hardly talks to anyone Geth. Still.' The deflection left his father smiling. The words seemed assured. They seemed to be saying Francis will see sense, he'll carry it through, that things were as they had always been. Francis sensed that. He shook his head. I've changed, his mind was saying, pleading now. See it, understand it, comprehend, he urged. But his father stayed smiling. 'Bloody Geth,' his father's voice was saying.

The shearers' room wasn't in as bad a state as his father made out. It was damp, but all rooms were damp when they were left unused for a time. Francis quickly acted on that. He moved in calor gas fires. He rolled them like tanks into position and opened fire. He worked around them, checking floorboards, ripping out the worn, putting in the new. He worked frantically, standing back now and then to appreciate the room. It was better than he had anticipated. It had recesses and hallways that connected with the shearing shed. That made the shape irregular. He liked that. He liked the appliances and furniture that was left too. 1950's but usable, he thought, running a cloth over an old sink and kitchen units. He cleaned up the chrome, removing cobwebs and a bag of wool that was home to a family of mice. When he tried the stove, having brought in a new canister of gas, it worked. 'I can cook,' he laughed. 'How about washing?' There was a bathroom down a small corridor that led to the adjoining shearing shed. But the bath had cracked. 'Yes,' he said to himself when he found the toilet worked. 'No need to write that down.' He referred to a list he was making. It highlighted what was needed: new bath, electricity. He added to it daily, noting the big things first and then the smaller issues like curtains and cups, the more personal touches that made it homely.

Francis particularly liked such touches. He liked the detail. He enjoyed the creativity of matching and the excitement of coming up with some essential niceness that is distinctive. The water tower had offered more in that respect. It gave him more to work with. The shearers' room was barer, colder. It felt disliked, as though the people who had been in it hadn't cared, which they probably hadn't given that they were shearers and transient. It needed a Jefferson quote. Something that was like an aroma, a sense of previous occupation, of being enjoyed. The lack of that made Francis feel it would take longer to attach to him. But that didn't deter him. No matter how bare, he knew there were qualities that appealed to him. The window, for example. A large rectangle where he could sit and stare out at the farmyard. He had warmed to that. Already Toggie and Zoon had sidled up and stared in. Once, in sunlight, when Francis had jarred back the window and opened it, showering rust on the sill, Toggie had approached. An apple on the window sill had rewarded his curiosity. Francis and Toggie had rubbed heads then. Francis moaning as the goat's bony pate had ground against his forehead. 'There Toggie. Hey.' He laughed as the goat searched for the soap Francis had learned to leave on his ear. Sniff, sniff, lick, lick, wee, wee. Francis knew the rhythm of the goat world well. He knew what would be appreciated too. 'Ok, Ok,' he said when Toggie stretched his head in. 'Wait a minute. There now. Hold it there.' Francis went out and confused the animal. His first approach was sensibly revoked with a shake of the head. Confusion took hold then. It manifested itself in a movement of ears that upset the goat's facial symmetry, leaving one ear forward and one back. What is wanted?, the look said, wanting meaning to be opened out, for the unusual to become the normal. 'This way. Come on.' Francis knew a push on the base of the goat's back would propel the animal forward. He applied it after Toggie had backed away from the window. The push moved him to the door. 'In you go.'

The goat was strutting now. The Egyptian look of the walk amused Francis. He knew it signified suspicion. Less obtrusive was a certain look, harder than normal, piercing even. What's wanted, it said, carrying a belief in Francis, a trust he had never really felt in humans. 'Go on,' urged Francis. 'No? Ok. Ok.' Francis moved in front of the goat and pulled back a magazine he had placed on a small coffee table. A slice of green appeared. It was enough to dispel the goat's doubts. An apple. The goat approached it and dug its teeth into it. 'Got it?' asked Francis, sitting down on the chair by the table. They were the only pieces of furniture in the room. 'Go on then. That's it,' he said, watching Toggie crane his neck to reach an apple by the matches at the side of the stove. 'My room. Apples,' said Francis. 'It means apples,' he added, laughing as a full apple shot out of the side of Toggie's mouth. The goat looked disapprovingly his way. 'Apples,' said Francis, picking up the apple and smiling at the goat.

It was the goats as much as the furniture that warmed the room. He thanked them for that. He shouted at them too when they knocked something over and left a smashed cup on the floor, but, at least, that uneven behaviour was nearly always remarkable. Not like his parents who occasionally showed themselves. His father tutting. His mother moaning. 'You can't put a bloody bed in here,' his father would say. 'Be damp in a bloody day. You'll ruin the bloody thing.'

'The shearers slept here.'

'Aye for a night or two once a bloody year.' His father shook his head at the transformation. His expression looked as though it was propped up. Disgust, thought Francis, trying to imagine what it was supposed to achieve. 'You can't stay here. Your mother'll break her heart. What's she supposed to think, eh? That this is better. Better than her house.'

'I like it.'

'Aye for a night or two. Ok.'

'The shearers used to like it.'

'Always bloody drunk they were. You could have put them in with the pigs and they'd have been smiling. But you. Bloody particular, you are.'

Francis couldn't compete with that. He knew what he wanted. He wanted to create layers, to talk of space and his need of it. He wanted to be precise, to talk of privacy and thought and expression, the need for freedom that travel fuelled. He wanted to take his father by the hand and be a good teacher, asking questions, giving praise, restating issues, but he knew his father wouldn't listen. There was no point. No point, thought Francis, staying silent.

The lack of response infuriated his father. He threw up his hands and sighed. His mother, too, was unaware of the issue. She spoke of food, washing, cleaning, but couldn't apply herself to the symbolism of such issues. It was the practicality that concerned her. 'Ridiculous,' she'd say, considering the suggestion of separate meals or washes. The interconnection and intimacy seemed secondary to her. They were hidden. Perhaps she didn't understand how they were assembled, what looseness allowed or meant and how affection could be maintained.

'Any more Francis? So what did he say?' Francis' mother turned her attention back across the table to his father. Francis was used to her eyes and ears having to divert back and fore at mealtimes, watching and listening while his father and he or his father and Gethin or Uncle Gwyn talked.

His mother enjoyed such times. She was in her element, controlling portions, directing what should be eaten and when. His dutiful mother. Francis considered her ambitions. The repression. The way it intruded on her relationships with people, yet somehow bounced off his father. He was unaware. Francis was sure of that. He was sure his father saw her as contented. The wanting, the desiring must have seemed a game to him. He discarded it easily. He walked away from it into the fields and treated it as derisively when he returned home. It was always there, but somehow the perspective of the day taught his father to ignore it, to let it have its moment and fade away. The contrasts, the friction made Francis wonder about the relationship. Was it just sex that had kept them together? He thought of all he had overheard when he was young, when he would sit on the landing listening. He had no comprehension of what it meant at the time. The secret life. The bedroom. He began to wish he hadn't intruded.

'I said no. What else could I say? I mean if he wants to play silly buggers than I can be the silliest bugger of them all. Doubled the price he had, blamed it on some chemical disaster in France. So I told him. I mean he wants the bun and the tuppence. The bun and the bloody tuppence,' repeated his father.

Francis smiled. He had expected a saying. He knew the pattern. It allowed him to think ahead and judge the applicability. This time he wasn't sure whether an apposite saying had been chosen. Others within his father's repertoire seemed more appropriate. Banana boat, he thought. I didn't come in on a banana boat. Even Clarence. That was used at any time when nothing appropriate was available. It was a sort of all-weather expression. 'So he won't be called Clarence any more,' thought Francis. The expression prolonged his smile.

'I'll be looking at his bill.' His father was still talking. 'Every bloody figure on it. If that bloody feed's gone up without him telling me, he can have it back.'

'You can't do that!' exclaimed his mother, pouring tea now.

'Can't I? You bloody wait. Willie bloody no arms.'

Francis smiled again. This time at the nickname. It was like a saying. It was certainly as good as a saying. The image it left was clear. It rang true as Francis thought over all his father had said about the feed salesman, about the meetings in the pub and his father paying. Francis always found that difficult to believe. Generosity had never seemed like one of his father's most prominent traits, though he always gave his father the benefit of the doubt. Money's tight, Francis would think.

'So not a good day. More Francis?' His mother was tempting him with a slice of lemon meringue pie. The prompting made Francis realise how easy it was to succumb to the three or four puddings his mother would provide for lunch and supper every day. He hadn't missed them in the States.

'You're not eating much,' remarked his mother still talking to him.

'Changed my diet,' he said slowly. 'Didn't eat half as much over there.'

'Eat like bloody horses, the Americans,' said his father. 'That's what Ena says.'

'Practices what she preaches too.' His mother suffixed his father's statement. 'Can't keep up with her when she's here.'

'Particularly the bloody gin,' laughed his father. 'How many bottles this time? Three, four. A couple of days she was here mind. Liquid bloody liver she's got. Bloody kill her it will.'

'You've been saying that for years.' remarked his mother. 'She's seventy six now.'

Francis laughed. He shook his head thinking how announcing he would be eating in his own room was difficult under such circumstances. It was probably badly timed, though Francis doubted if any time was congenial. After all he knew the announcement would be greeted with derision. Silence would be nice, he thought, something that signified understanding. But, when he managed the words, there was nothing like that. In its place were words which could have been grunts or groans.

'Bloody hell,' his father said, responding. 'You pick your bloody moments. I mean this is a bloody meal time.'

'So?'

'Well you make it sound like a meeting. I'm going to eat alone.' His father sounded disgusted as he managed an imitation. 'Point one on the bloody agenda, eh. What about an explanation?'

Francis sighed. He tried to contain the disdain he wanted to exhibit. He had to make an effort. He had to be considerate. He had to be reasonable. He told himself that, but he wondered if his father would facilitate such moderation, whether some sort of pitch of discontent would rise easily and early into the conversation. Francis took a deep breath and tried to find some words that would be acceptable. 'It's easier,' he said.

'No it bloody isn't. What do you mean easier?' His father shook his head. A salvo of looks passed back and fore between Francis' parents. They kept his mother silent. She looked hurt. His father looked mad. He was seething. Francis recognised that. He remembered the look.

'Bloody hell, so you can't eat with us now. What the hell's it coming to? And what do you mean easier?' his father asked again.

'I eat different things.'

'So? Tell your mother. She'll cook what you want.'

'I know that. I just need some space. Come on dad. I work with you all day long.'

'And what about your mother? Eh? What about your mother? You thought about her?'

Francis sighed again. He couldn't understand the argument about proximity, about being available to sit together at meal times. He was next door, across a farmyard. He made the point. 'Dad, I'll be twenty yards away. I'll see mum. It's not as though I'm in the States.'

'Ok. Ok.' His mother had sensed the need for intervention She brought both her hands down onto the table tapping it in a way that signified the end. It was time to be constructive. For her that meant acceptance of what Francis had said. The gesture seemed to work. It silenced his father. 'Right. You want to move. Fine. You want to eat your own meals. Fine. That's Ok.' She raised a hand to intercept any disagreement voiced by his father. 'You want independence. Ok. We should accept that. You'll need more money. We'll have to pay you a proper wage –'

'We can't afford it.' His father started to raise objections.

'We'll have to afford it,' said his mother matter of factly.

'I'll pay you rent.'

'We'll have to talk about that,' said his mother, a paragon of reasonableness now in Francis' eyes. He recognised the sense she had shown and smiled.

'Talk about it! See? It is like a meeting. A bloody union meeting. I tell you what, why don't we draw up a contract.? Would you like that? Would it suit you? Eh? Can't bloody answer that, can you? You're so bloody difficult. Thought you'd have learned.'

'What do you mean?'

'America. You came back. You came bloody back. Don't you see? I told you you would. All this I'll be away for bloody months.' His father laughed. 'You said that. In your bloody letters. You said it.'

'I was away nine months.' Francis sounded exasperated now.

'Aye, but you made it sound like years, bloody years. Then you're suddenly back here. No bloody letter. You just bloody turn up and we all know why.' His father nodded as his mother placed his meal in front of him. 'Not a bloody word,' his father tutted. It made Francis realise he had said nothing of his departure, of its haste. No excuses had been given. His father had just assumed some sort of acute home-sickness had struck or a nagging conscience picking on responsibility and duty had broken through. 'And now you're back, you've gone bloody silly again. Living in the shearers' shed. Not having meals with us.'

'I just want some independence. I'm used to it now. I've had nine months of it.'

His father chewed on the first fork load of food that had entered his mouth. He continued to hold up the fork, pointing it at Francis. 'That's what you bloody call it, is it? Independence,' he scoffed. 'You just want to make things bloody difficult. Always have done.'

'I'm going to do it.'

'What?'

'Eat by myself.'

'Yes, yes.'

'I am.'

'Right we'll start now then shall we?' His father smashed his right fist with the fork in its grasp onto the table. 'Keep that warm for me mother will you? I'll be in the big barn.'

It was the following day at supper time when Francis found himself writing. He had been out at lunch time buying bread and cheese in the village and had cut himself a sandwich and settled by the window. Immediately he saw he needed some sort of bench and chairs that could accommodate himself and pens, paper, sandwiches and coffee. He made a note of that, adding the items to a list and at the bottom of the page placed a reminder: ask dad for a budget. He began to think how he could broach that, how he could sort out the economics in a way his father could comprehend. Rent and property and responsibility suddenly seemed so urban, too modern for his father to untangle and make sense of. Something took over then. A thought. Toggie perhaps. Toggie entering the courtyard and lying on some dry hay in a sunny corner. Spotting Francis' attention, the goat momentarily stopped its ruminating, giving Francis an inquisitive gaze. Almost one of its stern looks, thought Francis, waiting for the gulp that would bring some more food up from its stomach. That was the sign that told Francis that his sitting in the window staring out had been accepted. It was the sign that Francis could join the tranquillity.

He was thinking of that, trying to choose a time and place and words to approach his father when he began to write. He had expected to draw. Like in the water tower. Fred perhaps or something more in tune with Brynlas. Something Welsh. A farmer. Fred the farmer, he thought. Or better still his father. Dai. Dai the farmer. That made him smile. But when the pencil touched the paper only words were produced. Somehow they seemed more necessary, fundamental to his understanding of where he was and what had happened. They started like a diary entry. Three weeks after America, he wrote on a file. He wrote about the flight home, about how he had changed, about work and the farm and Wales. Side after side were filled. He stopped now and then to read through the words. He conferred with them, laughed with them. Throughout, the words seemed to say going to America had been a starting point. It had shown him what could be attained. The elasticity of emotion. The dreams. The horizons. It gave him something to say. Particularly about the unknown. He focused on that. The collusion. Fritz and Zelda. What had they planned? How had they done it? When did they come together? There was nothing concrete there. He needed something to build on, some reality. Just a location would do. The meeting, he thought. The meeting after Zelda left the prison, the meeting between Zelda and Fritz. A conversation came to him. He tried to write it down, but the words were too quick. So he sat back. He enjoyed the intricacies of the words. The way they probed. The familiarity they gave Fritz and Zelda. It was as though they were there. It was as though he was hiding, listening. He imagined Fritz's voice.

'So he denied it?'

Francis smiled, filling in the features around the voice, the fat, smiling face looking as serious as it could. The 'he' was himself. Francis. Fritz's friend. Why not say Francis, he thought, a little disappointed with the formality. He concentrated again.

'So Francis denied it.'

That didn't work. It didn't fit the situation. Zelda's lounge. There was a necessary sombreness about the feel of it. This was her returning home. This was Fritz waiting. This was Fritz waiting to be told what was said, how Francis had responded. They were checking themselves too, checking they had done what was necessary, that they had been as fair as they could be to all parties, namely Francis and Ronnie, particularly Ronnie, and themselves.

Francis tried again. He closed his eyes, seeing where Fritz would sit, where Zelda would appear. Entrance left, he thought, directing it like a stage play. Enter Zelda, dressed for outdoors, looking white, shaken.

'So he denied it?'

'Yeh. You want a drink? Scotch? I have a scotch and soda every day at this time. Does you good, the doctor says. So I say fine. I mean if he's telling me, I'm listening. Boy am I listening.' Zelda left him and moved towards the kitchen. She kicked off her shoes as she walked. They fell against the chair with such precision that the movement looked rehearsed. It impressed Fritz.

'Hey that was some trick. How'd you do that? I mean without stopping. That's some trick. Jees.'

'What? Oh the shoes,' said Zelda, looking back. She kept the laughter going as she walked on into the kitchen and poured the drinks. 'Some trick,' she could hear Fritz say. It kept her laughing. 'Do it every day. When I come in,' she shouted, beginning the walk back to the main room. She moderated the tone of her voice as she walked into the room. 'I'm normally opening the mail, so I don't look. Gee I guess I hit the target, yeh?'

'Sure.' Fritz looked again at the shoes. They were facing outwards, leaning back on the chair. 'That sure is something. Top Gun Zelda, eh?' He laughed himself this time. Again he looked at the shoes. 'Wish I'd had a camcorder. Could play it back. View it in slo mo. You know like they do on the football games.'

'Football. You watch that shit?'

'Hey come on a man's gotta have his little pleasures, yeh?'

'Well try this.' Zelda offered him a glass with a generous portion of scotch. Fritz moved forward in his chair, smiled and accepted the glass. He maintained the smile as he closed his eyes and drank the whisky.

'Good?' asked Zelda as she turned and moved over to the double windows. She breathed deeply. 'It's so hot for heavensakes. Did they say it would be like this? Hey what you watching?' She felt Fritz's gaze on her as she moved away.

'I'm just watching you.'

'Me? What do you mean me?'

'You. I mean you.'

'Which bit of me?' Zelda giggled as she opened the window further.

'You wanna know.' Fritz took a slug of whisky and fell back in his chair.

'You like what you see?' Zelda's laugh covered a mix of excitement and gratitude. It said thanks for the compliment. She liked his honesty, his directness.

'Yeh, not bad at all.'

'You a connoisseur?'

'Yeh. Guess I am.'

'It's my best feature,' said Zelda, hitching up her skirt and wiggling provocatively. She had never felt such freedom with a man before. Somehow Fritz's manner and tone conducted it, brought it out and fine tuned it. She enjoyed the passion it provoked, the desire it cultivated.

'Hey come here.'

'Not now,' she said, turning and smiling. 'I'm going to sit here, a sofa's length away. You got long arms as well?'

'As well,' laughed Fritz, enjoying the nuances. 'Say you're a fuckin' wild lady. Someone out there should put a fence around this house with a sign saying scary woman. Yeh, beware scary woman.'

Zelda smoothed out her dress and reached forward to cup a glass. She took a swig of whisky and shut her eyes. 'So what do you think?'

'What about?'

'About the Welshman.'

'What's there to think? He's a pervert.'

'The nicest god damn pervert I've ever known.'

'Maybe. Yeh, s'pose. Yeh, he's nice. But doing things to little girls ain't nice. And what do you mean the nicest pervert you've ever known?' Fritz was laughing wildly now. 'So you know other perverts, yeh?'

Unlikely, thought Francis when it was over. Too intimate, he thought. He considered the lack of compatibility. A distance would be maintained. He was certain of that. Fritz would be in awe too. Francis suspected female company alone would censure his speech patterns and inhibit his expression. He would check his words, lose the spontaneity that made him appealing. Perhaps Zelda would sense the constraints and try to relax him. Francis wondered if that had already happened, whether during the week that Fritz had kept away from the water tower there were meetings with Zelda, whether a strategy had evolved. 'He couldn't fit it in,' Francis said softly to himself. Betty, the kids, golf, the garden, work. There was no slack in Fritz's life. One meeting, perhaps two, thought Francis. That seemed crucial. It meant formality would still be prominent, withering a little perhaps, but it would still be there. 'Ok, let's try again,' Francis said to himself, settling back in the chair. He closed his eyes, decided on a strategy and began to write.

'So he denied it?'

'Yeh.'

'You look shocked.' Fritz shuffled in the seat. He was on his best behaviour. The house had demanded that. Fritz had never seen such a slick look. Minimalist, he had thought. Certainly it was economical in its use of colour and furniture. The clean, large gaps cried out for imagination, yet seemed imaginative. Their placement did that. They trapped the eye. They held it while imagination roamed.

When Zelda poured a drink, Fritz's imagination considered the light touch, skittish almost, that had developed the room, how it had contrived to make it empty, yet full. The sculpture made it full. Sculpture needs space. Fritz saw that. He liked the way it provoked. It took over almost. It demanded concentration.

'You think he did it?' Zelda shouted as a spoon hit the side of a glass. The noise stopped and she reappeared.

'He had the opportunity. Hey listen to me. I sound like Perry Mason.'

'More like Colombo.'

'You think? Hey I like him. Betty likes him too. He's one of the few guys who stops her dancing.'

'Betty?'

'Mrs. Semmler. My wife.'

'She dances?'

'Perpetual motion,' laughed Fritz. 'Except for Colombo and anything with Warren Beatty in it. She loves Warren Beatty. Says he reminds her of me. And I believe anything.'

Zelda laughed. She sat back on her seat and put a hand through her hair. 'You remind me of someone,' she said suddenly, leaning forward to grab the copy of Halliwells that was on the edge of the table. 'Could be Colombo.'

'Me? No. He's clever.'

'No, I mean looks.'

'Looks? God he's cross-eyed. No. Look. See? I look straight.' He held up one finger, indicating some sort of test. 'Yeh I see fine. Two fingers, yeh?'

Again Zelda laughed. 'Oh yeh,' she said, turning the page of Halliwells. 'Joe Pesci. You seen him? *Goodfellas.* Yeh *Goodfellas*, that's it. I bet you speak like him too.'

'What d'you mean? You hear how I speak.'

'You haven't seen the film. He swears a lot. I mean Joe Pesci does. In the film.'

'Oh yeh, so how do you know I don't fuckin' swear?'

The laughter told Fritz he was free to swear, that the overwhelming control that stifled him could be left aside. He could relax now. He felt an immediate sense of relief and enjoyment.

'Ok, Ok. That's enough of me. What about Francis?'

'What about him?' emphasised Zelda. 'He's gone. Simple as that.' She was reading through the credits and comments on *Goodfellas*. 'What's there to say?'

Francis began to think of Ronnie too. Ronnie with Brad, Ronnie talking about Brad, Ronnie resembling Brad. All thoughts of Ronnie were linked with Brad. That was the key relationship now. It demanded scrutiny, though Francis wasn't sure what triggered a thought or recollection pertaining to it. Something major like a situation, something minor like a word could trigger it. Hearing his mother talk of Ena and her relationship with her father certainly did. Father, daughter, difficulties. The ingredients were perfect. It made him make excuses and make for the shearers' shed. He wrote there, scribbling dialogue, transcribing the words Ronnie said in the tower, how she had once started to take off her clothes.

'Hey what you doing?'

'It's hot.'

'So?'

Ronnie gave him a look that said she was appalled that he didn't link heat and bare bodies. Her eyes displayed disbelief. They were half closed, puzzled looking. 'Daddy takes his clothes off.'

'So?'

'So I do too. I always have up here. It gets so hot.'

'Yes but you can't stay. Not today.'

'Why not?' She looked disappointed now. Her face adopted a glummer look. It did that by dropping the edges of her mouth. Her eyes stayed almost the same. Quizzical, thought Francis, but with slightly more strain.

'I'm due out.'

'So? I can stay. I'll read or draw.'

'If you want.' Francis didn't want to sound severe or school-masterly. He smiled.

'And I can take my clothes off, yeh? It's no big deal.' Ronnie laughed at the look of concern on Francis' face. She didn't understand its source.

'I know about boys and girls,' she said slowly.

'You do,' said Francis, not understanding what she meant. He was used to moments like this. The logic crossed. The child on some other wavelength, smiling away, thinking they were communicating easily. Ronnie smiled now. He saw it and smiled back.

'Yeh. Boys have willies, girls have flowers. I know that.'

'Good,' said Francis, unsure how to react, whether he should make something of the point or stay calm, relaxed. He decided on the latter. 'You'll be Ok?,' he asked. 'I mean by yourself? You know what I've said about over there.' He waited for the girl to acknowledge the question. She nodded. 'Right. You don't touch anything.' Anything was the stove, which he would disconnect anyway before he left when Ronnie wasn't looking.

'Daddy used to leave me here. I'll be fine. I like it here.' She began to unbutton her blouse.

'You sure?'

'Gee yeh. This is better than the house. No boys here. And no mum. Mum makes me wear shorts and things. I tell her it's too hot.'

'Ok,' said Francis, embarrassed and hurrying. He stood for a second to take in the abandon of the girl. The lack of inhibitions seemed healthy. He couldn't denounce it, yet it made him edgy. He looked away from the girl. She was naked now. Flowers and willies, he thought, wanting to laugh as he looked for a pullover.

Somehow returning from the fields the next day to find Toggie in the shearers' room eating bananas also stirred memories. Toggie just looked around. He gave Francis one long look and then continued to munch away. Francis continued to stare at him. His annoyance at the loss of a bowl of bananas gave way to intrigue. Why did the goat leave the stalks? Every one was left, discarded with a disdainful shake of the mouth. What was wrong with stalks? Goats are so rarely discriminating, thought Francis, watching Toggie spit out another stalk. Francis thought how nice it was for him to find something beneath the skin. The goat was normally only given the skins. To find flesh inside and such lovely flesh was a real treat.

'Toggie,' said Francis in a mocking way, picking up the stalks and the paper, pens and calculator, all of which had been knocked over by the goat in his struggle with the bowl. Somehow the fruit bowl had stayed on top of the table. Francis wondered how, taking out the remainder of the bananas and hand feeding them to the goat. 'Another,' he said. 'Just one more then. Used to be Ronnie waiting for me,' he said, remembering coming home early from work in Texas. That one thought developed the memory. The silence of the wood. The empty look of the wooden bungalow. He recalled crying out. There was no reply. He remembered climbing up the ladder of the tower, dropping in, seeing Ronnie.

'Hi.'

'How you doing? Nobody about?'

'Momma is,' said Ronnie

'She didn't reply,' said Francis, laying his coat on the bed.

'She's waiting for Miss Pitton.'

'Miss Pitton?'

'My music teacher. Picks me up on the way to singing. I hate Miss Pitton. That's why I'm here. I've got my dolls. See? You have dolls?'

'Me?'

Ronnie's laugh acknowledged her mistake. 'Hey you're a boy. I forget that. Boys don't have dolls.'

'Don't they?'

'No. Boys have cars and things.'

Francis smiled at Ronnie. He took it as a compliment. It was like being accepted. Part of the crowd, he thought. He decided he liked the feeling. He felt it on his face. The lines. His eyes widely open. He moved his head back, the smile becoming faint. It would need detection to find it now. A long look, perhaps. A glance wouldn't do. Neither would any approach that was partly in tune with the conversation. Total involvement was needed.

'You're quiet,' observed Ronnie.

'Am I?' To Francis it seemed a strange observation. It was something most children would have missed. Ronnie, though, was different from most children. She seemed more aware of moods and tensions, more aware of atmospheres. Francis wondered why. He pressed the inquiry. 'What makes you think that?' he asked.

'Oh I don't know. You just are. You're like me when I've got to be good.'

Francis smiled. 'When have you got to be good?'

'When I want something. When I want some candy. Or a new doll. Or some clothes. You know. Momma makes me sit in a corner and count under my breath.'

'Count?'

'Yeh. Like this.' She moved to a corner, closed her eyes and began to count.

'Right,' said Francis, trying to restore her to the conversation.

'Hey I only got to ten,' she objected. The objection turned into a laugh. Don't be so silly, it said. It stopped and started. Like a struggling engine. Francis was glad when it died, then alarmed when it rose up again. Suddenly it seemed indulgent. He wondered what it was prompting, whether he should say something. He hoped it would peter out or be taken over by something.

'Sometimes I get to forty,' Ronnie said, regaining control. 'Sometimes sixty. Depends.'

Francis was left to imagine when it would be used. He considered the scene. A distraught Pam. Ronnie taunting. Like now. Keep quiet, Pam's voice would say. Ronnie would be investigating, probing, demanding attention when all Pam wanted was blandness. There was comfort for her in that. A moment to herself. It wasn't much to ask for, so she thought up schemes, ways of acquiring silence that wouldn't offend Ronnie, ways of getting Ronnie to go to her room and play with her dolls. There could be anything up to half an hour in that. Enough time to get working on a quilt, thought Francis.

'Dad does it too,' said Ronnie suddenly, breaking up Francis' thoughts.

'Brad?'

'Yeh. He pays me.'

'For keeping quiet?'

'Can't say,' she said with a laugh, throwing herself back onto the floor. She looked around at her dolls. A black one was selected and put down, then a blond, long-haired doll was picked up. She felt the dress. 'Mum made this,' she said. 'She's good at that. Making things. Do you make things?'

After the recall he would assess what he had learnt, putting it in the context of the accusation of abuse and the way it may have incriminated Brad. Brad, Brad, Brad, he'd think, all the time focusing, almost cutting Ronnie out as he profiled the man. Brad who had isolated him, Brad who had made him friendless and numb. Brad.

'I know about boys and girls.... Daddy takes his clothes off.... I can take my clothes off, it's no big deal....'

Francis used Ronnie's words like a cross examination. They were questioning Brad, saying what does this mean? They all pointed to

213

what was going on. But it seemed too easy. Francis thought that. Draw back, a voice in his head was saying. It was telling him the importance of context, the importance of bearing in mind just what a relationship between a father and child could involve. Perhaps it was all his own experience with his father had lacked. With them there had been no closeness, no hint of any form of intimacy. Building what Ronnie had intimated onto what he knew of his own relationship with his father almost made Francis cry. He would have liked a water tower for his father and himself, a place where they would have shared some space and taken notice of what each other was doing. Cowboy books and maps, thought Francis, laughing at the activities. But at least there were activities: they were possibilities that could have connected them. We could have had secrets, he thought, shaking his head.

The moment passed. What he learnt ushered it on. It left him believing Zelda and Fritz would have become contemplative too, that they would have thought over occasions when Brad said something or did something out of place. Something would have given him away. Something would have made Zelda or Fritz sense the truth. Especially Fritz, thought Francis. Fritz knew Brad as well as he did. Francis took comfort in that. It made him reach for a pen. He abbreviated what came to him, concentrating only on dialogue. Like a play, he thought, hearing the words. His mind played them, forcing them out into a scene. Lights, action, he thought, settling back, waiting for Fritz's voice to arrive on cue.

'So he denied it?'

'Yeh.' Zelda sat down and pushed a hand over her dress. She smoothed it out. 'You like it?'

'The dress?' Fritz followed the nod that told him to sit down. He fell back into the nearest chair and slumped against its back. He found it hard to imagine Francis was no longer in the States, that he was on his way home. It made him want to recover the past and reorder it, to firm up a dominant meaning. Love. Affection. He began to pin down associations and put the people in. It seemed to work. He hadn't sensed any evil, any wrongdoing. He felt a little ashamed for missing that. 'Why didn't we see it? You think it was him?'

'Who else could it have been? Of course it was him.' Zelda was quick to sense a need to provide balance. She, too, had been caught out, the consummate charm of Francis' vulnerability dominating her view of him.

'He seemed too... well, too nice,' said Fritz.

'Naive?'

'Yes –'

'My mom always said, don't trust the quiet ones.'

'It wasn't that,' Fritz objected. He stopped short of going on. Some instinct had interrupted him. It dealt in simplicities, feelings. Francis was good, it said. Francis could harm no-one. It was like a labelling. It made him wonder how others viewed him. What label he wore. 'Gee I'm not sure I can explain.'

'I understand,' said Zelda, quite softly.

'You do?' Fritz laughed.

'Yes, yes I do. You mean...well... You mean he was sort of child-like, vulnerable. He trusted people.'

'Yeh, yeh that's right. He did.' Fritz was surprised by Zelda's assessment. He hadn't thought her capable of it. She seemed too absorbed to observe and consider. Self, self, self, he thought. The epitome of individuality. He hadn't expected any semblance of sensitivity or perception. But she was right. Spot-on, in fact, he thought. Francis was naive. Francis was quiet. Francis was vulnerable. Francis did trust people.

'Dominated by his mother probably. He was kind of strange. Don't you think? I mean you guys hung around together. He used to tell me that.'

'He liked his mother,' remarked Fritz. 'I mean he sort of told me he got on with her. Didn't get on with his father.'

'See. Gee I knew it. I guess all the Oedipus stuff applies.'

'Hey hold on. I like my mother,' objected Fritz.

'Yeh, yeh. I guess most people do. So what was it then, repression?'

'Guess so. But we can't be sure.' Fritz's tone conveyed his doubts. 'What about Brad? We know more about him.'

'That's what rules him out. Heavensakes he was too darn macho. Don't you see that?'

'Macho?' Fritz almost laughed. 'What's macho got to do with it?'

Zelda's expression showed surprise. She hadn't expected such a remark. Fritz could see that. He could sense her confusion. He could see the disbelief in her eyes. He knew she was suspicious of him. The joker. The wild man. He knew what she thought of him. But he had tried to dispel such doubts. Now he had blown it. He had surprised her. She was wondering now what line he would take.

'Don't you see?' asked Fritz, quite slowly. 'Don't you see the danger?'

'Danger? Hey hold on now what are you saying? What do you mean danger?'

'I mean danger. The danger of instincts.' Fritz took care over his

215

choice of words.' God damn it Zelda Brad had no controls, no shield. He had no shyness, no fear. Christ most of us are afraid of consequences, of trying things out. Brad wasn't. He had confidence. He was the big man. Look at me, that's what his body language said, you know, when he walked in the room. Look at me, that's what he said. He had drive, he had initiative. He thrived on instincts.'

'So you think he could have done it? To Ronnie?'

'Sure.'

Zelda shook her head. 'But you saw what he was like with those kids.'

Fritz nodded. He thought of the tree house, how Brad had called him in to find it, how he had asked him to pretend not to see it, even when it was obvious where it was and his status with the boys was likely to diminish. Fritz had agreed. He remembered turning circles in the wood, calling out, the boys half giggling in their hideaway. He felt stupid. He realised that now. He hated the performance. It grated. The self-castigation was severe, particularly as only Brad knew the truth and the boys' pre-eminence kept him quiet. To them, Fritz had not seen it.

'I'll get you a drink.' Zelda broke the silence. She stood up and moved to the kitchen.

'Sorry,' Fritz shouted.

'Sorry?'

'I guess you're right. He wouldn't harm them. I mean he'd do anything for them.'

'Yeh. That's right. It's kind of chilling really. But yeh, he loved them.'

Sounds took over. Cups being found, switches being pressed, kettles being filled. Fritz listened and slumped back, staring at the ceiling. He felt as though he was turning again, how Zelda was conveniently drawing him to focus on the boys. What about the boys? What about the Jim MacDonalds, the men he fought with in bars? That was his real life. It made his relationship with the boys seem to have more to do with his reconstructed battles of the Civil War than with life in the bungalow with its two bedrooms and a water tower. The common ground was imagination. He was abdicating reality.

'Here.'

'What about Pam?' Fritz asked, accepting the glass.

'Oh shit that's another story.'

'Brad's fault?'

Zelda stirred in sugar and moved slowly in her seat. It was as though she was rocking herself. Like a child, thought Fritz. Calming herself. Giving herself a sense of security, a sense that all was well. He smiled, trying to help the feeling along. It seemed to work. Zelda stopped moving and stared at the wall. She thought how there was a touch of irritability about the mixing of the images – Brad with the boys; Brad with Pam. They didn't go. They seemed like different people. Control against impotence, she thought. She shrugged knowing how he reacted to such forces. Fantasy and reality, she thought, shaking her head, unhappy with the divorcing of the two.

'What do you think? I mean you must have some opinion. You know, leaving bias aside. I mean forgetting about blood and all that shit. What do you think?'

'Brad's fault,' she said emphatically.

'Yeh,' Fritz accepted the point and let it rest. He didn't want to push the persecution, to detail all he knew because he felt the immaturity he would convey would be seen as building a case against Brad. Somehow the dual personality of Brad that he and Zelda recognised, seemed to separate the bad and the good in him. The two never mixed. He was sure of that, as sure as Zelda seemed to be.

'Brad's,' she said again, emphasising the point.

Christmas came. Francis made up lists. Shopping lists. Christmas presents mostly. He talked to himself as he ran through the possibilities. 'Dad? A jumper. What did I get him last year? Not a jumper? No. Those bloody American wellingtons. Right. So it will have to be grey. Wool. No patterns. He hates patterns. Good,' he said above the Radio 3 music his mother loved listening to. 'Now Mum. Always difficult, mum. Another jumper, perhaps. Yes, why not. Patterns this time. Something stripy. Doesn't like dots. Remember that. No dots.'

It was in Swansea after a series of ticks filled his list that he found himself looking at model farms in a toy shop. 'We can put your name on the house,' an assistant, hovering behind him said. He held a long smile as Francis turned towards him.

'You'll paint it on?'

'That's what it means, custom made.'

'One name?'

'Yes.'

'My name?'

'If you want?'

'No,' smiled Francis. 'I mean my house name'

'Yes. Whatever you want. It's nine pounds extra.'

'For the name?' Francis opened up his eyes and shook his head. 'That's one pound something a letter. Better leave it blank.'

The assistant smiled and, seeing more likely opportunities of a sale elsewhere, moved away. Francis felt better then. He preferred selling the farm to himself. He liked marking the details, finding fault with anatomy and questioning the pose the modeller had chosen. Cows were sitting, lambs were running, goats were butting. 'No,' said Francis, picking up the male Saanen goat. He looked it over, examining details. 'Ah,' he said as a male Toggenburg caught his eye.

'You like it sir?' said another assistant approaching him.

'Toggenburg meadowlark,' said Francis, thinking of Toggie. He transferred Toggie's smile to the model's face. He imagined him breaking into gardens and picnics, jumping into the air to fight with Zoon.

'Comes in various sizes. I mean you pay for the number of pieces you have with the farm. The farm's basic.'

'I'll take him –'

'Him?'

'Just him. Just the one. The Toggenburg.'

Francis went back and bought the set. The biggest set. It was perfect for Ronnie. He knew that. He smiled at it. It made him feel pleased with himself. It was like finding the right expression when writing or detecting the right moment to move into conversation. Like waiting for the kill, he thought, applying one of his father's analogies. It gave him pleasure. He knew the farm worked. He could imagine Ronnie sitting in front of it. 'Where's that Toggie? Toggie's got his coat on,' she would say, talking to it. She would enhance the contents, bringing sounds and smells to animals. She would see beyond the poses. Francis knew that. He knew that she would mix it with nature, that she would take it through the seasons. The languor of summer, the gambol of spring, he thought. She would milk the cows and ride the horses.

He packed it in Christmas paper. Red paper with white dots for falling snow and small Christmas trees with candles on branches to light up the snow. Brown paper was placed over the wrapping. He sent it to Fritz with a note saying: 'Ronnie's present. Make sure she has it. If you can't put my name on it, put yours. She'll enjoy it. I know she will.'

It took him ages to write the note. He kept stopping at full stops, ending sentences and thinking of the water tower, of the time Ronnie had drunk orange juice and stared at some of his photos. Brynlas seemed to astonish her. The look on her face told Francis she had never seen a house like it. 'You live there?' she shrieked. The photograph was taken from the valley. The perspective made it look as though it was perched on a mountain top. It could just be picked out through the verdant, summer look of the trees. 'Gee. It looks so different.'

'To the houses here? It is. Can you see what its made of?'

'Squares, I guess' laughed Ronnie, looking more closely at the photograph. 'Yeh. Sort of big squares. All sizes.'

'Stone. It's stone.'

'Aren't all houses stone?'

'Yours isn't,' laughed Francis. He shook his head thinking how Ronnie had a habit of observing small things and overlooking the major. He wondered what processes filtered what was significant.

'Oh no,' laughed Ronnie. She was giggling now, absorbing a thought that was correcting her. 'No. It's wood. Yeh. Wooden deck, wooden walls. Yeh, it's wood.'

'That's right.'

'Why? Why's it wood? Why not stone?'

'Depends where you are, I suppose. What the weather's like. What materials are available.'

'So we've got better weather.'

Francis' face pulled a look of surprise. He wondered where such a conclusion came from. He wanted to ask. He thought quickly. Phrasing, phrasing, phrasing, his mind was saying as he tried to find the words that would make his inquiry meaningful to Ronnie.

'Oh yeh. I see,' she said, still staring at the photograph. 'Big trees,' she observed. 'So green. Much greener than here. We're just a little bit green. What does that mean?'

'Worse weather?' suggested Francis. 'What do plants need?'

Ronnie looked serious. She thought over the question. 'Ground,' she said. 'Dirt, I guess.'

Francis decided to help her. 'Why's it so dry here?' he asked.

'Oh rain. Yeh.' She suddenly got excited. It told Francis she liked the rain. 'Hey I like the rain, don't you? My pa doesn't. He gets annoyed. He chases me up here.'

'When it rains?'

'No. When I get wet.'

'Why?' Francis could see the question didn't impress Ronnie. It put an exasperated look on her face.

'Because momma doesn't like me getting my clothes wet. Gee I love the rain. So I get wet. I like playing in the rain, splashing in puddles and things. Oh yeh.'

Francis began to wonder how Brad fitted in. 'So why does your father get annoyed?'

'Oh he's not really annoyed. Just sort of annoyed. Because be knew momma would shout. So he'd take me up here to change. Kept spare sets of clothes up here. Pretty clothes. I'd only wear them up here. He'd dry my clothes in the drier. He used to like to see me in my pretty clothes, I guess. He'd buy them for me. They were my secret clothes. Momma never saw them.'

Francis came to question the sense of sending the present. It was more for himself than Ronnie. That was its fundamental flaw. But somehow it had to go. It was the present he had always wanted to give her. That makes it Ok then, he thought. His doubts came from the way it made her seem younger. Younger than eight, he thought, working on it, convincing himself that it didn't matter, that it was easier to regress than progress, that there was always comfort in picking up old toys and immediately conquering them. Instances from his own childhood immediately came to mind. They supported the view. He recalled how he had always enjoyed toys. They were like old friends. He thought how there was reassurance in knowing the game or how the toy would behave, whether it would move or make a noise. Even then life seemed messy. Permanently messy, he thought, switching back to adult life and the new comfort factors: his writing, Toggie and Zoon, his father. His father! That surprised him. It was as much confirmation of the power of communication, of the benefits of making an effort. One conversation had done it. One relaxed moment when something unremarkable – he couldn't remember what – had opened things up. Ideas and views had flowed in then. They had found a meeting place.

And it was that that had compounded his belief in the need for familiarity and change. Resilience and experiment, he thought, all sorts of images coming and going. An image of his railway set stayed. The one that filled a room and was too big ever to be put out, the one his father stayed up all night one Christmas Eve assembling. He remembered Christmas morning. The anticipation. The joy. The disappointment as his father monopolised the controls. The way frustration led him to power the Orient Express through the closed gates of the level crossing when he was finally given a go. 'Upstairs you!' his father bellowed. 'I've been up all bloody night putting that together. All bloody night mark you.'

He could laugh at that now. It was easy. He knew his father would laugh too.

'Francis –'

'Hey that's good timing.'

'What do you mean?' His father walked into the room. Concern came across his face. It seemed to hit him whenever he visited the shearers' shed that Francis now occupied. Francis wondered whether it was prompted by the Spartan look of the room or the smell. 'Goat wee,' said Francis. 'I like them coming in, but there's a price to pay.'

'No carpets here then,' his father remarked. 'Be bloody cold in winter. Bare concrete.' Francis' father enjoyed pointing out the faults and the hassles. He believed Francis would be back in the main house by winter.

Francis nodded. He smiled too. He respected the concern. It was genuine. 'You remember that Christmas with the train set?'

'Train set! Is that what you called it. More like a bloody model of the British railway system.'

'The pre-Beeching railway system,' laughed Francis, remembering how his father had previously described it.

'God aye. It was huge.' Francis' father stopped and thought. The reflection suited his ageing face. It touched humour into it, warming it up. 'You crashed it. You bugger. I remember now. Took a bend too fast.'

'No I didn't'

'You did.'

'No. It wasn't a bend.'

'What was it then?'

'A level crossing.'

'Oh hell aye. I remember now.' A broad grin filled his father's face. 'I didn't shout though.'

'You did. You shouted and shouted. You called it your set. Said you'd been up all night putting it together.'

'I had,' said his father sounding reflective as though he was reclaiming that night, assembling the moments. He seemed to enjoy it, seeing Francis as he was, seeing himself as he was. There was a burden about it, the responsibility clinging. The pride clinging too. Francis knew where such thoughts led, how his father always focused on how Francis was like him, how physically there had been a resemblance. It had faded with time. Francis was more like his mother now. Angular, sharp. The puppy fat shed. Transferred almost thought Francis catching a glimpse of his father's ever fattening face in the mirror.

As he studied it, Francis saw the gaze and sensed the abstraction. 'What's wrong?' he asked softly.

'Nothing. Nothing wrong.' Francis' father shifted his attention back to Francis. 'No nothing wrong. Just seeing you as you were, doing a now and then. You were like me, you know?'

'Was I?'

'God aye. Used to take you out in the pram.'

'You?'

'Yes. Course I did. You wouldn't remember. Too bloody young you were. Used to take you down the village. Hey why you laughing?'

'Oh nothing,' said Francis, shaking his head. There was something calming about the image, something cosmetic and manufactured. It was what all fathers did, up until now all except his.

'Oh I was proud of you. I was. You looked like me. My son. And you bloody looked like me. Only one bull in that field they used to say.'

'What?' laughed Francis, surprised at hearing a new saying.

'Only one bull in the field. It's a saying.'

'Hello.' His mother's voice led her body into the room. She was smiling, pleased to sense the growing association of father and son. 'Thought I'd bring you the mail. Looks as though there's a card from Texas.'

Surprisingly Francis didn't rush to mull over the words. Rather, he stared at the front of the card. It surprised him. It seemed un-Fritz-like. He expected something humorous, something saying how daft Christmas was. The card disappointed him. It was sober, dull. Ordinary thought Francis. It could have sat amongst the other cards that draped the mantelpiece. He looked at the illustration on the card a second time. There was a car running downhill. A Victorian looking man was driving his family, the implication being they were rushing home for the festivities. The implication seemed like the only link with Texan life, the rest was a cold, crisp English Christmas, the sort the rest of the world seemed to dream of.

Francis thought the message wouldn't be as disappointing. It couldn't be. It's from Fritz, he kept telling himself. The message would be powerful, open. He was sure of that. It would tell him what had happened after his departure. It would allow him to write the scene definitively, to get the nuances right. Nothing would be stifled there, he told himself. Nothing would be compromised. He was sure of that. Before he opened the card, he thought too how he would be satisfied with a yearly instalment, a Christmas update. It would be like a height chart in a room, a marker labelling a date, the chart monitoring progress. He would enjoy that.

'So he denied it?'

'Yeh.' Zelda nodded and put her coat away. She smoothed down her dress, surreptitiously stealing looks in the mirror to check for creases. Nodding an approval she moved away. 'He denied it. God, what do you make of it? He knows the truth. He knows the situation he's in. So why god damn lie? Why not come clean?'

'Because he's got to fight it. He's got nothing to lose. He's got to sort himself out, get a story together. God he's got the time for that. All those hours. Shit.'

'Hey don't feel sorry for him. I saw him. You gotta believe he's coping.' Zelda's hard gaze tried to chase away the sympathy Fritz had offered.

'You put it on,' said Fritz, laughing.

'Put it on?'

'Yeh. You cover it up. You feel sorry too. Sometimes you do.'

'You know, do you?'

'Seen it.'

Zelda laughed. She thought back over the interview room. Table, chair, she thought, nothing else. The bareness stayed with her. It echoed in the words she remembered. The click of the door. The shutter to look through. The detail returned. The touch of fright on Francis' face. His reaction to her words. Relief. Pain.

'Ok, Ok.' Fritz looked a little unsettled. He fidgeted, touching his face, rubbing his chin, then the side of his nose. 'But he's not going to say yeh man I did it. Would you? Hell no. Particularly Francis.'

'What do you mean particularly Francis? What's so special about Francis?'

'I tell you what was important. Trust. That's what. It's what he felt he never had. I know. He told me.'

Zelda listened acutely. She had never heard details of Francis' home and life. That was remote. Too intimate and distant from the focus of their interaction which had always been Ronnie. Ronnie, Ronnie, Ronnie, thought Zelda. Nothing but Ronnie, Ronnie this, Ronnie that. She thought of the evasion, the trickery. The long tales. The spoofs.

'He wouldn't do it.' Fritz seemed definite now. His head was shaking. Zelda tried to concentrate on his face. It seemed intense, focused. She imagined his mind calling up situations, replaying conversations, emphases were being analysed and taken in. It was all manipulating, developing opinions.

'You seem sure,' she finally said. An extended pause had developed. She had watched a smile on Fritz's face come and go.

'I just sort of sense he wouldn't do it. He's not the type.'

'And Brad is?'

'Jesus!' The possibility seemed to take Fritz by surprise. He abhorred the idea. Brad. Brad the father. Brad the friend, his best friend. God no. He couldn't even consider the possibility. It made him close his eyes. Zelda spotted the look. It indicated how distasteful Fritz found the possibility. She thought how the light look of meditation suited him best. He readopted it. A slight nervousness brought tremors of movements to his eyes and lips. The movements were irregular and unpredictable. It was like a game, as though features of his face were pitted against each other. His eyes win, she thought, seeing them adopt a steely look that was cold and clear. It gave nothing away.

'Did Brad use the room?' he asked.

'Don't know. Hey how would I know?'

She waited a moment and tried to interpret any movement in Fritz's face. 'He did, didn't he? He had his fucking battles there before he moved them to the shed. Did Ronnie go there?'

'Don't know.' Zelda raised her voice emphatically. She covered her thoughts of battles, of the way Brad would talk through them with her and their brother, how each year Brad had a new battle or greater knowledge of a battle already discussed. Paul encouraged it. He made Brad bring in plans or papers and plastic soldiers. He made Brad go beyond a commentary. She remembered feeling bored. She remembered the way he would get excited, the way his stories were like sermons. 'I don't know,' she repeated. 'I mean I don't know him. I don't know whether he could do it.'

'Hey come on. You know what he did to Pam.'

'Yeh. Yeh I know. I also know what he was like with the boys –'

'But not with Ronnie?'

'No.' Quickly she ran through their meetings, the way words skirted around Ronnie, how she was always fine, nothing more or less, just fine. 'No. Not with Ronnie,' she said.

While he considered the scene and smiled at the way he had moved Brad into the frame, all Francis wrote on the paper in front of him was 'No reply'. Nothing else. Instead of writing, he let the scene flow. He let it fill his mind. The words that were left on the page were like a doodle. Sometimes they were insignificant; sometimes they showed what was bothering him. Francis thought how the latter applied in this case. Fritz hadn't written. 'No reply,' he said, reading his words. They were in capitals sprawled across an A3 sheet. He underlined the words in red. Double underlined them. Then he picked up a ruler and drew lines up the sides of the words, the front and the back, and across the top. Like a box. The lines contained the words. Then he shaded the area outside the box black. He made it look like a car number plate.

'Surprised,' he said to himself. It summed up all he was thinking. He knew Fritz wasn't a correspondent, but to be asked to say yes or no didn't seem overly demanding. He couldn't work it out. He knew it was all down to discipline and that Fritz was always chasing rather than leading, that he was never in command. The kids, the wife, golf, work, the garden, something was always calling. Realisation of that should have made him picture his letter on a breakfast table or a desk. Coffee cups perched on it, perhaps. Round stains circling words.

Yet none of that could keep the disappointment away. He wanted to write again. He wanted to tell Fritz he was his only link, the only voice he had left in the world. He wanted to pull the harshest look he had ever pulled, to find the most threatening word, but something pulled him back and told him how volatile Fritz was, how it would all be counterproductive. At least he sent a Christmas card, he told himself. At least once a year his name would be on a list and Fritz would say, 'Fuck you Welshman. How you doing?'

Lambing was starting. Always late here, thought Francis looking at his home-made calendar on the wall. He liked his calendar. It was one of the first things he made when he moved into the shearers' shed. He remembered setting it up. He wrote out the dates, carefully checking when the month started and ended, and used photos of Brynlas to illustrate the month. Subtle, he thought, evaluating its role in the room's conversion to something warmer, something more intimate.

He thought that as he turned the page of the calendar over, transforming February into March. Toggie smiling with his ears sticking out as he rubbed heads with Gethin became Toggie jumping over a fence. The grace of the goat momentarily held Francis. Goat elegance always captivated him. It was so easily acquired. Each movement was long and exaggerated. Even closing an eye is lovely, he was thinking, when his mother opened the door.

'Forty minutes.'

'Ok,' said Francis, knowing what was meant. 'How's it going?' he asked referring to the lambing.

'Good. Not sure of numbers. But your father seemed happy. I can tell,' laughed his mother, recognising the knowing look on Francis' face. 'Just one look and I know.'

'You know him well.'

'Course. He's easy to know. Remember last year when he lost those twins? God the look. Horror? Pity? I don't know.'

Francis nodded at the memory. He recalled how his mother had written to him in America saying lambing had started badly, that his father had blamed Gethin and the weather, but mostly Gethin. There had been no explanations. Complications didn't come into it. Gethin had been there. Guilt by connection, rage by association, his mother had written.

'Don't be late,' she warned.

'Not me. I know better,' smiled Francis.

'Mind you he's going soft –'

'Dad?'

'Aye. He's talking about changing the heating. About getting oil in. He's heard it's good.'

'Oh has he?' said Francis, wanting to laugh at the confusion on his mother's face. She shrugged and moved away. He watched her cross the yard. The wellingtons too large for her. The waterproof jacket too large too. She would like to be graceful, he thought. She would have liked a little gentility. 'Thirty nine minutes,' he said to himself, his eye catching the clock. He wondered where Toggie was, then what he should do. Shaking his head, he moved over to the bed in the corner and sat down. 'No reply,' he said, remembering the letter he was owed by Fritz. 'Yes or no. All he had to say. Yes or no. One word,' he said, tutting. 'Guilty conscience,' he said to himself, returning to thoughts of Brad. Culpable Brad, Brad the baddie, he thought, letting his mind see Zelda's room with the sculpture and Halliwell's and Fritz and Zelda.

'So he denied it?'

'Yeh.'

'Guess I'll have to write,' said Fritz, moving off the chair. 'You sit down. You're bushed. Hell of a place, jail. I'll get you a drink. Don't say you could murder one,' laughed Fritz.

'Thanks.' Zelda smiled. She sat back and closed her eyes. It was all for effect. She hoped Fritz saw it, that he wouldn't know her well enough to class it as self-conscious or self-absorbed. She sighed. And yawned. The movements of her face timed to catch an eye before it pulled away.

'Right then. Coffee. Hey and I've got a pizza booked. That Ok? For ten to eight.'

'That was five minutes ago.'

226

'Was it? Hell it was. Guess those guys are always late.' Fritz turned and double checked the clock. 'You want an appetiser?'

'No. There's no need. A pizza will be just fine.' The words opened Zelda's eyes. She strained her features into a smile. 'So will you write?'

'If I knew his name.'

'You know his name.'

'Oh yeh I know he's Francis. But Francis what? Francis Drake? Hey this could be a game. You give me clues.'

'His last name?' Zelda thought for a moment. She screwed up her eyes, looked puzzled and then smiled warmly. 'It's Williams. You know it's Williams.'

'Oh yeh. Francis Williams.' Fritz returned the smile and began to walk towards the kitchen. 'Yeh Francis Williams,' he repeated.

'So now you know,' laughed Zelda. She kicked off her shoes and stretched back. 'He says he didn't do it.'

'Shit he did it.' Fritz shouted back. There was a hiss of pouring water. A click of plugs going in and being switched on. 'Oh yeh. He did it alright. I saw her there.'

'Ronnie?'

'Yeh. She was there. Once when I went to the tower. I said hi and she answered me. Fuckin' scary, you know? I guess I never knew she was there.'

'She went there a lot.'

'What?' he said, realising she had spoken over his voice. He moved back and stood by the door of the lounge.

'You go there with Brad?' asked Zelda.

'Brad? Hell no. Not with Brad. He wouldn't take me there. It was private. Real private. No way in there with Brad. No way. Only Grant and Lincoln were allowed up there with Brad.'

Zelda laughed once more. There was no lengthy and complex process when getting to know Fritz. There was nothing hidden to probe and flush out. Or so she thought. Others knew better. Francis knew. Brad knew. There were secrets, declarations that Fritz would have chosen to make. He was too open about most things. That lulled others into not bothering. They left him alone. He liked that.

'So you'll write?'

'Yeh? Why not?' He pulled another face, an inquiring face. It doubted himself, disagreed with the words he was saying.

Zelda shook her head. 'Shit, he's, well you know what he's done.'

'Yeh, yeh. He's got problems. Let's leave that alone. Let's sort of cut around it. Know what I mean? Hey the rest of him's alright.'

'Oh come on.' Zelda wasn't impressed. She sat forward now. Fritz could see she was concentrating. Like a person with a finger on the trigger. Francis was in her sights. 'Hey you're not serious. You can't be.'

'Yeh I'm gonna write.'

'But he's not alright. You know he's not. And you can't cut around corners.' She stuttered a little, struggling with the analogy. 'It spreads. Sure as hell it does. It spreads.'

'Like a cancer,' suggested Fritz.

'Yeh that's it. Like a cancer,' Zelda agreed.

His father looked tired when Francis reached the barn. He found him in a corner, staring at an ewe. He was sitting in a chair, a flask of tea was propped up against its front left leg. His arms were folded. Trying to keep flesh on flesh, thought Francis, sensing the temperature and realising the need to retain heat.

'You Ok?' he asked, creeping up behind his father, whispering.

'She's nearly ready,' said his father. The concerned tone grabbed Francis' attention.

'I meant you,' he replied.

'Me? God aye, I'm Ok. Got a headache. Touch of vertigo I think. That's why I'm sitting. Bloody ears. Doctor says it stays with you through life. You know that?' For the first time his father took his eyes off the ewe and looked back over his shoulder at Francis. He smiled when he saw Francis shake his head. 'Want a tea? May's well finish it. I'll have a break then. Here.'

Francis watched his father pour the tea from the flask into the cup that had been its top. His father passed it to him. 'Bloody cold in here. Lovely in summer see. When we're out. Thick walls. Thick bloody walls.'

Francis took a long sip and thought over the laconic explanations. The cold seemed to energise him. He felt like moving, tapping a foot or shaking an arm. His father by his side seemed to find the cold enervating. He sat huddled up, staring at the ewe.

'You enjoy this?' asked Francis.

'Course.' His father chuckled and shook his head. A quick look was spent on Francis. It said how could he have doubted it, how could he have thought anything other than enjoyment filled his father's days. It had been the same for generations of Williamses. It would be the same for Francis in the future. Another shake of the head ended his father's stream of thoughts. 'It ain't what you do it's the way that you do it,' his father said, laughing again.

Francis nodded. He looked around the barn. He liked it. He always had. Its coolness in summer had always drawn him. He remembered standing where he stood now, watching the swallows swoop and glide through the arrow slit windows. In and out, they'd move, getting food; their young in a nest on the rafter. Beneath them Toggie would have been trying to open the food bins. Always Toggie, Francis thought. He pictured him trying to bite open the clips on the bins. He laughed remembering the goat's frustration when he found Francis had used bicycle elastics to hold the clips in place. Toggie reacted by butting the bin and knocking it over. Then the bin would roll away down slope. That was enough to frighten the goat who hated anything that moved suddenly and unexpectedly.

'You're thinking,' said his father, breaking into the thought. He recognised the abstraction, the involvement. He approved of it. It made him smile.

'No, no. I was just...'

'Thinking. That's what you were doing. About this place, yes?'

Francis nodded. Such involvement helped him understand his father. It helped him recognise more of his qualities. The enthusiasm. The desire. The unselfconscious sitting and staring at ewes in labour.

'Be glad when this is over,' said Francis' father interrupting Francis' thoughts again. 'Bloody difficult lambing.'

'You don't mean that,' said Francis sounding surprised.

'Oh yes, yes I do.' His father smiled. 'Mind you I just moan. Always have.'

'So what's difficult?'

'Oh I don't know. The waiting, I suppose. I'm not good at waiting. Never have been. You end up doing something daft like watching the rain drip in, telling yourself there's a bloody slate missing. Geth will have to get up there I tell myself. Did you know I can't stand heights?' He stopped talking to let Francis respond. Nothing was offered. 'See. And I talk to myself. Got to. I mean it's just me and them. And they don't say much. Do you?' he asked the sheep. 'Thank God they trust me. I know they do. God knows why. I mean the way I bloody treat them.' He sighed as he stood up. 'Hell,' he said, feeling a little dizzy again.

'You better get some sleep.'

'Perhaps I will,' he admitted, moving away, smiling again.

His father fell ill that night. He said he was dying. His terror of mutability easily got the better of him. Francis wasn't aware how the illness developed. He had gone from the barn to his room. Gethin had taken over from him. 'I'll have a sleep,' he said thinking of what he would do. He was awake when his mother put her head around the door. 'Francis can you come?' She looked bothered. 'Your father's not well. I've had the doctor. She said it was vertigo, but I'm not so sure.'

The second doctor, witnessing a cycle of vomiting and moans, sensed the deterioration. 'I can see what Doctor Jenkins meant,' she said. 'The vomiting, the lightheadedness, but the pain? Does he get stomach pains often?'

'No,' Francis' mother said.

'He doesn't get it with the vertigo?'

'No. Never before.'

'Take me through it again.'

Francis mother took a deep breath and unravelled the events of the day. The dizziness. The way he came home and sat down. How she had found him in the kitchen on his knees. How he threw up. How the pain in his stomach developed. 'That was about ten. He's been in bed ever since then. He's been sort of out of it.'

'Delirious?'

Moans came from the bed. Something about dying. 'I'm bloody dying,' Francis' father said.

The doctor turned her attention back his way. 'Now you take it easy Mr. Williams. You know me? Doctor Hopkins.'

'Aled's daughter?'

She wasn't, but the doctor nodded an agreement. 'We're getting you an ambulance. You'll be in Bronllys in half an hour. You take it easy.'

His father had an embolism. Nobody told Francis what it meant. To him it seemed grave. The intensive care unit emphasised that. He was surprised though: the mawkish stayed well away; a fear pervaded. He felt like a cornered animal. The trap was the farm. He felt it creeping in, its responsibilities were pressing. He would have to take it over, a voice in his head was telling him. He would have to organise and delegate and make money. The emotions he experienced considering that were wide ranging: shame, guilt, sorrow and sadness all in turn arrived. They took a bow and made their mark. Some dwelt in recollections – mostly trivial, but poignant. Recent events in particular were prominent. They were important. There were smiles there. There was trust. There was jubilation. They emphasised the change since his return. They emphasised it had been a change for the better. It was constructive. It seemed an uncompromising view. A realistic one, he thought, holding his father's hand. His touch was gentle. The wires and tubes conveyed a fragility. It matched their relationship. He pressed into the hand. He tried to find the moment of friendliness that had drawn them back together. The delicacy of it had astonished him, but now he couldn't find it. Come on you, he urged. The process was engrossing. He considered the plane home, the party with Ena, the negotiations, the independence. There was little affinity with his father through that, yet something had suddenly changed. What? he thought. How did it happen? He couldn't say. All he knew was there was a paradox now, a mix of disagreement and respect for his decision-making was clear. The disapproval had subsided. He had thought that in the barn when he was cradling the cup of tea and thinking of Toggie. Only warmth now, he had thought. No hostility. No doubts. No ridicule. Not real ridicule, thought Francis, comparing his father's recent jibes with the onslaughts of old. Such changes had taken them, father and son, back into the pack, normalising their relationship. To an extent, Francis had wanted that, but he missed the excitement of vitriol. The words that were meted out now were more measured. The frontiers that had once been near were now out of sight. Suddenly everything was typical.

'Grazing in the last bloody field, I am.' His father's words drained into a cough.

'Easy,' said Francis flinching at the way the cough seemed to ripple through his father's body.

'No I mean it.' The cough returned. It seemed to rack his father's system. He put a hand to his throat as though he would cut it off and contain it. 'Bloody dry see. No windows open. Can't sleep without the windows open. Those doctors,' he tutted. 'What do they know? They don't know a potato about sleeping.'

'A what?' Francis laughed. He hadn't heard the expression before.

'A potato about. It's a saying. Gwyn brought it back from Spain. Why are you laughing?' Francis' face managed a smile. The cough returned.

'I'll get you some water.'

'In the jug. The jug.' He coughed again and pointed to the desk-top like structure that was at the end of the bed. He quickly drank the water Francis poured. 'You alright with the lambs?'

Francis nodded and tried to think of something reassuring to say.

'You sure now? You be careful. Watch the bloody weather. Watch it like a hawk. Wet and cold it looked yesterday. Bloody lethal that.'

'It's warmer today.'

'So you bloody say.'

'It is.' Francis laughed. It was a laugh of relief. The doom and gloom of the past week momentarily seemed to pass.

'See the feed man as well,' his father demanded. 'You do that?'

'Yes, Ok.' Francis sounded impatient.

'Good. Now tell me how long have I been here? Lose track of time see. Sleeping. All I bloody do is sleep. It's not good for you. You die in bed, my father used to say.' Francis' father shook his head as he thought. A glance Francis' way indicated a response was needed.

'A week. Six days.'

'A week! Christ!' More head shaking followed. It seemed he had no recall of the time or the machines and doctors that had kept him alive. 'There's a diary in the kitchen. His name and number'll be there.'

'Whose?'

'The feed man. The bloody feed man. Are you listening to me?' Again his father shook his head. 'And don't let him talk you into ordering any more than we had last year. He'll try. Always bloody does. And no new products.'

His father fell asleep then. Francis was used to that. The coming and going. It was a sign of weakness. It left Francis thinking of the significance of the diary. It was like being let in. It was like a handing over, a ritual. It reminded him of the photo album when he was little. It provided the same tension, the same sense of drama. Do I want it?, he asked himself. He thought of his mother. She should deal with it. After all this was temporary. Soon his father would be up and about, ordering and developing, doing all that he had done before the illness.

'Mr. Williams.' A voice called to him. A soft, female voice. It came from behind him. 'Would you like a word? With the doctor? He's doing his rounds.'

Francis turned to see a nurse. The smiling face seemed a little out of place. It emitted reassurance. It made him smile too.

'Your mother's been trying to see him, but he's not been here when she's been here. You know how it is.'

'Yes. Of course.'

The news was not good. Francis was put in a chair to listen. There was talk of a long recovery period, about the work being too physical, about a slight problem with blood sugar levels that could give bouts of faintness. They would monitor that. Francis just nodded. No questions came to him. He was numb. 'A full recovery,' tugged him back. 'He can get back to where he was,' the doctor said, 'but there may be difficulties if he works too hard. Farming's so physical. I think the burden of work may be too much. We'll have to see.'

'You got time for this? You're going to say now that it doesn't matter, but it does matter. You're in charge remember? And there's always work to be done. I've done it for forty years so I should bloody know.'

Francis sat at the edge of the bed. He was surprised by the length

232

and the strength of his father's words. It was more than he usually managed, ill or not. There was a tension in the words. Francis recognised it was represented by the need to stay in touch with what was going on and by the desire to call for company. Such an approach seemed a natural prelude to either sending Francis out or giving him something to do at the bedside. It also conveyed who was in charge. His father smiled when Francis poured him a cup of tea.

'Good of you to bring it up.'

'You like it fresh.'

'Aye,' his father agreed, putting the book he had been reading down at his side. 'You could read to me if you like. Only if you've got time mind. I find it difficult holding the book up. Makes me sleepy.'

'Ok.' Francis poured the tea. He started to pass it to his father, but saw the likely difficulty. He paused, his eyes searching for a solution. The tray provided it. He removed the teapot on it and placed the empty tray in front of his father. The cup was placed on it. 'Now what's this you're reading? *Slim Revenge*,' said Francis, picking up the book and looking at the title. The cover had a weak drawing of a man on a horse riding out of a poorly constructed town. Francis tutted.

'I need to think,' said his father adopting a defensive tone.

'Think?'

'Imagine. You know.'

Francis nodded. He thought of the alien land and experience the book would contain, how his father colonised such ideas.

'I can see America,' his father said. 'Know what I mean? God you're lucky. You've been there.'

Francis smiled. He knew what his father meant. He knew also what he was working with. The farm. The gun. The events that were read weren't bare in his imagination. He had tools to work with. Equivalents.

'His wife's gone. Off with some prospector. Dirty bitch. He's chasing them. He's called Slim.'

'Oh I see.'

'That's it. Slim's Revenge. Well Slim Revenge. They've cut it down a bit.'

Francis nodded and smiled. The corner of his eye saw his father settling down. He lay back, pulling up the bedclothes. There seemed little left to do but read. Francis pulled on the bookmark and eyed the page. He read with a comfortable confidence, managing a good Texas accent.

'Good,' said his father at the end of the chapter. 'Made it come alive. Good,' he said again.

'You like this?' Francis dismissed the book.

'Course I bloody like it. Wouldn't read it otherwise.'

Francis shook his head. He re-read a paragraph to check what he thought of it. Little structure, lifeless characters, contrived plot. The review confirmed his verdict.

'Ok,' said his father, smiling. 'I know it's not much good.'

'I didn't say that.'

'You don't have to. You smiled it.'

'Laughed it.'

'Ok. Laughed it.' His father laughed too. More wildly than Francis had ever known. Uninhibited, thought Francis, free. The sound made him believe what was possible when the burden of the farm was lifted. He listened closely to it, deciding there was a directness about it, an accuracy that set it out. It marked a confidence in their relationship. His father could laugh with him now. That touched Francis.

'You know what I really like?' His father tried to regain control. Stutters of laughter punctuated the words. 'Oh,' he said, calming down. 'What I really like is the comparison.'

'With what? With Wales?'

'No. Not bloody Wales. This is all settled here. Bloody long haired goats coming in here. Andorras.'

'Angoras.'

'Angoras then. Bloody angoras. Still, better than bloody prospectors I expect.' The laughter stopped. A seriousness resumed. 'I mean with the sort of books you buy me. You know. Black cowboys. That sort of thing.'

Francis nodded. The movement contained his surprise. The mythical and the real seemed an odd consideration for his father. It gave him a depth Francis hadn't thought possible. It left Francis wondering what to say.

'You know?'

'Oh aye. I bloody know. It's all formulas see. No surprises.'

'Is that what you want? Wouldn't you like some surprises.'

'At my age? Hell no. Like to know where I am. You know me,' he said, his eyes almost twinkling. As he spoke he tapped his finger on the book. It drew Francis back to the page.

'Right,' said Francis coughing and clearing his throat. He began to read. He read about a ride in a canyon, about eyes on a hillside following the figures, about water canteens and camp fires. It made him think about myths that were closer to home. Wales and the sheep farm. Fathers and sons. His father. Himself. They seemed like a myth. Perhaps reality was around them. Not in Brynlas, he thought. He looked at his father. His eyes were closed now. A look of satisfaction had set on his face.

'So he denied it?'

'Yeh.'

'Could be he got railroaded.'

Zelda sat down and stretched. She looked puzzled. Her thoughts were seeing and considering connections. They were asking who was involved and what was meant. Railroaded, railroaded, railroaded, her mind was repeating. Who? Francis? By whom? Fritz seemed a step ahead.

'I mean he could have done it. She'd remembered the place as much as the person I guess. Hey what am I saying? What the hell. I mean what do I know?'

'Speculation.'

'It's all fuckin' speculation.' Fritz was nodding now. He saw the strength and sense in it. There were assumptions and presumptions. Things qualified and connected other things. Important things. There was compatibility. But, at its best, it was a mishmash. He and Zelda continued to probe it, but only Francis and Ronnie really knew what had gone on. Perhaps there was more they could do. Perhaps there were weak openings and conclusions that had passed their eyes and infiltrated. Perhaps the isolation and estrangement of Ronnie had made it harder for them to pin down what had gone on. All they really knew was that they would continue wondering, checking Ronnie.

'He'll struggle,' said Fritz coming out of thought.

'Struggle!' exclaimed Zelda. 'What do you mean struggle?'

'Adapting. I mean for chrissakes it's difficult. Going home.'

'Going home's easy.'

Fritz shook his head. There was something about his look that conveyed he had done it, that he knew what a predatory world home could be, how people would ask what had happened and why an early return had been made. 'All those explanations. I mean having to say why you came home quickly. Gee.' He shook his head.

'Ran out of money.'

'What?'

'All those difficult explanations. Ran out of work, Ran out of money.' Zelda smiled. 'Easy! Hey why we talking about him?'

'Why?' Fritz seemed surprised by the question. He didn't know what to make of it. 'Because we've, well I guess we've accused him or found him guilty of, well...'

'I know.' Zelda's hard look told Fritz she knew full well how they had dramatised Francis' stay in Texas, how they had accused him and passed sentence. 'I know what he did. I can't forgive. But I can forget. I guess that's what I think. We should forget. Ronnie will.'

'You sure?'

'Oh yeh. Of course. Give her a month or two and she won't remember a thing.'

'I'm not so sure.'

'You wait.'

'Well, we'll see.' Fritz stayed calm. He was slightly shocked by the clarification of what Zelda felt. Forgetting not forgiving, he thought. It seemed severe. Forgetting. One mistake, he thought. One aberration. It was the other parts of Francis' behaviour they needed to remember and consider. It made the issue seem two faced: the grotesque indecency of the indiscretion and the smiling generosity of the friend he knew. 'I don't know,' said Fritz trying to deal with the divergence.

'You need help?' Zelda stood up. She smiled enticingly and held the tray as she walked towards the kitchen. The expression on her face changed as she moved. 'Just imagine it's your daughter. You wouldn't forgive would you? You just think about that.'

Something urged Francis on. He wasn't sure what. It seemed to hide in some sort of confusion. I'm so moody, he thought, recognising the mix of elation and deflation, the way plans were decimated by such polarisation. He felt in limbo, going for things then turning back, returning to the same place, a starting point, over and over again. He was going forward now, starting again. It felt like a launch, the expectation caused him to tingle.

Writing was the starting gun. He understood that now. One syllable and he was off, leaving behind home life. The past and the future seemed preferable now. He would spend half the day thinking of the water tower and Ronnie, considering the subtlety of those days, the way it was like following a path without knowing where it was going. At least there was a path, he thought. Being at Brynlas was like seeing all the possibilities around him without being able to move. Brynlas was like a quagmire weighing him down. The letters to Fritz were like the visions. 'No need to reply,' he'd write. 'I'm Ok. Nothing more than that. Just Ok. But that's good enough. How are you?'

The touch of self pity was mandatory. It maintained the big issue that would run and run and establish its full significance through time. Whenever he mentioned it he wondered whether Fritz jumped the paragraph or whether his feelings fell in amongst the words. Any association would make Fritz sense injustice. Francis was sure of that. So sure that he used ruses to trap Fritz, making little jokes about their time together when they spoke about Ronnie, drawing comparisons with Welsh life. Any way of disrupting the predictability was seized upon and used. He knew full well eventually it would open up and some sort of interplay would give volume to how dismal Brynlas was. His father's illness fattened that out. It played for sympathy. It put emphasis on his captivity, upon being upstaged, as though he lost equilibrium, as though the return had made him lose his footing. That was what he wanted Fritz to see. Not that Fritz would sense anger in that. Fritz would tolerate a little chaos. Francis knew that.

'So he's ill in bed and I read him stories. Cowboy stories. They could be San Antonio. The hero could be your father's father. In fact it could be you!' Francis laughed as he read out the latest letter. He read it out loud. Toggie listened. He looked Francis' way trying to work out the significance of the intonation. The highs normally signified annoyance, some complaints about his behaviour. He'd look up when a shrill tone came. And down a few seconds later. He'd paw the ground then wanting it to turn at a touch into hay.

'Ok,' said Francis seeing the goat's annoyed look. 'Ok.' A second attempt by Francis to move the goat failed. The goat started to butt the door. No patience, thought Francis, considering how Zoon was different, how she could stay in one position for minutes on end. Inscrutable, he thought, closing the door after Toggie had gone out. Through the window, he watched the goat move steadily across the yard. It made him pick up a pen. 'Toggie is Ronnie,' he wrote. 'He comes and goes just like she did. He's the surprise of the day.'

Francis wasn't required to read the following day. He offered, but was sent away with a wave of a hand. For a minute or two he sat and watched his father propped up in bed, earphones on, listening to something. Cassette cases were laid out on the floor by the side of the bed. Mario Lanza, Glenn Miller, The Bachelors. Francis wondered what was playing. He tried to work it out from the look on his father's face and the syllables he was miming. 'I...I...I... Me.... Me....' He laughed as his father's eyebrows lifted and a look of pleasure crept into the side of his eyes. His father smiled, his head bobbed with the rhythm.

Francis enjoyed the exercise. It was like sitting a test. He enjoyed being the spectator, catching a private moment. He enjoyed working it out too. He would imitate his father, closing his eyes conducting an orchestra or singing the song, belting it out. He thought too of the role music had played in the States, of the tapes he had taken, how it was like *Desert Island Discs*, how the songs and recordings were like best friends. They were there, available, calming, sometimes translating what had gone on and what would go on. He thought too of the discovery in the water tower, how he had moved the mattress to reveal a stack of four cassettes marked 'Bus'.

He hadn't played the cassettes. In fact he forgot about them. They stayed at the base of the mattress for two or three days, then one morning he stepped on one. The cover cracked. 'Shit!' The exclamation accompanied crab handed efforts to piece together the broken cover. Sellotape was tried. Glue too. 'Shit!' It bothered him then. He wanted to find Brad, to drag him up to the tower and show him the tape. Somehow it seemed so significant. It was a leftover from Brad's use of the room. It was like a secret that had been broken into.

'You play it boy?' laughed Brad when Francis eventually found him. 'You haven't, have you? Gee you should have. Used to love making tapes. I tell you boy?'

Francis shook his head. The tapes were still in his hand. He placed them on the kitchen table.

'Let's play one, yeh?'

'Ok,' said Francis a little alarmed by the excitement Brad was showing. He couldn't match that. If anything he managed to contain the intrigue that wanted to push more enthusiasm into his tone. 'Fine. Yeh I'd like to hear it.'

'So would I boy,' laughed Brad. He moved out of the room for a second or two, looking for the ghetto blaster that the boys used for Michael Jackson. 'Ok. Let's go,' he said, returning with the machine. He placed it alongside the tapes and plunged the plug into a socket above the toaster. 'What is it? Oh Jesus.' He looked at the cover. 'Jesus,' he repeated, emphasising the syllables. 'Ok, Ok. You wanna hear it? Right. Some real cookies on this.'

Francis watched him pick up the tape and read the cover. 'So what's it about?' asked Francis.

'What do you mean?'

'I mean is it music?'

'Music!' Brad laughed fully. The misunderstanding amused him. It made him wonder how Francis interpreted Bus. 'Bus,' he said under his breath. 'You think... Oh Jees boy, you think... You do. You think Bus is a band.'

'Good name for a band,' remarked Francis, wishing he had kept quiet while he waited for an explanation. It would have come. He could see that now. Brad wouldn't have resisted. His sense of self importance would have persisted until he had asked questions and given answers.

'Bus,' Brad laughed again. It was a stertorous laugh. Air was pushed through his nose. The laugh stuttered to a stop. 'It means what it says. Bus. I was putting together a file on the bus service into San Antonio. The local company ran it. Wasn't any good. I mean the service. That was the trouble.'

'That's why you made the tape?'

'Yeh, yeh. That's it. Hey have a listen.' Brad pressed the button marked 'Play' and sat down opposite Francis. He smiled. The composure astonished Francis. He couldn't believe anyone could expose himself in this way. The thought heightened the sense of anticipation. He felt it. Brad felt it. He could see that in the nervous movements Brad was making. He moved his hands over the table, shuffling them back and fore. 'Evidence,' a voice said on the tape. 'Elmore Harris, forty five years, occupation shopkeeper.' The link voice was Brad's. He indicated that by pointing to himself, whispering, 'That's me.' Complaints followed. Mostly mundane, they listed occasions of lateness or non appearance. Some picked on characters, employees. Angel King was the chief figure. 'The baddie,' said Brad. 'Threatened to skin me alive.' He raised his eyebrows to convey a sense of shock. 'Bit of a mad man. Hey listen to this one,' he demanded. A woman's voice came on. 'Well I just laughed,' it said. 'I held the baby and got on. The driver said, 'Hey baby, we'll have you in town no time at all.' And off he went. I was so shocked. I couldn't get my words out. I just smiled. Well we went two blocks and I said, 'Hey what you gonna do with this baby?' He turned round and said, 'What d'ya mean? What d'ya mean what am I gonna do with the baby? The baby's yours lady. You saying it's got something to do with me. I mean I think I'd know if I had something to do with it, wouldn't I?' he said. I said, 'Well it sure ain't mine. I just held it while a woman sorted out her buggy. You closed the doors on her.' Funny now I guess, but it wasn't at the time. No sir...'

Somehow recalling the tapes brought a stream of memories. Francis wondered how they arrived, what drew them. Some came to him several times. The first night in Texas did. He remembered waiting on the veranda. The building up of strength. 'Come over at seven,' Brad had said. What did that mean? Six thirty for seven, Francis had heard people say in the films. That was etiquette. English or American? he wondered. He settled for the time he felt most at ease with after laying out his clothes and combing his hair. He washed too, smiling at himself in the mirror. Then he made his move, stopping on the veranda when he heard voices.

'I'm just being friendly. You said be friendly. I remember you saying it. So I am. I ask her how she likes her eggs, what she likes doing. Just conversation. I'm just being friendly.'

'Oh yeh?'

'Yeh the girl needs friends. I'm her friend.' Brad sounded insistent.

The admission taunted Pam. 'You would be,' Francis heard her say. She knew the way it played on truth, asking questions about the breadth of the definition of friend.

'You think about it. It's kind of clear. I mean she came here, you can't find the time to take her into town.'

'I can.' Pam put down her mixing bowl and placed her hands on the table. She stared up at Brad as though she were waiting for a retraction.

'No. No you can't,' he said, shaking his head. 'You can't get away with that. No Pam. You turned her down. I heard. I was standing right here.'

'Shit Brad I was going to the doctor's.'

'You never said.'

'Do I have to?'

'Yeh. Yeh I think you should.' Again Brad laughed. He liked exposure. The way people moved towards it. The way people got caught. He liked setting the trap.

'So what you do with her?'

'What do you mean do with her? What you saying?' Brad raised his voice. He moved to the fridge, pulling out a can of beer. 'This is what you do things with.' He pulled on the ring of the can.

The first angry word made Francis stand perfectly still. Brad and Pam hadn't heard him. Their attention was elsewhere. Francis decided to wait. The first lengthy silence would be like a green light calling him on. He counted in his mind. Ten...Twenty... Thirty. He moved. His hand was reaching for the door when the next syllable was uttered.

'Thank God she's gone.' The words were Pam's. They concluded as Francis pushed on the door.

'Hi boy, hey you're quite a mover.' Brad smiled widely. 'Gee normally that wood out there creaks and croaks. Nearly snaps when ol' Fritz walks on it.'

'Fritz is a friend,' explained Pam. She was used to the need for explanation. Brad was one of those people who dropped names into conversation as though the participant should know whom he is talking about and what they are like.

'You stick round boy and you'll meet Fritz.'

'You won't be able to miss him,' said Pam, again qualifying Brad's words.

'Fritz is Ok.'

'Yeh. Fritz is lovely.' She smiled in agreement with her husband.

'I'll look forward to that.' Francis tried to find the diplomacy that would pre-empt a re-run of the verbal hostility he had heard from the balcony. It made Pam smile. She recognised how quickly Francis had come to understand their relationship.

'Hey, you're learning quickly,' she said, nodding and walking out of the room. 'I'll be in the bedroom if you want me.'

'Knitting,' said Brad. 'She's always knitting. Hey what does she mean you're learning quickly. What's up?'

Francis shrugged. He thought quickly, but no appropriate response came to mind.

'She's always in the bedroom. But not with me. That's the trouble. Always with her knitting. I mean it's not normal. Kind of spooky don't you think? A grown woman. An intelligent woman for chrissakes.' He went to the fridge, claimed a can of beer and threw it towards Francis.

'We all have hobbies,' remarked Francis, catching the can and sitting at the table. 'Thanks,' he said, pulling on the ring of the can.

'Oh yeh I accept that. Yeh we all have interests. It's good to have an interest. Keeps the mind sort of healthy, yeh? Keeps you motivated. But you've got to keep a balance. I mean she's forever knitting. Then when I take ol' Esme –'

'Esme?' Francis made it quite clear he had no knowledge of who Esme was.

'God yeh. She went just before you arrived. We took her to the station. Shit she probably got on the bus you got off boy. You probably saw her. Cute kid with big brown eyes. Yeh she's cute, real cute.'

'So's Pam.'

'Yeh Pam's a good looking woman. Jealous as shit though. You'll see that.' Brad didn't follow up his words with looks. He took it for granted Francis nodded or said yes. 'People always notice. I tell her. I say you gonna show us up. I say you got to be careful. She just clams up. Doesn't say a word to me. No sir, not a word.' Brad shook his head and smiled. His hand half raised his beer. A thought arrived. He put the beer down. 'I like girls. Gee.' He laughed again. 'They're a gift from God boy. Hey why am I whispering? Shit I like girls,' he shouted, screwing up his eyes and waiting, expecting some reaction. A re-entry, thought Francis, a wonderfully theatrical dressing down. But nothing happened. It puzzled Brad. Francis could see that. 'Ok, Ok.

You like girls boy, yeh? Course you do. Well Esme's great. And I mean great. You know? Yeh, right, you know.' He nodded and looked at his beer, smiling to himself. There was a smugness. Francis sensed satisfaction. 'Gee girls.' Brad shook his head. 'Young girls, yeh. The younger the better. Yeh. Girls...'

He also remembered being in the woods with Brad. In summer. Evening time. The shade was as welcome as a long, cool drink. He remembered the drop in temperature, the sensation on the skin. It was like a soft breath blowing on it, cooling it. Francis would sit at the edge, looking out at the stretch of fields that waved in the heat. The clouds were like woods to them. Thick, impenetrable summer clouds. Like forests. Francis was always excited by it. It was so extreme. It made Wales seem moderate, controlled. It gave it harmony and balance. Texas, by contrast, seemed in disarray. Like the clothes of the workers who had to endure the heat. It bred untidiness. He recognised that when he saw Brad coming towards the woods.

'Brad!' he shouted.

Brad almost jumped. The startled look on his face softened when Francis waved. 'Hi. Hey what you doing in the wood?' He moved the branches of a shrub and looked in at Francis. 'You hiding? Those kids got you playing?'

Francis laughed. Brad seemed a little discomposed. It went with the bedraggled look of the land. 'Hiding from the weather,' admitted Francis.

'That a game? You English. Guess you're not used to it, the heat. That a drink?' Brad saw a line of cans alongside Francis. They produced a grin on his face. 'Hey hold on boy. I'll join you.'

'Yeh. Come in,' urged Francis. 'Sit down.' He waved his hand over the cans, gesturing to Brad to choose one. The inducement brought an opening of the eyes and a nod of approval.

'You come here often boy?' asked Brad.

'When it's hot. When Davison doesn't want me. It's a good place. Slightly raised.'

'Yeh,' agreed Brad. 'You can see the land. He was swigging at a can of beer now, wiping his lips. 'Hey that's mighty welcome boy. Thanks.' There was a compliance about him. He was submitting to the weather, stretching out. He lay flat on his back, pulling his cowboy hat down over his face. 'So you like it here?' he asked, almost automatically.

'Keeps me cool.'

'No.' Brad laughed. The familiar, sterterous laugh. The wisps of breath puffing through his nose. They made most of the noise. 'No I mean here. Texas. Shit sometimes we sort of miss each other. You know what I mean boy?'

Francis nodded and laughed. A short laugh. He wondered whether there really were two languages, whether they touched at some tangent that barely connected them.

'See you're laughing now boy. What's funny?'

'Just thinking.'

'I'm thinking too,' admitted Brad.

'So what are you thinking?'

There was a snigger and a little hesitation. Francis also sensed some agitation. It came in a fidget. A scratch on the knee, a rub of the nose. a twist of the hip. 'Hm,' went Brad, stalling.

'Come on,' urged Francis.

'Ok boy, Ok. The kids.'

'The kids?'

'Yeh. I think of them a lot.'

'The boys.'

Again there was a pause. This time for effect. It made Francis think that Brad had never differentiated. 'No, I mean yeh, yeh I think of the boys, but I wasn't then, understand? I mean I was thinking of Ronnie, thinking what a swell kid she is. I guess I was trying to picture what she'll be like when she's older. That's important. I mean boys, they can look after themselves. Girls. They gotta look good. An' I mean good.'

Francis laughed.

'No she has. I'm serious, real serious. I mean she can't play hooky. She's got to get in there. Make the best of it, you understand? Ronnie's got to be the best looking girl around. That's what she's got to be. Ain't no use being one of the crowd.'

Francis tried to untangle what was being said. He wondered about equality. It seemed more likely here. At no time had he sensed a dual structure. Admittedly there was a strong sense of the traditional in areas like this, but San Antonio and modernity were a step away. Most girls would opt for that, he thought.

'Hope she has a cute bum,' laughed Brad, giggling now. 'I like a good bum. Zelda my sister's got a good bum. I guess Pam's too short. I'd be mighty proud if she had a cute bum. I'd be taking her into town, parading her about. Yeh, I'd be proud, real proud.'

'So he denied it?'

'Yeh?'

'Well, well.' Fritz didn't sound surprised. He sat back, looking tired, lulled by a general feeling of well being. He enjoyed being Zelda's friend, associating with a lady as he put it, a classy lady. He liked the role. It shook him when he considered its importance. It sat him up, left him straight backed like a sentinel overlooking the conversation.

'I thought he would.' Zelda shook her hair as she spoke. She threw her coat onto a chair. 'He's as guilty as shit. You know he expected me to say, Ok Francis, Ok we believe you. Yeh we believe you.'

'Like shit we do.'

'Yeh. That's right. Schmuck.' Zelda seemed suddenly annoyed. Recollections of her conversation with Francis jostled in her mind. They funnelled into her awareness, changing perspective. 'Should be shot. Pervert.'

'You sure now?' Fritz seemed suddenly doubtful. A look on his face conveyed that to Zelda.

'What do you mean?' she asked. 'Sure? Course I'm sure. We're sure. You're sure. You said yourself.'

'Oh yeh, I'm sure. I'm real sure.'

'Well then,' said Zelda a little worried by Fritz's wavering. He didn't sound convincing. He wanted to, but something had begun to nag away. It made him think over the events of the last few weeks. The confidence of Zelda, their meetings, their interpretations, their talks with Ronnie, the piecing together of what had gone on. It also made him think how he had avoided Francis, how he had lied to him, hiding away. He was surprised Francis had worked out he was on to him. But there had been no indication of concern, no strange reaction. He stopped. He started again, recalling Francis' behaviour. Francis had been relaxed. There was no biting of the lip or becoming garrulous. It was the same old Francis. Fritz tried to change that. He tried to liven him up, to get him to kill a debate on something or the other, but there was nothing but a smile and a laugh and a promise to see him soon. There was no concern or fretting. Fritz wondered why. 'Guess it was him,' he said, coming out of thought.

'Hey what's bugging you?' Zelda had sensed the abstraction. She recognised it from the time they had sat down and considered what had gone on. It was always Francis. The finger always pointed his way. Now some doubt had moved in. It troubled Zelda. She wondered what had caused the change. The amiable Fritz would tell her. Ask him, her mind kept saying, knowing she could manipulate him. But first she wondered whether she had missed something, whether something in their conversation had spread new lines of enquiry. A suspicious stare began to take over her face. It accompanied her words. It alerted Fritz. He moved nervously, raising a hand. Undaunted he tried to explain.

'I don't know. I mean the boy, Francis... That's just it. He's just a boy. He's so innocent. You said yourself.'

'Yeh, well I thought he was innocent. I mean he looked it.' Zelda shook her head slowly. The movement was precise. The precision gathered a significance. It said more than words could have. 'Besides who else could have done it? ·

'Brad?' The name surprised Fritz. He had thought it all along. He was sure Zelda had considered it too, but the consequences of Brad's involvement were so desperate. They both sheered away from it, thinking they could deal with the suspicion, that they could keep it away from themselves, that they wouldn't have to investigate it. Its gravity had worked on Fritz. 'I mean we haven't discussed it, have we? We should have.' Fritz began to ramble. He was a little shaken by Zelda's lack of reaction. She just stared. 'I mean he liked sex and I know there's sex and sex, if you know what I mean, but he liked young girls. He told me.'

'Told you?'

'Yeh he told me he liked young girls.'

'How young?'

Zelda listened. She thought she should, but the more she listened the more she thought there was no basis for the link with Ronnie. Still she should listen. She told herself that. She would listen and check it through thoroughly. 'So how young?' she asked again.

'Sixteen, seventeen, I guess. Yeh.'

'Sixteen,' repeated Zelda.

'Yeh.'

'Ronnie's eight for chrissakes. Eight.'

On his home-made calendar May had Toggie and Zoon grazing. They were looking as though they were enjoying themselves, facing each other, down on their front knees. Francis looked at them and laughed. Toggie had that effect. No matter how grave Francis felt, Toggie's mood was constant. Mischievous, thought Francis. He realised the goat was ever engaging, possessing some undefined quality which concealed sadness and always used a mannerism to lighten a moment. June next, thought Francis. June was his favourite month. He pictured it. The photograph of Toggie in his box feeling the summer heat. He acted the pose, stretching his head up. 'Up,' he said. He began to wish for a longer neck. That was where the grace came from. The ability

245

to make a right angle between shoulders and neck was crucial. It eluded him. 'Toggie, Toggie, Toggie,' he said, turning the page of the calendar over to June. There it was. Loose lines of body. Ears limp. Nose and chin straight as his neck rested on the side of the box. The left front leg languid, extending out of the box. It was so expressive. It said summer and added an exclamation mark.

The pose made him write. He tried to tell Fritz about his father, about the illness and the problem with blood sugar. Custard creams are the answer, he wrote, wondering immediately if there was such a thing in the States. 'Change it,' he said, deleting custard creams and writing cookies. He found perspective then, telling Fritz what it meant to him: a central role on the farm, managing, taking decisions. It also meant he had temporarily returned to sleeping in his old room. 'Hate the symbolism of that,' he wrote, explaining how it was necessary to support his mother.

Finishing the letter, he realised no mention had been made of Ronnie. He tried to understand why. Different places. Events moving on. Time. Pressure. On scrap paper he wrote down reasons. He ordered them, putting lines through some, underlining others. They made him see Ronnie was competing with more immediate places and events. She had to raise her voice to compete. She did that in a variety of ways. A letter from Fritz would have helped. A letter like his conversation. Francis missed the panache of Fritz's words. The wildness of his opinions would have brought Texas to life. Without such commitment Francis had to search within. He decided adding a paragraph was the least he could do. That's it, he thought, that will do it. He knew it would furnish a glimpse of the way recollection and speculation played a prominent role in his thoughts. It would make Fritz see that a response would help even if it came spasmodically. That's it, he thought, stopping to check his conclusions. That will do it.

The doctor was happy with his father's progress. She came on Mondays and listened to his father's stories and told tales of her own about change and progress. Coming down the stairs she would be shaking her head, giggling, smiling broadly at Francis or his mother, whoever was home.

'He'll live forever. He's got the humour for it.'

'I'm not sure it's humour,' said Francis, thinking how some people abjure charm. It made his father seem rather exotic. He thought too how easy it was to miscategorise his father's love of the past. How it was and how it is, thought Francis, understanding how his father's mind worked. The comparisons overrode everything. It accounted for the delay too. The need to think, to link back. Cows, sheep, bushes, roads, people – everything was compared, normally unfavourably, so stimulating a diatribe.

'Rambling a bit,' the doctor said. 'Does he read?'

Francis took his time answering. He wondered what to say. Eventually, discarding the cowboy stories, he shook his head.

'Listen to music?'

'No.'

The doctor stopped on the bottom stair. She became thoughtful.. 'He needs stimulation,' she said. 'The hills gave it to him. The problems. I think he enjoyed the problems. It's all he talks about.'

Francis laughed. How right she was. Astute, he thought, realising his father needed something to be neurotic about. He saw that the illness may succeed the day-to-day problems of running the farm. His father's behaviour told him that. He had already asked for the family health book and was checking and correcting symptoms, talking blood sugar levels and hypoglycaemia.

'Has she bloody gone?' his father asked when Francis returned upstairs. 'Bloody woman. She laughs at me. She was telling me about being on call. You know being called out at night. So I told her about the milk round. Every day, I said. Every bloody day. Three o'clock I'd be up.'

'Three?'

'Yes, three.'

'Used to be four,' remarked Francis.

'Four,' his father sighed. He pulled himself up in bed. Somehow, upright, he looked less vulnerable. 'Three, four. It was nearer three. Twenty five past, perhaps,' he said, laughing, smiling at the white lies. He enjoyed the bombast, the play acting.

Francis smiled too. There was a softer side to his father now. Francis saw it and liked it. Its development seemed to coincide with Francis' return. The illness supported it. Shaving off responsibilities, thought Francis. Momentarily it turned day-to-day work into a distraction, something that had deflected humour and soured him.

Francis' visit was brief. He put down the coffee and made excuses. Work was something his father didn't argue with. He knew that. So he used it.

'Is he alright?' Francis passed his mother on the stairs. He answered her question and told her how the doctor had called and how everything was stable.

'Stable. Good,' said his mother, passing judgement. 'He's coming on then.'

'Yes, she was pleased. She likes him.'

'Does she now. How do you know?'

'Oh you know. You can tell. With some people you can tell.'

His mother began to walk up the stairs. 'D'you want coffee when I make it?'

'No. No thanks. Things to do.'

It seemed strange to Francis that he could just leave thoughts of America alone, that he could just put them to one side and store them away. He wondered how he could do that. Then he tried to dismiss it, blaming it on energy, saying to himself that he was busy, that there was too much to do, that there was no room for it. Besides it didn't worry him. He thought it would come back. Like a treat. Like a comfort food. The bare diet of Brynlas, Brynlas and Brynlas had left him jaded. It couldn't go on and on. He knew that. Not like America. America could have. The friendships, the foils, the discoveries. It was the chemistry for exhilaration. He tried to fix into that and work it out. There were similarities. He saw them. The commitments at Brynlas were similar. Energy. Dedication. Intrigue. But in America there was less to worry about because ultimately he was responsible only for himself. Brynlas broadened the base. Toggie, Zoon, Bess, the sheep, the farm, the buildings, a mother, a father and occasionally Gethin and Gwyn. Perhaps there were simply too many concerns.

'Could be,' he said, staring at the list he made. He thought of Fritz and Zelda, about the scene that had cornered him and had seemed so vital, straining his consciousness, how it came and went too quickly. Perhaps it was mixed up. All those versions. All those interpretations. He was oblivious of many of the nuances now. Somehow Fritz and Zelda had returned to the plain reality where he had left them some months before: Fritz at the bus station, Zelda at the prison. It was almost as though they had stayed there, fixed in time, that nothing had moved on. That confined the characters. They were left with what he knew. And that was little. It shocked him when he realised that. Oral felicity couldn't have been Fritz's only quality. A liking for football. A love-hate relationship with his wife. A shrewdness. A secrecy. A generosity. He began another list of all he knew, then he stopped, realising the qualities were playing off each other, that Fritz's verbal assaults played on things like relationships. They were there for Fritz to beat the shit out of. Nothing else. Francis laughed at that.

What an influence. The mere thought of Fritz changed his words, littering them with expletives. And that was Fritz's charm. He had likeability. In abundance, thought Francis. Enough, perhaps, to ingratiate himself with Zelda. Ok there had been some sort of connivance. There had been some sort of plotting. Circumstances dictated the need for that. It was a necessity. And that shocked Francis. It seemed like a resolution. Unsatisfactory, he thought, trying to engage it, wanting it to return. He needed the continuity of perception, to feel there was a target. 'The need to unravel,' he said, 'the need to sort it out.' But that couldn't be based on delusion, so why try? Why fashion arguments and reason out of small shreds of evidence? It was speculation, comforting perhaps, but working within strict confines. The rat catcher and the publicist, he thought. The family man and the single woman. The art lover and the football addict. No common ground there, he thought. Nothing to make conversation or friendship out of. Nothing to make them friends or lovers. The only link was Ronnie.

'So how is he?'

'Your father? He's fine. Talking about going out, helping you.' The positive burst was muzzled by a tone that doubted the wisdom of such a move. The ghosts of previous turns and the state of collapse it put him in were lurking, qualifying everything.

'We'll see,' said Francis, thinking it best to be non-committal. It made his mother sense how he feared such a return, how it would be difficult to deal with. As she considered what she meant, she nodded.

'Have to have a pack of custard creams on the tractor, eh?' laughed Francis.

'Go on. He'll be OK. You know he will.' His mother walked over to the stove and looked into the saucepans. Something about the amount of steam or the state of the bubbles told her practised eyes how long it would be. 'Five minutes, Ok?'

'Yes fine. Shall I go and see him?'

'He's sleeping. I'd leave him be for now. Have your food.'

Francis nodded and sat at the table. He stared at his mother. She seemed to be stooping slightly now, as if the burden of the last few weeks had adopted a physical presence. The curve was quite pronounced. Francis felt himself looking at it as she turned towards him.

'We should thank you son.'

'Thank me?'

'For all you've done. I mean helping your father when he has a turn, getting him to bed. I couldn't do it.'

'You don't need to. The doctor said. Said he could stay wherever he has the turn, said he'd come through it. You heard her.' Francis smiled. He tried to be as positive as possible whenever his mother mentioned his father.

'Oh I could see that. Your father lying there.'

'Where?'

'Wherever he had the turn. No he couldn't do that.'

'Too untidy,' joked Francis.

'No. Just not comfortable. He needs to be comfortable. Doctor said. Get him comfortable, she said.'

'She meant make him tea, get him biscuits, wipe him down. That's what she meant.'

'Did she?' His mother smiled fully now. The recuperative qualities of custard creams always amused her. It was quite a revelation. She shook herself, recollecting the point of the conversation. 'It mustn't tie you,' she said quickly. 'You know if you want to move on. You see that, don't you?'

Francis nodded. The experiences of America made it difficult for him to be unsentimental, to be fresh and clear. There was always America. There was always Ronnie. She was prominent. She flitted in and out of his thoughts, settling with Brad and Fritz and Zelda. She was pervasive.

'So you understand?'

'What?' said Francis, closing down his mind, chasing away the glimpses of a strange world. He was back with his mother again. His arrival being matched by a smile. 'Oh yes, yes. Of course. I'm fine at the moment.'

'You sure?' His mother recognised the change in tone and manner. She must have wondered what it meant, whether the changed world with his ill father and his new responsibilities were a challenge or a bore. Something in between, Francis thought she would have concluded from the look. It bordered on resignation. It was exactly what his mother wouldn't have wanted to have seen.

The following day at lunch time Francis went to the pub. He was picking up bread and potatoes and buying stamps and was hoping to see Dilwyn who had phoned to ask about a course Francis had attended on environmental farming. He knew Dilwyn sometimes went to the pub, so he took the chance. When he got there, he thought how strange it was sitting there, never having been in the pub during all the years of growing up, the teenage years, the father and son years, the years when fathers showed off sons like an initiation, a ceremony.

He thought of that as he stood at the bar. 'Dilwyn in?'

'Which Dilwyn? Hey you're Dai's lad, aren't you?'

'Which Dai?' said Francis laughing.

The barman laughed too. He enjoyed the moment. 'Touché' he said, recovering. 'How is Dai? The boys miss him. Tell him the domino table sends their regards. Good at dominoes your father. Some say there's no skill in it. All luck. They should see your father play. Pint is it?'

'Dark.'

'Your father's drink.' The barman laughed again. Francis smiled. He liked such discordance. He liked the way it helped tell a story, filling the detail in. It somehow helped him decide what to take with him in his thoughts and what to leave behind. Dominoes. Good player. Competitive. Likes mild. He ran through what the conversation told him, building his new knowledge into what he knew, attaching it carefully, making sure it adhered, that it was accurate and true.

'There you go.'

Francis accepted the drink and smiled.

'Now which Dilwyn?' asked the barman, wanting to appear helpful and friendly.

'Dilwyn Davies, Dilwyn from Fair fach, up by us. Over the hill.'

'Oh Dilwyn. No. Not today. Comes down on Tuesdays normally. Has a drink with Vic from the café. You know Vic? Your father's dominoes partner.'

Francis had heard of Vic. He was Italian with an old café that spouted steam and had a line of Milk Tray boxes on the top shelf behind the counter. He had spoken to him on the phone. A high, shrill voice. 'He said he might be in,' said Francis.

'Then he might,' smiled the man. The look was used as an apology as he moved away. It told Francis that he enjoyed his work, that he particularly enjoyed the way it was capable of producing the unexpected. Francis could appreciate the allure of manifold reason, the multiplicities, possibilities rather than probabilities. The smile said nothing surprises me.

Francis began to smile too. He moved over to a seat by a long table. It was scratched by glasses and money and dust on jackets. He remembered such a table where they had lunch in Texas. Davison had provided it. A room with a table and a pool table and sofas and a coffee machine. Sometimes they would go back to the room. Other times they would sit in a field or in a truck and eat on the spot. That was why it was important to know where you were working. For Francis it didn't matter. He took some fruit and a flask of coffee. It was the same every day.

'Hey is that all you eat?' the other men joked.

'I've offered,' Brad said, looking as though Francis' repetitive diet reflected on him. 'Ol Pam she thinks the world of him. Wants to fatten him up. She tells him. All those calories. All those calories he's using up. I said, hey you seen him work?'

Francis would nod his way through the salvo. He wasn't bothered by it. It was mild, gentle for them. He had seen their rougher side, the shouting and spitting side which frequently became apparent at lunch times. There's something about the time, he thought. Half way through the day. Enough time to pick faults in work completed or think over some loose comment from the previous day.

'So what you got today?'

'Beef, I guess.'

'What do you mean you guess? You always have beef on Tuesdays. Every Tuesday you have beef. Tuesday is beef day.'

There were openings for each day. All predictable. All preliminaries for role play. They all had roles. Francis was the fall guy. The innocent abroad. Vulnerable. Swamped. Overwhelmed, they must have thought. They were waiting for him to toughen up. They knew how it worked, how they pushed and felt no resistance for a while. Push, push, push. They would go on and on, unravelling traits, revealing weaknesses, until some tender point was prodded. Francis had resisted for longer than anyone else. He made them nonchalant, flitting ideas, turning them over like cards in a pack. They waited for a reaction. Like snap, thought Francis. But he was aware, prepared. That drew attention. It eased out the characteristics of the English. For to them, Francis was English: Wales was unheard of and, for all Francis' efforts to educate them, they continued to say 'Yeh' and call it England. So the English were calm, distant, inscrutable even. No emotions were unleashed. Certainly no anger. Even indignity was counted out by a voice under his breath. Count to ten, count to ten it would say. One. Two. Three. Four. Five.

It never made ten. A voice interfered. 'You know what you've done.' It was the barman. It was the pub. His father's local. 'Listen, you'll have to excuse us. I mean we shouldn't say, but we had to laugh. Like father like son, I suppose.'

Francis smiled. He switched back to the dark Welsh pub. The small lounge reverberating to the chatter of two men in the corner, laughing occasionally and the undertone of the barman exchanging pleasantries. This time with Bill, whoever he was. Francis had heard them ask each other if they had seen so and so recently, whether they were well.

'Of all the places.' The barman laughed again. It was like a prompt for Francis to smile. 'Well there's not that many, but there's a choice. A good choice. And you pick there.'

'There?' Francis seemed a little alarmed. It was as though he was back in Texas. Texas at lunch time, he thought, the men testing him, becoming more and more ridiculous in their efforts to rile him. 'You mean here?' Francis seemed rattled, more so than he ever let himself appear in Texas. He looked at the table, he looked over the shoulder at the back of the chair.

'Should have given you your father's mug. It's that one up there. Silver.' The barman nodded towards a tankard. 'Don't you see what you've done?'

'What?' Francis was lost now. The look on his face brought a reassuring smile from Bill at the bar.

'Just like his father,' said Bill, shaking his head.

'You've sat in his chair,' the barman finally said. 'You've come in and sat in his bloody chair.'

Perhaps Francis' father died that day not the following Tuesday while he sat up in bed reading about the Silverton Railway and eating his corn flakes. He always ate corn flakes and a banana, a banana cut up into pieces spread amongst the flakes under a deluge of milk. Francis would watch him, thinking of Toggie and how the banana skins would be for the goat.

The doctor said it was a painless death. Francis nodded, thinking it was what doctors said, that they needed something to ease the despair they frequently encountered. Impulse and conscience, thought Francis, what they'd like to say, the clinical, however gruesome, and the restraint, the need to launch some comfort. Quick. Painless. The adjectives were always picked out, chosen without any real care. Francis would have preferred the truth, what it was that made his father seem to choke, whether it was the effort of trying to stay alive, a fight for breath or some pain that needed an outlet. And why did his eyes seem to open? A look of astonishment? And what caused the contortion, the sharpening of features?

His mother saw none of that. She was in the kitchen buttering his toast, looking for the marmalade, getting a tray ready to take upstairs, the tray she dropped when Francis called. He called from the landing. Like he had the first time his father had experienced a turn. 'Not again,' his mother said to herself, hearing the call. She turned to look for the custard creams. Upstairs, Francis moved back into the bedroom. He saw the pain on his father's face was much sharper than any of the grimaces he had seen during the turns. This was different. It was disconcertingly clear, pure. There was nothing else in the expression. Just pain. It made Francis return to the landing and call out again. 'Mum! Mum!' He was running now, but, by the time he raced back into the bedroom, it was too late. When he reached his father, he grabbed a hand. It was soft. That was a surprise. All those years of farming and his father's skin was soft. Not baby soft, but leaf soft, spring soft. He wanted to pull on it, to drag his father to the window, to fill his father's eyes with a glimpse of the valley between the trees. Somehow that seemed appropriate. Glimpsing. It was all his father did. But all his father's goals, all his values and beliefs, his motivation, was out there. He would have enjoyed it. Instead his eyes opened and closed and his chin fell and he looked as though he was falling into one of his long sleeps.

The funeral brought back memories. Brynlas' parlour became Zelda's back lawn, Brynlas' kitchen the temporary bar. Like in San Antonio there were people to meet and talk to, but the mystery of meeting the friends and family of Brad and Pam couldn't be matched by conversations with Uncle Gwyn or the cousins that surfaced for funerals. Francis was polite. Just like his old self in fact. He'd say hello, ask whoever confronted him how they were and let them talk. Most stories he had heard over and over. Not that there were many. From that he realised his father mostly kept himself to himself. He had suspected that. He knew there were ventures, but only to The Feathers or Vic's. Most encounters were linked to dominoes and market days. It was from there that stories came. Remonstrations mostly were recounted. What Francis' father had called an auctioneer at such and such a mart, how he duped the man from the ministry. Much was hearsay, but, from what Francis knew of his father, much was probably true. His father didn't believe in cultivating mystique or myths. He was forthright, clear, thought Francis. Admirable in a way.

'He was a bugger. Don't mind me saying that do you? I mean it in the nicest way.' The voice was Dilwyn's. 'And I owe you a thank you.'

'What?' Francis couldn't place the words in perspective.

'You seen Owain? He's here.'

Francis recognised the flow of questions. It was Dilwyn's way. He spoke in sequences. Owain did it too, even as a young boy. Francis thought it was something to do with isolation. The loneliness. The storing up of words. Given the chance they ran free. The words shifting and wriggling with the life the opportunities gave them. Sometimes they didn't settle, leaving incoherence. That made Francis nervous. He never knew what to answer, where to start.

'I said to Owain how is he? You seen Francis? But I should have rung. I meant to, but I never got there. And now, well. It's not good enough. Wouldn't have happened years ago. God I sound like an old man.'

'No,' said Francis, easing his way in. He smiled. It wasn't at the words or at the sense of what was being said, but at the way such people seemed to come out of nature. It made the hills seem like a web. They were caught there, held in a sort of sadness that suspended them. They wriggled free at times like this, times when they had to.

'I found him difficult. Have to say that. I'm here out of admiration.' Dilwyn paused momentarily. He seemed to be expecting Francis to interject, to ask what precise qualities were admired.

A far away look greeted his gaze. Francis was thinking deeply now, He was thinking of the incident with Owain's dog, the way his father made Dilwyn jittery, how his father stopped the long flow of words, reducing Dilwyn to responses rather than questions, monosyllabic responses. Yes. No. Francis remembered that. The silences. The looks. It showed him. It made him understand. His father said what he meant. Francis wondered whether that was rare in the hills.

'Thanks for the info by the way,' Dilwyn's voice rose now. 'Intriguing, eh? I mean it seemed very clear, but there must be a catch. Always is. You'd have a better idea. I mean having been there, having sat through it. Hey why don't you come up and talk it through with me. I'd like that. You could see Owain too. He's here till Tuesday. Has to go back then.'

'I will,' said Francis. He smiled again. 'Actually there's something I wanted to ask you. About the co-operative.'

'You want in?'

'Maybe. I mean I think I do.'

Dilwyn shook his head. Francis knew what it meant, that he was thinking of Francis' father, of his independence. 'Your father didn't want to know. Bloody co-operative, he used to say. He didn't trust the people from over Brecon way. Too distant, he said. Said decisions should be taken closer to home.' Dilwyn laughed. It stressed the dimensions of Francis' father's world. The valley. The village. Anything else was distant. It made Francis wonder what his father would have made of America.

'In a way he was right. Bad decisions see. Got in with the wrong firm.'

'Haven't heard about that,' remarked Francis.

'Your father heard about it. Smug he was. Mind you that's all sorted now.'

'Joining will save us money?'

'God aye.'

'A lot?'

'Oh yes, you'll cut your feed bill. You can sell through the co-operative too. You'll get a good deal there. Both ends better. You think about it. Chat to Meirion.'

'Meirion?'

'Meirion. Meirion Williams. Over there. By the window. Not that window, that one,' said Dilwyn, his eyes redirecting Francis to a grey haired man who was talking to Gethin.

Brynlas took over then. It demanded so much. It gave Francis so little time. Organising, working, negotiating. Business dominated. Any thoughts of America were like jottings. They came and went, seeming much less significant. It was as though Francis was adopting or inheriting his father's scheme, as though America was receding, losing its influence and detail. Domesticity, he thought. America was a violation of that. Its vestiges of freedom were losing familiarity. Instead ordinariness was clinging to him, settling him down amongst the autumn leaves and the frost and the fences he was mending. 'Circumstances,' he'd say. Coming home, father dying, the patching up of relationships. Logic backed up the inheritance. It also set him in Brynlas for some time, possibly to the end of his days. He couldn't believe that. He couldn't let himself believe it. From liberation to captivity. He'd shake his head. How did it happen? he'd ask himself, wanting to write, wanting someone or something to intervene.

Christmas 1994.

Fritz. Hi!

My father died last May. It was sudden. Painless the doctor said. But death means so much to everyone. Not just the grief, but the reorganisation. I'm doing it all now, running this and that and trying not to change too much. The one thing I'd like to do is to diversify a little. So I'm looking for a specialisation. Any ideas? The best I've come up with is ewe's cheese, special ewe's cheese with herbs and bits of fruit and nuts in it. You have that in Texas? It would be the first in Wales. Everybody I mention it to thinks it's daft. They say that if it could work, by now it would have been done. That's a bit Welsh. I'm sure people in the States would have said, yeh man go for it. I miss all that. It helps me when I say to myself someone's got to be the first, so why not me?

I still think of Ronnie. I know you're expecting me to ask of her and I am, but I'm getting through it. Other things have sort of taken over. The farm in particular. My future's here now, so any worries you and Zelda have about me showing up or trying to pull some stunt or other are unnecessary. I'm staying here. I had thought of travelling again – Australia not the USA – but the thought never developed and events sort of overtook it. Boring as it sounds, I'm happy now. The responsibility is wonderful. I decide what to buy, when to sell and I deal with the ministry. My mother leaves me alone (I live in a shed adjacent to the farmhouse, it's water tower-like and cosy) and the goats visit me. That's when I think of Ronnie. Still they come in and help me make decisions and consider what's gone on. If there's a gap in my life, I don't notice it.

Trust you're all well. You must write. Tell me about Zelda and Ronnie and Davison and, of course, Betty. Is she playing golf yet?

Merry Christmas, Francis.

Hello Welshman, Sorry about your dad. Thought you didn't get on with him? Must have got it wrong. I get most things wrong, but at least I've managed to write this card without swearing once. Merry Fucking Christmas, Fritz.

Christmas 1995

How are you? I'm well. Nothing changes here. I'm still relishing the challenge and things are beginning to turn. We're doing well. I joined a co-operative in March. My dad would have killed me. He was an independent so and so. To him, look after yourself meant keep away from everybody. He trusted no one, not even me or my mother. That is not until towards the end of his life. Something happened then. I've thought about it off and on all this year. I think something changed when I returned to Wales. I didn't realise it at the time, because it was sort of vague. I was aware of it, but it wasn't strong enough to reach out and say hey this is different. I knew it was different and I knew I was taking over and that he approved. That was the main thing: he approved. I heard it in his voice, I saw it in his face. I think America did that. I think he saw a change. Perhaps he doubted a need for continuity, for me to find a place and, perhaps he saw me as someone returning to a dream, coming home. He always thought I would, but must have wondered about the mechanism. How could it happen? How could it be the same? What he discovered was it wasn't. It changed me in some respects, but it changed him more profoundly. He came to respect me. He respected me because it was something he could never have done.

Toggie's just come in now. Toggie's my goat. Have I mentioned him? He does a Ronnie, visiting me whenever he feels like. He's rubbing heads with me now. Ouch! The force tells me he's in good shape. I'm glad of that. In the summer I was a bit concerned about his condition. His summer coat was very thin, so much so that I had to rub in a little sun tan oil along his back. Factor 35, I think. Hugely expensive, but only the best's good enough for Toggie. He's my best friend now.

Talking of friends, how's Ronnie? You didn't say? And how are you? Is Betty still dancing?

Merry Christmas, Francis.

Hi, Hell of a year here. No cold winds from the interior. No winds means warmer weather; warmer weather means more fucking rats. They're everywhere now and, because they're everywhere, I'm fucking everywhere.

Betty broke her leg dancing last week. Danced out of the house across the deck and fell down the stairs. Ended up in my fern garden. Squashed my fucking osmunda regalis. Merry fucking Christmas, I said. Who's gonna do the shopping?, she said. Who do you think? I said. Santa Fuckin' Claus I guess.

Season's greetings, Fritz.

Christmas 1996,

Hope Betty doesn't try her old trick again this year. Tie her down. Get her basting or plum pudding-making. Something seasonal and sedentary (is that the right word?).

I'm fine. The farm's fine too. We've had our best year ever. The co-operative is working well and I'm to be on the committee next year. I'm glad of that because I think I can help strengthen the marketing. We really have more clout than we think, so somehow we've got to appear stronger and, as you would say, tell them that we'll take no shit. I think the States taught me all I know about respect and strength and the way mutual strength can be accommodating. I'm sure you know what I mean.

Strange year here. I think the weather you spoke about last Christmas must have drifted our way. Spring was unusually cold and dry. Everything was late and ever since we've been struggling to catch up. I've spent a lot of time converting the room I was living in (did I tell you about it? it's small, detached from the main house and very much like the water tower) into the cheese making plant. That's cost lots of money, but we were much better off after dad's death than anyone anticipated, including my mum. So we're spending it – mum's had a central heating and appliance blitz and I've had the cheese-making plant.

As ever Toggie's next to me trying to eat the letter. He's been a bit down in the dumps recently. He hurt his leg. He really is a baby. For a few weeks he just held it off the ground whenever anyone looked his way. He'd shake and shiver a little too. It meant I couldn't cut his toenails for six weeks, till he began to turn in on his feet and slide around my room. He got better then. Wise old goat.

Talking of wise old goats, how's Betty? (couldn't resist that, forgive me). Here's hoping she doesn't dance across the veranda and fall on your osmunda regalis again this year. Didn't know you were into ferns and gardens in a big way. Fancy you knowing the Latin names. I guess there's a lot of things I don't know about you.

Merry Christmas, Francis.

Hi, Hope Christmas is better than Thanksgiving. We bought a bird and I mean a bird – one that makes noises and tries to fly. It ate too. Fucking thing saw off the astilbes in a week. Then it started on the azaleas, so I had to buy a cage. Betty said, 'Now don't you go getting something expensive. Remember you've got to kill it soon.'

'What!' I mean just because I put down poison and use gas doesn't mean I'm a natural born killer. As I said to Betty, 'A rat is different to a duck.' Fucking profound, yeh?

Merry Christmas, Fritz.

Christmas 1997
Sad year. Toggie died. It's dominated everything. I wanted him to be a new millennial goat. He nearly made it, just a couple of years. I

should have expected it. His condition had been deteriorating and he became very stiff, so much so that last winter I had to haul him up onto his legs once or twice. Whenever that happened, I got worried and called the vet. He checked him out and said he had some arthritis in his elbow joint. At the time, more worrying was the state of Toggie's teeth. The vet said, 'I'll just have a quick look at his teeth.' 'Oh they're fine,' I said, watching the vet force Toggie's mouth open. Only three and a half teeth came into view and the half tooth fell out when the vet touched it. I think it was then I realised he wasn't well.

I gave him evening primrose after that. It didn't make him sprout new teeth, but it did help his arthritis. His spirit improved too. He began to do all the things he used to do – he grazed on his knees, he came for walks, he had a gambol or two on spring mornings. Then, one Saturday, early summer, I saw him kick his stomach. He died four days after that. I stayed the night with him before he died. He binged on chocolate dessert and baked beans (all mixed together of course) and I told him stories about our long walks at blackberry time when his beard would be black and how he'd battle with Zoon and how I'd hide apples.

I miss him terribly. Even more than I missed you and Zelda and Ronnie and Brad and Pam and the water tower. Forgive me for saying that. I think you'll understand.

Merry Christmas, Francis.

Too bad about the goat. Guess I can't appreciate it. God I didn't cry when my mother died. She had a brain haemorrhage on Christmas Eve and died after my father went to Church to pray for her on Christmas Day. Still think of that when we go to Church Christmas Day and watch the television and visit friends and eat and eat and eat. I couldn't cry. Why?

Merry Christmas, Fritz.

Christmas 1998,

How are you all? I'm still here with my mum and Zoon, the goat, and the cheese-making plant and one hundred and seventy three sheep. Quite a family.

Everything's working well here apart from the government. I should have known it would happen. My Dad always said it would. He always had trouble with the man from the ministry. Mind you it was mostly of his own doing. He couldn't keep records. Perhaps I should say wouldn't keep records. The outcome was that he'd have to bluster his way through encounters using tricks and geography, the only things on his side. Still he'd always win. Now I'm having to do the same. Win, I mean. The battle I have is something the Europeans have drummed up. In short they feel threatened by my little cheese making plant so they're after me. I suppose they think if I can do it, so can one hundred or two hundred other Welsh sheep farmers. They're afraid of it. So they're drawing up charges of problems with the way I'm doing it. You know all the normal scares about soft cheese and bacteria. In short they're trying to close me down and I'm simply NOT having it.

How are you? I still think of you and Betty and, of course, Zelda and Ronnie. My months with you are so important now. A different world, I suppose. A world that encouraged me and showed me what I'm capable of.

Take care. And write.

Merry Christmas, Francis.

Hi Welshman, No strength for words. I've got some bug. My temperature is 101, there's a football bouncing on my brain and Betty's gone to San Antonio. Christmas shopping, she says, so I'm ten times worse and wanting to kiss the life out of her. No Christmas shopping for Fritz! Who's the big shot in this house, eh? Don't answer that.

Bad year. Firm taken over. New contracts. 20% less holidays, 20% less pay, 20% more work. Globalisation, the union says. Fucking union. It has to say something. What does it know? Globalisation. How can you globalise rats?

Merry Christmas, Fritz.

Christmas 1999

Dear Fritz,

Hope you recovered in time for last Christmas. You've probably forgotten your illness by now. I haven't, but I suppose that's how it is for us – a year is five minutes' conversation. Perhaps we should double our efforts. I'm sure we could manage ten minutes a year. How about July 4th? I'll write early to prompt you. Do we have a deal?

It's been a quite year here. The ministry seems to have backed down (thank God!) and wool and lamb prices have been encouragingly high (hurrah!). But the quietness makes me edgy. I'm looking around for ideas now. Trekking, perhaps. Holiday homes. Farm holidays. Everyone says the service sector is here to say. So why not bring it to Brynlas? The location is right, so is the climate, the economic climate that is. Perhaps I'll give one of them a go. Watch this space.

It's six years now since I left Texas. Ronnie will be going on 15. That's unimaginable. I suppose the separation and the one letter a year from you maintains a time warp. You're the same, I'm the same, Ronnie's the same; nothing's moved on, yet it has and we're all so different. Mind you what you write in your Christmas cards always supports the theory – you sound exactly the same. Thank God for that. Merry Christmas, Francis.

Hi Welshman, You heard of cellulite? Do you have it over there? Well I've got it here. It's sort of like a bubble around my stomach. Betty says I'm full of ice cream. Ben and Jerry's, I guess. It's still the best.

She's got it too – the cellulite I mean. It's on her thighs. Ice cream on her fucking thighs. She must be massaging it in. No wonder we're getting through six buckets a week.

You're right. We've changed, but we haven't changed. How's the cellulite over there in Wales? That Zoon got it?

Merry Christmas. Roll on July 4, Fritz.

Francis was writing his July letter to Fritz when his mother walked in.

'You've got a visitor,' she said, a happy look suffused over her face.

'I heard a car.'

'Yes.'

'Didn't recognise it.'

'No.' She smiled again. 'You wouldn't,' she added. Her words stopped Francis. They made him look up. He needed to scrutinise expressions more thoroughly now, to interpret the significance of what was being said. 'You'll be pleased,' said his mother, waiting for his words.

'I will?'

'Think so. I'll leave you to it. They're in the kitchen.'

Why didn't I ask who, thought Francis when he heard his mother close the door. It was as though he was fearful of surprises. That was a legacy. He associated surprises with accusations, with finger pointing and cold looks. They stopped him. Like he had stopped now. They made him remember. So he sat considering America. Late afternoon America. With Fritz. Fritz with his unflinching face. The straight delivery. The need for defence. His mind saying, 'They'll see. They'll see.' And all the other comfort phrases. They know me. They know me. The reiteration. The pushing, the prodding. The attempts at infiltration.

He shook his head as he put the top on his pen. He read through the first sentence of the words he had been writing while covering the piece of paper they were on. Why am I covering up? he thought. He questioned that, wondering what he was doing, sighing as he stood up. They're in the kitchen, a voice in his head was saying.

The Ronnie he saw in the kitchen was taller than he had imagined Ronnie would be at fifteen. She was slightly thinner too, more sinewy. She looked as though she had been stretched. Colt-like, his father would have said. She was certainly all limbs. He wondered whether he should say any of that, whether he should tell her how he had aged her, how in his mind she had gone through gangly and filling out stages, how such stages were somehow part and parcel of his analysis of what had gone on. Analysis, he thought, relishing the prospect. Now he could ask her. Now he could examine what she knew.

'Good God,' he said excitedly. 'Well, well.' He shook his head, covered his eyes with his hands and as quickly took them away. 'Just checking. My God. It is you. Ronnie! Hey I can't believe this.' A smile arrived now. It said welcome. 'So why are you here? What's got you here? Nothing wrong is there?'

'No. There's nothing wrong.' The tone of her voice conveyed how Francis' reasoning had surprised her. 'By the way this is Rhoda,' said Ronnie, standing behind the kitchen table. Rhoda moved to her side. The table hid half their bodies. Behind it Ronnie could almost still be the little girl he had known.

'Hi,' said Rhoda.

'Hi,' said Francis, looking at the taller, darker girl who half smiled. She looked older than Ronnie. And she was. Francis should have worked that out. The car should have told him that Ronnie was too young to drive and that the driver must be older. He looked at the round clear eyes that dominated Rhoda's features. They made her look intelligent. They directed her expressions. They were smiling now. 'Coffee. We'll have some coffee, yeh?' Francis remembered the need for civility. 'You sit down. Ok, Ok, well let's see what we can do.'

Ronnie laughed. 'Hey I remember you.'

'You do?'

'Yeh. You know Aunt Zelda denied you existed. I mean she said you never came to the States, but I said I thought I'd met you. Something told me I had. Don't know what. But something stuck. Then I did a bit of research. Confronted her with it.'

Francis' hands roamed around the kitchen top, picking up and putting down containers and cups. He wished his mother was with him. She would deal with this. She would have left him to sit and talk and take in what was said. 'How'd you know?' he managed to say, finding the filters for the machine. 'I mean about Brynlas?'

'Looked it up,' said Ronnie.

'What?' said Rhoda interrupting her. Francis turned and smiled her way. Rhoda looked rather serious now. A fair girl with round glasses. Nervous, thought Francis, protracting his smile, trying to make her feel comfortable.

'The fire. I told you.' Ronnie directed her words solely at Rhoda.

'Oh yeh,' Rhoda nodded.

'Why did you look it up?' Francis poured water into the coffee machine as he spoke. He plugged the machine in quickly and turned back towards the table. Immediately he felt calmer. It allowed him to concentrate again.

'Oh we were doing a project in school. You know the sort of thing. Find an event, look it up. I did the Paseo del Rio.' Again Ronnie spoke more to Rhoda than Francis. She waited for Rhoda to nod before continuing. 'You know that Francis? The Paseo del Rio. The river walkway in San Antonio. You know it?' She waited for Francis to nod a response. 'Well anyway, I went to the library in San Antonio and I thought hell I could do this for the fire.'

'You knew about it?'

'Oh yeh,' Ronnie looked puzzled by Francis' question. 'You're kind of cute you know that? I mean you're asking all the wrong questions. Gee I thought it would be why're you here, what you doing.'

'So why are you here?' Francis obliged. He realised how much he wanted to know answers to what Ronnie was prompting. 'You staying? I mean we can fix you up over night. Stay a few days.'

'No we've got to go back to Swansea. We fly home tomorrow,' said Rhoda in a matter of fact way.

Francis' disappointment was obvious. He breathed deeply, thinking how he should have guessed he would only ever be allowed a glimpse, a peep at the reality he had been questioning. It all called for refinement, for the words in his mind to be bolstered by a sharpness and directness that was fine tuned and would miss little.

'Yeh, it's been good,' said Rhoda. 'We like your country. God the people. So quaint. That's a good English word, yeh?'

Francis nodded. He could sense Rhoda had a capacity for talking, for going on and on. He needed to check that, to circumvent any openings that may have presented themselves.

'Yeh I'd heard of Wales.'

'Really,' said Francis, trying to be polite.

'Remember Richmond, Ronnie? That concert. The tour of Virginia. The jamboree.' Rhoda looked hard at Ronnie. It urged her to respond. It said come on. In turn Ronnie looked puzzled and sighed. 'You remember,' said Rhoda. 'Yeh you remember. The conductor was from Wales. And if you can't remember him you'll remember Tommy McCarry's cello, yeh?' She almost demanded the recall.

'Oh my God, yeh. Hey Francis you should have heard it.'

'God I wish we'd seen it. I mean I wish we'd been in the audience. They could see it.'

'Yeh it sort of disappeared,' remarked Ronnie.

'It's thing was in a crack.' Rhoda tried to explain the source of their mirth.

'Thing?' said Francis.

'You know. The thing. At the end.'

'The spike,' said Ronnie, finding an acceptable description of what Rhoda was trying to ascribe a noun to.

'Yeh the spike,' said Rhoda, reclaiming the story. 'Tommy got it stuck in a crack between the pieces of the stage. It was one of those stages that were built. Sort of in bits. Yeh? You must have seen them. They have them in schools, yeh?' Rhoda looked for some recognition from Francis. A nod said he understood. 'We could see the cello getting lower and lower. Tommy sort of managed to play on.'

'Went down with his cello,' joked Ronnie, laughing wildly now. She always laughed well, Francis thought. It was a full laugh, infectious. Rhoda joined her. The sound seemed to build as though it was coalescing, gaining volume.

'Real funny that,' Rhoda said, disturbing the sound. It broke into splutters and ended as Ronnie coughed.

'Oh,' said Ronnie, starting to laugh again. She was almost crying now.

'So you're here to sing?' asked Francis.

'Texas State Youth Choir,' replied Rhoda. 'British tour.'

'First and last British tour,' added Ronnie.

'That bad?' asked Francis, affected by the sudden change in her tone.

'Oh no, no. Nothing wrong with us or the people. You Welsh have been great. Just the old story.'

'And what's that?' asked Francis.

'Francis!' screeched Ronnie, surprised at Francis' naïvety. 'Money. That's the trouble. It's always the trouble.'

265

Ronnie had found the name of the farm on the back of a photo. An old photo she said. It must have been one Francis had been given by his father. His father always dated the photo and on its back made comments. Francis ran through the sort of description in his mind. 'Uncle Eiron in the dairy. Brynlas Farm, Wernfawr, Powys. March 11th, 1940.' The full address. The precise date. It was as though his father was preparing the photos like documents for future generations. They were to be admired, to be learnt from.

'I knew it was the place,' Ronnie said. 'I mean Aunt Zelda told me about dad going off for a few years before he met my mother. I guess it sort of helps me understand him.'

'Coming here,' said Francis, qualifying what she was saying.

'Yeh. Aunt Zelda said he always had an adventurous spirit. I like that.'

'You need things like that,' Rhoda said, trying to ease her way back into the conversation. 'I guess you need to build a picture.'

'Oh yeh,' Ronnie agreed. She was nodding now. Her eyes wide open, appreciating what was being said, agreeing with it. 'Yeh, yeh. I've spent years building a picture. The pictures of Wales were real helpful. They were so cute. So warm. You understand?'

Francis and Rhoda nodded. Neither spoke. Neither felt the need to interrupt Ronnie's flow. They kept out of it: Rhoda hoping the topic would change or broaden out; Francis wanting Ronnie to go deeper and deeper into detail.

'It was the photos that told me how much I needed to know. I wanted to know him. I mean God, he was my father.' Ronnie shrugged. She wasn't pleased with her explanation. She tried to sort it out. 'I mean everything I knew about him came from Aunt Zelda. To find something out for myself was great. I was so pleased. That's what encouraged me to go to the paper office and research the fire. And it was so easy. I gave them a date and ten minutes later I had a copy of the paper. And there it was. Gee. I'll never forget the names and the photo.'

'Be easier next year,' said Rhoda, interrupting Ronnie's flow.

'Hey what d'you mean?' asked Ronnie.

'CD Rom. They're putting the paper on CD Rom. They announced it the other day. All the years. Back to 1960 to begin with.'

Francis nodded. He didn't understand the significance of that, but he tried to look as though he understood the implications. He smiled and nodded, raising his eyebrows appreciatively.

'I'll go back and try it again,' said Ronnie excitedly. 'God it will be so easy. Type in fire or water tower or Brad Stubbs or Francis Williams and see what comes up. That will be sure interesting. God.' She shook her head. A thought pulled her back. 'Anyway that's how I found you.' She laughed again and looked at Francis.

'Me?' Francis latched onto the direction of the look.

'Yeh. The foreign national who saved me.'

'I didn't save you. You were with me. You used to come up to the tower. You used to visit me.'

'I did? I was wondering about that. What were you doing in the tower?'

'I stayed there for a while.'

'I remember my dad there. He'd sort of play games there, yeh? Battles, I think. He used to draw too. I think I just went there to see him. He must have been good to be with.'

Francis smiled. 'He was,' he found himself saying. 'He was good with you kids.'

Ronnie was shaking her head now. Something had come to her. It was what she had travelled to Brynlas for. A revelation. A memory. 'You came on holiday, yeh? Hey, I remember now. Dad invited you over. Aunt Zelda took her time to admit you visited. Don't know why. I guess she didn't want to complicate it. I mean it was real complicated as it was. The fires, the deaths. You came for a month, yeh?' Ronnie was excited now. Her interpretation of events seemed to her to be correct. Francis was confirming it, sitting and nodding, knowing somehow that he should go along with whatever she said. 'Oh God what a holiday. I mean you coming all that way and well the fire. Gee. And the police questioning you.'

'Helping with their enquiries.' Francis remembered his discovery of it from the papers Davison had brought him, the way the reports changed the significance of the police visit. The pleasant policeman, he thought, the genial questions. The concentration. The preamble. The talk of England.

'And you didn't say goodbye,' said Ronnie, interfering. 'No time, I guess.' Ronnie smiled offering an easy way out. 'I guess you wanted to get home.' Francis nodded, not wanting to upset her view of how things were. So he had gone, he thought. He had left her. It seemed calculated, cold. She must have wondered why such an event hadn't devastated him. Normal people would have been devastated. He went home. Simple. Clinical. Francis shook his head and tried to find something that would put him in a better light.

'Aunt Zelda said you had commitments yeh?'

'Yes. Sort of. It was complicated.' Francis stumbled on words. Excuse, excuse, excuse, he thought, find an excuse. Work, visa. The visa, he thought, the visa. He settled on that. Something came to mind. 'It was the visa.' Francis made it sound like a throwaway comment. He made it sound unimportant. 'Shouldn't have been working.'

'I see,' said Ronnie, looking serious. 'Yeh I understand. I didn't at the time. I mean you were a sort of link. More so than Aunt Zelda. More so than Fritz.'

'Fritz. How is he?' Francis was glad of the break. He wanted to ask about Fritz.

'Fritz is fat. Oh God is he fat, but he's funny, gee he's seriously funny.'

'Tell Francis the story about *Don Giovanni*,' urged Rhoda, laughing to herself.

'*Don Giovanni*? Oh yeh. God.' Ronnie laughed too. 'Ok, Ok,' she said, composing herself. 'This was just before we left. He came over to see Aunt Zelda and I was in watching *Don Giovanni* on tape. I was sort of looking for something to say so I said, Hey you like opera? He says, yeh her shows are great. Her shows are great!'

Rhoda laughed more fully. Francis followed, not really understanding the joke. 'Oh Jesus,' spluttered Rhoda. 'He meant Oprah. Oprah Winfrey. My God. What did you do? I've never asked you what you did?'

'I laughed,' admitted Ronnie. 'Couldn't help it. He's gotten a big problem with culture. Golf and gardening's all he knows. Gee he needs educating. I laugh whenever I see him. He's funny.'

Fat Fritz, thought Francis, thinking back to the last Christmas card. He would have something to write now, something that Fritz would have to keep to himself. Could he be trusted? Francis didn't dwell on that. He probed further.

'You see him often?' he asked.

'Oh yeh. Once a week. Sometimes twice a week. Gets on well with Aunt Zelda.' Ronnie laughed again. She shook her head. It indicated she couldn't understand their connection. 'They watch movies. All sorts of things. Fritz doesn't know what to make of them. He sits and watches and goes on about taking her to football.'

'They're friends then?'

'Oh yeh they're pals. Hey you didn't think that.... Fritz and Aunt Zelda? Oh God. No.' Again she laughed fully. Rhoda laughed too. It was clear she, too, knew Fritz and considered any liaison between him and Zelda to be preposterous. Rhoda's laugh seemed more cruel. It lacked any affection. It conveyed to Francis that she thought much less of Fritz than Ronnie did.

'You didn't think...' Rhoda laughed again briefly but fully.

Ronnie hadn't stopped laughing. 'Oh Francis,' she said, slowly regaining control. 'I mean Fritz is lovely, but he and Zelda. God all they want to do is sit on the deck and watch films. God knows what he tells his wife.'

'Betty? She's nice,' said Francis.

'She's probably like you thinking something's going on there.'

'Betty? No.' Francis disagreed. He wanted to explain his intuition, but found it difficult. He gathered thoughts. The pause extended into a silence. An uncomfortable silence. Come on, thought Francis. Come on Rhoda, he said under his breath. He would have been grateful if she had offered something now. He looked her way. She smiled back. A nervous smile. His eyes shifted down, away.

'Hey can I see the animals?' Ronnie was animated again. 'Before we go, I mean. We'll have coffee first. Yeh I'd like that. Then the animals. They're so cute. I've lived with them for years. You know that? Dad told me all about them.'

'Your dad did?'

'Oh yeh. Who else?' Ronnie let a flutter of a look touch her face. Bewilderment thought Francis. It was shaken quickly away. The reaffirmation of her beliefs. It struck Francis. Such depth of belief. He wondered where its depth came from, how it was so effective as a foundation for all she knew. He smiled. She returned the smile. 'Dad told me in the water tower. He used to plan battles there and draw. Have I told you that?' asked Ronnie, thinking the words familiar.

'Draw?'

'Yeh. Little cartoons. I've got some. Bald headed guys. I mean guy.'

'Hey they're good.' Rhoda recognised the description and realised she had seen the cartoons. 'You like those. They're on your wall, yeh? They're kind of clever. I mean in a simple way. Makes you wonder why he did that. It's got to be a cry, you know?'

'Yeh I guess so,' agreed Ronnie. 'Don't get that feeling from anything else though. The priest said he was well loved. I've got a typescript of his speech, what he said about my Pa.'

Again Francis found himself reconstructing the events, recalling phrases and words. He focused on the priest. The speech. The wall, he thought. The bloody wall.

'Hey what I'd really like is to wander round the farm for a while. Check out the animals, take in the charm.'

Francis laughed. He knew already that he liked her, that she was little changed. Perhaps little bits of Zelda had rubbed off on her. She

269

seemed more middle class now, a touch of snobbery was evident. Like Zelda, he thought.

'Hey, you guys go off,' suggested Rhoda. 'I'll stay here. A cow's a cow to me.'

'No you come too,' cried Ronnie.

'No, I'll be fine. I've got my book in the car. Yeh I'll be fine. We shouldn't be late, remember,' she warned Ronnie. 'Sue Ellen said she'd wait for us before going out and discovering Swansea. We shouldn't miss that. It's our last night remember.'

'Party, party, party,' said Ronnie.

Francis took Ronnie to the room by the shearers' shed. It was an office now, an office for the cheese making plant, but he still thought of it as his room. It was still like the water tower. A private place. As he offered her a seat, he wondered whether something she said or he said would change what was set in her mind, whether she would recall something out of their reacquaintance that would question what she had been told. He wondered what the ice breaker could be. He knew the realisation would have to come from within her. He couldn't feed it. He would have to wait. She would be certain then. She would see the truth.

'That's Texas,' Ronnie said, looking at a map. 'We on there?'

'The wood? The water tower?'

'No. Aunt Zelda's. The old house. She still goes back to look at it. Prefers it to where we live now. More space, I guess.' Ronnie shrugged. The look told Francis that she didn't understand it. She looked at the map again.

'The wood's there,' said Francis, surprised by the way her focus had changed. He was the same, he thought. His focus had changed. Why? Place, people. Zelda, he thought, but he wouldn't blame her for that. Connections, life, he thought. That seemed more reasonable.

'So what did my dad do here?'

'He lived here,' said Francis, lying calmly. 'He milked the cows.'

'You have cows?'

'Not any more.'

'Oh I'd have liked to have seen some cows.' Ronnie looked disappointed. She turned to face Francis and moved to the door. Its simple catch attracted her. She played with it.

'You push it up,' said Francis, explaining the mechanism.

'Never seen anything like this,' she said, laughing. It was a calculated laugh. It told Francis how primitive she found it. 'And this works?'

'To a degree,' said Francis, thinking of Toggie's dexterity, how the goat had mastered it quickly and how Zoon had never quite worked it out.

'So he did the milking, yeh?'

'The milking. And he'd help with the sheep. Mainly worked on maintenance though.'

'That's what he did in Texas,' said Ronnie, welcoming Francis' answer.

'Yes.' Francis felt calm now. Texas, he thought, remembering the wall again, the wall Brad had built. And the priest. And the fence he had climbed over after the fight. And Jim MacDonald. And Jim MacDonald's words. He remembered the ditches he and Brad had dug together. He remembered the tapes he had found under the bed. The bus tapes. And with the memories came a smugness. It was as though he was giving himself marks for his answers. Ronnie stared at him. She couldn't sense such mischief. She wanted belligerence. She wanted to be told. Francis wondered whether that was frustrating her, whether at some stage she would give him a look and say cut the shit. The problem was he couldn't.

'Gee how could he leave those animals. Are the goats still here? They were my favourites.'

'Toggie and Zoon.'

'Yeh.'

'Toggie died.'

'Oh that's too bad. Guess Rhoda was right. All she said about turning up. You know. About uncovering things. She said it's best to leave it as it is. You understand?'

Francis nodded. Of course he understood. It was what he had practised, not so much by choice, but through the circumstances that continued to leer at him. They were still doing that. Even now. He would have liked to turn her way. He would have liked to divulge all that he knew, to tell Ronnie about Brad beating Pam, about Brad's shortcomings at work, about his fighting and squabbling, about his obsessions. The little reality Zelda had fed her would make her scorn that. He knew she would protest and wriggle and stop listening, that she would just leave, thinking him bitter. She wouldn't wonder why. Why should she? Why should she bother? He was unimportant to her, at least he was intrinsically. She needed him only to be anecdotal and amusing about Brad. But Francis couldn't be that. He could only be luke warm. A candle rather than an electric light, he thought, considering what he should say.

'Kept himself to himself,' he said slowly. 'Didn't really mix. Saw

271

more of the animals than us.' He laughed warmly, convincingly.

'He loved those goats. Lots of photos of them. Photos of you too.'

'Me?'

'Oh yeh. You with Toggie and Zoon, with Bess too. Yeh lots of you, well one or two. Seems like a lot because there's none of him, I guess.' She paused and laughed at herself. 'Hey you look so young in those photos.'

'I was young. They were taken when I was fourteen or fifteen.'

'My age. Aunt Zelda said you were some young farmhand, someone my pa made friends with.'

Francis smiled again. More to himself this time than Ronnie. Opportunity, he thought, opportunity after opportunity to be sententious and revealing. He checked himself again.

'Gee I'm sure he liked it here.' Ronnie kept surveying everything around her. She did it as she moved through the farmyard. She did it when she reached the trees. She did it when she came out of the thin line of trees and faced the drop down to the valley. 'This all yours?' she asked.

Francis nodded.

'You're lucky. So green.'

'Like an apple,' laughed Francis, thinking how pleased he was that Ronnie could still be emotional. That warmed him. Yet something about her manner also made him keep his distance. Personal and impersonal, he thought, somehow they were linked in Ronnie and, as if constantly in turmoil, at any time either could be ascendant.

'Our apples are normally red,' Ronnie said, smiling. 'But yeh, I guess they're green over here, so yeh let's go with the local.'

'So are you happy?' Francis laughed, a little impatient now. He wanted to store the trivia away, to move onto something deeper.

'Oh yeh. It's so interesting. You know I can picture him here. I can almost feel him here. Yeh, that's it.' Ronnie was excited now. She was open mouthed, considering. Any problems were being eclipsed.

'I meant with your life in Texas,' said Francis, quite directly.

'Oh yeh. Why shouldn't I be? Hey you know something?' Ronnie laughed. Again she couldn't follow the line of questions. She stopped and thought. She began to re-evaluate what she had said, she began to question what, if anything she was missing. 'Yeh, I'm happy. Zelda's good to me. The house is luxurious. I go to a good school. I guess I'm doing fine.'

Francis wondered if that was all she would say. He kept hoping that something would trigger a memory and that the memory would drive her to find out about Francis and Brad and Wales and the water tower.

'And I'm grateful. She's been good. Gee so good. She's a sweet lady. Don't know that she's happy though. I mean it's a hell of a thing to have taken me on. One hell of a commitment. I mean it must have held her up. That sort of worries me.'

'Why?' asked Francis, egging her on.

'Don't know. That's the stupid thing. I just don't know. Something to do with the way she values her freedom, I guess. Something to do with me getting in the way, stopping her doing this and that. No wonder she was pleased when I was at Uncle Paul's. Can't blame her. I mean, gee she loves freedom. Made me feel a little awkward. You know?'

Francis nodded. The words matched what he would have expected. He thought back to the early signs of impatience and intolerance. The symptoms of that were masked by excuses and apologies. They flowed with Ronnie's words now, leaving a sense of selfishness. Rather graceless thought Francis, recreating scenes and dialogue, remembering the sense of relief that Zelda couldn't contain when Ronnie stayed on at Paul's. Where's the tenderness? thought Francis.

'She got better. I mean as I got older. She could leave me then.' Ronnie laughed. 'She kept trying to entertain me, taking me here, putting me in clubs and things. She'd take me and pick me up. Just to have an hour to herself, I guess.' Another laugh told Francis memories were coming and going. Commonplace, light memories too insignificant to bother him with. She smiled warmly. 'Ok enough of me,' she said.

'But she kept your singing going?'

'Oh yeh,' Ronnie found herself saying, a little annoyed with Francis' persistence. 'I was a bit naughty mind, kind of didn't mention it for a while. I mean she didn't know me and I didn't like it. That was cool.' Ronnie pulled a face. 'Hey did you meet my teacher? Miss Pitton. What a demon. Oh yeh!' The exclamation secured Miss Pitton in Francis' memory. He recalled her now. Friday evenings after school. The scales. The songs. All the songs Ronnie didn't want to sing. 'Oh God, Beth Pitton. You know what dad called her.'

'Don't tell me. I should remember.' Francis grated his teeth as he tried to recall. Pitton, Pitton. He knew it was something to do with her name. A play on the sound. The sound, he thought, trying again. Pitton, Pitton.

'Miss Spitton,' laughed Ronnie. 'Gee that was funny at the time. Started out as Miss Spittoon, but he said it didn't work. Didn't rhyme or something. God I hated her.'

'I know.'

'Did I tell you?'

Francis nodded. He saw a look of surprise on her face. It lingered. It made him wonder what it covered, what thoughts were constructing the look. Austerity, thought Francis, wishing it was delving into a cognate criticism that was sharper and stronger than the look. Perhaps she was seeing now, really seeing.

'Hey that seems strange,' remarked Ronnie.

'Strange?'

'Me telling you about ol' Spitton.'

'You did tell me.'

'You sure? So what else did I tell you?'

Francis thought quickly. Incisive thought was crucial now. Something that would show how close they had been, how histories were swopped, how intimacies were revealed. 'Morris the Realm,' said Francis, remembering something Brad had said.

'Oh yeh,' laughed Ronnie. 'Oh yeh. What a place! Everything there. All under a roof. Every small town in America has a Morris the Realm.'

'You can say it,' laughed Francis.

'Now I can. Oh yeh. Couldn't then.'

'Morris eleven,' said Francis, timing the words well.

'Yeh. Hey you know lots. You know everything.' Ronnie shook her head.

Francis smiled. He thought how the conversation sounded like something they would have enjoyed when she was eight. It was loose and free, wandering, delving into the unexpected which seemed to attract it. Away from Ronnie such conversation always seemed in danger of attenuation. It needed youth, he thought. He could see that now. He could see it in Ronnie's eyes. Amplifying, clarifying. More than anything believing what she was saying. They were so supportive. Like an act of faith, thought Francis. They could change quickly too. Like now. Francis walked on as confusion crept in.

'You really remember?' she was asking.

'What?' Francis sounded confused. The thoughts had detached him momentarily from the conversation.

'Me telling you about Pitton.'

Francis nodded. 'You said she had a crumpled nose. Used to squeeze it up to keep her glasses on. Had a moaning voice. Yeh? And she took no breath between words. She used to wheeze.' Francis was surprised at the recall. Somehow pressure had produced it, dredging it up to the point that the image he had of Pitton was resurrected. It was Ronnie's image. She had painted it. Now he was offering it back to her. And she was shocked. He could see that. He wanted to ask why, but realised it was all to do with the degree of exposition. How did he know all that? She wouldn't have told him. Not in a month. In a month she wouldn't have told him. In two or three months, then yes, possibly. Over time, then yes, he would come to know. But surely not in four weeks. Not in twenty eight days.

Ronnie had no time to develop that. All that was left was to ask to see Bess and Zoon. She had an hour for that. It was all they were designated. To her it was all they were worth. Small pieces in the jigsaw, thought Francis, taking her down to the valley and the field where Bess had roamed since his father's death. Half an hour for Zoon, two hours for me, he thought, summing up. He smiled through the summary. He wanted to give her enough to want to return, to call back, to impress upon her that Brynlas is welcoming, a place she could enjoy. Francis began to play for time.

'You take care,' he said when they got back to the farmhouse.

'We'd better go,' said Rhoda, greeting them.

'Yeh, Ok. Be with you now.' Ronnie stopped and turned to face Francis who was following her through the courtyard.

'So you'll come again?' he asked

'Yeh, maybe. I'd sure like to. It's nice here. And all those links make me feel at home.' She nodded and smiled, a full smile. 'And you've been so kind. God I haven't said thank you properly yet.'

'For what?' asked Francis.

'For keeping me alive. It was kind of important I came over and said that. Thanks.'

'Pleasure,' said Francis, accepting her for a hug.

'Now you look after yourself.'

'And you.'

Francis turned as the car moved away. He kept watching as it began to descend into the valley. When it dipped out of sight, he ran back indoors. He had to write now. He had to recall the words, the thoughts. He had to record what he remembered and what he had learnt. Beth Pitton, Zelda, Zelda saying he hadn't visited, Zelda saying Brad visited Wales, Zelda saying Brad could draw. Those bald headed guys. Toggie and Zoon. 'Brad's animals,' he said to himself, picking up a pen. As soon as he began to write, he realised the image he now had in his mind was confused. The visit had obliterated the Ronnie he had developed. Smudged it, blurred it, over-exposed it, he thought, discarding it. In its place was something less pure and slightly less beautiful but still strong. The sense of humour, the fun, the youth pervaded. Life, thought Francis, admiring the power, the force. It was the life in her that tracked him down. He thought of the papers again. The papers Davison brought. The bundle in the plastic bag. The news of the fire was like a wave washing up on the front page; the backwash drawing it back, making it unnewsworthy such a short time after its impact. It would have been the same for her, he thought, turning it into a shared experience. He relished that. The cutting of the string. The springing of the paper. The newsprint on the fingers.

There was nothing threatening in that. But there was something else she had said. He wondered why the danger didn't strike him at the time. He had seen it. Like a snake, he thought. But he hadn't considered the bite, the venom. 'CD Rom,' he said to himself, musing it over. 'CD Rom.' He wondered what it was, what it looked like. He imagined it was like a bomb. 'Rom, Bomb,' he thought, exploding information. 'Type in your name,' she had said. So you type it on a screen, then bang, everything comes up, a complete exposition. It didn't worry him at first, but then he realised. The arrest. The charges. They would come up. He imagined it. 'In Mobile, Tennessee, the foreign national, who was deemed a hero last month in the San Antonio wood fire that caused four deaths, was arrested. He is charged with abduction.' But it would be more than that. Much more. Much more depth. Much more detail. What he was like. A physical description. A photo perhaps. One that he had given Ronnie, perhaps one with him and Toggie and Zoon. And words from someone. An acquaintance. Or a friend. Fritz perhaps. Fritz saying he was just a regular guy, nothing more or less, that he loved Ronnie, that he just wanted to see her.

On and on, thought Francis, anticipating questions. Why? Why did he want to see her? Why was he denied access to her? He anticipated the illumination. The exposé. The speculation. The revelation. He also knew it had never got that far, that something put up a barrier and held the investigation in check. If it hadn't, they would have got to him, phoning, questioning. His release must have done that. But that offered little relief. The fact was he was there, abductor and more. Type in Francis Williams and out it would come. 'She'll find it,' he thought, assessing her tenacity and how the past motivated her. 'She'll find it.'

Being a detective came easily to Francis. He tracked Ronnie down by phoning the concert hall in Swansea where the choir had played. A telephonist told him where they were staying without any prompting.

That surprised him. He had expected her to be suspicious, to ask questions regarding his interest. So he had planned a spiel. It was on a piece of paper in front of him. Ronnie Stubbs and Rhoda Fisher, two friends. He was to be away. On business. So he hadn't planned to see them. But he had returned early and they had one last night in Wales, so he could see them. As it was, there was no need for any of that. All that had happened was that he asked a question and the telephonist responded.

'Could you hold the line a minute?' was all that was asked, then in the background there was a salvo of questions and someone called Gerald was whispering. The telephonist confirmed what Francis had heard. 'Apparently they're at the Ocean Crest,' she said. 'You know it?'

'No, but I'll find it,' Francis answered.

'It's on the front. Oystermouth Road. You know Swansea?'

'Yes,' answered Francis confidently. 'Down by the jail.'

'That's it,' said the telephonist.

His mother asked who he had been talking to when she entered the room. He told his mother about it. He sensed she needed to know who the girls were, to link them into what she knew of Texas and the water tower and the fire and the deaths. Her question made Francis realise that she must have been curious, that his answers must have pleased her. A nod confirmed that. Another nod seemed to suggest she was pleased to hear more about the fire. She never pushed the issue, thought Francis. She never broached it. 'So what did you think of her?'

'Nice.'

'She is. Lovely.' His smile told her he hadn't been let down, that the reality of her form and presence in terms of its humour and spirit was as lovely as he remembered it. That pleased her. She returned his smile.

'She Ok?' she asked.

'Fine.'

'Good.' His mother bit her tongue. Francis sensed she wanted to ask more, perhaps about how Ronnie had coped, how she had maintained a balance and endured, how she could start from scratch and not change. How could she have done that? With all the problems. With all the pain. Francis considered the question and wondered whether it was easier at eight, whether starting again was less daunting. Perhaps it was exciting even.

'She's staying in Swansea.'

'I know.'

'Leaving tomorrow. Thought I might see her again. For breakfast. What do you think?'

'If you want.' His mother left it open. She made him consider again whether leaving things alone was the best policy, whether now it was time to change, to become a playmaker rather than be sidelined. Somehow he felt Ronnie had brought him back in. She had chosen to do that. She had searched him out. She had considered him.

'What do you think?' he asked, struggling with perspective.

'I can't say. I mean I don't know. Only you know.'

Francis checked himself. She was right. How could she know, without the detail, without all the problems and solutions and all that was left unsaid and unknown. It was unfair of him. He knew it. Open up, a voice in his head said. Unleash the full story. His mother would support him. He was sure of that, yet at the same time it would be hard for his mother to fit him into the intricacies of the events, particularly as so much was unresolved. Only Francis knew the truth. Francis and Ronnie. And they were back together now. As it was and is, he thought.

'I'll probably go. Leave early. That Ok?'

'Yes, whatever,' said his mother turning away.

He went early. Over and over in his mind he considered what he needed to say. The order, the timing, the stress, the way he would need to dominate, to have his say, to be strong. He scribbled the words down, refining them, composing a note that articulated all that needed to be said. He read it over and over, at one point deciding to opt for it, to leave it at reception. It would do the job, he thought. But the coldness of that made him draw back. He realised that he had to see her, that he had to face her.

'Be confident, be easy,' he told himself when he arrived at the hotel. He explained to the receptionist who he was, where he was from and what he wanted. The receptionist consulted the manager and showed him to a seat. He stared at the chairs and the table and the rack of magazines. *Punch. Country Life. Homes and Gardens*. It all seemed too middle class for the cheap, uncomfortable chairs with their garish red and blue striped covers, slightly worn with plain pieces for the arms. It made him smile. It made him think of appearance and reality, how such considerations were like a familiar landscape to him now. He knew the way they worked, the way they were assembled. He wanted to deconstruct them, to lay open the reality and not graft on inconsistencies and abnormalities. He wanted it to be straight and simple.

He was thinking of that when Ronnie came down the stairs. Rhoda was with her. He stood up. At first she didn't notice the figure in the lounge. It was a left turn from reception to the dining room; the lounge was to the right. The lack of recognition made him call after her. 'Ronnie!'

'Oh hi,' she said turning. 'Francis! Well what a surprise.'

'Hi,' said Rhoda. 'We forgot something?'

'No,' Francis laughed. He thought how Rhoda fell into the inconsistencies and abnormalities. He smiled. 'No. I was coming to Swansea later in the week. I forgot. Got the date mixed up. My mum reminded me. Thought it was next week. So I've put it forward a day or two. Thought I could meet up with you before you left.' He wasn't a good liar. He knew it. It made him search their faces for a response. As he looked he thought how the fabrication of stories made him talk in a staccato way. Stop, start. Never knowing when to stop, how much to tell, how to tell it. He started to speak again, still smiling. 'So I've come early. Thought we could have breakfast.'

'Hey it's a week of surprises,' laughed Ronnie. 'So this is sort of getting your own back,' she added.

'That's neat,' said Rhoda, feeling uncomfortable. She knew now Ronnie was comfortable with Francis, that she could jettison her role as chaperone. 'Yeh you guys go ahead,' she said, seeing her chance. 'We leave at nine remember. You got that. Hey you've got enough time to check out that hotel we were in last night. They'll serve breakfast. Sure to. See that hunk Gwyn or Jim or whatever he called himself. Some guy. He liked you. I could see that.'

Ronnie giggled. 'You sure?' she asked. Rhoda nodded and smiled.

Croissants and coffee were followed by Francis' words. They didn't have the finesse of those that made up his letter. They cracked and grunted and broke up occasionally and were interspersed with sighs and sniffs, big intakes of air that signalled his degree of nervousness. They made his voice seem a little weak and inconsistent.

'Thanks,' he said softly.

'What for? Hey it was me who came to say thanks. It's my pilgrimage.' Ronnie laughed. She played with her croissant, pressing the crumbs on the plate together, then eating them quickly.

'Hey you're hungry. You want some more?'

She nodded. 'Please. Missed dinner. Got back too late. God did we dance. Jees that Rhoda.' Ronnie laughed. 'And I've no voice left this morning. You noticed? YMCA,' she started singing. 'You know it?'

Francis smiled. 'Will you tell Zelda?' he asked.

'What? That I saw you? Oh I don't know. God I'd like to. I mean I'll have to tell someone. It's so exciting. It's awesome. Being here, meeting you. God!' Ronnie shook her head. It checked what she had been saying. 'But I didn't tell her. I mean I didn't tell her we were coming to Wales. Scotland, yes. And England, yeh. But I didn't mention Wales. I don't know why. I mean I don't know what she's afraid of.'

Now, thought Francis, now. The opportunity was there. She had given him the opening, the crucial link with Texas. Wales, Texas, thought Francis. The tower. Ronnie. The accusations. The manipulation.

'Shall I tell you? Do you want to know?'

'Want to know?'

'What frightened her,' said Francis. He spoke slowly, carefully. Time for precision now, he thought. He took a deep breath. 'Ronnie I'm telling you this because I know you're going to find things out and because, well I know, as things stand, if you find things out you'll draw the wrong conclusions.'

'What! Hey what is this?' There was a touch of shock in her voice. Francis knew his words must have seemed too severe, too considered. Rehearsed, he thought, drawing breath again before continuing. 'All I'm saying is just don't believe everything. Don't take it at face value. Will you remember that?'

'Yes,' Ronnie sighed and pulled a face that told Francis she thought she deserved more, that she believed she was being sold well short, that there was much more to be revealed.

'Good. Just don't accept what you're told. Question it. Yeh?'

Ronnie nodded her head. The sharp expression on her face made her look disgruntled, at odds with her experience of Wales. She still didn't understand.

'Look I'll give you an example.'

'Yeh I think you should.'

'Ok, Ok. Your father couldn't draw.'

'What?'

'The Fred cartoons. I drew them. Your father couldn't draw. He had no idea. The Fred cartoons were mine. I drew them'

'You?' Ronnie looked more dismayed than shocked. The expression disturbed Francis. He had expected her to show that she couldn't cope with such questioning of truth. It struck at the core of what she knew. Francis thought how she had striven to understand, to work it all out. The fire. Her mother. Her father. The foreign national. The understanding she had was precious. It demanded faith. It told Francis she would resist. 'No. No I can't believe that.'

'You believed your father drew them.'

'He did.'

'See. You were only told that. Who told you?'

'I remember him there.'

'In the water tower?'

'Yes. In the water tower. He was there,' she said definitely.

'Oh yes he was there.' Francis nodded. He smiled too, reassuringly, kindly. 'But you never saw him draw. Zelda told you he could draw, didn't she?'

'No.' She shook her head. 'He did draw.' She adopted an aggressive tone now. It said she was adamant, that she knew the truth. 'Look. Jees why am I listening to this? I should go.'

'No, no you shouldn't.'

'Look I've got the drawings. I've got them at home. November, March, July. They're mine.'

'And I drew them.'

'But you couldn't have. Aunt Zelda told me. Fritz told me. They wouldn't lie.'

Francis sensed there was a need to take the heat out of the argument, to let rationality creep in and assume control. He considered ways of welcoming it. 'Ok, Ok. Let's see.' He bit his lip. 'Now let's think. Remember November? The gunpowder plot. November 5th. Guy Fawkes. Fred working out what went wrong, blowing up his home.' Francis paused. He was pleased with his delivery. He liked its speed, its precision.

'So?' Ronnie brooded on her thoughts. She couldn't keep track with the logic that was assaulting her.

'So it's British,' said Francis almost exploding the words. 'So's June. Remember that? Cricket.'

'Yeh, but that was learned by my dad when he was over here. Zelda said he drew all the time when he was over here. She said he was a good artist. She said he did oils too. Landscapes of Wales.'

'You seen them?'

'No he sold them.' She sounded insistent.

'That good huh?' Francis shook his head and reached inside a pocket. He pulled out an envelope. He turned it upside down and emptied its contents onto the table. 'Go on,' he urged, begging Ronnie to pick them up, to examine them. 'You remember these?'

'Giraffes,' laughed Ronnie. 'Oh they're neat.' She examined them fully. 'I like giraffes. The way they move. Oh gee. You seen them move? Wow.' She shook her head for effect.

'I gave you drawings like these.' He watched her pull a small piece of paper from beneath a larger piece. The drawing emerged. Fred. Fred mowing the lawn. Then another. Fred skydiving. Another. Fred doing a handstand and simultaneously reading a letter. Fred gets word from down under, the caption read. 'See,' said Francis, coaxing a response.

'You took them,' accused Ronnie.

'No. Look.' Francis took out a biro and pressed on its top. Frantically he drew. A round shape and limbs, a bald head, the hair dragged up and over the top of the head.

Ronnie watched. She was speechless. She shook her head and sighed. The urgency seemed subversive. It was acting against her, not giving her time to think. It was so different from what she was used to. In the past, mention of her father had always been met with calm. Now there was no sense of consideration. The truth seemed to ride with the words. The twists and turns were connected.

'You see?' asked Francis, finishing with a flourish. 'I drew them. You remember them? Do you remember the giraffes? The one that went over two pages. Remember?' He pressed for a reply.

Ronnie smiled. A vague recollection seemed to come to her, but it didn't seem to convince her. Francis saw the familiarity subside. Her expression cooled. 'Oh come on. You knew him. You knew what he could do. So you can draw too. Gee. Big deal. Most people can draw. I could with a bit of practice. Yeh, I'm sure I could. And my dad would know, wouldn't he?'

'Know what?'

'About cricket and things. I mean he lived in Wales for a time.'

'Ronnie your father never lived in Wales.' Francis checked for a reaction before going on. 'He never set foot in Wales. For heaven's sake he never set foot outside of Texas.'

Ronnie shook her head. She looked more distraught than dismayed now. Words had failed to counter Francis so she turned to thoughts. Ideas were floated. All that she knew about her father's trip came to her. She used them like weapons. 'Yeh. Course he did,' she said somewhat belatedly. 'He had a good time. You said so yourself yesterday. You said he worked in the dairy, that he fixed machines.'

'I did and I was wrong to do that. I was lying.'

'And Aunt Zelda and Fritz said that he visited Wales. Uncle Paul said so too.'

'They were lying too. Ronnie, he never visited Wales. Believe me,' Francis spoke emphatically.

'But Toggie and Zoon.'

'Mine.'

'The photos?'

'Mine too.' Francis shook his head at that. He could sense Ronnie was fidgeting, that she wanted him to be more expansive again, to develop issues and make points, to prove his case. The fact she was quiet and still with him confirmed to Francis that she suspected something, that she was beginning to consider his version of events. 'You said yourself he was never in the photos. I was. They were mine. I was showing you them when the fire started. I even promised to buy you a goat like Toggie if you moved quickly. Remember?'

Ronnie shook her head. She still couldn't bring herself to consider the new version of events. Francis draws. Francis loves animals, has animals, gorgeous animals. It all took too much away from her father. It depleted what she knew of him and left him like a husk, lifeless, skeletal. It extinguished the glow.

'You think about what I've said. It's the truth. He didn't visit Wales, he didn't draw Fred. He didn't know Toggie and Zoon. He never set eyes on them. Apart from the photos that is.'

'So?' asked Ronnie, suddenly moving on, wondering where such revelations were leading.

Francis breathed deeply. 'I don't know,' he said.

'What do you mean?'

'I mean I just don't know. I don't know what you'll find out. I'll let you do that.'

'Like a game.'

Francis nodded. He thought how that was what it had become, how it should have never developed in such a way, how reality and its compromises had pushed it into another realm. 'All I'm saying is you mustn't take things at face value. You could find things out. Like you found out about the fire and me. You may find out more.'

'I will now,' she said quite adamantly.

'Yes I'm sure you will. But take care. Analyse it a little. Think there could be some myths working on the truth. Yeh? You do that?'

'So they're lying?'

'Fritz, Zelda, Paul? Yeh like I did.'

'But why?'

'Why'd you think?' Francis chastised himself. He shouldn't have held back. Make it explicit a voice was saying, sort it out. But he wanted her to join in, to move with his ideas, to see their worth.

'Hey are you saying there's some kind of conspiracy?' blurted Ronnie.

'Perhaps.'

'A cover up.' Something was filling Ronnie's mind. She stopped to consider what she had said and Francis' reaction to it. She dwelt on it, calling up evidence, dismissing it and calling it back as something favourable or inappropriate came to mind. She shook her head. She sighed. 'But why? Tell me. Why?'

Francis shook his head. He decided he had said enough, that he should leave it to her. She would find the answers. He believed that. He believed she would uncover the abduction and the accusations. At least now she may doubt Zelda and Fritz and Paul and the newspapers. At least now she would have some independence, he thought.

'More croissants,' she suggested, coming out of thought, smiling. Francis nodded, wondering all the time what he would say to Zelda. Something came to mind then. Would she know? What would Ronnie say? Would she let on that she knew another version of what had happened? Francis had to find out. He had to ask. He coughed before speaking. 'Will you tell Zelda? I mean you don't have to. It will only lead to a confrontation. Perhaps you shouldn't. Perhaps you should just work it out for yourself. You'll find the truth.' Francis sighed. He thought how most of the problems had developed because nobody wanted to consider the reality of Brad's obsessions, of his moods, of his inadequacies. Where were they in Zelda's film, in her reconstruction?, thought Francis. 'Oh God listen to me. I don't want to tell you what to do.'

'Seems everyone else has,' laughed Ronnie, cutting open the croissant.

Francis watched her spread on too much butter and wondered if he had gone too far, if what he was doing was more than a subtle prompt. That was all it was meant to be. 'I don't want to intervene,' he said, watching her eat.

'But you have,' said Ronnie, reaching for the jar of marmalade. 'You already have.'

He was smiling when he arrived home. He felt as though he had done something that had been hanging over him for years. Now he had acted. Being decisive impressed him. He liked the way it seemed to move things on. Now Ronnie had an alternative. He wondered how far she would take it. 'Down to me,' he said, sitting in his room. He began to assess his performance. Better than he would have expected was the verdict. It broadened his smile.

'Francis! You back?' His mother called. She had arrived back from the village. Francis heard the shopping bags being placed on the kitchen table. He heard her begin to unpack. 'Hello,' she said, anticipating his approach. 'You Ok? Ronnie phoned.'

'Ronnie?'

'Yes. She said she'd seen you and that you'd had a good breakfast. She's very nice. I like the way she talks, don't you?'

'The way she talks?'

'The accent.'

'So why'd she phone?' Francis seemed nervous now. He hadn't expected this. He had thought he had said goodbye forever and that she would walk away and laugh at his story, that he would never see her again.

'Just saying goodbye. Asked one strange question though?'

'Did she? What?'

'Asked whether her father had ever stayed at Brynlas. Strange question.'

'Yes,' agreed Francis. A smile followed. He knew the call meant she had already started to check things out.

'So he denied it?'

'Yeh.' Zelda nodded. She felt tired now. The jail had done that. Wearing, she thought, reconsidering the experience. She had found it distressing. Somehow the environment had seemed aggressive. It had almost accosted her. It made her see how freedom was everything to her. To get up when she felt like, to read a long paper, to go for a walk or see a friend or go shopping. The only constraint in her case was that she was a slave to the dictates of fashion. That frequently told her what she should do. Perhaps, more to the point, it told her what she should not do.

'So he looked alright?' asked Fritz.

'Oh yeh. He looked fine.'

'What do you mean, Oh yeh, he looked fine?' Fritz's imitation dwelt more on her tone. It told him she was holding back, being economical with the truth.

'I mean he was sort of inhibited. You understand?' Zelda shrugged, disappointed with her attempt at words. She couldn't convey Francis' predicament. She didn't fully understand it.

'So that's it, is it? I mean he's free to go.'

Zelda nodded. She thought how it seemed wrong to draw lines under events, to say that's it and deem it over. It was too straightforward. It rode over explanations. Thinking of that she opened her eyes fully and shook her head from side to side. She looked as though she were weighing something up, considering a word or a look, some hint or clue to Francis' guilt or innocence. There had been nothing condemning in her prison conversation with him, no inadvertent slip of the tongue, no overwhelming admission. 'Stronger than I thought,' she admitted.

'The Welshman? Oh yeh. That doesn't surprise me. Quiet types are. My old momma said that.'

Zelda smiled. She was still doubtful. She nodded again, replaying Francis' words over and over. Convincing, she thought, then she censured herself and came to think how she hardly knew him, how a few conversations didn't constitute anything substantial when it came to drawing a characterisation. Fritz knew him better, she thought. Fritz would have more to go on. 'You like him?' she asked.

'Oh yeh. Yeh I do. I admire him. Tough guy. Strong. I mean coming all that way. Getting on. Yeh, good guy.'

'Sounds very macho.'

'Francis?' Fritz laughed.

'So what was he like?' Zelda wanted more. She needed to know and understand motivation, why he was in Texas, why he wasn't in Wales.

'Yeh. Yeh I like him,' Fritz said thoughtfully.

'Why? What was it you liked?' Fritz's laconic answers drove Zelda on. She wanted words that conveyed condition, that pointed to a state of mind. She wanted to move Francis from the particular to the general, to categorise, to place Francis in a group that would allow her to make sense of him. It was what he shared with others that would enlighten her. 'Ok, Ok,' she said quickly, deciding to help out Fritz. 'Was he ambitious?'

'No. No I don't think so. I mean he was kind of adventurous. I mean to come here. Yeh, Betty said she could never do it, leave her records, leave her home.'

'And you.'

'What?'

'You. She'd leave you.'

'Oh yeh!' Fritz laughed. To him Zelda's remarks seemed ludicrously serious. 'Yeh, you're right. Me and Betty. The dream ticket, yeh?' He laughed again. He thought how he would be low down on the list of reasons why Betty couldn't leave.

'So what did he want?' Again Zelda stepped in to redirect Fritz.

'I think he had problems. At home. I think he kind of couldn't get anyone to take him seriously. You know how it is when you're out of line. But to him that was a big problem because man he is serious.'

Fritz paused. It was an unusual act for Fritz. He was normally fluent, rapidly weaving words so that some inconsistency occasionally rode over them. Now he was thinking, considering, evaluating. Continuity, he thought. Francis. Serious. Wanting to be valued. Lighten him up, a voice in his mind was saying.

'I mean he could joke and play. You mustn't get me wrong on that. No I mean he could laugh. I mean he had to. Otherwise he and me, well we wouldn't have got on. No way. Everyone I know has to be like that. Except perhaps Brad. Now he was serious. He had issues. Big fuckin' issues. Buses. Drains. Civil Wars. Jesus was he focused.'

'Intense?'

'Brad? Oh yeh. He was glued down in issues. You couldn't shake him. Except football games. An' me. Pam said I could lighten him. Oh yeh and I could, but only for a second. For a fuckin' second. No more.' Fritz smiled and raised his eyebrows as if to say can you believe that? He enjoyed the nod Zelda gave him. 'Oh he was fuckin' deep man.'

'And Francis wasn't?'

'Oh Francis was nice. He liked animals. He liked people.'

'Girls?'

'Don't know.'

'What do you mean? Don't know!' Zelda was intrigued now. She was confronted by an imprecision that went against Fritz's normal strident answers. Flaws, she thought, realising that was what she needed, to compare options, to reject and accept, to compose. Francis, Francis, Francis, she thought, trying to connect with something Fritz was saying, trying to make him come to life.

For his part, Fritz thought of conversations. Nights at Oscars, Talk of girls. Francis' words. Francis' reactions. Words. Looks. 'I mean he said some nice things.'

'Nice things? Do men say nice things?'

'You mean when they're together?'

'Yeh.'

'Men talk?'

Zelda looked a little coy now. It wasn't a look that was normally associated with her. It wasn't a look she normally let herself associate with. 'Yeh,' she said, trying to regain a little brashness.

'No,' Fritz was quite blunt. 'We sort of insult. We know we do it. But it's macho. You know. Cute bum, nice tits. An' a few things that are worse than that. That worry you?'

Zelda blushed, but quickly regained control, 'No. Not at all,' she said.

'Bet it does.'

'And Francis talked that way?'

'Jees no. Francis would stay real quiet.'

'A gentleman?'

'Guess so.' Fritz smirked. He blew out through his nose and laughed a little like the way Brad used to, though more quietly and less irritatingly. 'Can't remember him saying much about girls. I mean he kind of listened more than he talked. Hey he said some nice things about Pam. I remember that. But everyone said nice things about Pam.'

'Did he look at girls? You know?' Zelda smiled. She led Fritz on. 'Did he stare at girls.'

'Give them the come on you mean?'

'Yeh.'

'No. I mean I didn't notice. You notice?'

'Why me? I hardly knew him.'

'But you're a woman. You should sense what a man's like, whether he'll try it on, whether he's available. You get a feel for that?'

Zelda shook her head and produced a look that conveyed the fact she had sensed little. 'You think he's repressed?' she asked.

'Jees no. No he was kind of shy I guess. He lacked a little confidence. Always did lack it. That's why he came over here. But he was genuine. I'm sure of that. You knew that when you were with him. You sort of felt it.'

'Meaning?'

'Meaning others lead you on, cut you short. Get my drift.'

'Brad?' Zelda said excitedly. She found it all rather exhilarating, the way Fritz liked Francis, the way he tolerated Brad, how much he trusted Francis. There was a grace about Fritz's guile. There was a speed and skill to the rhythm of his words. She rode with them, learning to skim off the shrill polemic and accept the deeper tones within. 'So you prefer Francis,' she concluded.

'I'm not saying that. I'm just saying that if you were looking for a friend then Francis would be the one.'

'Or a father?'

'You can't choose a father,' objected Fritz.

'Can't you?' laughed Zelda.

Francis tried it out that night in front of the television. *Robin Hood Prince of Thieves* was playing. The television, he thought. Zelda's film. Brad the wall maker. Brad the family man. Brad the hero. He imagined him on the screen. Brad replacing Kevin Costner. 'This is my father,' Francis said to himself. He turned down the television and played sounds in his mind. The laughter of reunions. The curses of wall building. This is my father, he kept saying, imagining Ronnie remembering Brad and the tower and her knitting. 'This is my father,' he said. She would remember him drawing her giraffes and goats and making up cartoons. She would remember laughing. Zelda would encourage that. She would tell her how Brad had told her stories of foreign lands, that he had lived in Wales for some time, that her mother's family came from Wales. She would show her the photograph album. Toggie. Zoon. Bess. Her father's quaint old English van. She would tell her how he had taken Ronnie to the pictures.

'Yeh, yeh I remember that,' Ronnie would say, smiling at the image of the prince in Snow White. She would recall how her father at the end of the film had promised to buy her Grumpy, her favourite dwarf. 'He was nice,' she would say. 'Gee he was real nice. I wish he was here today. Don't you Aunt Zelda? Don't you wish he was here? Wouldn't that be just fine?'